CHILDREN OF THE GATES

Baen Books
by
Andre Norton

✿ ✿ ✿ ✿

Time Traders
Time Traders II
Star Soldiers
Warlock
Janus
Darkness & Dawn
Gods & Androids
Dark Companion
Masks of the Outcasts
Moonsinger
Crosstime
From the Sea to the Stars
Star Flight
Search for the Star Stones
The Game of Stars and Comets
Deadly Dreams
Children of the Gates

To purchase these and all other Baen Book titles in e-book format,
please go to www.baenebooks.com

CHILDREN OF THE GATES

ANDRE NORTON

BAEN

CHILDREN OF THE GATES

Here Abide Monsters copyright © 1973 by Andre Norton. Yurth Burden copyright © 1978 by Andre Norton.

A Baen Books Original

Baen Publishing Enterprises
P.O. Box 1403
Riverdale, NY 10471
www.baen.com

ISBN: 978-1-4516-3889-9

Cover art by Stephen Hickman

First Baen paperback printing, May 2013

Distributed by Simon & Schuster
1230 Avenue of the Americas
New York, NY 10020

Library of Congress Cataloging-in-Publication Data:

Printed in the United States of America

10 9 8 7 6 5 4 3 2 1

❖ Contents ❖

Here Abide Monsters

For Bee Lowry,
who suggested that Lung Hsin
be one of the adventurers
in Avalon.

❋ 1 ❋

To Nick's left the sun had hardly topped the low trees. It was a ball of red fire; today was going to be a scorcher. He hoped he could make it into the woods road before the heat really hit. Of course he had wanted to start earlier, but there was always some good reason why— Behind the faceplate of his helmet Nick scowled at the road ahead.

Always some *good* reason why the things *he* wanted to do did not fit in with plans, not *his* plans, naturally. Did Margo actually sit down and think it out, arrange somehow ahead of time so that what Nick had counted on was just what was not going to happen? He had suspected that for some time. Yet her excuses why this or that could not be done were so perfectly logical and reasonable that Dad always went along with them.

At least she had not ruined this weekend. Maybe because she and Dad had their own plans, or rather her plans. Give Nick another year—just one—and Margo could talk to the thin air. He would not be there to listen to her. That—he relished the satisfaction that thought presented—was the day he was going to start living!

Dad—Nick's thoughts squirmed hurriedly away from that path. Dad—he had chosen Margo, he agreed with Margo's sweet reasonableness. All right, let him live with it and her! Nick was not going to a minute longer than he had to.

The trees along the road were taller now, closer together. But the surface over which the motorbike roared was clear and smooth. He could make good time here. Once he turned into the lake road it would be different. But in any event he would reach the cabin by noon.

His thoughts soared away from what lay behind, already seeking the peace ahead. The weekend, and it was a long one from Friday to Monday, was his alone. Margo did not like the lake cottage. Nick wondered why she had never talked Dad into selling it. Maybe she just did not care. There was plenty else for her to own. Just as she owned Dad.

Nick's scowl deepened, his black brows drawing together, his lips thinly stretched against his teeth. That scowl line now never completely faded, it had had too much use over the past three years. He swayed and adjusted to the swing of the machine under him as an earlier generation would have ridden a horse, the metal framework he bestrode seemingly a part of his own person. The bubble safety helmet covered his head front and back. Below that he wore a tee shirt, already dust streaked, and faded jeans, his feet thrust into boots.

Saddlebags, tightly strapped against loss, held the rest of his weekend wardrobe and supplies, save for the canned food at the cabin and what he would buy at the store going in. He had a full tank of gas, he had his freedom for four days—he had himself! Nick Shaw as he was, not Douglas Shaw's son, not Margo's stepson (though, of course, that relationship was hardly ever mentioned). Nick Shaw, himself, personal, private and alone.

A twisting curve downhill brought him to the store at the foot of the bend, a straggle of houses beyond. This was Rochester, unincorporated, with no "Pop." on the sign Nick flashed past. He came to a stop at the store. A Coke would go good. Ham Hodges always had those on ice.

Bread, cheese, Nick had no list, just had to remember to get things that would not be affected by the bumpy ride in. His boots thumped on the porch as he reached for the knob of the screen door. Behind the screening a black shape opened its jaws in an almost inaudible but plainly warning hiss.

Nick jerked off his helmet. "I'm no Martian invader, Rufus," he said to the big tomcat.

Unblinking blue eyes stared back but the jaws closed. "Rufe, you there—move away from the door. How many times am I going to tell you if you sit there you're going to be stepped on someday—"

Nick laughed. "By whom, Ham? Some customer pounding in for bargains, or one going out because you ran the prices up on him?"

The cat moved disdainfully back a little, allowing him to pass by.

"Nick Shaw!" The youngish man moved out from behind the counter on the left. "Your folks up for the weekend?"

Nick shook his head. "Just me."

"Sorry your Dad couldn't make it, Larry Green sighted some big ones in the cove. He was just saying to me no more'n an hour ago that Mr. Shaw sure ought to come up and cast a line for one of those. He hasn't been here for a long time now."

Ham was being tactful, but not tactful enough. Nick shifted his feet. They never mentioned Margo, but she was always right there, in their minds as well as his, when they talked about Dad. Before Margo Dad had loved the lake, had been here in the summer and the fall every minute he could get away. How much longer will he even keep the cabin now?

"No," Nick answered in a voice he kept even with an effort. "He's been pretty busy, Ham, you know how it is."

"Don't suppose I can sell *you* any bait—"

Nick managed a smile. "You know me, Ham. I'm about as much a fisherman as Rufus is a dog lover. What I do want is some stuff to eat—what I can carry on the bike without a smashup. Any of Amy's bread to go?"

"I'll see. No reason why we can't spare some baking—"

Hodges turned to the back of the store and Nick moved around to pick other items. A package of bacon from the freezer bin, some cheese. From all the years he had been stopping at Ham's he knew where most things were. Rufus was back on guard at the screen door. He was about the biggest cat Nick had ever seen, but not fat. Instead, in spite of the plates of cat food he could and did lick clean each day, he was rather gaunt. His conformation was that of his Siamese father, though his color was the black of the half-breed.

"How's hunting, Rufus?" Nick asked as he returned to the counter.

An ear twitched, but the cat's head did not turn even a fraction. His interest in what lay outside was so intent that Nick moved up behind him to look out, too. There must be a bird, even a snake—something in the road. But he could see nothing.

Which did not mean that nothing was there. Cats saw above and below the human range of sight. There could be something there all right, something invisible—

Nick wondered just how much truth there was in some of the books he had read—those that speculated about different kinds of existence. Such as the one that had suggested we share this world with other kinds of life as invisible to us as we might be to them. Not altogether a comfortable thought. You had enough trouble with what you *could* see.

"What's out there, Rufus? Something out of a UFO?"

The cat's attention was manifestly so engaged that it made Nick a little uneasy. Then suddenly Rufus yawned widely, relaxed. Whatever had intrigued him so was gone.

He returned to the counter. There was a paperback turned upside down open, to mark the reader's place. Nick turned it around to read the title—*Our Haunted Planet*—by somebody named Keel. And there was another book pushed to one side—*More "Things"* by Sanderson. That one he knew, he had read it himself, urged by Ham to do so.

Ham Hodges had a whole library of that type of reading, starting with Charles Fort's collections of unexplainable happenings. They made you wonder all right. And Ham had a good reason for wondering—his cousin and the Commer Cut-Off.

"Got you a loaf of whole wheat, a raisin one, and a half-dozen rolls," Ham announced coming into sight again. "Amy says give the rolls a warm-up, they're a day old."

"They could be two weeks old and still be good if they're hers. I'm lucky she can spare so much a day ahead of baking."

"Well, we had some company who was going to come and didn't, so she was overstocked in the bread box this week. Funny about that." Ham thudded the bread and rolls down in a plastic bag before Nick. "This fellow called up last Friday—just a week ago. He said he was from the Hasentine Institute and they were gathering material about the Cut-Off. Wanted to come out here and ask around Ted and Ben—" Ham paused. "Hard to think of it being all this time since they disappeared. At least it scared people off from trying that road for a while. Only somebody's taken the Wilson place for the summer and, since the new highway to Shockton went in, the Cut-Off's the only road to reach that side of the lake now. So it's getting traveled again.

"Anyway, this fellow said he was doing research and asked about a place to stay. We've that cabin, so we said we'd put him up. Only he never showed up or called again."

"How long has it been, Ham?"

"Since July 24, 1970. Why, you and your Dad and Mom were up here at the lake that summer. I remember your Dad was out with the search party. I was just home from the army. We sure gave that land a going over—Ted was a good guy and he knew the country like it was his own backyard. Ben was no fool either, he'd buddied with Ted in the Navy and came up for some fishing. No, they just disappeared like all the others—that Caldwell and his wife and two kids in 1956, and before them there were Latimer and Johnson. I made it my business to look it all up. Got out my notebook and read it through this week so I could answer any questions the fellow from the Institute might want to ask. You know, going as far back as the newspapers had any mention of it, there's been about thirty people just up and disappeared on the Cut-Off. Even before it was ever a road, they disappeared in that section. It's like that Bermuda Triangle thing. Only not so often as to get people all excited about it. There's always a good long stretch of time between disappearances so people sort of forget in between. But they should never have opened up that road again. Jim Samuels tried to talk the new people out of it. Heard they didn't quite laugh in his face, but I guess they took it as some superstition us local yokels believe in."

"But if it's the only way to get into the Wilson place—" Nick knew the legend of the Cut-Off, but he could also understand the frustration of outsiders needing an easy access.

"Yes, I guess it is a case of needs drive. You can't get the county interested in laying out a new road to serve just a few summer cabins because there's a queer story about the one already there and waiting to be used. You know, this writer"—Ham tapped the book with a fingertip—"has some mighty interesting things to say. And this one"—he indicated the More "Things" volume—"makes it plain, for instance, that we think we know all about this world, that it's all been explored. But that isn't the truth, there are whole sections we know nothing about at all, mountains never climbed, places where nobody civilized has ever been."

"'Here abide monsters,'" Nick quoted.

"What's that?" Ham looked up sharply.

"Dad's got a real old map he bought in London last year—had it framed and hung it down in his office. It shows England and part of Europe, but on our side of the ocean just some markings and dragons or sea serpents, with lettering—'Here abide monsters.' They filled up the unknown then with what they imagined might be there."

"Well, we don't know a lot, and most people don't want to learn more'n what's right before their eyes. You point out things that don't fit into what they've always accepted, and they say it's all your imagination and nothing like that is real. Only we know about the Cut-Off and what's happened there."

"What do you think really happened, Ham?" Nick had taken a Coke from the ice chest, snapped off the cap, and now drank.

"There's this Bermuda Triangle, only this writer Sanderson says it's no 'triangle,' but much larger, and also they've made some tests and it's only one of ten such places all around the world. Ships and people and planes disappear there regularly—nothing ever found to say what happened to them. A whole flight of Navy planes once and then the rescue plane that went out after them! It may have something to do with magnetic forces at those points. He makes a suggestion about breaking into another space-time. Maybe we have one of these 'triangles' right here. I sure wish that Hasentine guy had shown up. About time some of the brains did some serious investigating. And . . ."

What he was about to say was drowned out by a wild yapping from without. Rufus, his back arched, his tail a brush, gave a warning yowl in reply. Ham swung around.

"Now what the heck's all that about?" He headed for the door.

Rufus, ears flattened against his skull, his Siamese blue eyes slitted, was hissing, giving now and then a throaty growl of threat. The yapping outside was apparently not in the least intimidated.

A car, or rather a jeep, had drawn up, and a girl slid from under the wheel, but had not yet stepped out. She was too busy trying to restrain a very excited and apparently furious Pekingese that fought against her hold, its popping eyes fixed on Rufus.

She glanced up at Ham behind the screen, Nick looking over his shoulder.

"Please," she was laughing a little. "Can you cope with your warrior? I want to come in and I certainly can't let go of Lung Hsin!"

"Sorry." Ham stopped to catch up Rufus with practiced ease in avoiding the claws the big cat had already extended to promise battle. "Sorry, Rufe, you for the storeroom temporarily." He departed with the kicking and growling cat, and Nick opened the door for the girl. She still held the Peke who had fallen silent upon witnessing the unwilling exit of the enemy.

"He's mighty little to think of taking on Rufus," Nick commented. "Rufe would take one good swipe at him and that would be that."

The girl frowned. "Don't be too sure about that! This breed were once known as dragon dogs, lion dogs—they helped guard palaces. For their size they're about the bravest animals alive. Hush now, Lung, you've made your point. We all know you're a brave, brave Dragon Heart." The Peke shot out a tongue and licked her cheek, then stared about him imperiously as if, having chased the enemy from the field, this was now his domain.

"Now what can I do for you?" Ham came back, licking one finger where Rufus had apparently scored before being exiled.

"I need some directions, and a couple cases of Coke and . . ." She had Lung Hsin under one arm now as he no longer fought for freedom, and with her other hand she pawed into the depths of her shoulder bag. "Here it is," she said with relief. "Thought it might have gone down for the third time and I would have to empty this thing to find it."

She had a list ready now. "If I can just make out Jane's writing. She really ought to print, at least with that you can make educated guesses. That's right, two cases of Coke, one of Canada Dry, one of Pepsi. And she said you'd be holding melons—oh, I should have told you, I'm Linda Durant and I'm picking all this up for Jane Ridgewell—they've taken over the Wilson place. She said she'd call and tell you."

Ham nodded. "She did and I've got it all together. Won't take us long to load it up for you—" He glanced to Nick who obligingly moved away from the counter again. He was willing to give Ham a hand. Though they should be in no hurry to speed this one off.

This Linda was almost as tall as Nick. A lot of girls were tall nowadays. Her hair had been tied back from her face with a twist of bright red wool, but it was still long enough to lie on her shoulders in very dark strands. Her skin was creamy pale. If she tanned she had not started that process yet this season.

Her jeans were as red as her hair tie and she had a sleeveless blouse of white with blue dolphins leaping up and down on it. Sunglasses swung pendant from another red tie about her neck and she wore thong sandals on her feet. He was not usually so aware of a girl's clothes, but these fitted her as if to complete a picture.

Nick shouldered one of the melons Ham pointed out and took a second under his arm, carrying them out to the waiting jeep. Ham was busy stowing in Coke.

"Wait 'til I get some sacks," he told Nick. "Shake those melons around and you'll get them stove in."

Linda Durant had followed them out. "That sounds," she commented, "as if I have a rough road ahead. You'll have to give directions, Jane's are vague."

For the first time Nick realized that she meant to travel the Cut-Off. He glanced at Ham who looked sober. After what Ham had just been saying—to send a stranger, and a girl, down the Cut-Off—But if there was no other way in now—only Nick had a queer feeling about it.

There was one thing—he could take that way, too. It was really shorter to his own cabin when you came to think about it. And it had been almost his whole lifetime since Ted and Ben had disappeared. This was broad daylight and these Ridgeways must have been up and down there maybe a hundred times since they moved in. So, why look for monsters that did not exist?

"Look here," Nick suggested as Ham reappeared with sacks and newspapers and proceeded to wedge in the cargo. "I'm heading that way. It's rough and we'll have to take it slow, but if you'll match your speed to mine"—he motioned at the waiting bike—"I'll guide you in. I'm Nick—Nicholas Shaw—Mr. Hodges here knows me. My people have had a cabin on the lake for a long time."

Linda gave him a long, intent survey. Then she nodded and smiled.

"That's fine! From what Jane said the road's pretty rough and I could miss it. I'm very glad of your company."

Ham packed the last of the papers in, and Nick gathered up his own purchases and bagged them in a bundle he could tie over the saddlebags. Several indignant yowls from the storeroom brought an instant sharp response from the Peke.

Linda adjusted her sunglasses and got behind the wheel. But Ham spoke to Nick in a low voice.

"Take it easy now. I have a funny feeling—"

"Not much else we can do if she's going to get to the Wilson place," Nick pointed out.

As he gunned the bike to life he wondered what looming danger one could watch for along the Cut-Off. No one who had ever met whatever peril lurked there had ever returned to explain what he or she had faced. No, Nick was not going to let his imagination take over. He'd end up seeing a UFO or something lurking behind every tree, he waved to Linda and swung out. She nodded and followed.

They turned off the highway about a half-mile farther on and Nick cut speed, concentrating on the rough surface ahead. He had come this road enough times to memorize every rut and bump, but the heavy rains last week would have done damage, and he had no intention of being spilled through carelessness.

A mile and a half to the Cut-Off. In all the years he had been coming up here he had always looked for the overgrown entrance to what had become a sinister road to nowhere. Could she get the jeep in there at all? But they had been using it, so they must have cleared a passage through. July 24, 1970—he'd been too little then to realize what had gone on. But he'd heard plenty about it ever since. All that searching—the neighbors, the sheriff and his deputies. And not so much as a track to tell them why two young men in the best of health had vanished from a half-mile strip of road one sunny morning.

They had been seen entering, had stopped and talked to Jim Anderson about the best place to fish. Jim had been going into the store. He had watched them turn into the Cut-Off. But they never came out at the lake where a couple of guys were waiting to join them.

Mouth of the Cut-Off—like a snake with jaws wide open to swallow them down.

Nick took firm control of his imagination. If he did not see Linda to the lake she would go by herself. And he somehow could not let that happen and be able to look at himself in the mirror when shaving tomorrow.

It was only a half-mile, perhaps a little more. They could run it in minutes, even if it were rough. The sooner they got through the better. He wondered what this Linda would say if she knew his thoughts. She'd probably decide he'd been smoking pot. Only when you heard about the Cut-Off all your life—well, you had a different point of view.

He had borrowed a lot of Ham's books, bought some of his own, knew all the things that did happen now and then that nobody seemed able to explain. Maybe Fort and those other writers who hunted out such stories had the right of it. The scientists, the brains who might have solved, or at least tried to solve, such puzzles, refused even to look at evidence before their eyes because it did not fit in with rational "facts." There could be facts that were neither rational nor logical at all.

There was the turnoff ahead. And there certainly had been changes since the last time he was here. Looked as if someone had run a bulldozer in to break trail. Nick gave a sigh of relief at the raw opening. There was a healthy difference between wriggling down an almost closed and ill-reputed trail and this open scraped side road, which now looked as good as the one leading to his own cabin. He flagged the jeep as he came to a stop.

"This is it," he called. Something in him still shrank a little from entering that way, but he refused to admit it.

Only he continued to feel that odd uneasiness, which had come to him earlier as he had seen Rufus watch something invisible that Nick had been convinced against his will was there.

"Take it slow," he cautioned, also against his will. He wanted to take that road at the best speed they could make. "I don't know how good the surface is."

"Yes." The dark glasses masked her face. She surely did not need them here in the shade of the trees, but she had not let them slide off as she had at the store. The Peke was on the seat, his forepaws resting on the dashboard, looking ahead with some of Rufus' intensity. He did not bark, but there was an eagerness in every line of his small, silky body, as if he wanted to urge them on.

Nick gunned his motor, swung into the Cut-Off, his speed well down. The jeep snorted along behind him at hardly better than a walking pace. The road crew had run the scraper along, but the rain had cut gullies across, here and there, and those had not been refilled.

The lane was all rawly new, bushes and even saplings gouged and cut out and flung back to wither and die on either side. It looked ugly—wrong, Nick decided. He supposed it had to be done to open up the road, but it was queer the road crew had not cleaned up more. Maybe the guys who had worked here knew about the sinister history of the Cut-Off and had not wanted to stay around any longer than they had to.

That broken stuff walled them in as if it were intended to keep them in the middle of the road, allow them no chance to reach the woods. Nick felt more and more trapped. Uneasiness was rising in him so that he had to exert even more control. This was plain stupid!

He must keep a grip on his imagination. Just watch the road for those ruts and lumps so he would not hit something—do that and keep going. They would be there in no time at all.

It was still, not a leaf moved. But the trees arched over well enough to keep out the sun. Probably it was very quiet, too, if the noise of the bike and the jeep had not advertised their coming. Advertised it to what? Nick hoped only to those in the Wilson place.

Right ahead was the turn, a blind one. And this was a narrow road. No place to meet anyone coming the other way. But surely they were making enough noise—

Noise! The Peke had begun to yap, almost as when he had challenged Rufus. Nick heard the girl call out: "Down, Lung! Down!"

He half-turned his head, the bike hit something and wobbled. Nick had to fight to keep it away from a mass of dying brush. But there was something else, a cloud—like a fog trapped under the trees. It was thickening, coming down like a blanket—fast!

Nick thought he cried out. Behind him he heard an answering scream and a crash. Then he hit something, was thrown, and skidded painfully into total darkness.

❋ 2 ❋

Nick lay with his feet higher than his head, the whole left side of his face smarting. Groggily he levered himself up on his hands and blinked, then shook his head to banish the queer not-here feeling. He could hear a whimpering sound from behind, but at first he was so much occupied with his own aches and pains that it had no meaning.

He looked around.

The bike lay entangled in broken brush into which it must have slammed with force. Nick sat up farther. Bike—the jeep! Where was the jeep? Now the whimpering alerted him to what might be a serious accident. He had no idea what had happened—memory seemed at fault. They had just come around the turn in the Cut-Off and then . . .

Nick got shakily to his feet.

There was no road.

He staggered toward the jeep. That was there, yes, slammed against a tree. A tree that had no business being there at all, for seemingly it had sprung up right in the middle of what had been a newly cleared road.

There was no road!

He reached the jeep, supported himself against it. His aching head still seeming foggy. Fog—mist—cloud—there was something

17

18   *Andre Norton*

about that he could faintly remember. But that did not matter now. What did was the girl behind the wheel of the jeep.

She was supported partly by her seat belt, partly by the wheel itself. Her eyes were still covered with those sunglasses. With an effort Nick reached over and jerked them off. She was unconscious, he decided.

The whimpering came from the Peke huddled against her, licking at her arm. Lung growled at Nick but only halfheartedly, as he slid in beside Linda.

As far as Nick could see she had no open wounds, but—broken bones? His hands were shaking with a tremor he found hard to control, as he eased her back in the seat so he could get at the fastening of the seat belt.

"What—what—" She opened her eyes but, though they were turned in his direction, they did not seem to focus on him.

"Hold still!" Nick ordered. "Let me get this open—"

A few minutes later he sighed with relief. She had no broken bones. The side of his face, where it had scraped gravel, was raw, but that was minor. They could have been killed. Looking about him now, with eyes entirely aware, he wet his lips with the tip of his tongue.

Killed—if they had been going any faster—slammed up against these trees. But where—where did the trees come from?

They were huge, giants, and the underbrush beneath them was thin as if their mighty roofing overhead of leaves and branches kept any weaker growth from developing. The jeep was trapped between the one against which its nose was stuck, and a log of a fallen giant behind it, boxed in neatly so there was no hope of getting it out. Impossible, but that was the way it was.

Nick moved slowly around the machine, ran his hands across the top of the log, dislodging moss and fallen leaves. It was very apparent that this had been here, half sunk in the mucky soil, for a long, long time. But—there was the jeep—and—where was the road?

"Please—" Linda had edged around on the seat and was looking at him, her eyes very wide and frightened. "Please—where are we—what—happened?" She cuddled Lung against her. Now and then the small dog whined. He was shivering.

"I don't know," Nick answered slowly. Only he suspected what was so frightening he did not want to face the fact that it might be the truth.

"But—there's no road." Linda turned her head from side to side, searching. "We were just driving along and then—Where is this?" Her voice slid up the scale; Nick judged she was close to panic.

He was not far from that himself. But they had to hold on, to lose control would do no good. He hurried back to climb into the jeep.

"You—you know—!" She did have her voice under control now, was watching him narrowly. "What has happened? If you know—tell me!"

But he still hated to face what must be the truth. "I don't know," he said carefully. "It is only a guess." He hesitated. Those trees there were certainly good evidence. What more did he want? They were out of the Cut-Off, in such woods as had not been seen in this part of the country for two hundred years or more when the first settlers had attacked the great forests to carve out mastery of the land.

"Did your friends know anything about the history of the Cut-Off?" he began. How could you explain to anyone what might have happened, something so bizarre, so improbable?

"No." Linda cradled Lung in her arms, murmuring soothingly to him now and again. Her one-word reply was uncompromising. It was apparent she wanted the truth, or what he thought might be the truth.

"Well, the Cut-Off has a history of disappearances—running back as long as records were kept around here—"

("Around here." But surely this "here" was not the "here" of a short time ago.)

"The last time it happened was in 1970, two men going out to the lake to fish. But before that there were others. That's why the Cut-Off wasn't in use. Not until they built the new freeway and closed off the other road in."

"Disappearances to where?" Linda demanded sharply.

"That's it, nobody knows—knew. There are places . . ." Nick paused again. Would she believe him? She had to believe the evidence now before them at least. "Places where people do disappear—like the Bermuda Triangle—a whole flight of Navy planes went there, and the rescue ships after them. There have been planes and ships and people—and on land, in other places, army regiments even." Though he did not want to remember, all the stories he had read flooded back into his mind. "They just flew, or rode, or walked into—nowhere."

Linda sat very still. She no longer watched him. Her gaze was straight ahead at that giant tree trunk against which the jeep was nosed.

"What—what is the theory about it then?" Her voice quivered a little. Nick could sense her effort at control.

"One is that there is a magnetic field like a whirlpool—that anything caught in it may be thrown into another space-time continuum."

"And—that may be what has happened to us? How do we get back?"

There was no answer to that. There never had been through all the centuries of such disappearances. Nick stared at the tree too now, fiercely willing it to vanish, for them to be back in the Cut-Off.

"There is no return." Linda made that a flat statement rather than a question. "We—we're trapped in this—this *place!*"

"No!" Nick exploded. "We're not sure of that! Anyway we can try—we can always try—but"—he regarded the dim, shadowed places under the trees uneasily—"let's get out of here. On to the lake—"

He had a feeling that they were under observation, not that he could detect any movement, any sign they were not alone. To get out of this place of trees, where a man was dwarfed and lost, into the open was a desire goading him to action.

"We can't take the jeep." Linda stated the obvious.

"No, but I can the bike—push it now—and we can ride if the road gets better and you are willing to hold on."

"Yes! Yes, let's get out of here!" Her reply was feverishly eager.

She opened her shoulder bag, took out a leash she hooked to Lung's collar. "My bag—it's small." She reached into the back of the jeep, pulled out a canvas duffel bag. Then she laughed, though that sound was a little ragged. "All that stuff back there for the party tonight. Jane—Jane may have to wait some for it."

Nick's foreboding lightened. Linda was taking it well. Did she really believe him? Did he believe himself? But his first panic had subsided. And action drew him. Maybe if they could just find the lake, a familiar landmark—Don't think of any future beyond the next few minutes, he warned himself.

Mentally he inventoried the contents of his saddlebags—first-aid kit, sweater, swimming trunks, matches, a hunting knife, flashlight, chocolate bars, water canteen, two shirts, tool kit for the bike— transistor radio—Radio!

He was out of the jeep, hurrying back to the bike. Radio—if they could hear anything on that—Nick fumbled with the buckles of the saddlebag as Linda joined him.

"What is it?"

"My radio—if we can pick up anything—"

"Oh, hurry!" She shifted from one foot to the other impatiently as he untangled the gear and brought out the small transistor.

Three stations, he flipped the switch from one to the next. Only silence. Then—A gabble of sound, not static, more like speech. But not in any language he had picked up before.

"There! Turn it up!" Linda urged. "You've got something!"

"But what?" Nick asked.

"But what" was right. This sounded like gasps, clicks, and even a gabbled singing, but it made no sense. He thumbed the set off.

"Whatever that was, it was no broadcast of ours," he said bleakly.

"But somebody was broadcasting," Linda pointed out. "Which means we aren't alone here. Maybe if we can find people they will be able to help us."

Nick was not too sure. The language, if language that had been, was far removed from anything he had ever heard in his life and he had monitored a lot of foreign broadcasts with Gary Langford when Gary had his ham outfit. But Linda was right about getting out of here. He had the small compass and the lake was northeast—or it should be—if there was still any lake at all.

They could not keep to a straight line, but the lack of heavy underbrush was a help. And with the compass to steer by they wove a path among the towering trees, rounding boles that the two of them together could not have hoped to span with out stretched arms.

The bike seemed uninjured, but Nick had to wheel it along, walking beside it. There was no opening through which they dared ride. Linda carried her duffel bag slung over her shoulder by its cords and had let Lung down to patter along over the thick layers of countless years of fallen leaves. The little dog seemed to have lost his fear. But, while he sniffed at a moldering branch now and then, or snuffled into a pile of last season's leaves, he made no effort to pull to the end of his leash, staying close to Linda.

Though the trees about them were awe-inspiring, there were sounds in this forest familiar enough to allay some of their distrust. For there were not only birds to be heard and sometimes seen, but those winged inhabitants appeared unusually fearless as well as curious about the intruders.

Intruders Nick felt they were. This was a place that did not know man and had no idea of his species' destructiveness. The barked giants about them had never felt the bite of axe and stood in arrogant pride. Had it not been for that gabble from the transistor, Nick would have suspicions that the phenomena which haunted the Cut-Off had brought them to a space where his kind had never existed at all.

"It—it is so quiet." Linda moved closer, laid one hand on the bike near his. "Except for the birds. I never saw woods like this before. The trees—they are huge! When I was little my aunt had an old copy of *Swiss Family Robinson*—there was a tree in it that they turned into a house. You could do that with most of these."

Nick had one eye on the compass. They had had to make a good many detours, but they were still heading for the lake. Only here among all these trees it was hard to judge distance. Surely they couldn't be too far away from it now. But—what if there was no lake here?

He wanted that lake, he *had* to see it. The body of water was a promise of security somehow—without the lake they would be lost entirely. Nick hardly heard Linda's comment, he was so intent on willing the lake to be waiting for them, hoping that the stand of trees would soon thin so they could glimpse it.

"Nick!" Linda's hand flew from the bike to his wrist, tightened about it in a convulsive grip.

But he had seen it too.

They closed ranks, the bike between them. Lung lunged to the full length of his leash, set up a frenzied barking, not unlike that with which he had challenged Rufus. It was plain what he saw he resented.

Where it had come from was a minor mystery. For it was such a shimmering, dazzling white in this greenish gloom that it caught and held the eye almost at once. Yet they were so suddenly aware of it that it might have emerged from the tree against whose bark it was now framed.

"I—don't—believe—" Linda's voice trailed away. She saw it, Nick saw it. And so did Lung, still dancing on two hind feet at the farthest reach of his leash, jerking the strap in her hands, waving his forepaws in the air with his furious desire to be at this new enemy.

"What do you see?" Nick's wrist was still in her tight grasp. They had both taken knocks back there in their rough transition into this alien world. Perhaps this was a collective hallucination. Only—would the dog share it?

"A unicorn," she answered. "Don't—don't you see it, too?"

The creature was about the size of a large pony, not a horse, Nick thought. Its coat was that dazzling white, almost a source of light. The mane and tail were also white. But that single spiraled horn set just between and above the creature's wide dark' eyes was golden. And it, too, glowed. This was certainly the fabled unicorn, as Nick had seen it in reproductions of medieval paintings.

It stared back at them and then tossed its head, so that the forehead fringe of mane about the base of the incredible horn lifted. Then the creature pawed the earth with one slender hoof, lowered its head, and snorted at Lung as if replying to the Peke's shrill challenge. To all appearances, Nick thought it real enough.

Once more it tossed its head and then turned and paced away among the tree trunks, its white glow speedily lost.

"But unicorns—they are not—they never were alive," Linda said in a voice hardly above a whisper.

Something he had read came to Nick's mind then. All the old

legends of dragons and griffins, the People of the Hills, the very core of folklore and myth—men had believed in them for a long time, had sworn oaths in court that they had seen such, had had converse with the more humanlike figures of an unnatural, magical world. Could it have been that, just as he, Linda and Lung had been caught up in some force that had deposited them here, some of the creatures native to this world had been dropped into theirs? But a unicorn! Now that it was gone Nick had already begun to doubt what he had seen, to try to rationalize it.

"Wait here!" he ordered Linda and started for the place where the animal had stood. There he went down on one knee to examine the thick leaf mold. Then he wished he had not, for it was cut and patterned by tracks. Something had been there, unicorn or not.

Nick hurried back to Linda and the bike. They must get out of this woods as quickly as they could. For that sensation which had come upon him earlier was back full force. They were under observation—by the unicorn? It did not matter. Nick was aware they were invaders in this place. And sometimes intruders meet with active retaliation.

"I did see a unicorn," Linda was repeating, apparently to herself. "It was right there, under that tree. I have to believe that I saw it—believe that or—I just have to believe it!" She had picked up Lung, holding him high on her breast so his silken head was right under her chin. The Peke had stopped barking and was licking her face, or as much of it as his tongue could reach.

"Let's get going." Nick's tone was rough. They must get away—out into the open, if they could find any open.

The compass did bring them out a few minutes later into a space where the giant trees ceased and brush took their places. They pushed through the thinnest section of this and came to an expanse of tall grass, which in turn gave way to reeds bordering the lake—or a lake.

Along the shoreline, they could see no cabins, though by now Nick had ceased to hope to find those, or any sign that their own species had ever been there. Wading through the shallows were several herons that paid no attention to the newcomers. And in a rough pasture farther to the south animals were grazing. They were so light of hide Nick wondered if they had chanced upon a small herd of unicorns. Then one raised its head and showed branched antlers. But who had ever heard of silver-gray deer?

"There're no cabins—" Linda loosed her hold on the bike, let her duffel bag thump to the ground. "Nick, what are we going to do?"

He shrugged. "I don't know." He was no superman, no use in her turning to him as if he could get them out of this by flexing his muscles or something like that. "If you want to know the truth, I'm hungry. We might as well eat."

By the angle of the sun it must be close to noon. And he was hungry. It appeared that even a jump across time (if that was what had really happened to them) was not enough to subdue one's appetite.

"Hungry!" Linda repeated. Then she laughed, even if it was a small and difficult sound. "Why, I guess I am, too."

The grazing deer paid no attention to them. And, here in the open, nothing could sneak up on them without attracting attention. Linda moved on to a place where the grass did not appear as tall.

"Here's a good place." She beckoned as if this were an ordinary picnic. But Nick thought now about food. Not of how hungry he was, but of the meagerness of the rations they carried.

He had been depending on the store of canned goods at the cabin, and all else he had was what he had picked up at the store. That would not last long. Then they would have to live off the country. But what if they could not?

Even in the countryside of his own world he did not know much about what could be eaten in the way of berries (if any could be found) or other growing things, except those from gardens. There were survival books supposed to explain just how you could live off the wild, but such knowledge had never appealed to him and he had never read one. No, they would have to go light on their provisions. Back in the jeep—if they could find their way back— were the two melons and all those cases of drinks. But that was not much.

He squatted down on his heels, facing Linda who had settled cross-legged in the grass.

"Listen—about food—I don't have much. You have anything in that?" He pointed to her bag.

"You mean—" He could see from the expression on her face that she understood. Then she went on, steadily enough. "You mean we might not be able to find anything to eat here?"

"Well, there might be fish in the lake. And there are blackberries—at least there were blackberries near our cabin. But this isn't our lake. We had better go easy with what we have until we know the score."

Linda pulled at the knotted drawstring of the duffel bag. "I don't have much, but I was taking two boxes of peanut brittle up to Jane, and a tin of English toffee—Jane loves peanut brittle and Ron has this thing about toffee—the rum-flavored kind. There're the melons and all that Coke and stuff back in the jeep. But it's heavy to carry. I don't think we can pack it along with us. Nick, where will we go? There're no houses here, and beyond there"—she pointed to the far side of the lake—"it looks like more woods."

She was right. There was a dark rise of trees over there, matching that from which they had just emerged. In fact, as far as Nick could see, though the lake curved farther south and that end of it was now hidden, the water was ringed by forest. Suppose they did work through that, and they had no idea how many miles of it there were, what lay beyond? He had a hazy idea, from a novel he had read concerning the early American wilderness, that such growth could extend across a state with very few breaks.

"I don't know," he said frankly again. "But I'd rather be here in the open than under the trees. We can move down to the end of the lake—there's an outlet—the Deep Run—there, if this is like our lake. Maybe we could work out of the woods using that for a guide." He was rather proud of himself for remembering that.

"*If* this lake is like the one you know," she commented. "Does it look like it, really, Nick?"

He stood up, shading his eyes against the glare of the sun, which was hot now, but not as hot, he thought, as it might have been in their world. Slowly he studied the part of the lake visible from here. It was hard to equate this untouched, wild land with that where cabins and small docks were visible. But he was almost certain the contours of the shoreline were not too dissimilar from those he had known since he was small. And he said so.

"Do you suppose," Linda asked, "that we have gone back in time—that we're in the country that existed long before our people came into it? That—that we may meet Indians?" She shot another wary glance at the woods.

"That would not explain the unicorn. Nor gray deer—" Nick indicated the peacefully grazing herd. "We could be in an alternate world." He was unrolling the package of food from the store, but now his hands were still as he thought of what he was saying. Alternate worlds, time travel—such things did not exist! They could not—not for Nick Shaw, a very ordinary person who only wanted a quiet weekend for himself. He was Nick Shaw, he was alive, yet this was happening! Unless, of course, he had really knocked himself out back there with the bike and maybe now was in a hospital with a vivid dream—

"Alternate world? But unicorns—they never existed at all. They are only fairy tales." Linda shook her head. "Nick!" For the second time her voice soared up and she caught at him. "Nick, look there! Isn't that smoke?"

She pointed south beyond the deer and he followed her finger with his gaze. She was right! From somewhere in the brush beyond the meadowland a beacon of smoke was rising. And smoke could mean only one thing—people! Ted and Ben—trapped here all those years! Nick's thought flew first to them. But company—company to help them, to let them know they were not alone in a nightmare!

Hastily he repacked the food, put the bag back on the bike. He wished they dared ride, but it would be folly to try. And they had better be careful about getting around those deer. The animals looked harmless enough but that was not saying they would remain so if alarmed.

They wanted to run, but the grass tangled and pulled at their feet and the bike wheels, so that they floundered along at little better than a walking pace. Also, at Nick's insistence, they made a detour around the edge of the open space where the deer were, putting a screen of brush between them and the animals. And they froze once as the stag that was the leader flung up its head and stared straight at the bush behind which they happened to be.

Nick felt very naked and exposed then. He had heard that if you were absolutely still animals would lose interest in you and he scowled a warning at Linda. She nodded, holding her hand about Lung's muzzle. But the Peke appeared to understand and did not fight for his freedom and a chance to bark.

The stag watched them, or at least Nick thought they were its quarry. But after a time when the two dared hardly draw a full breath, the stag grunted and trotted toward the lake. When it was what seemed to Nick a safe distance away they hurried on.

But this closer sight of the deer presented another puzzle. Surely these gray animals were larger than those of Nick's own world, differing in size as they did in color. He wished he knew more, could get enough hints to answer some of his questions, if those might be answered at all.

They moved on, around the curve in the lake. Yes, there was the opening to Deep Run. So this place did follow the general pattern of their own world. And the smoke rose near the mouth of the Run. Nick felt some return of satisfaction at being proved right on one point of geography. But his triumph was speedily dashed.

"Stand where you are, chums!"

✳ 3 ✳

Lung broke into a wild barking, facing the bush screen from behind which that order had come. Nick halted, though Linda took a step or two as if the plunging of the now aroused Peke pulled her ahead.

Nick touched her arm with one hand, with the other he steadied the bike.

"Who are you?" he demanded of the bush and was inwardly glad his voice was so even and controlled. Ted—Ben? Some other who had preceded them into this alien world?

There was a moment of silence, so prolonged that Nick wondered if the challenger had faded into deeper cover, tricking them into a halt while he withdrew. But why would anyone be so elusive? The stranger in hiding could certainly see they were harmless.

Then the bushes parted and a man came into the open. He was very ordinary looking, a little shorter than Nick, but broader of shoulder, his bulk of body enhanced by the garment he wore, a coverall. Perched on his head was a helmet rather like a inverted basin, and he had on thick boots.

His face was round and there was a thick brush of moustache, grayish red, half hiding his mouth. In one hand he carried—

A slingshot!

Viewing that, Nick could have laughed, except there was something in the stranger's attitude that did not permit such a reaction to his childish weapon. And there was a very faint stir of

29

memory deep in Nick's mind. Somewhere, sometime, he had seen a man wearing just such clothing. But where and when?

As yet the newcomer had given no answer to Nick's question. Instead he eyed them narrowly. Lung, straining to the very end of his leash, was sniffing, his barking having subsided, sniffing as if to set this stranger's scent deep in his catalog of such odors.

If the stranger intended to overawe them with such a beginning, Nick refused to yield.

"I asked," he said, "who are you?"

"And I heard you, chum. I ain't lost the use of m' ears, not yet. I'm Sam Stroud, Warden of Harkaway Place, if it's anything to you. Which I'm laying odds, it ain't. There's just the two of you?"

He watched them closely, almost as if he expected them to be the van of a larger party. Linda broke in:

"Warden! Nick, he's dressed like an air raid warden—one of those in the picture about the Battle of Britain they showed in our history course."

English! That explained his accent. But what was an Englishman in the uniform of a service over forty years in the past doing here? Nick did not want to accept the suggestion the discovery brought.

"Is she right?" He added a second question to the first. "You are that kind of warden?"

"That's so. Supposin', m'lad, you speak up now. Who are you? An' this young lady here?"

"She's Linda Durant and I'm Nick Shaw. We're—we're Americans."

Stroud raised a thick hand and rubbed his jaw. "Well, now—Americans, hey? Caught right in your own country?"

"Yes. We were just heading for a lake—like this lake—then suddenly we were here. Where is here?"

Stroud made a sound that might have been intended for a bark of laughter, except there was very little humor in it.

"Now that's a question, Shaw, which nobody seems able to answer. The Vicar, he's got one or two ideas—pretty wide they are—but we've never been able to prove them one way or another. When did you come through?"

"Not too long ago," Linda answered. "Is that your fire making the smoke? We're awfully hungry and we were just going to eat when we saw it and came along . . ."

"You have some supplies?" Stroud rammed the slingshot back under the belt of his boiler suit. "All right, come ahead." He turned a little toward the bush from which he had emerged, put two fingers to his lips and gave a low but carrying whistle. "You ain't bait as far as I can see."

"Bait?" Nick did not like the sound of that.

Again Stroud gave his crow of laughter. "Bait, yes. You'll learn, m' lad, you'll learn. This way now, an' mind the bushes . . ."

He pushed ahead and they followed in a way which to Nick's eyes used all available cover. But if there was such a need to hide, why then did they allow smoke to rise like a banner in the air? Only a moment later, he realized that they were not heading toward the site of that fire, but well to the left of it.

Linda must have made the same discovery, for now she asked: "Aren't we going to your camp?"

"Right ahead—" Stroud's deep voice reached them. "Mind this vine, enough to trip a man up it is."

Nick had to mind the vine, a tough cover on the ground, with attention. It caught at the bike, as well as at his feet, with such persistence one could almost believe it a set trap. Twice he had to stop and untangle it, so that Stroud and Linda had disappeared and he had only the marks of their passing to guide him on a trail that took them farther and farther from the site of the fire and then curved again toward the Run.

He came out at last in a clearing walled by what seemed a solid siding of thick brush. And there he found Stroud, Linda, and three others. Two were men, the third a woman. They had been facing Linda, but, as Nick pushed his way through with a crackling of brush, they turned almost as one to stare at him.

The men were in contrast to each other as well as to Stroud. One was elderly, very tall and gaunt, his white hair in a fluff about his head as if it were too fine to be controlled. He had a great forward hook of a nose that was matched by the firmness of the jaw beneath. But his eyes, under the shadow of bushy brows, did not have the fierce hawk glare Nick expected. They were intelligent and full of interest, but they also held an acceptance of others, not the need for dominance that the rest of his face suggested.

He wore a dark gray suit, much the worse for hard usage, and a sweater underneath its coat that did not come high enough to hide a clergyman's roundabout collar. On his feet were rough hide moccasins, which were in strange contrast to the rest of his clothing, shabby as that was.

The younger man was an inch or two taller than Nick and, like Stroud, he was in uniform, but not that of a warden. His blue tunic was much worn, but there were wings on its breast, and he had pushed to the back of his blond head a pilot's cap.

Their feminine companion was almost as tall as the pilot and she, too, was in uniform, with badges Nick did not recognize on the shoulder. A helmet like the Warden's crowned a mass of unruly dark hair. Her figure was almost as lean as that of the clergyman, and her face, weathered and brown, made no pretense to good looks. Yet there was an air of competence and authority about her that was impressive.

"Americans," she commented. "Then," she spoke to the clergyman, "you were entirely right in your surmise, Adrian. We did travel farther than we thought in that cage."

The blond pilot also fingered a slingshot. "We'd better shove off." His eyes had gone from Nick to the brush. He had the attitude of one listening. "No use watching the trap any longer—"

"Barry is correct," the clergyman nodded. "We may not have had the kind of success we hoped to obtain. But by attracting our young friends here we have excellent results."

"Better introduce ourselves," the woman said briskly. "Adrian Hadlett, Vicar of Minton Parva." The clergyman gave an old-fashioned and rather majestic inclination of his head. "Pilot Officer Barry Crocker, and I'm Diana Ramsay—"

"Lady Diana Ramsay," Stroud growled as if that was important.

She made an impatient gesture with one hand. The other, Nick noted, held a third slingshot.

"There're a couple more of us," she continued. "You'll meet them at the camp."

Once more, this time with Nick and Linda in the midst of this energetic group, they pushed on, to come out on the bank of the Run. And not too much farther on was their camp.

Logs had been rolled into place and reinforced with rocks, forming what was half-hut, half-cave. Lung set to barking as a huge, gray-furred shape, which had been sunning by the entrance, reared back and showed a brush of tail. With ears flattened to its skull, the cat faced the excited Peke with a warning hiss that deepened into a growl. Linda dropped her bag to catch up the willing warrior, holding him despite his struggles.

"Now then, Jeremiah, m'dear, that be no proper way to say good day, not at all it ben't."

From the door issued a small woman to catch up the cat, a hefty armload, and soothe him gently with hands crook-jointed by arthritis, patched with the brown spots of age. Her hair, as white as the Vicar's, was twisted into a tight little bun above a round face with a mere knob of a nose that gave very precarious perch room to a pair of metal-framed glasses.

She lisped a little as she spoke, perhaps because her teeth seemed uncertainly anchored in her mouth, but there was a bright and interested welcome in the way she regarded the newcomers. Her dress was covered in part by an apron of sacking and an old mackintosh which swung cloak wise from her shoulders. On her feet were the same kind of crude moccasins as the Vicar wore.

"Jean," she called back over her shoulder. "We've got company."

The girl who came at the summons was perhaps only a little older than Linda herself. She also wore a dark blue uniform, though over it she had pinned apronlike a piece of dingy cloth, as if she hoped so to protect the only clothing she had. Her hair was brown and sprang in waves about her tanned face, a face that was pretty enough to make a man look a second time, Nick thought.

"Americans." Lady Diana again carried through the ritual of introductions. "Linda Durant, Nicholas Shaw. And this is Mrs. Maude Clapp and Jean Richards, who is a WREN."

"WREN?" repeated Nick, a little bewildered.

The girl smiled. "Women's Royal Naval Service—I believe you call yours WAVES."

"Well now, didn't I tell you that the dream I had me last night was a true one?" Mrs. Clapp's voice was cheery with open friendliness. "Company comin', that it was. An' we've fish all ready to fry out nice'n crisp. Couldn't have been luckier, now, could it?" she asked of the company at large, but not as if she expected any real answer. "Jeremiah here, he won't take at your little dog, Miss, if the dog don't take at him. Jeremiah, he ain't a quarrelsome beast."

"I hope Lung isn't." In Linda's hold the Peke had become quiet. Now she swung him up so she could view him eye to eye. "Lung, friend, friend!" She spoke with emphasis, then turned the dog around to face the big cat whom Mrs. Clapp had put on the ground once more. "Friend, Lung!"

The Peke flashed his tongue across his own nose. But when Linda set him down he settled by her feet, quiet, as if he had not been only moments earlier in a frenzy against a tribal enemy.

Nick offered his own supplies.

"Bread!" Mrs. Clapp opened the bag and sniffed ecstatically at its contents. "Fresh bread! Lands, I almost forgot what it smells like, let alone tastes."

Nick had grounded the bike. Now he stood a little to one side glancing from the pilot Crocker to the girl Jean, then on to Stroud in his warden's uniform. Crocker, unless Nick was a very poor judge of ages, was in his early twenties, Jean even younger. They could not be as old as Stroud's uniform suggested. But—

"Something bothers you, my boy?" It was the Vicar. And without thinking Nick asked his question baldly:

"Do you mind telling me, sir—how long have you been here?"

The Vicar smiled wearily. "That—that may be impossible. We tried to keep a record in the beginning, but after they captured us and brought us here—" He shrugged. "By a matter of seasons, I should judge about four years. The raid hit Minton Parva the evening of July 24, 1942. I think we all have reason to remember that. We were in the crypt shelter of the church. Mrs. Clapp is, was, my housekeeper.

Lady Diana had come to see me about the hospital fund. Jean and Barry were on their way down to the station to take the train back, they were both returning from leave. And Stroud had come to check up on our supplies—when the alert sounded and we all went into the crypt. There was a sound—frankly, Shaw, we all believed it was the end. And then—somehow we were out of the church, out of even the England that we knew . . ."

He hesitated. Those tired but very keen eyes had been watching Nick's face. Now the Vicar's expression changed.

"You know something, don't you, my boy? Something that is disturbing you. What is it?"

"Time, sir. You say you think you have been here about four years. But today is—was—July 21, 1985."

He expected the Vicar to challenge him on that. It was not believable, not if Hadlett had been speaking the truth. And Nick was sure he had.

"July 21, 1985," repeated the Vicar slowly. "No, I do not doubt you, my boy, as I think you are expecting. It is too apt, it bears out all the old tales. But—1985—forty-three years—What happened there—forty years back?"

"Forty years what? . . ." Crocker lounged over to them. He had been more intent on the motorbike than he had on their conversation, but now he looked at Hadlett alertly. "What is this about forty years?"

"Tell him your date," the Vicar said to Nick as if his saying it would make the deeper impression.

"The date today—it's July 21, 1985," Nick returned. Hadlett had accepted that without question, but would the others?

"Nineteen eighty-five," repeated the pilot blankly. "But—it's impossible—Padre, it's about 1946, unless we counted wrong, and a man can't tick off forty years that way without knowing it!"

It was Lady Diana who had listened this time. "Adrian, then you were right. It's like the old tales, isn't it? Over forty—" She looked beyond them to where the water curled around the stones in the even flowing Run. "Ninety-eight—but I'm not, Adrian, I'm no older—"

"That, too, was part of those same old tales, Diana," he said.

"No!" Crocker protested. "This kid has it all wrong, he's one of *Them* maybe. How do we know—" He was backing away from Nick, the sling again in his hand. "He's working for *Them*, sent to break us down with a story like that!"

"Here—what's goin' on?" Stroud bore down on them. "What's this talk about *Them*?"

Crocker burst out with his accusation. And there was open anger in his voice as he turned on the Warden. "We brought these two here—next *They* will be coming! Tell us that we've been here forty-plus years! That's a lie no one's going to believe."

"Now, then." Stroud's hand was on Crocker's shoulder. "Take a reef on that there tongue of yours, Barry. These don't smell like the Herald do they? An' when did the flying devils use bait? They zooms right in an' takes what they wants, no frills about it. All right, you say it's 1985 back there—what happened to the war?"

Stroud's rumble had drawn them all. They made a semicircle, looking at Nick, some with speculative, Crocker with accusing, eyes.

"That ended in '45." Nick searched memory for an account of the conflict that had ended long before he was born, but that to this handful was still vividly a threat.

"Who won?" demanded Crocker angrily, as if by his answer Nick would be judged.

"We did—the allies. We invaded and took Germany from one side, the Russians came in from the other—they got Berlin. Hitler killed himself before they got to him. And we dropped the atom bomb on Hiroshima and Nagasaki—then the Japanese surrendered that same year."

"Atom bomb?" Crocker no longer sounded angry, but rather dazed.

"Yes. Wiped out both cities." Nick remembered the accounts of that and hoped he would not have to go into details.

"And now—?" the Vicar asked after a pause, while his companions stared at Nick as if he were speaking a foreign language.

"Well, there's still trouble. There was the Korean War and the one in Vietnam, and now there's trouble in South America. China has gone Communist, and Russia still has half of Germany under control—the eastern part. But we've made manned landings on the Moon." He tried to think of what had been progress and not just dreary wrangling. "And now we are planning to put a permanent station into space—besides Skylab. But—I can't tell you everything that happened. England—they've given up the Empire, and they had a Labor government for a long time—it's been tough over there—awfully high taxes and slipping back—"

"Forty years, yes, a lot can happen." The Vicar nodded. "And still wars—"

"Please." Linda broke into the quiet that followed his comment. "If you came here from England and we from Ohio—Did you get across the ocean some way? Or is this all just one country?"

The Vicar shook his head. "No, the general contours of this world seem geographically aligned to those of our own. This continent and England appear much as they must have in a very remote past before men began to tame the land. We were brought to this continent as prisoners. Only by the grace of God were we able to escape. Since then we have been trying to devise a way to return. Only I fear that this world has no ships to offer us. But ours is a very long and complicated story and I would suggest we tell it by degrees, perhaps over some of Mrs. Clapp's excellently cooked fish. Shall we?"

Perhaps it was the return to tasks they all knew and had shared for some time that relieved the tension. They got ready for the meal. And passing around the bread Nick had brought apparently made this a feast.

Hadlett turned a roll about in his fingers. "You never know how much you miss the small things of life"—he used a cliché to express the truth—"until they are taken from you. Bread we cannot produce here. Though Mrs. Clapp has experimented with ground nuts and seeds from a wild grass not unlike oats. It is good to eat bread again."

"You said you were brought here as prisoners." Nick wanted to know the worst of what might now menace them.

"Ah, yes. It is best that you be warned." The Vicar swallowed a bite of roll. "This is a very strange world and, though it has not been for want of trying, we have not penetrated very far into its secrets. But we believe that it is somehow parallel with our own, though obviously different. Sometime in the past, we do not know how far past, there was apparently a force set into being that could reach into our own world at special places and draw out people. There are many stories in our own world of mysterious disappearances."

Nick nodded. "More and more of those have been collected recently into books. We came from a place that has such a reputation—many disappearances over the years."

"Just so. And our church at Minton Parva was situated near a fairy mound—"

"Fairy mound?" Nick was startled. What was the meaning of that?

"No, I am not trying in any fashion to be amusing, my boy. In Britain we have a very long history—considered today to be legend— of disappearances near such sites. People 'fairy taken,' who sometimes reappeared years, even generations, after their disappearances, with an explanation of spending a day, or a month, or a year in another world, these are common in our folklore."

"Then," Linda broke in, "we can go back!" She had been holding Lung, and perhaps her hands closed too tightly on the small dog, for he gave a whine of protest.

"That," the Vicar told her gravely, "we do not know. But our own efforts have failed. And—we have seen enough here during our wanderings to suggest that such escapes, or returns, must be very exceptional."

Linda, still holding Lung in her arms, was on her feet. She stood so for a moment, her glance sweeping from face to face, ending with Nick. And it was to him that she spoke directly, as if she was prepared to believe him over whatever the others might say.

"Do you think we can get back?"

He had the choice of lying, of trying to be easy with her. But somehow he could not do it.

"No one ever went back through the Cut-Off that we knew of." In his own ears his voice sounded harsh.

Her face was blank of expression. She turned abruptly and began to walk away, her walk becoming swifter as she went. Nick got up to start after her.

"No." She did not turn to look at him, but it was as if she knew he would follow. "Let me alone—just let me alone for a while!"

And such was the force of the way she spoke that he stopped, uncertain as to whether he should force his company on her or not.

"Jean." It was Hadlett who spoke. "See that she is safe, but let her be. We must all face our truths as best we can."

The English girl passed Nick. He turned to the others.

"See that she is safe?" he repeated. "And you were prisoners. Who and what do you have to fear? Let's have it straight!"

"Good enough." Stroud had been eating stolidly. Now he leaned back against one of the logs helping to form their shelter. "We're not alone here, you must have guessed that. And as far as we've been able to find out there's three kinds of people—or things—or whatever you want to name 'em.

"There's some like us who have been caught. We tried to make talk with a couple of crowds like ours—or we think they're like us. But they don't understand. The last time it was soldiers, an' we got shot at. Not our soldiers—they looked Chinese.

"Then there's the Herald an' those who listen to him an' change—" He spat out that last word as if it were some obscenity. "The Herald—he may always have been here, native to this world. He has the cities an' the People with him. He wants us. Soon as he finds out about you two he will come snoopin'. All we know is if you take what he has to offer, then you change. After that you're not a man or a woman anymore, you're something different. We aren't havin' any of that. You won't either, if you have sense.

"Third—there's the flyer hunters. They ain't o' this world any more than we are. Only in their flyers they can get in an' out. One of their planes winks into the air an', 'fore you know it, they have you netted. I don't know what they do with the poor devils they catch, outside of shut 'em up in cages like we was. But we were lucky. The ship that caged us, it got something wrong. Made a crash landin' here an' we escaped 'cause the crew were wiped out. That's when we found out they'd brought us out of England."

"But your smoke—you talked about bait. What—or who—were you trying to catch?'"

Stroud grunted. "Not the flyers or the Herald, you can bet. No, we came across some tracks yesterday, mixed, women an' children. We got to thinkin' it was another crowd we could meet up with an' not get shot at. Of course, they might be dream things. But we figured it wouldn't do no harm to set up a signal an' see what came lookin'."

"They set traps," Crocker commented. "We thought we'd try one, but not for *Them*."

"You meant the hunters?" Nick was confused. After Stroud's story of the flyers he wondered that these people wanted to pull such a menace down on them.

"No, either the other drifters, or else the changed ones—if they were changed an' not just born that way."

"We saw—or thought we saw," Nick said slowly, "a unicorn when we were back in the woods. Was that what you mean by changed ones?"

"Not quite," the Vicar answered him. "We've seen a good many strange beasts and birds and things that combine two or more species. But such do not threaten us, and we believe they are native here. Perhaps from time to time in the past they strayed into our world to leave legends behind them. We have yet to meet a dragon, but I would not swear that none exist here. The changed ones—they are human for the most part in general appearance. It is the small details—certainly their 'powers,' which is the best word to use for their abilities—that betray them. The People of the Hills are very old."

"We stay near the woods"—Stroud nodded at a stand of trees not more than a few strides away—"because the flyers can't get in under those to reach us. So far we haven't seen many of 'em. They come in waves like—we'll have a sky full of them for a few days—then they're gone. An' as long as we keep away from the cities we're all right. The flyers got a hate for the cities—try to bomb 'em."

"Not bomb, I told you, Stroud!" Crocker cut in. "They don't bomb. In fact I don't see what they do—though it must be some type of raid the way they come over. Whatever they try to accomplish, it doesn't cause any damage—none that we can see. The cities are safe."

"For them as wants to be changed," Mrs. Clapp observed. "But we ain't them."

Nick felt as if his head was spinning. It would seem that life here was complicated past even the many perils that now threatened his own time and space. This band, which had continued existence together as a group, displayed great hardiness and determination. Undoubtedly he and Linda had been lucky in this meeting. What if they had wandered on, on their own, to face all these threats without warning?

He tried to express his relief at their good fortune, and the Vicar smiled gently.

"You, yourself, have a part in your future, my boy. You have managed to adjust to a situation that might indeed have threatened your reason. We have seen the pitiful ending of one man who could not accept his transition. Acceptance is necessary."

Nick saw Linda and Jean coming back along the bank of the Run. So much had happened. Had he really accepted as Hadlett said, or was this all some kind of crazy dream from which he could not wake? Would there come a time when it would hit him as it had Linda, and he must make his peace with what seemed insanity?

❖ 4 ❖

Outside the rain was falling steadily. It had begun at sunset and had continued. Nick could hear the even breathing of those asleep around him in what was now a crowded shelter. But he could not sleep, rather lay close to the door staring out into the dark, listening.

The sound had started some time ago, very faint and far away. But it had caught his attention and now, tense, he listened with all his might, trying to separate that rise and fall of distant melody from the gurgle of the Run, the rain.

Nick could not tell whether it was singing or music, he could not even be sure it had not died away upon occasion and then begun again, faint, far away—drawing— For, the longer he listened, the more he was caught in a net of desire. A need to answer moved him, in spite of the rain, the utter dark of the night in a hostile land.

Sweet—low—but now and then clear and true. Nick thought he could almost distinguish words. And when that happened his inner excitement grew until he could hardly control it. Run—out into the night—answer—

Nick sat up now, his breath coming faster as if he had already been running. There was movement behind him in the shelter.

"Lorelei—" Hadlett's precise, gentle voice was a whisper.

"Lorelei," Nick repeated and swallowed. He was not going, he dared not. Caution born of his basic sense of self-preservation was alert, warning—He dared not.

"A lure," the Vicar continued. "The rain appears to produce it. Or else the proximity of water. There is this you must understand—part of those who are the permanent inhabitants are well intentioned toward us, or neutral; others are merely maliciously spiteful. A few are blackly evil. Since we cannot guess which are which, we must be ever on guard. But we have proof of the Lorelei—we witnessed the results of its—feeding. Oh, not on flesh and blood—it feeds on the life-force. What is left is an empty husk. Yet its lure is so strong that, even knowing what it may do, men have gone to it."

"I know why," Nick said. His hands were balled into fists so tightly that his nails, short as they were, cut into his skin. For even as Hadlett had been talking that sound swelled. Now, in growing fear, he raised his fingers to his ears, plugged out the melody.

How long he sat so, or if the Vicar continued to talk to him, Nick did not know. But at last he allowed his hands to fall, dared to listen again. There was nothing now but the rain and the stream. With a sigh of relief he settled back on the pile of dried stuff that formed his bed. Later he slept and dreamed. But as important as those dreams seemed, he could not remember them past waking.

For two days thereafter they might have been camping out on a normal countryside with no sign that they shared the land, untouched as it was by ax, uncut by road.

Fishing was good, and in addition there were ripe berries and a variety of headed grass close to the grain of their own world, which could be harvested. Nick learned that this shelter by the river was not the permanent base of the party, but that they had a cave further north they considered their headquarters. They were engaged now in making a series of exploratory trips.

Using the compass on the second day Nick managed to guide Stroud and Crocker back to the jeep.

"Tidy little jumper." The Warden considered the machine regretfully. "No getting it out of that pinch though."

Nick had gone straight to the cargo, those cases of drinks and the melons. But someone or something had been there before him. All that remained were a couple of smashed bottles.

"Pity," Stroud commented. "Not a pint of the old stuff, maybe, but we could've used it. What do you say, Barry—who nosed in ahead of us?"

The pilot had been inspecting the leaf mold around the stranded jeep.

"Boots—army issue, I'd say. Those Chinese maybe. They could have drifted down this way. But it was in the early part of the evening, maybe the afternoon." He squatted on his heels, using a twig to point out what he could read stamped into the ground. "There's been a slinker here, its pads cover one of the boot marks, and those don't go prowling until dark. Anything else worth taking?"

Stroud was searching the jeep with the care of an experienced scrounger.

"Tool kit." He had unrolled a bundle that he had found under the seat to reveal a couple of wrenches and some other tools. "That's all, I'd say."

Nick stood near the tree against which the jeep nosed. This had been the middle of the Cut-Off. Yet looking around now he could not believe it.

"What caused it—our coming through?" he asked, though he did not expect any answer.

Stroud had rewrapped the tools, his face mirroring his satisfaction in the find. Now he looked up.

"There was a talk I heard—about our world running on electromagnetism. This brain who was talkin', he said we were all— every one of us, men, animals, trees, grass, everything—really electrical devices, we vibrate somehow. Though most of us don't know it. Then he went on to say as how we have been using more an' more electricity an' how now some small thing like a radio or such can throw out force enough to stop a much larger power source without meanin' to.

"He was warnin' us, said we were usin' forces we didn't fully understand without carin'. An' something might just happen to lead to a big blowup some day. Maybe these places we come through work that way. The Vicar, he thinks a lot about it, an' he said that once."

"But we've been using electricity only close to a hundred years, and people disappeared this way before that. Right here." Nick pointed to the trapped jeep. "We had records of people disappearing here going as far back as when the white men first moved in, and that's about one hundred seventy years. According to your Vicar it goes much farther back in your country."

Stroud shrugged. "Don't know what works the traps. But we're here, ain't we? An' we'll probably stay, seein' as how we ain't goin' to get back across the ocean by wadin'. An' what about you, Shaw, any chance of your findin' a way back from here?"

Nick shook his head. The solidity of the tree he could touch, the scene about him, was manifest. And no one had ever returned from the Cut-Off once they had gone. The sudden realization of that closed in on him as it must have on Linda earlier. He wanted to scream, to run, to allow his panic some physical expression. Somehow he did not dare, for if he lost control now, he was sure, he could never regain it.

His fingers dug into tree bark. No—he was *not* going to scream—was not going to break!

There was a sharp sound from the jeep. Stroud threw himself flat on the seat. Crocker went to earth as quickly. Nick stared, not understanding. Then he saw it lying on the ground. A spear—They were under attack. He crouched, sought cover.

Nick listened for another sound, warning of an outright attack. He had no weapon, not even a stone, with which to defend himself. The quiet was absolute, no birdcall, not even a rustle of breeze in the foliage above them. Stroud and Crocker had their slingshots—but what use were those here?

Nick studied the spear. It had made a dent in the side of the jeep. That he could see. But the weapon was outside his own experience. In the first place the shaft was shorter than he would imagine it should be. The point was metal with four corners united. He knew next to nothing of primitive weapons but he thought it was not American Indian—if Indians did roam this world.

The spear, the silence—Nick found himself trying to breathe as lightly as possible. This waiting—when would come the attack? And from which direction? They could be completely surrounded right now. His back felt very naked, as if at any moment another of those weapons might thud home in his own body.

He could see neither Stroud (who must have squeezed himself to the floorboards of the jeep), nor Crocker. The pilot must have had training in such warfare, he had gone to earth so well. What did they do, just sit here and wait for death to come out, either silent, or in a wild roaring charge they could not counter with bare hands?

Nick's mouth was dry, his hands were so sweaty he wanted to wipe them on his shirt, yet dared not move. What were *They* waiting for?

What did break the silence was the last thing he expected to hear—laughter.

So this enemy was so sure of them it could laugh! That cut through his fear, made him angry. Funny was it?

Laughter and then a voice calling out in some incomprehensible tongue. A demand for their surrender, a listing of what would happen to them when they were overrun and taken? It could be either, but Nick noted that neither of his companions made any response to it. He could only follow their lead, hoping that their hard-learned lessons might in turn teach him some answer to the local perils.

Again laughter, light, mocking—But was it threatening? It seemed rather to have the spirit of mischief in it. Something in that tone made Nick less tense. So he was not startled when again a voice called, this time speaking his own language:

"Out of hiding, fearful men! Did you believe the Dark Ones were upon you? Scatter and hide, is that the way to greet us, you who came tramping into our land without asking? No courtesy?"

Nick watched Stroud heave his bulk out of concealment. Apparently the Warden was willing to accept the harmlessness of the questioner, or else there was a truce on. Crocker crawled out also, and, still wanting some reassurance, Nick was shamed into joining him in open sight.

He was beginning to wonder how good the aim of the unseen might be. That spear had struck well away from any of them. It could have been intended as a warning, a drastic announcement of arrival.

"We're waiting." Stroud's voice held a very audible note of

exasperation. Nick could believe that the Warden was angry at his own reaction moments earlier, though Nick would think it was better in this country to cling to caution.

"No courtesy—yes," countered the unseen. "So you are waiting. What if we make a wall of waiting to enclose you, spin a cage?" Now the voice was sharp in return.

Nick stared in the direction from which it appeared to come. There was space there between the massive trees, but the speaker could well be concealed behind any trunk. He could detect no movement.

Stroud shrugged. "I don't know who you are, or what you are. You offered attack—" He was making a visible effort to reply calmly, not to cause any more annoyance to the concealed speaker. "We've shown ourselves—now it's your move."

"Move, move, move!" the voice repeated in a rising chant. "A game—the heavy-footed stumblers would play a game, would they?"

Out of nowhere flashed a ball of light. It almost touched Stroud, then halted in midair, bobbed up and down in a wild dance around him. The Warden stood still, his hands loose at his sides. Though he blinked when the ball seemed ready to dash into his very face, he did not try to dodge its swift flurries of seeming attack.

"A game—you play then, stumbler. Take your courage in your thoughts and play!" The ball went into a dazzling flurry of movement, becoming nearly too blinding to watch.

With a sudden leap it abandoned Stroud, made the same threat of attack about Crocker, who presented a like impassive front. Now it changed color with eye-searing rapidity—green, blue, yellow, violet, and all shades rippling in between. Never red, Nick noted, nor any shades of yellow bordering on that color, nor did it reach pure white.

"You do not care to play then? But the sport would be poor with you, stumblers!" The ball withdrew, bobbed up and down vertically some distance away. The glow increased so its movement wove a pillar of light, a light that continued to hold when the ball itself disappeared.

Now the column of light winked out as a blown candle flame, leaving a small figure. Perhaps he did not top Nick's shoulder, even with the upstanding feather in his cap, a feather that quivered with every slight movement. But he was completely humanoid in form, and by his appearance an adult male. His face was smooth, young, and yet about him was the feeling of age and boredom. He wore dull green breeches, the color of the leaves. They were very tight-fitting breeches and they were matched by calf-high boots of the same color, only visible because they were topped with wide turn-over cuffs.

His tunic, which laced up the front and had no sleeves, was green also and exposed his small muscular arms. The lacings were glinting gold, as was the elaborate buckle of his belt, and the clasp that fastened his cloak, which was flung back over his shoulders to allow his arms full freedom.

The cloak was scarlet, lined with green, and his cap was of the same shade. Fair hair fell to his shoulder. And the hair held a light of its own, surrounding his head with a gleaming mist. He had well-cut, handsome features, only Nick saw, where the locks of hair were swung back behind his ears, that those were large out of proportion, rising to very discernible points.

There was a short sword, or long knife, sheathed at his belt, and he carried a second spear, twin to the one lying by the jeep. His expression was one of malicious amusement. But he did not speak. Instead he pursed his lips to whistle. And there was movement behind him, shadows detached themselves from the tree boles to flit forward.

Humanoid the little man might be, but the force he captained was not. There was a shambling bear that sat up on its haunches, its forepaws dangling, its red tongue lolling between only too-evident teeth. Beside that crouched a spotted cat—but what was a leopard doing in these woods? Those two of the company Nick could readily identify—but there were others—

What name did you give a creature with a catlike, spotted body, but with four limbs ending in hooves, a canine-inclined head, bearing great upstanding twin fangs in its lower jaw and double horns sprouting at the beginning of a horse mane just above its wide, fierce eyes? There was a second beast beside it that might be very remotely related to a wolf, save that it had a more foxlike head, a very slender body, the talons of a giant bird in place of forepaws; the hind paws and bushy tail normal enough, if anything might be termed normal in such a mixture.

The four creatures sat at ease, their glowing eyes, for even the bear's eyes glowed red, intent upon the three by the jeep.

"You see," the small man with a graceful wave of his hand had indicated his hoofed and clawed and pawed companions, "our strength. Now we ask of you your absence. This is our domain and you have not asked our permission to enter it."

To his own surprise Nick found himself answering:

"We did not want entrance. We came without it being our will." He pointed to the jeep. "One minute that was on a road in my own world—the next it was here."

The small man lost the smile that was close to a taunt. In fact all expression faded from his face. He held out his hand and the spear he had flung earlier arose in the air, went to him, fitting its haft neatly into his grasp. If he made some sign to his company Nick did not catch it. But the four oddly assorted animals arose and faded away into the gloom, where they were instantly lost as if they had turned into nothingness.

"You are, being what you are," the stranger said slowly, "not for our governing. But I say to you, get you hence, for this is a forest under rule and not a wild wood open to wanderers."

He lifted the spear once again as if about to cast it. But it would appear that was only to underline his order. For a moment he held it so, then the blaze of his cloak, the mist about his hair billowed out like smoke from a fire, clouding his body to hide it utterly. The vapor drew back again on a center core, then vanished. They were alone. Nick turned to his companions.

"Who—what—?"

Stroud reached back into the jeep and jerked out the bundle of tools, hurrying so fast to unwrap it again that he almost dropped it. He drew out a small wrench and a screwdriver. Crocker grabbed the latter, holding it at chest level as if it were a weapon or shield. Stroud thrust the wrench at Nick who accepted it with surprise.

"Hold that in plain sight," the Warden ordered.

"Why? What—what was that?"

"Why—because it's iron. An' iron is out an' out poison as far as the People are concerned. If we'd had this in sight he wouldn't have dared even sling that toothpicker at us. As to who or what he is— you'd better ask the Vicar. We've seen his like a couple of times before. People of the Hills, the Vicar calls 'em—the Old Ones who have always been here according to what he says. They can get at a man all right—not with those spears an' swords of theirs—but in his mind—makin' him see whatever they want him to. An' if they say this place is theirs they mean it. We'd better get out—"

Stroud was already two strides along the back trail, Crocker matching him. Nick hurried to follow. The others did not look around. If they feared any ambush they showed no sign of that. He would be governed by them. Iron—iron was poison, was it? He held the wrench in sight. Good enough—if showing this was a form of protection he was willing to comply.

He could not draw level with the others until they were well away from the jeep. Nick himself kept looking around suspiciously, certain at one time or another he would catch a glimpse of one of the animals slinking behind to make sure they were leaving what was a haunted forest. Yet he never saw anything except the trees. Not even a unicorn this time.

When he finally joined Stroud he had another question.

"What about the animals? I can understand a bear—though leopards are African animals. But those other two—they weren't real—they couldn't be—"

He heard Crocker grunt. "You tapped it right there, Yank. But it doesn't matter how 'real' they are, you know. Here they'll be real enough to tear your throat out if that Green Man back there gave the order. You'll see worse than them. You heard him mention the Dark Ones? Those nobody wants to see! They have most power in the dark as far as we can tell—" He turned his head to look full at Nick, his face haunted by some memory. "Iron beats them, too. Ask Jean and Lady Diana sometime. They were berry picking and came upon a tower—it looked like a tower. That was late afternoon an' a cloudy day, so perhaps those in there were more active than they would have normally been. Jean saw one—full on—an' she, well, we had to wake her up at night for awhile. She had nightmares that near sent her around the bend! We've learned a lot—mostly the hard way—about what you can an' can't do here. An' you've just had your first lesson—when you're warned off you go!"

In spite of their zigzag path they made far better time getting out of the forest than Nick and Linda on their first journey. But when they came out into the comparative open Crocker gave a cry of alarm.

"Down!"

Seeing Stroud throw himself belly flat and half roll under a bush almost large enough to give him complete coverage, Nick tried to follow suit, though his own hastily won protection was smaller and thinner than that which sheltered the Warden. He saw Crocker a little beyond, also flat, but with his head supported on his crooked arm, looking out and up over the water.

"No—not a flying saucer!" Nick's protest was said aloud. And a vengeful-sounding hiss from his left reminded him to keep his mouth shut. Only he could not believe what he was seeing. Somehow this was harder to accept than those mixed-up beasts in the forest.

The thing—machine—illusion—whatever it was—hung silver bright and stationary well above the surface of the water. It was saucer shaped in part, though the upper half swelled to near dome proportions.

Unmoving, it hung. Then, from the south, there sped another sky craft of an entirely different model. This one was cigar shaped and moving at such speed it arrived almost in the wink of an eye. It swooped at the waiting saucer and from it shot a brilliant beam that should have struck full upon the swelling upper half. Instead the beam hit an invisible wall a good distance from the skin of the vessel.

The cigar backed off in another of those incredibly swift maneuvers, rose over the stationary craft to strike from a different angle. This was not a duel, for the saucer made no attempt to retaliate. It merely hung there in the open, well protected by whatever shield it carried, while the other craft, in a frenzy of effort, aimed its weapon-beam from various angles. Nick could imagine the frustration building up in the attacker—to launch his—or its—greatest power and not even awaken a slight response from the attacked must be infuriating.

Finally the cigar climbed directly above the saucer and hung there as motionless as the craft beneath it. There were no rays stabbing downward from it now. Instead there was an instant of sparkling light, a flash that was gone so quickly Nick could not even be sure he had sighted it at all.

Slowly the cigar began to descend, straight down on the saucer. What this maneuver might be Nick could not guess, nor had he any help from his companions. So slow was the descent that it was plainly ominous. The pilot of the upper ship now must be using the ultimate weapon at his command.

Down, down—was he going to ram the other—as did the Japanese pilots of World War II who died willingly to take an enemy plane or battleship with them? Down—

Nick saw a tremor in the lower ship. And then—

It was gone!

Exploded? But there had been no sound, no shock wave, no debris. It was just gone.

The cigar lurched, gave an upward jump. It circled the lake twice as if trying to make sure the enemy was no longer there. Once more it returned to hover over the site of the attack. Then it left, streaking away with a speed that took it out of sight in seconds.

Crocker sat up, holding his screwdriver in one hand before him as a worshipper in church might hold a candle.

"Fun and games," he commented. "So they're out to burn each other down now. That good or bad for us, I wonder?"

"What was he trying?" Nick wanted to know. "Coming down on the saucer that way?"

"I would guess, and it's just a guess, mind you, that he was going to use his force field against whatever one that other ship had. The flyers—they're years—centuries ahead of us with their technology— just as the People are with their 'magic.' Anyway the other plane decided it couldn't take it."

"I know one thing"—Stroud crawled on hands and knees between them—"that's plain now, m'boyos. We're gettin' out of this here country. With the Nasties back flyin' overhead, this ain't a healthy place for us to be. An' we've been warned out of the woods so we can't go kitin' in there to be safe. Get started out as soon as we can." He was on his feet, his pace near a run, as he headed up the open land toward the river camp. Yet even if it were needful to make speed, Nick noticed, he kept as much as he could to cover, as did Crocker. And Nick copied their caution.

5

Nick ran his hands along the handlebars of the motorbike. To leave it here would be like closing the door yet tighter on any chance of return. But Stroud was right, he could not take it through rough country ahead and it would be worthless anyway when the gas was exhausted. He wheeled it to the back of the shelter and there concealed it as best as he could.

They had waited until close to dawn of the next day before preparing for their trek back to what the English party considered their best haven of safety. But the night had not been an easy one. They had taken guard duty by turns, alert for any sky sign to prove the hunters' return, or any noise at ground level to suggest they were watched.

There had been a moon and the night was cloudless. And the light had drawn strange shadows, to look upon, which stirred the imagination, Nick believed, in a manner that did not allay uneasiness.

He had not been helped to confidence when, during his watch, an hour after midnight, the furred shape of Jeremiah flowed past him into the open just beyond his reach. Out there the big cat sat down, his tail stretched out straight behind him, his attitude one of listening. Then, without warning, the tail lashed from side to side, and there was a low growl. The sound never arose to that squall meaning a challenge, but kept on a low note, while the tail beat the sandy soil.

Nick wanted to use the flashlight he had taken from his saddlebags. But, though he longed to see what had so affected the cat, he did not want to run the risk of drawing the attention of what might be prowling out there.

He could hear nothing at all except what were, as far as he could tell, normal noises of the night. What Jeremiah could see, or hear, remained lost to his less efficient senses.

The cat cowered to the ground, tail still. He no longer growled. Across the sky something large and dark moved silently. There was a slow, single flap of wings, and it was gone. Jeremiah streaked back, leaping Nick's knees to reach the interior of the shelter.

But the sound that followed his return—Was it laughter? Not loud, hardly above an evil chuckle, it sounded. And it seemed to Nick to come out of the air, not from ground level. That flying thing? Nick drew on logic, reason—though logic and reason from the past had little to do with this world. How much was real, how much imagination?

Now that it was morning and they were preparing to leave, he found disbelief easier.

"Too bad you're havin' to leave your fine big bike." Mrs. Clapp was inducing Jeremiah to enter a woven basket, a form of imprisonment he was protesting. The cat turned his head suddenly and seized her hand between his jaws, though he did not apply the pressure of a true bite.

"Now, now. would you be left here, old man?" She scratched behind Jeremiah's ears. "Get in with no more fuss about it. It is me who'll have the carryin' as you well know. An' when have I ever made it the worse for you?"

She closed the lid, fastened it with quick efficiency.

"Yes." She spoke to Nick again. "A fine big bike an' one that cost you a good penny too, if I have eyes in m' head to guess. This country's not for ridin' though—less'n we get ourselves some of the white ones—"

"White ones?" He slung his saddlebags together over his shoulder and turned his back on the bike, trying to put it out of mind.

"Them what belong to the People. Ah, a fine proud sight they are, ridin' on their white ones. Horses those are, or enough like horses to give 'em the name. We've seen 'em twice at their ridin', always between the goin' of the sun an' the comin' of dark. A fine sight." She reached for a small pack to one side, but Nick had his hand on it before her fingers closed on its carrying loop.

"You have enough to look after with Jeremiah," he said.

Mrs. Clapp chuckled. "That I have. A big old man he is—ten years about. No . . ." Her round eyes showed a trace of distress. "Over forty years back—that's how you said it now, didn't you? Forty years—that I can't believe somehow. Almost a hundred and ten that would make me, an' I'm no granny in front of a fire. An' Jeremiah— by rights he'd be long gone. But he's here an' I'm as spry as ever. So I ain't goin' to believe in your forty years."

"Why should you?" Nick returned. "It's a time that does not hold here, that's certain. I read something once—does time pass us, or do we pass it? And we can add to that now—how fast or slow?"

"Slow, I'll speak up for the slow!" She smiled. "Ah, now, hand me over m' collectin' tote. I'll just have that handy. It's a good lot of things to fill the stomach snug, like you can find just marchin' along. Drop 'em into a stew an' you'll be smackin' your lips an' passin' up your bowl for more."

She slung the woven grass band supporting what was a cross between a basket and a tote bag made of reeds over her stooped shoulder. And, with Jeremiah's basket firmly in hand, trotted out, Nick following.

They all carried by shoulder bands, or knapsack fashion, similar bags. And Nick noted each also kept close to hand the iron defense, either in the form of one of the small tools from the jeep, or, in the case of Stroud, a small knife, blade bared.

Linda had Lung on a leash again. The Peke kept close to his mistress, but he held his head high, turning it from side to side as if he were defining and cataloging the various scents of the land.

The Run's bank was their road. And along it they went in an order that apparently was customary to them, Hadlett and Stroud to the fore, then Mrs. Clapp and Jean Richards, with Linda, Crocker and Lady Diana playing rear guard. Nick joined the latter.

"Running water." Lady Diana looked down into the Run. "That has more than one use here, young man. You drink, you wash, and it can be a barrier for some of the Dark Ones."

Crocker grunted. "Except you never know with a new type whether it's water-shy or not."

"There's that of course," Lady Diana agreed. "But here everything's really a matter of luck or chance. We've had more than our share of luck so far. There have been very difficult times—"

Again Crocker had an addition. "That's one way to see it. I'd say we've just squeaked through, more than once. I'd thought we'd used up all our luck when we walked away from the crash."

"What is *that?*" Nick had been only half listening, more intent upon the land around them than the conversation. He was staring with stark amazement at what lay half on the bank, half in the Run on the opposite side of the water.

A boat, canted over a little so its lower deck was awash on one side. But such a boat! And how had it come into the Run, which was manifestly too narrow and shallow to give it water room?

Now that they were closer he could see that it had been nearly gutted by fire, which had eaten in places into the great stern wheel that had been its method of propulsion. But how had it come here—and when?

He had seen a cruising sternwheeler on the Ohio River that took passengers for nostalgic rides during the summer. One such caught now in time?

"It's too big for this stream—" He protested against the evidence his eyes supplied.

"Not in flood time." Lady Diana carried a stout staff and with this she pointed to evidence, higher up the bank they traveled, that some time in the past there had indeed been a far greater rush of water here.

"We went over that coming down the first time," Crocker supplied. "Looks as if there had been an explosion. Hadlett said those things often blew up if they were pushed too hard. If there were any survivors"—the pilot shrugged—"they must have gone off. It's been here for some time."

"This stream must join a larger one farther south." Lady Diana nodded. "It drains the lake and flows southeast. If they came through and were lost, they could have turned into it, hunting—" She shook her head. "Panic came, and they pushed the engines harder all the time—then the end here."

"Those were in use," Nick had no desire to view the charred hulk closer, "more than one hundred years ago."

"We've seen stranger than that." Lady Diana strode along at an even pace Nick was trying hard to match.

"Overseas." She did not enlarge upon her statement and Nick did not ask questions.

About a mile beyond the wreck of the sternwheeler, their party turned aside from the riverbank, to shortly after climb a rise overlooking fields. There Nick had his second shock of the morning.

For there were lines bisecting this open land. They were straggling and in some places nearly gone, but this had been walled once, with fieldstone divisions, into recognizable fields! And down the slope directly before them was evidence of a road, drifted with soil, overgrown by grass, yet still a road that had once run straight between those deserted fields.

Stroud's arm swung up. In instantaneous answer the whole party dropped, flattened themselves in the shrubs growing here. From across the fields came another band of wanderers.

There were horses, undersized when compared to those Nick knew—some bearing riders, others running loose, herded along by the same riders. Behind them crawled an object so totally beyond his experience that he could not put name to it. On a platform to which had been hitched a massive team—if you could refer to some twenty straining animals as a "team"—was a domed construction. The vehicle was awkward, yet it did cover ground, a guard of horsemen around it reining in their restive mounts to keep pace with the lumbering wagon.

The band had turned into the road, avoiding the walled fields which would be an obstruction it could not hope to overcome. Nick was thankful the whole caravan was heading away. He marked the bows and lances that equipped the horsemen, who presented so barbaric a sight he could not believe they would make comfortable fellow travelers.

"Mongols." Lady Diana lay shoulder to shoulder with him. "True Mongols—a clan or family perhaps."

"You mean," Nick demanded, "the people of Genghis Khan— *here?*"

The stern wheeler had been a shock. But a Mongol party was almost as severe a dislocation of logic as the strange animals of the wood. And they had not the awesome feeling of the forest to cloak them with the air of being where they belonged.

"That is a yurt—one of their traveling houses," Lady Diana continued.

He glanced around. Her weatherbeaten, strong-featured face was alive with interest.

"Here the past comes alive." She seemed to be talking to herself. "Perhaps those warriors down there really did ride with the Great Khan. If we could talk to them—"

"Get a lance through us if we tried it," Crocker replied. "If I remember rightly they had a talent as bowmen, too."

"They were good enough," Lady Diana agreed, "to wipe out half the chivalry of Europe. And they could have mastered the whole continent if they had pressed on."

"I'd rather," Nick commented, "see the last of them now."

But they had to lie in their hastily found hiding places (which perhaps would be no shelter at all should one of the horsemen choose to come scouting) for some time until the Mongols passed out of sight. How many more remnants of the past had been caught here?

"Those fields, the road—" Nick strained to see how far he could trace that highway. "Who built those?"

"Who knows?" Crocker answered. "There are a lot of such places. We've seen a complete castle. And there are the cities of the People."

"Cities?" Nick remembered mention of those before. "The ones the flyers bomb?"

"Not bomb." Crocker sounded exasperated. "They fly over and hover and shoot rays down. Not that that seems to accomplish anything. But it's not bombing as we know it. I can testify to that."

"The cities," Lady Diana mused, "they are different. Our own cities sprawl. You ride for miles through gradually thickening masses of little box houses swallowing up the country, you see less and less open. These cities are not like that at all, they have no environs, no suburbs, they are just there—in the open."

"All towers," murmured Crocker, "and such colors as you wouldn't think people could use in buildings. No smoke—all light and color. But if Hadlett's right—they're traps. And traps can be attractive—we're in no mind to prove that."

"Traps?"

"We believe," Lady Diana explained, "that the Herald comes from one. And that can be the source of energy or whatever it is that draws us—all of us—from our own world. Whatever governs our coming has been going on for a long time."

"We saw a Roman cohort. If that wasn't one of their dream spinnings," Crocker said. "You can't be sure of what is real and what isn't, not here with the People around."

Stroud rose to his feet, and the rest came out of hiding. They used what cover was available to cross the road where the ruts left by the yurt and the hoofprints were deep set, coming into the fields. At the edge of a small copse they laid down their packs to rest and eat.

"That's an orchard over there." The Vicar pointed to another stand of trees a field away. "Apples, I believe—perhaps early ones."

He glanced at Stroud inquiringly. It was apparent that, on the march at least, the Warden was in command.

Stroud squinted into the sun. "We've got to make the farm before dusk. And with them around"—he glanced in the direction the horsemen had vanished—"it's a risk to stop."

"Not too big a one," the Vicar answered. "We'll be under cover of the trees."

"The wall"—Lady Diana stood, measuring the distance ahead as if this was something she knew well how to do—"runs along to the trees. And it grows higher all the way."

"We could do with some fruit." Mrs. Clapp patted her harvest tote as if she already felt it lumpy with plunder.

"All right," Stroud decided. "We set guards though an'—"

"I am afraid that we shall do nothing now," Hadlett cut in. "Look there."

As usual Stroud had steered them to cover. If they kept near to ground level they would escape sighting from any distance.

Bearing down from the same general direction that the Mongols had come was a second party. These were on foot and Nick could see they moved with the caution of those who expected either ambush or attack. They were in uniform and some had rifles, though the majority were not so armed. Their clothing was dull, earth brown, ill fitting, and he could not identify them.

"The Chinese," Hadlett said softly.

Those in the woods watched the cautious advance, as the newcomers went along the same route as the Mongols. Nick wondered if they were in pursuit of the former band. If so, he was not sure of their chances when or if they did catch up. Somehow those rifles looked less efficient than the bows of the horsemen who in their time, as Lady Diana had observed, had accounted for armored knights.

"The whole country," commented Crocker, "is getting a little too crowded."

"Yes. And what is the reason for all this activity?" Hadlett added.

"It's got a nasty kind o' smell to it," Stroud broke in. "The sooner we get under cover, I'd say, the better. Maybe there's a huntin' party out."

They spent no time in a fruit harvest. As soon as the Chinese squad was well gone, they broke from the copse and traveled at a jogging pace along the protection of a wall, pushing to reach a ridge about a mile and a half away. Nick thought that most of them could make that effort without difficulty, but he wondered about Mrs. Clapp and the Vicar. He saw Jean fall in beside the older woman and take Jeremiah's basket, to carry herself.

There was a straggling growth of vegetation in the fields, resembling self-sown grain, though its like was new to Nick, for the ripe heads were red with protuberant seeds or grains. It also possessed narrow leaves studded on the edges with tiny hooks that caught at their clothing with amazing strength so they had to constantly jerk free.

Nick swallowed. He was thirsty, but he had no time to drink from his canteen. The need for speed was so manifest in the attitude of the others that he kept steadily on. Linda had taken Lung up to carry him, though the Peke had walked most of the morning.

Luckily the rise of the ridge was a gradual one, but it taxed their strength after that trot across the open. Stroud signaled a rest. There was plenty of cover and from here one could see some distance.

"More drifters!" Jean and Linda were on either side of Nick, and the English girl indicated, at a distance too far to see details of clothing or accoutrements, another band of travelers.

Stroud and Crocker, Nick noted, had flopped over, shading their eyes against the sun, studying not the country beyond but the sky above.

"No sign of 'em," the Warden said.

"Not yet. But there's too much movement. If a big hunt was on—"

"We stay flat an' under cover until dusk," Stroud decided. "Yes, that's pushin' it," he added at an exclamation from Lady Diana. "But I don't see how else we can do it—'less we spend the night right here."

"How far are we," Nick ventured to ask, "from your place?"

"About three miles straight. But keepin' under cover adds to that. We've seen more drifters today than we have in weeks before—"

"And now we see something else!" the Vicar interrupted. "The Herald—we are not too far from the city."

There was no concealment, no hunting for cover by that colorful figure below. As the Mongols, he was mounted. But he did not bestride any rough-coated half-pony. The animal bore a general resemblance to a horse right enough, save that its legs were longer and thinner. And its white coat had about it a halo of light such as had been cast by the hair of the Green Man in the forest.

Mounted on this creature, which skimmed the ground at so swift a pace as made Nick stare, was a man, or at least a humanoid. His clothing was as dazzling as the brilliant coat of his steed, a kind of patchwork of bright colors centering in a stiff and sleeveless tabard that flared out over his hips as if boned. Under that were breeches such as the Green Man had worn. And on his head was a four-cornered cap, the points of which projected.

Unlike the forest man, his hair was short, sleeked to his head. And what little showed was very dark. On his face, a line of hair, as fine as if it had been drawn on with a delicately handled brush, crossed his upper lip, to bracket either end of his mouth.

There was purpose in the way he rode, in the wide, ground-covering strides of his horse. And then, watching their going more carefully, Nick perceived what he had not at first sighted. The "horse" was not hooved, but had clawed paws not unlike those of a hound.

And—they did not touch the surface of the ground over which it passed. The thing galloped as if it followed some invisible pathway some inches above the foundation. It did not swerve or even appear to leap as it came to one of the walls about the fields. Instead it simply rose higher in the air, crossing the obstruction, climbing a little more with each pace, heading for the ridge some distance away.

Up and up, always well above the ground now. The paws worked evenly, without effort. It was gaining altitude steadily, ready to cross the ridge. Now Nick heard a whining hum—from the rider?

No, that came from overhead.

"Hunter!" Stroud warned.

They cowered within their cover as there appeared, as suddenly as if the sky parted to drop it through, a flyer. This was like the saucer they had witnessed in battle beside the lake, but very much smaller. And from its bubble top a ray of light shot groundward.

Nick felt a choking sensation. He could not move, was rooted to the ground on which he lay. There was a tingling close to pain through his body.

The ray held steadily on the climbing-horse thing and its rider. But neither looked up to their attacker. Nor did the gallop of the beast fail. The ray increased in intensity. Nick heard a whimper from Lung, a growl from the cat basket. Yet neither animal protested more loudly.

However, the beam was centered on the rider, strengthening until Nick had to glance away from that searing brightness. When he dared look again it was to see the rider slowly descending on the other side of the ridge. Whatever weapon the flyer used had no effect on the Herald. He continued to speed on, completely disregarding the attack as if the alien had no existence.

Yet the saucer followed, training the beam on the Herald, as if by the persistence of its power it could eventually win. When both were well gone, the Herald only a spot of color rapidly disappearing into the distance, the saucer relentlessly in his wake, Nick discovered that he felt better. He hunched up to watch the strange hunt go out of sight.

"A hunter, but it didn't get him," Crocker said. "And he's heading for the city. Defense, not attack—"

"What do you mean?" Nick wanted to know.

"Just that. The hunters try to break down the cities, but the cities never retaliate. They don't let off ack-ack, never send a bolt back. It's as if they don't care, as if the hunters can't touch them, and so they needn't bother to fight. You saw the Herald—he never even looked up to see who or what was strafing him! If we only had a defense like that—"

"We can accept their offer," the Vicar said quietly, "You know that, Barry."

"No!" The pilot's return was violent. "I'm me, Barry Crocker, and I'm going to stay me. Even if I have to run and hide all over this country!"

"What happens if one accepts a Herald's offer?" pushed Nick. "You said that one changes—how?"

Crocker did not allow the Vicar to answer. He scowled at Nick.

"You just change. We saw it in Rita." And he closed his mouth as if he could not be forced to add to that.

"You see," Hadlett answered slowly, gently, as if there was some emotion here he feared to awaken fully, "there was another one of us once, Barry's fiancée. She met the Herald before we understood, and she accepted what he offered. Then she came to us to urge us to do likewise—"

"She was better dead!" Crocker pushed away from them.

"But what happened to her?" Nick persisted. "I think we, Linda and I, have a right to know—if the same choice should be offered to us."

"It will be," Lady Diana replied sharply. "But the boy's right, Adrian. Give him the truth."

"There were"—the Vicar hesitated as if he found giving that truth a difficult, almost painful matter—"certain physical changes. Perhaps those could be accepted. But there were mental, emotional ones also. To our belief, Rita—the Rita who returned to us—was no longer human. Men have an inborn fear of death that very few of us are able to overcome, we shrink from even the thought. This change is like a kind of death. For the one who accepts it crosses a division between our life and another. There is no return. We have in us such an aversion to what they become that we cannot stand their presence near us. I am trying to find the proper words, but in reality this change must be faced to be fully understood."

The Vicar met Nick's eyes, but all the rest, save Linda, looked away, almost as if they were afraid, or ashamed of what he said. The Lady Diana spoke again, a rough note in her voice:

"Well, Stroud, do we sit here much longer?"

❄ 6 ❄

In spite of the cover about them Nick felt exposed, helplessly defenseless before whatever might come from the sky, or pad across the land. Yet the way he could overlook from the ridge was far too open. Down there he thought they had no way of passing unseen.

Stroud was making a careful survey of the same territory. "We can work along there." His finger indicated the slope of the ridge far to the right. "When we get that far we can see better what's still ahead—"

The journey along the ridge was a rough one. They had to take part of it on their hands and knees, scuttling from one patch of brush to the next. It was hardest on Mrs. Clapp. But she made no complaint and the rest took turns by her side, giving what unobtrusive help they could. At least they did not witness the return of the hunting saucer, nor did they see any more drifters in the country below. However, by the time they reached Stroud's halting point, the sun was well west. Mrs. Clapp's face was deeply flushed and she breathed in small gasps. Her hands, as they lay across her knees, were shaking. Privately Nick thought she would never make it without a good rest.

"We wait 'til dusk," Stroud said. "Eat and wait."

Nick's canteen and another Stroud carried made the rounds and they ate from their supplies. To all sighting, the land below appeared deserted now. But, as the sun crawled down the sky, Nick became aware of another light radiant in the northeast.

He was sharing the watch with Jean. Now he touched her shoulder lightly and pointed to the glow.

"The city," she answered his unasked question. "At night it is all alight—you have never seen anything like it."

He wondered if he detected a wistfulness in her voice.

"How close have you seen it?" The mysterious city, or cities, intrigued him. Apparently they were secure havens of safety for their inhabitants.

"Close enough," she returned, "close enough to be afraid." For a moment she was silent and then she added:

"What the Vicar said about Rita—is true. She was—different. But she was crying that last time she tried to come to us. She didn't mean us any harm—she wanted to help—"

Her voice was uneasy, as if in some way she felt guilt.

"But you all turned her away." Nick regretted his words the moment he spoke.

Jean turned her head to look straight at him. "We sent her away," she said harshly.

Nick was disconcerted. Why had he said that? These people knew what they were doing, what they had to do to survive here. And what he had voiced sounded like an accusation.

Jean had turned away again to watch the dusk creeping across the land. Though she lay within easy touching distance, Nick sensed that in one way she had totally withdrawn.

"If we go on"—he wanted to break that silence—"how can Mrs. Clapp make it? She is exhausted—"

"I know." Her tone was remote. "But she will have to try and we can all give her a hand. We must get to a place we can trust before nightfall."

"See anything?" asked Stroud from behind them.

Jean shook her head. "It's been clear. The city's turned up tonight."

The glow in the sky strengthened as the natural light failed.

"But the far ridge will cut that off." Stroud appeared satisfied at that thought. "We'd best be gettin' to it."

The descent from the ridge was gradual. Jean again had

Jeremiah's basket. And Linda, carrying Lung, had closed in on Mrs. Clapp's left. When they hit the more level country Stroud set a brisk pace and the Vicar dropped back to the three women.

They took breaks at intervals, and Mrs. Clapp made no complaint. But it was plain to see that only her determination kept her going. Even her collecting tote now swung from Linda's shoulder to balance her own duffel bag.

Lady Diana moved in, setting her hand firmly, without any word, under Mrs. Clapp's arm. What they would do when the full dark came Nick could not tell. Luckily this was the season when twilight held. And the land also had light from the glow in the sky.

The night was not quiet. Nick's tense nerves twitched in answer to the sounds. There were cries, sometimes wailing. None of the sweet, beguiling singing such as he had heard the night of the rain. Rather these held an abiding terror to feed one's fears, made one look at intervals over one's shoulder to see what sniffed along one's trail. He longed to ask what this or that noise meant. But as his companions accepted them he would not.

"We're well along," Stroud announced at one halt. "We've only a short bit now, then we'll lie snug."

They were out of the fields, nearly at the foot of the ridge above which blazed the radiance of the city. As Stroud led right again, they followed a smoother path between more tumbled walls—this could be a lane.

So they arrived at a black bulk of building, its walls also stone, though now the twilight was so subdued Nick could not be sure just what it was like. With the ease of familiarity Stroud opened a door and entered.

"Praise be," Nick heard Mrs. Clapp's breathy voice. "Not one minute too soon for these old legs o' mine. Just get me in, m'lady, an' let me sit a little. Then I'll be as right as right again. I'm a mite too old for all this scramblin' about, that I am."

"Nonsense!" Lady Diana propelled her forward with a right good will. "Don't you forget, Maude, we all took a dose of that hunter's ray back there. That doesn't do anyone any good."

There was a glimmer of light in the doorway. As Nick crossed the threshold, Crocker behind him thudded shut a stout door to close out the night. The light was feeble, but it showed the American most of a single big room with a fireplace double the size of any he had ever seen, a bench, some stools and a table—all made of wood and massively heavy.

Mrs. Clapp dropped rather than sat on one of the stools, and Jean hastened to put Jeremiah's basket down beside her. There was a pleading mew from the cat. Mrs. Clapp fumbled with the fastening to allow him out. He shook himself vigorously and then looked about, sniffing at the fireplace, and beginning a cautious exploration of the room.

There were windows, Nick could see, but each was covered with an inner barred shutter. Crocker had just dropped into place a similar but thicker bar across the door. Their light came from a bowl on the table where a cord burned in liquid. There was a pleasant scent from that burning and, in the room itself, an aura of peace and security that was relaxing.

"What is this place?" Linda put Lung on the floor and he flopped flat at once, his chin supported by his paws. "Somehow—it feels—good!"

The Vicar seated himself on the bench not too far from Mrs. Clapp. He smiled at the girl.

"A place to rest, yes, and more than rest, recruitment for the spirit. We have found several such. Some are the work of man's hands—others are of nature. But from them you may draw peace of mind and relaxation from all tensions. This was perhaps built by one who was an exile here, even as we are. We believe it was once a farm—in days when this land was not so troubled as it now is. There is iron set into the door bar and across the windows—which means that those who built were of our kind. But how they brought into their building this spirit of contentment, that we cannot tell. Perhaps all emotions are heightened in this time-space. We meet terror in some places, this blessed quietude in others. While in our own world, if such exist, our senses are not attuned to recognize them."

Stroud had subsided on a stool, his thick legs stretched out before him, his craggy face only partially lighted by the lamp.

"We could stay, weren't it so close to the city. At least we can hole up for now."

That feeling of peace lulled them all. Nick's legs ached, he could not remember when he had walked so far. And while the pressure of the need to escape had kept him going, now that that was removed his fatigue settled all at once, bringing every ache and pain of misused and seldom-used muscle with it. A little later he was glad enough to stretch out flat on one of the heaps of dried leaves along the wall to which Crocker pointed him. And sleep came quickly.

There were dreams, not frightening, but rather the kind one longs to hold onto, to prolong. Even when he drifted awake and knew he was awake, he held his eyes shut and reached again for the dream. However, it was not only gone, but he could not remember it at all.

"Nick! Oh, why doesn't he wake up! Nick!" A fierce whisper, a hand on his shoulder.

Reluctantly he opened his eyes. Linda crouched by him. Though the lamp was out he could see her face in the thin gray light that came from a small opening very high in the walls.

"Nick!" She shook him harder.

It took a great effort of will to answer her.

"Yes—"

"Be quiet!" She leaned closer. "You'll wake one of them."

The urgency in her tone was enough to make him sit up. It banished the peace of this place.

"What is it?"

"Lung—he's gone!" Now that he showed himself fully aroused, Linda withdrew a little. "There was a whistling and he went!"

"Went how? The door's barred—" It was true. The bar Crocker had put there last night was still firmly in place.

"In the other room—" She jerked at his arm. "There's an open window. Lung ran—I got there just in time to see him squeeze through—"

He followed as silently as possible in her wake. Around him he could hear snores, the heavy breathing of those deep in slumber. Linda's hand reached back for him, drew him on. They passed the fireplace and turned right. There was a brighter glimmer of the gray light.

Here was another room, the door to it a little open. Inside there was no furniture, but there was the square of an open, barred window, set quite low in the wall. Nick did not have to be told that the bars were iron.

Linda dropped his hand, ran to the window, her hands gripping those bars as she pressed against them, striving to see out into the light of pre-sunrise.

Perhaps time had eaten away the strength of that metal barrier, or perhaps there was some concealed catch the girl's weight activated. The crisscross of bars swung outward and Linda half fell, half scrambled through.

Nick hurled himself after her. "Linda, don't be a fool! Come back here!"

If she heard him she was not about to obey. As he banged into the lattice that had fallen into place again, Nick could see her moving out into the yard calling Lung softly. The bars now seemed solid, but he beat his fist against them, and once more the lattice gave and he went through.

"Linda!" he shouted. If it awakened the others, all the better.

He could see her by an opening in the wall.

"I see him," she called back. "Don't follow me, he's being naughty—he'll run again unless I can coax him. And he certainly won't come if he sees you."

There was no way Nick could reach her in time. Unheeding of her surroundings, she was already through that gap, now calling again.

"Lung—here, Lung—Lung—Lung—"

In spite of her admonition, Nick pushed open the window bars again and went after her. Maybe what she said was true and, seeing him, the Peke would be wary. But he had to reach her, make her understand the danger of wandering out this way. If necessary she would have to abandon Lung for her own safety.

However, even as he knew the logic of that, Nick also realized he could never make Linda agree to it. It might take physical force to return her to safety.

"Lung—Lung, you bad, bad boy! Lung—" Linda crouched in the lane, her hand out, her voice coaxing. "Lung—" With her hand she dug into the big patch pocket on her jeans. "Lung—goodies—the kind you like—goodies, Lung!"

Nick could see the Peke. He had stopped, was looking back at Linda. Nick slowed to a halt. If Linda could coax him to her—

"Goodies, Lung—" She spoke as if this was a game she had had to play before.

Lung turned a little, his pink tongue showing, as if he already tasted what she had to offer.

"Goodies—" Linda made the word a drawn-out drawl.

One step, and then two, the Peke was returning. Nick held his breath. As soon as Linda could get her hands on Lung it would be his turn to hurry them both back to the house.

"Good—good—Lung—" The Peke was almost within reaching distance of her hands now. On the palm of one were some broken pieces of brown biscuit. "Good Lung—"

Sharp, shrill, a whistle.

Instantly the Peke whirled, looked toward the stand of trees to their left, from which the sound had come. He barked and was gone in a flash.

Linda cried out, stumbled to her feet, and dashed after him, aware of nothing but the running dog. Nick called, and then went after her, prudence thrown away, knowing that somehow he must stop Linda before she met whatever summoned Lung.

The Peke was still barking. And Linda shouted in return, calling his name at the top of her voice. Nick kept silent. No use wasting breath when she would not listen.

He might have caught her, but a stone half-embedded in the ground proved his downfall. As the toe of his boot met that, he sprawled forward, hitting the ground hard enough to knock the breath from his body.

It was a moment or two before he could claw his way to his feet again. Linda had gone, only a swinging branch guided him. But he could still hear the barking and her calls. The little fool—stronger names came to his mind as he went on. Doubtless his folly was as great as hers in following. But if he went back for help she could be lost. He would have to take the chance as it was the only one he had.

Thrusting his way through bushes at the cost of bloody scratches, Nick won to an open space under the trees. Though the direction of those barks and calls might mislead, they were all he had to guide him. And somehow the sounds were reassuring, at least they were both able yet to make them.

"Lung—Lung!" Between those two words there was a change in tone. The first utterance had been a call, the second—what? A protest?

Nick pushed on at the best pace he could, and, without warning, stepped into an open, treeless glade. Before him stood Linda, but she was making no effort to capture Lung.

The small dog was still barking, sitting up on his haunches, waving his forepaws excitedly in the air. While she whom he was wooing with all his might smiled and enticed him with something held tantalizingly in her hand.

Linda moved just as Nick caught up with her. Before he could reach out to restrain her—

"No!" she shouted. Her hand swept through the air to strike at the other's.

Swept out—and passed through!

Linda screamed. The other shrank back. But Linda threw herself to the ground and seized the Peke who struggled wildly in her hold, actually snapping at her in fury.

Nick pushed her behind him, confronting the other—perhaps a phantom.

There was a nebula of light about her, seemingly thrown off by the unusual white skin of her face and hands. In part that light misted her, made her from time to time harder to see. But, in spite of what had happened when Linda had tried to strike the morsel from her hand, she seemed to be entirely real and solid. And she looked more human than had the Green Man.

Her hair was a warm chestnut brown, reaching a little below her shoulders. She wore breeches of forest green, with matching boots and shirt, the sleeves of which showed from beneath a tabard like the

Herald's. Only hers was not multicolored but green, bearing across the breast glittering embroidery, in silver and gold, of a branch of silver leaves and golden apples.

"Who are you?" Nick demanded. "What do you want?"

But the stranger continued to back away, and, as she went, the mist about her deepened, clung tighter to her body, until all that could be seen was her face. There was nothing there of threat. Instead from her eyes came the slow drip of tears. And her mouth moved as if she spoke, only he heard nothing. Then the mist covered ail of her, dwindled again to nothingness and they were alone.

"She wanted Lung!" Linda still held the dog to her with tight protectiveness. "She tried to take Lung!"

"She didn't get him," Nick pointed out. "Get up! We have to get out of here quick."

"Yes." For the first time Linda seemed to realize how far they might have ventured into danger. "Nick, she tried to take Lung!"

"Maybe—"

"Maybe? You saw her! She was going to give him something— You saw her!"

"She was teasing him with it. But she might have had a bigger capture than Lung in mind. You followed him, didn't you?"

"Me?" Linda stared at him. "But she didn't even look at me—it was Lung she called—"

"Could it be she knew you would follow him?" Nick persisted. Looking back he could not swear that the girl had seemed any menace at all. But he had no way of evaluating the many traps this world could offer. At any rate Linda had better be well frightened now so that she would not be so reckless again.

"Do you really believe that, Nick?"

"More than I can believe she was only after Lung. And—"

He had been looking ahead, his grasp on Linda's arm hurrying her along, intent on regaining the safety of the house with all possible speed. But now he realized that he was not sure of the direction. Though it was much lighter than when he had set forth, he could sight nothing here as a landmark he remembered. As he studied the ground he hoped for some mark there to guide them.

Yes! His momentary uneasiness passed—here—and there—He need only follow those quite distinct marks and they would lead them back to safety.

Odd, he would not have believed they were so far from the house. It had seemed, remembering, that he had not been too long under the trees before he had caught up with Linda. But the tracks were plain enough to keep him going.

Until they pushed under the last tree, past the last bush to face not the building, but an open meadow with knee-high grass and tall spikes of yellow flowers. There were more trees a distance away, but to Nick all of this was totally unfamiliar.

He had retraced their own tracks—then how—Their tracks? A small chill grew inside him—whose tracks? Or had those been tracks at all? As the lure of the singing, and the whistling that had drawn Lung, had those been signs deliberately made to draw them on, away from safety?

"What are we doing here, Nick?"

Linda was caressing the now subdued Lung. Perhaps she had not even paid attention to where they had headed.

"I thought we were headed for the house. We must have been turned around back there."

The only thing to do, of course, was to return in the opposite direction. But he had the greatest reluctance to do that. Fear of the ill-omened glade made him unwilling to voluntarily enter it again. What was happening to him that he was afraid—actually afraid—of the woods?

"We'll have to try to go through it." He spoke his thoughts aloud, more than to her. Nick was determined not to yield to that growing aversion to the necessity for retracing their way.

"No, Nick!" Linda jerked back when he would have drawn her with him. "Not in there."

"Don't be silly! We have to get back to the house."

She shook her head. "Nick, are you sure, absolutely sure, that you can?"

"What do you mean? This is no forest. We got through it one way, and that didn't take us hours. Sure we can go back."

"I don't believe it. And I won't." It was as if she braced herself against his will. "I won't go back in there!"

Nick was hot with exasperation. But he could not drag her, and he was sure he would have to if they went in that direction.

"We've got to get back to the house," he repeated.

"Then we'll go around." Linda turned her back on him and began to walk along the outer fringe of the brush and trees.

Nick scowled. He could not leave her here alone, and short of knocking her out and carrying her—

Kicking at a clod of earth, though that hardly relieved his feelings, he set out after her.

"We're going to have to go a long way around."

"So we're going the long way around," Linda snapped. "At least we can see where we are going. Nothing is going to get behind some tree to pick us off as we go by. Nick, the woods—had things in it besides *her!* I could feel them, if I couldn't see them."

"The tracks." He brought into words his own fear. "They led us out here—perhaps to trap us."

"I don't care! I can see anything that comes here."

But she was willing to hurry, Nick noted. And they followed the edge of the woods, heading south, at a pace that was close to a trot. He hoped this detour would not take long, he was hungry and he was also worried as to how the others would accept their absence. The English might believe that he and Linda had cut out on their own.

No, they had left their bags, everything they owned now. A little reassured at that thought, Nick decided that the others would not clear out and leave them. Maybe right now they were in a search party, hunting. Suppose he called?

But he could not. If Linda was not just running from her own imagination, they could be watched by things from the trees. Or hunted by those to whom his calls would serve as a guide. Though the grass was so tall it was hard to tramp through, he thought he saw ahead the end of the woods.

"Nick—there's water." Linda angled to the left across his path.

The hollow was not a pond, but rather a basin that the hand of man, or some intelligence, had had a part in devising. For the water trickled from a pipe set in a wall about a hollow. Then that was cupped in a rounded half-bowl and fed once more into a runnel that ran on out into the meadow and disappeared.

Linda knelt, loosing Lung, who lapped avidly at the basin. She flipped the water over her flushed face and then drank from her palms cupped together. Seeing the water, Nick was struck by thirst, just as an ache within him signaled hunger. But he waited until the girl had drunk her fill, standing on guard, his attention swinging from woods, to sky, to open fields, watchful and alert. As Linda arose he ordered:

"Keep a lookout." He went down in her place, the clear, cold water on his hands and face, in his mouth, down his throat. He had never really *tasted* water before. This seemed to have a flavor—like mint—

"Nick!"

7

He choked and whirled about, water dribbling from the side of his mouth. One look was enough.

"Get back!" Nick forced Linda, by the weight of his body and his determination, into the brush fringe of the woods.

"Keep Lung quiet!" He added a second order.

They were no longer alone in the meadow. Two figures had rounded the rising bulwark of the ridge, were running, or rather wavering forward desperately. They were dressed alike in a yellow brown that could easily be seen against the vivid green of the grass. But they did not try to take cover. It was as if some great terror, or need, drove them by the most open ways where they could keep the best speed they could muster.

Both staggered, as if they kept erect and moved only with the greatest of efforts. One fell and Nick and Linda heard him call out hoarsely, saw him strive to pull up again. His companion came to a wavering halt, looked back, and then returned to help. Linked by their hands they went on.

"Nick—in the sky!"

"I see it. Keep down, out of sight!"

A small saucer craft, such as the one that had hunted the Herald, snapped into view. Now it was almost directly over the runners who may or may not have had an instant or so to realize their peril.

Both men continued forward, their agonized effort plain. It might have been that the grassy meadow had been transformed into a bog in which sucking mud held them fast. Then they wilted to the ground and lay very still.

The saucer hung motionless directly above them. From its underside dripped a mass of gleaming cords looped and netted together, lowered by cable that remained fastened to the ship. And swinging down that came another figure.

The saucer man (if man he was) was small, dwarfish. But little could be seen of him save a silver shape. For he wore suit and helmet not unlike those of an astronaut. A second such joined the first and they busied themselves with the net and the inert men on the ground. At a signal the net swung up, heavy with the runners, the suited crewmen riding with it.

The craft swallowed up captives and captors. But it did not disappear as Nick hoped desperately that it would. He began to fear that those on board had knowledge of their presence also. Who knew what devices the hunters might operate?

"Nick—!" Linda's whisper brought a warning scowl from him.

Her hand went to her mouth as if she needed to physically stifle her fear. Lung crouched beside her, shivering, but he did not utter a sound. Dare they try to move? Edge farther back into the woods where they were more protected by the trees? Nick was not sure they could make it—not now. It could be that they were needlessly alarmed. Still the saucer did not go.

Lung whined.

"I told you, keep—" Nick began hotly.

What he saw stunned him into silence in mid-sentence.

Between the bushes where they lay and the open meadow flashed a slender line of light. It broadened, became a mist, forming a wall before them.

Out of the saucer in turn came such a ray as had followed the Herald during his ride. It was aimed at them and once more Nick felt that sickening tingling. Where the ray met the vapor wall, the mist balled into a fiery spot. And from the centering of energy ran out lines of fire.

"Quick! This protection cannot be held. Into the woods!"

At that cry Nick did not hesitate. When he reached for Linda, his hand closed on emptiness, she was already retreating, fighting her way into the shadows of the trees. It was not until they were well under that leaf cover again that Nick demanded:

"Who called to us?"

"Nobody!" Linda leaned against a tree trunk as if she could no longer trust her own feet. "It—it was in our heads. Somebody—something—*thought* at us!"

He shook his head, not altogether denying what she had said, but as if to clear away the disorientation brought about by the realization that it was true. No one had shouted that order, it had rung in his mind!

Linda turned her head slowly from left to right and back again.

"Please, whoever—wherever you are"—her voice was low and not too steady—"we're grateful—"

But need they be? Nick's wariness was back full force. It might only be that they had been marked down as prey by one power who thus had defended them against another.

Something flashed into his memory as clearly as if he still saw the scene before him.

"She was crying," he said.

"Who?" Linda was startled.

"The girl with Lung. She was crying when she disappeared."

"You think she—" Linda was, he saw, prepared to protest.

"It might be. But why was she crying?"

Linda pressed Lung so closely to her the Peke whined. "I don't know. Maybe she wanted Lung so much—"

"No, it wasn't that." Nick shook his head again. That queer sensation frustrated him. It was as if he had been on the very edge of learning something important and then a door slammed, or communication was sharply broken, leaving him ignorant. "I don't think it had anything to do with Lung at all."

"She whistled him to her," Linda snapped. "Nick, what are we going to do? I don't like this woods any better than I did before, even if it shields us from that saucer."

He agreed with her. There was a feeling of life around them that had nothing to do with trees, or vines, moss, or the rest of the visible world. Which was the lesser of two evils—the unknown of the woods, or the open and the hunting saucer? Somehow, of the two, he was more inclined now to risk the woods and he said so.

Linda looked dubious and then reluctantly agreed.

"I suppose you are right. And we would have been netted just like those others if something hadn't interfered. But which way?"

There Nick was at a loss. The compass on which he had depended before was back at the house with the rest of his gear. And he no longer trusted his own ability to set any course, not after what had happened before.

"Too bad Lung isn't a hound—he might guide us—"

"But he might! Oh, why didn't I think of that?"

Linda actually seemed to believe the Peke could guide them, and Nick was amazed at her obsession with the dog.

"His leash! I need his leash—" She had put Lung down between her feet, was looking about her as if what she sought could be materialized out of the air by the strength of her desire.

"Wait—maybe this will do." She caught at a vine running along the ground. It was tough and resisted her efforts to wrench it loose.

Nick grabbed a good hold on it and jerked. He had no false optimism about Lung's ability to take them out of the woods, but perhaps Linda knew more about the Peke than he did.

Linda stripped off the leaves and small stems and fastened one end to Lung's collar. Then she picked up the small dog and held him so his slightly protruding eyes were on a level with her own.

"Lung—home—home—" She repeated that with solemn earnestness as if the small animal could understand. Lung barked twice. Linda put him down. Again she repeated:

"Home, Lung!"

The Peke turned without hesitation and headed into the woods. Linda looked back impatiently as Lung pulled at the improvised leash.

"Are you coming?"

Nick could refuse, but at the moment he had no alternative to offer. And there could be a chance she was right about Lung, that he might find the way back. Nick followed.

Apparently Lung had utter confidence in what he was doing. He wound his way among the trees never hesitating at all. And the very certainty of his steady progress promised something, Nick decided. But he was still only partly able to accept the fact that the Peke had such ability as a guide when they came out of the woods (it must have been a narrow tongue at this end) and could see, some distance to their right, the farmhouse.

"I told you!" Linda had such a note of triumphant relief in her voice that Nick guessed she had not been so firmly confident of Lung's abilities after all.

Now she ripped off the vine leash, picked up the Peke, and ran for the building that was more than ever a promise of safety. Nick halted for a moment to check the sky. The saucer people might have foreseen this move, could be cruising overhead, or snap suddenly into view—

But Linda was running faster, too far ahead for him to catch and suggest prudence. He set out after her. As they entered the space immediately before the door Nick saw it was not, luckily, barred to them but stood ajar. Did that mean that the others were gone—?

Linda crossed the threshold, he was now only two or three paces behind her. And Nick had hardly cleared the space of the door swing before that was clapped to and the bar clanged down.

The transition from sunlight to this darkened room was such that Nick could not see clearly. Someone seized his arm ungently. He knew Stroud's voice.

"What d'you think you're doin'?

"I ought to give you a good one!" the Warden continued, and his grasp tightened into a painful vise. "You haven't even the sense of a coney—not you!"

"Get your hand off me!" Nick flared. All his fears, frustrations, his anger against Linda for her foolishness, was hot in him. He struck out at the man he could only half see.

"Sam!" The Vicar pushed between them as the Warden ducked that badly aimed blow with the ease of one trained in such business.

Stroud loosed his grip, but Nick, breathing hard, did not draw back.

"You keep your hands off me," he said again between set teeth.

"Stop it!" Linda cried out. "Nick only came after me—"

"And what were you doing out there, girl?" Lady Diana asked.

"I went after Lung. Someone whistled and he went out—through the window in the other room. I had to go after him. It's a good thing I did or she would have had him!"

"She?" It was the Vicar who asked that. Nick's sight had adjusted to the gloom now. He saw that they were ringed by the rest of the party.

"The shining girl in the woods. She was going to give Lung something—something to eat, I think. When I tried to knock it out of her hand," Linda's voice faltered, "my—my hand went right through her arm!"

She stopped as if she thought they would not believe her and for the space of a breath or two she was met by silence. Then Crocker spoke, a roughness in his voice close to that which had hardened Stroud's when he accused Nick.

"What did she look like—this ghost girl of yours?"

"She—she was about my height," Linda said. "I was so afraid for Lung I didn't see her much to remember. I think she had brown hair and she was wearing green. Ask Nick—he saw her better than I did. When my hand went through her arm—" As her voice trailed into silence Nick saw them all turn to him.

"She—well, she had brown hair, only it had some red in it, too. And it was shoulder length." He tried to remember all the details he could. Crocker had pushed ahead of Stroud, was as intent upon what Nick said as if this was of utmost importance. "She wore green—with a coat like the Herald's—a silver and gold apple branch on it. And she was pretty—Yes," memory suddenly provided him with another small point, "she has a little dark mole, right about here." He touched his own face near his mouth. "You could see it because her skin was so very white."

He heard Crocker's breath hiss as if the pilot gasped.

"But—" Nick added what seemed to him to be most important, "when she faded away she was crying."

"Rita!" Crocker pulled away, his shoulders hunched, his back to them.

"Or an illusion," Hadlett said quietly. "We have seen illusions, many of them, Barry."

Crocker did not look around, his hands were covering his face.

"An illusion would be intended for us, we knew her. These two didn't! So what would be the purpose of feeding them an illusion?" His voice was low, toneless. Nick thought he fought to control it.

"Barry is right," Lady Diana agreed. "Unless the People want us to try and find her—and provide such an illusion to get us out of here."

"Which they won't, not that way!" Crocker replied. But he still did not look at them. "We let her—it—know that long ago—"

"What else happened?" Hadlett took over the questioning.

Nick supplied the account of the mist-hidden departure of the illusion (he thought the Vicar had the right identity there), their following the wrong tracks out into the open. As tersely as he could he gave them an account of the capture of the fugitives by the saucer, the strange wall of light that undoubtedly saved them from a like fate, and their return with Lung's aid.

Hadlett was more interested in the defense that saved them from the saucer than all else, and he took Nick through as full a description of that as he could give for a second time.

"Definitely a force field," the Vicar commented when he had pried every possible detail out of Nick. "But the People have never interfered before, not for one of us."

"Rita would—" Jean said. "I don't care," she added. "He said she was crying, and Rita did cry that last time. I believe it was Rita, not just an illusion sent to trap us. And I believe she did save them from the hunters."

"She's one of them!" There was ugly violence in that sentence Crocker hurled at Jean.

"Yes." Her agreement was bleak as if he advanced an argument no one could deny.

"We do not know," Hadlett commented, "how much of the human remains in those who accept. If Rita remembers us I do not believe it is in anger. We did what we had to do, being what and who we are. It seems plain that something well disposed to these two young people did save them this morning. And that is no small action."

"That's all past," rumbled Stroud. "What we've got to think of is that there's hunters here—not too far away. Something in the woods wanted you two free, but that don't mean that it's goin' to keep on fightin' for us. We can hole up here—for awhile—but not long. No supplies to keep us goin'. We've got to get back to the cave."

"We've the bolt hole," Crocker said as if he welcomed the change of subject. "That'll put us on the other side of the ridge."

"An' a sight too near that city for my thinkin'!" Stroud answered. "But it may be we won't have much choice."

They scanted on the rations they shared for breakfast. Luckily they did not lack for water, for in the far corner of the big room a round stone could be heaved up and there was a well below. It would seem, Nick decided, that the original inhabitants of this place had built to withstand sieges.

Stroud held a council of war, to which Nick and Linda could add very little. That they had returned safely from the morning's venture, now seemed to Nick to be better fortune than they deserved. But perhaps some good had come from it by their witnessing the capture by saucer, a warning of the trouble now hovering aloft. It was finally decided that they would wait out the day where they were, since their position here was safe. With dusk they would move again, this time through a secret exit of the house.

Hadlett suggested the advantages of resting all they could, since once they were on the move again they would have heavy demands made upon their strength. It was then that Mrs. Clapp spoke up.

"You are all goin' to listen to me now." She spoke with the same firmness as Stroud showed upon occasion. "The Vicar, he has the right of it when he says as how this is goin' to be a hard pull. Me, I ain't put by in a chair with a pap bowl under m' chin an' two shawls around me—not as yet. But I'm stiff in m'legs, an' when it comes to a spot o' runnin', I ain't no gal in m' teens, as it were. This is a safe place, as we all know. Best I bide here an' you take off where m' old feet won't be no hindrance to you. This is only proper sense an' you all know it!" She glanced from one to another, her face stubbornly set.

"Maude." The Vicar spoke gently. "This is something we decided long ago—"

"Not the same at all, it ain't!" she interrupted him. "It weren't no matter then o' one o' us havin' to lag so badly that she was a botheration an' handicap to put all the rest in danger. You can't make me be that, sir, you can't!"

"Perhaps not, Maude. But do you want to lay a worse burden on us then? To go and leave you and remember it?"

She stared now at the hands twisted together in her lap. "That's a hard—hard thing to say—"

"Would you go, Maude? If I broke a limb and could not travel, if Lady Diana, Jean, Sam, any of us said what you have just said, would you agree?"

He paused, she made no answer. Then he continued: "From the first we said it, and we mean it—we stay together, no matter what comes—"

"It ain't fair—sayin' that. Me an' Jeremiah, we're old, an' we're safe here. You could come back when it's safe again."

"*We* shall make it, Maude." Lady Diana moved up behind the stool on which Mrs. Clapp sat. Now her hands closed on the rounded shoulders of the older woman, and she gave her a small shake that had a rough caress in it. "We've been through a lot, and we've always made it."

"There's always a first time not to, m'lady. An' I don't want to be a burden—"

"You, Maude Clapp? What would we do without your knowledge of growing things? Remember how you pulled Barry through that fever when we had all given up? We can't do without you!"

"And don't forget what we owe Jeremiah." Jean knelt beside the stool, her brown hands laid over the gnarled, arthritis-crooked fingers clasped so tightly together. "He always knows when the People are around and tells us. You and Jeremiah, we couldn't do without either of you, and we're not going to!"

"It ain't right." Mrs. Clapp held to her view stubbornly. "But, if I say you 'no,' you're like to try to carry me. I wouldn't put it past your stuffin' me in a basket"—she smiled a little—"an' draggin' me along. An' a good hefty bit of draggin' I would make for the one who tried that, I'm tellin' you, should you have a thought in that direction."

"You'll go out on your own two feet, along with all of us," Hadlett assured her. "I foresee more skulking and hiding in our next journey than running. Is that not so, Sam?"

"You have the right words for it, Vicar. With them flyin' devils out an' bein' so close to the city, an' all. We go out through the bolt hole an' then we take to the country like Jas Haggis used to."

"Seein' as how we ain't no poachers nor night hiders like Jas," Mrs. Clapp commented, "I don't believe that for one minute, Sam. Me, I'm more used to a good comfortable kitchen than all this trampin'. Get back to the cave, I will, an' then you're goin' to have a good hard argufyin' on your hands do you talk about doin' this again."

Jean laughed. "I shall remind you of that, Maude, the next time you get down your herb bag and start talking about what you think may be waiting to be popped into it if you only have the chance to go and look."

"You do that, m'gal." Mrs. Clapp chuckled. "You just remind me about m' perishin' feet, an' aching back, an' all the rest of it. An' like as not I'll be a homebody as quick as I could scat Jeremiah—not that I am like ever to do that. Am I now, old man?" The gray cat had come to her knee and now stood on his hind legs, his forepaws braced against her, looking intently into her face as if he understood every word she said.

"So we wait and rest." The Vicar spoke briskly. "And go at dusk."

"Seems best," Stroud agreed.

But if the others could rest, Nick found that the day dragged. There was more light in the room, but it was stuffy, for the small slits under the eaves that admitted the light did not do the same for much air. The door to the room with the barred window was open and he could see the sun on the dusty floor there.

They had all retired once more to their beds, and he thought some were asleep. But he was sure that the pilot, whose pile of leaves adjoined his own, was not one of them. Crocker turned restlessly. Nick believed he heard him mutter once or twice. But his words were obviously not addressed to the American and the latter dared not break the silence between them.

Rita—Crocker's girl who had accepted what the Herald had to offer and so was no longer human. Nick would never forget seeing Linda's hand pass through the other's outstretched arm. Illusion, but, if so, created by one who knew Rita well. And why had an illusion been crying? Was that so he, Nick, could carry such a tale back here?

His head ached, the stuffiness of the room was unendurable. With as little noise as possible he got up, went into that other chamber and to the window guarded only by the grill, being careful not to touch the iron lattice. There was actually a breeze here and he filled his lungs gratefully with fresh air.

From this point he could not see the front lane nor the woods. That was east, this faced south.

Color—a shimmer of color at first. Then it—hardened was the only word Nick could supply for the process. Shaped, fully three dimensional, he saw brilliant details.

A man stood there, his eyes on the house, searching. Somehow Nick thought this stranger knew just where he was, even if the window's shadow might hide him. Out of an angle of the wall paced a white animal, its legs stilt thin, pawed where they should be hooved. But this time flat on the ground, not inches above the surface.

The stiff material of the Herald's tabard was divided by pattern into four sections, each rich with embroidery. Nick could guess where the English had gotten their name for the alien—the tabard had a strong likeness to a quartered coat of arms, a true "coat" since it was worn.

Herald and horse, interested in the house. Nick wondered if he should give the alarm. But, as he hesitated, he saw the Herald swing up on a saddle that was hardly more than a pad.

The "horse" took an upward leap, soaring as if it had spread wings. And, though Nick now pushed against the grating, he held the two in sight for only a second or two. As long as he could see them, the steed was still rising.

❈ 8 ❈

"What is it, my boy?"

Nick started. He had been so intent upon the disappearance of the Herald that he had not been aware of the Vicar's coming up behind him.

"The Herald was out there. Then he mounted, and his horse flew over the house." The rising of the mount that was able to climb in thin air still astounded him.

"The Horse of the Hills—" Hadlett joined Nick at the window. There was nothing to be seen out there now but part of the wall in the full sun. "Do you read Kipling, Shaw? He is not so fancied nowadays—the new thinkers hold his 'white man's burden' against him. But there is a bit in one of his tales about the People of the Hills out on their steeds in a stormy night—Kipling knew the old legends, perhaps he believed in them a little, too. You need only read his *Puck of Pook's Hill* to know how much the Old Things of England captured his imagination. Yes, the People of the Hills, and their airborne mounts. There were others before Kipling who knew—Thomas the Rhymer for one.

"In Britain they lingered, as in all the Celtic realms. You find them also in Brittany, which is akin more to Celtic Britain than to Gaulish France. There must have been dealings in the old days between our world and this one—"

"Sir"—Nick looked from the window to the old man's hawk face framed by that silver-white hair—"is the Herald, or what he represents, as much our enemy as the saucer people?"

Hadlett was not quick to answer. Nor did his eyes meet Nick's at that moment. Rather they looked beyond the American, out the window. When the Vicar did reply, he spoke slowly, as if he wished to be very sure of every word.

"The saucer people, as you call them, they threaten our bodies, and I do not dismiss that as a minor thing. But the Herald comes to us not in open threat, but as a tempter. If we accept his offer of alliance, or absorption, then we are truly absorbed. We become other than ourselves. There would—there could be no return to our present state. It would be an abdication of all our beliefs. Those who accept are as divorced from our state as if they were not our blood kin. It is, as I have told you, a type of death."

"Rita—if that was Rita we met . . ." Nick had heard the warning notes in the other's voice not to pursue this subject, but he could not let it alone, though neither could he understand what worked in him to so question. "She—she was crying. And it may have been she who saved us from the saucer."

"Yes. She wept also when she came to us the last time and Crocker would not look at her. In her, through the change, there lingered ties. That, too, exists in the legends. Fairy men and fairy maids and the mortals they loved. But never was there any happiness at the end, but sorrow, loss and defeat.

"But you say the Herald was watching the house. Which means he is aware of you and Linda, that he will offer his bargain. Be warned of that, my boy." Hadlett placed his hands on the window frame as he looked out.

"So fair and smiling a land. He who built here must have had untroubled years, for he was able to work these fields, sow his crops, raise this house as a bulwark against the night and that which prowls it. How long ago was that, I wonder?"

Nick was forced to accept the Vicar's change of subject. Hadlett being what he was, the American could not push further on a topic plainly so distasteful.

"Have you seen any places such as this where people live now?"

"No. This is a land under a blight. Perhaps it is the flying hunters who have made it so. The cities seem to flourish and stand intact. But the open land is full of traps. Not all the People were ever of a friendly or neutral nature. We have our tales of ogres, giants, black witches, trolls. And there are traces here of dark malignancy seen and unseen, though not to the extent we found them in England before we were captured. This is perhaps a younger land, one in which such inhabitants have not spread far. Still we have seen ruins—towers, a castle—that are certainly not of the America you must have known. This has been a fruitful, well-populated country. Now there are only the cities and such places as this. In the open move bands of drifters— in the sky, the hunters."

"Do the cities, or the Herald, control our coming here?" Nick had a need to know as much of the truth as Hadlett could or would tell him. He judged that the Vicar was the only one of the three men who might have tried to seek out the causes for action. Stroud was intent on a problem immediately at hand, and as yet Nick knew very little of Crocker.

"If we can accept old legends as a guide," Hadlett replied, "the People do have a manner of control. But according to all accounts they exercise that by appearing in our world, to achieve their purpose by forms of enticement or outright physical kidnapping. While our type of transference is different. Undoubtedly the cities represent a high form of what we might call, for want of a better term, technology. Though when you look upon them you cannot rationally identify them with our civilization. They may generate forces to operate a drawing power at certain sites."

"And if we could discover how they brought us in, we could reverse that?" Nick persisted.

Again the Vicar hesitated. "You are forgetting the time element, that your own arrival here made clear to us. We have counted seasons to reckon four years—you tell us it has been more than forty in our own world. Again there were legends of men who returned, to age and die quickly as they passed from one state of existence to another."

Nick counted days—three—no four—since they had found

themselves here. How long back there—weeks—months? He
shivered because that was so hard to believe. But doggedly he
returned to the subject at hand.

"But the cities are safe against the saucer hunters—"

"Yes. Twice we have witnessed an aerial attack. You yourself saw
them try to bring down the Herald. There appears to be a great anger
or fear working in the flyers—not only for the cities but for all that
pertains to them—such as the People."

Nick digested that. The cities were safe, the open countryside was
an invitation to danger. What if they could get into a city, without
accepting the Herald's bargain? He asked that.

Hadlett smiled. "But of course that is logical, and so do not think,
my boy, that that idea did not present itself to us early during our
existence here. Only, it cannot be achieved. For one must enter in the
company of a Herald, or else there is no way in. Around each city
there is an unseen wall of force. And the price for entrance is too high.
The Herald will come sooner or later, he will offer you that choice. It
will then be your decision to accept it, or refuse. But at that moment
you will know what one of our blood must do."

To be told a thing is one matter, to experience it another. After
another word or two the Vicar returned to the larger room. But Nick
remained. This insistence on the frightening change in those who
accepted the Herald's offer continued to interest him. The English
apparently agreed it should not be done. Yet all their words could not
bring home to Nick what was so horrible. To him the saucer hunters
were the greater menace—perhaps because he could understand
them better.

Looking back now he believed that Rita had offered them no
threat. He could not erase his memory of her tears. In fact every time
the scene came again to the fore of his mind it was clearer. Nick could
recall more and more details. And he was willing to accept the fact
that Rita's intervention had saved them from capture.

The safe cities—that could only be entered in the company of the
Herald. In the company of the Herald—that repeated itself. Could
one take the Herald as hostage?

But surely the English must have considered every possible angle.

None of them was stupid, and the need for survival sharpens the wits, bringing to the fore all one's native abilities. Yet he kept returning to that idea. Were the Herald's powers such—and in this world no powers whether improbable or incredible could be dismissed as impossible—that there was no possible way of capturing the air-riding messenger, or warden, or whatever he was?

Nick knew so little, except that the cities were safe, and he had a desire to find safety.

He slept awhile in the long afternoon on the floor by the window. When he roused it was to find Jeremiah beside him, an enigmatic, unmoving statue of a cat, his tail tip folded neatly over his paws, his green eyes unblinkingly set on Nick's face. There was something in the regard that made the young man uneasy. He had the impossible idea for a moment that the cat knew exactly what he was thinking and was superiorly amused, as one might be amused at the fumbling of a child striving to master some problem too adult for his comprehension.

Nick had always liked cats. He had had old George for twelve years. And one of the stoutest stakes in the barrier between him and Margo had been her having George "put to sleep" when Nick had been in New York a year ago. George was old, he had had to have checkups at the vet's, he was a "nuisance." So George went, with a surface-sweet explanation of how wrong it was to prolong life that was a burden for an old and ailing animal. But Nick knew that George could have been saved. He had never answered her, never given her the satisfaction of knowing his raw anger at that new defeat. George was gone, he could do nothing about that. But Nick could remember as he did now—in every detail.

Jeremiah growled, his ears folding down to his skull, his eyes still intent on Nick's. And Nick's breath hissed between his teeth, almost with the sound an angry or alarmed cat might make.

The cat—knew! Jeremiah was reading his mind! Nick was as certain of that fact as if Jeremiah had spoken aloud. But it was Nick who spoke.

"You know." What he expected in reply, he did not know. Would Jeremiah give some sign of complete understanding? But the cat made no move, did not utter a sound. And Nick's certainty of that exchange began to fade.

Imagination—Yet he could not altogether accept the fact that he had been wrong. One did not deny the idea of telepathy nowadays, of the paranormal talents some people possessed—the gift for psychometry, precognition, all the others. And animals were supposed to be psychic, especially cats. All the rational explanations for what he believed had just happened came to mind now. Yet they did not quite explain it—and *he* was not psychic in the least. So how could Jeremiah have read his thoughts, his memory, and reacted?

Whether Jeremiah could understand him or not, Nick went on speaking softly to the big gray cat.

"George didn't look like you. He was long-legged, and no matter how much he ate, and George was an eater all right"—Nick smiled at the memory of George enjoying a plate of turkey—"he never fattened up any. You'd have thought we kept him on short rations. He was a hunter, too. And liked to sleep on beds, but he didn't want you to turn over and disturb him, he could make that plain."

Jeremiah still watched him. Then the big cat yawned, stood up and walked away, his boredom plain in every movement. Nick felt foolish. It was obvious that Jeremiah was no longer interested in the least. His disdain of George, undoubtedly an inferior type of feline, obvious in every small flirt of his upheld tail as he went. Do not regale *him* with accounts of other cats, he seemed to be saying; there was, naturally, only *one* Jeremiah!

For the first time since his arrival in this world Nick laughed. Jeremiah could communicate all right—after his own fashion. And even if the cat had read Nick's mind, he still had the standards and logic of his own species. Nick could question, but he must also accept what he saw and not close his mind.

Their party made the move at dusk, having eaten. Nick's bread was long since gone, but some of the cheese and bacon were left. And the English carried small hard cakes made of ground nuts and dried berries pressed together, with strips of dried and tough meat.

The exit, Nick discovered, was via the fireplace. That was a cavern of an opening, the largest he had ever seen. At its back four great stones, fastened together, could be pulled out like a door. He tendered his flashlight and Stroud accepted it at once.

"Wait for me to beam up now," the Warden ordered. "These steps are tricky."

He disappeared and Nick caught sight of the beginning of a narrow stairway leading down. It was laid into the back of what must be a very thick chimney. They waited until from below a bright beam reached up. Then Lady Diana squeezed through with Jeremiah's basket, followed by Mrs. Clapp, Jean and Linda carrying Lung. Hadlett went next, and he was hardly through the low door before Crocker nudged Nick.

"Now you. I'll have to set the blocks back."

It was a narrow squeeze all right. Mrs. Clapp and Stroud with their greater bulks must have found it almost painful. But it was not too long. Then Nick was in a level passage, also stone-walled, elbowed aside by Stroud who still held the light steady for the pilot.

Crocker did not come at once. They caught a couple of mutters to suggest he was having difficulty in fitting the door back into place. At last he joined them and Stroud sent the light ahead, taking the lead in a passage that kept them going singly, but was wider than the cramped staircase.

Little of the light filtered back as far as Nick. The air was dank, the walls sweated drops of moisture, and there was an ill smell. The passage appeared to be endless as they tramped along. There were no breaks in the walls, the way did not give access to any cellar, or side passage. Nick wondered how those with whom he now traveled had ever come to discover it. They called it the "bolt hole" and that seemed apt. But much hard labor had gone into its making, which suggested that those who had fashioned it had felt the need for such a hidden exit to the outer world.

After a while the stone walls changed to upright stakes set close together with earth packed behind them, a cruder piece of work. Nick glanced up overhead and saw a crisscross of similar stakes, thick beams to support weight. He trusted that time and decay had not damaged them.

Then, after what seemed a very long time, the light revealed another flight of stairs, these far less finished than those in the chimney, resembling a crude ladder. Up these Stroud climbed. In a few moments the light swung down to show the hand-and footholds for those who would follow. Nick watched Hadlett and Lady Diana assist Mrs. Clapp all they could and it was a lengthy process.

But the way was then clear for the younger members of the party who made the climb with more agility and speed. They emerged in another stone-walled place. Above their heads, well above, was an opening to the night sky, with a star or two winking there in reassurance; and the fresh air felt good after that passage.

Before Stroud snapped off the light, Nick caught sight of the charred remnants of what must once have been beams protruding in places from the wall above, marking the sites of perhaps two upper floors. And there was a mass of fallen debris underfoot so they linked hands in the dark and moved with caution toward the open arch of a door.

Vegetation masked the ruin rankly on the outside. Bushes Stroud had been holding aside snapped back when the last person was through the door, covering the door from sight. Nick saw the rise of the ridge now at his back.

Outside the tower they had more light than the natural night offered. It sprang rainbow-hued from some ground-source ahead, hidden by the trees and brush which so well cloaked the ruin.

At Stroud's order they kept close together. If the Warden was no trained woodsman, he did his best, as did the others, following his example, to keep their passage as noiseless as possible. They were angling right, and with every step they took, the growth about them thinned, the light grew brighter—until at last there was only a thin screen of branches through which Nick saw the city.

The wonder of that sight stopped him short so that Crocker bumped into him. But he paid no attention to the pilot, he was entranced by what he saw.

It arose abruptly, without any outlying clusters of buildings, even as they had said. And it towered until he thought that its spires might well dispute the stars. For it was all towers and spires, reaching shafts like longing arms held up to the wonders of space.

What might be the material of those distant buildings Nick could not begin to speculate. He could not equate stone with the constant play of color. For that blaze of brilliance, which radiated from the walls to light the night, was not constant in any one place. Rainbow-mixed shades, light and dark, rippled and flared, to die down, before once more flaming up.

Strange as the city was it did not seem alien to the ground on which it rested. There was the green of woodlands in its sheen, the gold of meadow flowers, the rust red of bark, the blue, the silver gray of water, the pale pink of blossoming fruit trees, the ruddy, heavy splendor of that same fruit come to full ripeness. It was all the colors of the earth mingled joyfully together.

For the city did not frighten, it did not awe. The emotion that filled Nick as he gazed upon it was happy excitement. Something that had long been sought, that had been glimpsed imperfectly, perhaps in a dream, now stood proud and magnificent before him.

"Come on, you fool!" Crocker caught him, gave a jerk hard enough to break Nick's daze. "What's the matter with you?"

"It's wonderful!" Nick wanted to run straight across the open to the city.

"It's a trap!" The pilot was uncompromising, harsh. "They set it for us. Don't look at it."

Was Crocker right? Nick could not believe him. But the distant towers did draw him. And now that he had passed his initial wonder, he distrusted that longing a little.

Yet it was still with reluctance that he moved on, edging always to the east after Stroud and the rest. Crocker matched step with him as if he feared that Nick might suddenly take off.

They had not progressed far before Stroud hissed a warning and they halted. To the west, figures came into the light. There was no mistaking the long-legged creature that paced ahead of that group—a Herald "horse."

But there was no one on its back, rather the brilliantly coated one who was the creature's master walked behind. With him were three others, a strangely assorted group.

There was a man wearing the drab uniform of those Nick had

seen netted, and behind him—surely that was one of the suited aliens from a saucer. Yet here they walked as if they were not enemies, both with their eyes fixed on the Herald. The third was a woman.

"Rita!" Crocker cried.

Nick would have thought the party too far away for any to be recognized. But he could read on the pilot's face the conviction that the green figure was his lost friend.

A sharp noise in the sky. This time it was not one of the saucers that appeared out of nowhere, rather one of the cigar-shaped craft.

It shot earthward as if about to bury its nose in the soil. From it pulsated sharp bursts of light. They struck around the advancing party—who paid them no heed—bringing wisps of smoke from charred stretches of ground. The rays were obviously deflected and struck at angles to either side or the rear of those on foot.

Overhead the flyer made reckless darts, as if its pilot was determined to stop the others if he had to ram his craft into them. But in every one of those dives the ship wavered from side to side and the effort with which the pilot maintained control was manifest.

All this time it would appear that the four people and the "horse" were entirely oblivious to the attack. They did not turn from the straightest route to the city. And Nick could imagine the frustration of their attacker.

At length the flyer's pilot must have accepted defeat. The craft skimmed back toward the ridge, streaking off at incredible speed. But the party on foot continued their even-paced way, unruffled and undaunted.

Nick was impressed. He had a real safety blanket, did the Herald. With such protection he could travel anywhere and not worry. If a man could just discover how that worked! Nick watched the Herald speculatively, wondering why he now walked instead of rode. Was that so his protection covered those he led? If they only had his secret!

The Herald and the city, one or the other was the key. And Nick was sure they merited a detailed study. The Heralds went out of the city, so he would be easier to check on. A man could not enter the city without the Herald—but could a Herald be held for ransom?

That might be utterly impossible. They had just had a

demonstration of how impervious the Herald and those under his protection were to force. And there was no use in trying to talk the English into such an attempt—not until Nick had a plan that had an even chance of working. But he would continue to think about it.

The pace of the Herald's party must have been swifter than it seemed, or else the city was closer, for they were almost there now.

"That was Rita!" Crocker said. "She's helping them set their traps for poor fools, marching them in!" He balled one hand into a fist, struck it into the open palm of the other with force. "She's *helping* them!"

"Why not?" Jean asked. "She is one of them now."

She stood to the other side of Crocker, not looking at the pilot, but rather at the city. When she spoke again it was in a lower voice that embarrassed Nick for he could not move out of hearing and he knew it was not meant for him.

"She is gone, Barry. And you cannot bring her back—let her go. You won't be whole again until you do."

"Let me alone!" Crocker flung out his arm. He did not quite touch Jean, but the force of his voice was close to a blow. "I know she's gone—but let me alone!" He plunged past her and there was a stir among the rest where they huddled. Stroud started them moving to the east, and a little later they began to lose the glow of the city in a darkness that seemed twice as heavy and drear because it was away from the strange glory—the promise behind.

Nick caught at that half-conscious thought. No, he must not allow his momentary enchantment at the first sight of the city to influence him now. There were traps aplenty here without allowing himself to be beguiled by such an obvious one.

❖ 9 ❖

"We've never seen it like this before."

That "safe" stronghold, the one place in this alien and threatening land that they could call home, held them at last, had sheltered them now for several days. But conditions, Nick was quick to discover, were far from what the English had earlier faced. In the pile of tumbled rocks that masked the entrance to their hideout they had a sentry post. He now shared it with Crocker.

"We can't hunt or fish—not now," the pilot continued.

For the land was no longer seemingly deserted as the refugees had led Nick to believe was generally the case. It was rather as if a sweep was coming from the north, bringing past their place of concealment a tide of drifters.

Though they expected to see the drifters harassed by the saucers, there had been no sighting of those. Just the bands, which moved with unslacking determination as if they fled from fear. And the sight of them made the watchers uneasy. Yet they were not ready to desert their own stronghold.

The foundation of their refuge was a natural cave but it had been enlarged, embellished by the hand of man or some other intelligence. Walls had been smoothed. On their surfaces were incised lines, some filled in with ancient paint to make the designs fully visible.

There was light, too. A kind that puzzled Nick more than the rock paintings, for such as those were to be found in his own world. But these rods, based in the native stone, yet bearing on their tips flares of blue light, were of a civilization far more advanced technically than one that would have used caves for dwellings.

These lights were oddly controlled also. There was no apparent switch—one *thought* them alight. You need only face one of the slender rods, wish for a light, and the flames, like those of giant candles, flared aloft.

The patterns on the walls and the lights were the mysteries of this world. The rest was what the refugees had brought—beds of dried grass and leaves, a fireplace of small rocks, wooden bowls and spoons Stroud had carved, having the knowledge a hobby supplied. They were cave dwellers surrounded by the remnants of a vastly more advanced civilization. But so easily defended was the way into their stronghold, so safe its atmosphere, they clung to it.

If the land continued so occupied, Nick could understand Crocker's concern. Food supplies were dwindling, even though they had stocked up well in the days when this land had been their own. One could not hunt or fish and be constantly alert for attack.

They had been pent-up for two days now, unable to venture out because of the drifters. Those did not appear even to rest at night. Twice in the one just past they had witnessed flickerings of lights out there. Nick was impatient. They ought to do something—find out what was going on.

He had depended upon the English for guidance. Only an utterly stupid person would plunge ahead without learning what he might have to face. But, within the past few hours, he was sure they were just as baffled as he, that this mass migration was new.

Ill assorted, the drifters were. It was, Nick thought, like watching the flow of history stirred into a weird mixture. He had seen Indians once. And later three men with long-barreled rifles and the fringed hunting shirts of the early colonial frontier. But there were others— a party of bowmen with steel helmets accompanying two armored knights. And another band, this one with women (who were always rare), also in armor but of a far earlier period, the helmets topped with brushes of red-dyed bristles, bronze-embossed shields on their arms.

Stroud had slithered out that morning, using rocks and brush as cover. The Warden was, Nick gathered, the only one who appeared to have the ability to scout, limited as that might be. It was his intention to reach the river to the east and judge the traffic around it.

Though the cave had been their headquarters ever since they had first chanced upon it and they had other refuges, such as the camp by the lake and the farmhouse, they had never intended to make any of these a permanent base. Their plans had been to reach the sea and, if possible (which sounded hardly probable), find transportation back to their own land. In pursuit of this general plan they had begun work some time ago on a raft at the river, but had been forced to hide the results of their labor when there had been sudden saucer activity near that point.

Now Stroud was to discover if that section were still patrolled, or if they could hope that the movement of drifters had drawn the flyers after them. If so, and they could not wait out the migration, then the raft on the river might mean escape. It seemed a very slender hope to Nick, but he knew that they held to it.

The city continued to haunt his own thoughts. If one could just learn the secret of getting in—

"I'm going to the back post and relieve Jean," Crocker said. "Lady Diana will be here shortly."

The pilot was gone, Nick was alone. He was glad of that. Crocker was all right, but Nick knew that the pilot did not warm toward him, any more than Nick himself would have sought out Crocker back home. It was plain that the Englishman had problems, which kept him in a sullen, brooding state, and he did not welcome strange company.

Now the Vicar—Nick could warm to him. And he understood Stroud. The Warden reminded him vividly of several men he had known, the last being Coach Heffner at high school. Mrs. Clapp—he smiled—and Jean—but he was sure Jean had an eye only for Crocker. He wished her well in that direction but success seemed dubious.

Lady Diana was manager whether they welcomed it or not. She was one you would have to reckon with if you crossed her.

Linda—he thought about Linda. Before they met the English,

they had drawn together. Afterward, she had become more quickly absorbed in the other group than he had. And, following their adventure in the wood, she had avoided him. He had made no attempt to close the gap she had opened. Linda was all right, but he certainly was not going to make any effort to know her better. Just because they were fellow victims did not mean they were thereby joined in a relationship.

Nick tensed—movement out there, a shaking of bush not caused by any wind. During his sentry tours Nick had seen animals on the move also, disturbed by drifters.

And the animals had sometimes been grotesque. There were the light-colored deer, and twice wolves, giant ones as large as a small pony. Rabbits of a very ordinary type had come and a flock of wild turkeys. But there had been a pair of nightmare forms as weird as the two he had seen with the Green Man. Each had four limbs and a body not unlike that of a giant cat, though the fur was more like deerskin, and a long neck ending in the head of a beaked bird, an eagle, scaled instead of furred or feathered. From the shoulders had sprouted membranous wings like those of a bat, plainly too small and weak to support the bulk of the body. In the open the creatures stretched their wings with a clapping sound.

He described these two to Hadlett, and the Vicar nodded as if he recognized such an impossible mixture of bird and beast.

"An opinicus—"

"A what?"

"A fabulous beast used in heraldry. Just as the two you met in the forest were a yale and an enfield."

"But—" Nick was completely bewildered. He had an idea that heraldry had something to do with shields, coats-of-arms, the designs used in the Middle Ages to identify knights in battle, and used nowadays as a form of snobbery to make wall plaques, mugs, designs on stationery. But living animals—

"Yes," the Vicar continued. "Imagined beasts do not roam the countryside. But here they do! They are allied to the People and show no interest in us, unless they are directed to do so. Fortunately that seldom happens."

Now as Nick watched the movement down slope he speculated as to what might appear, a normal animal he could name, or one of the weird companions of the People. But what flowed out, with the sinuous grace of his species, was Jeremiah. The cat was experiencing some difficulty, having to keep his head at an angle unnatural for him, for he had mouthed and was drawing along a large bird. Twice on his way up the slope he had to pause to take a fresh hold. But his determination to bring in his catch never faltered.

He finally reached Nick and dropped his burden. His eyes fixed upon the man, he gave a warning growl. The limp bundle of now dusty feathers was vividly colored. Some of the long tail pinions were bent and broken. It seemed about the size of a chicken, but its plumage was far removed from the barnyard fowls Nick had known.

"Good catch," Nick observed. "You're a better hunter, Jeremiah, than we've been lately."

The cat lay down on his side, his forepaws outstretched. Now he dropped his head on these and gave a visible sigh. It was plain his endurance had been taxed by the effort of bringing home the fruits of his hunting. Nick put out a hand toward the bird, watching Jeremiah for any sign of resentment. But the cat merely watched him, did not again assert ownership.

He had killed the bird cleanly, there was not even any outward sign of a wound. Nick smoothed out the bedraggled plumage in wonder. The colors were as brilliant as those of a parrot, yet blended into one another in a subtle fashion. He was reminded of the glory of the Herald's tabard.

The Herald—holding the bird Nick no longer saw it. He was rather remembering that long moment in the farmhouse when he was sure the Herald had known he stood behind the window. And his thoughts moved to his own—well, you could not call it a plan—idea of somehow getting the Herald to use as a key to the city.

But the trouble was he would have to know so much more about the Herald himself. And Nick was well aware that such discussion was taboo as far as the English were concerned. Only Hadlett had given him bits and pieces, never as much as he needed to know, always changing the subject when he tried to find out more about the enigmatic master of the city. *Was* he master there, or a servant messenger? The status of the Herald could have a distinct bearing on what Nick wanted to do. If he only knew—

Hadlett had warned him that he and Linda would be the target for an offer. But so far that had not happened. And holed up here as they were now, how could it? If Nick could meet the Herald, perhaps he could learn for himself—But if a saucer attack could not trouble that alien, what could he do?

The need for action continued to gnaw at him. He did not believe they could indefinitely hide out here in the present state of the country. And what if whatever was driving the drifters south did arrive? The very flimsy hope of escaping via the raft was no hope at all, he was sure, rather a delusion that might prove fatal. No, the city was safe—

Nick was so certain of that that his very surety was a surprise. He had played with the idea ever since he had seen those glittering towers, but this was absolute conviction.

A soft rub against his hand. Jeremiah must want his trophy. But when Nick looked down at the cat, the animal had not reached for the bird at all. Rather he rubbed his head back and forth against Nick's hand and arm, and he was purring.

"Good boy!" Nick scratched behind the gray ears, rubbed along the furred jaw line. "You agree with me, don't you?"

The question had been asked in jest, but at that moment he knew he spoke the truth. Once more Jeremiah had reached into his thoughts, and the cat was agreeing in the way he could best express himself.

Nick's hand slipped gently Under the jaw, urged Jeremiah's head up, so he could meet those wide eyes straightly. "How much do you know—understand—Jeremiah?"

The cat's reaction was swift and sharp. A paw flashed up, claws raked across Nick's wrist. He jerked back. Plainly he had taken an unallowable liberty. There was a warning growl and Jeremiah once more mouthed the bird, pushed around Nick, and vanished into the cave. Again Nick was left unable to judge what was the truth, what imagination. He must ask Linda about Lung—did the Peke also give her the impression that here he was able to communicate if he wished?

He was still staring after Jeremiah when Lady Diana scrambled up.

"Anything to report?" she asked directly.

"Nothing except Jeremiah coming back with a big bird."

"That cat! Maude is right under his paw, which is where every cat wants you. Though I will admit he seems able to sniff out any of the People—"

"The Herald, too?" Nick asked.

She studied him. "What about the Herald?" There was a hostile note in her voice.

"Does Jeremiah know when he is around?"

"Now that"—his question appeared to be a surprise—"I don't know. He can point out one of the People whether we see them at first or not. But the Herald—Why are you so interested?"

"It would seem he's such good security, I just wondered."

"Ask Maude, she knows everything knowable about that animal. Your food is waiting, you had better get to it before it's cold."

"Yes, m'lady!" Nick sketched a half-salute, giving her the address Stroud used, and scrambled down into the cave entrance so well masked by the jumble of rocks.

He found Linda on K.P. duty. Mrs. Clapp was some distance away, Jeremiah's trophy laid across one knee, stroking the cat's head and telling him what a brave, smart boy he was. Jeremiah accepted this praise complacently, with a feline's estimate of his own worth.

Nick picked up a bowl and went to where Linda was stirring a pot sitting on a pier of stones over the fire. Lung was beside her, his head cocked a little to one side, apparently intent on watching the flames.

"Linda, have you noticed anything different about Lung?"

"Lung?" She had taken Nick's bowl to fill it from the pot. But she turned her head quickly to look down at the small dog. "What's the matter? Lung?"

At his name he sat up on his haunches, waving both small forepaws in the air, and gave a soft bark.

"Has—" Now that Nick was prepared to ask his question it sounded improbable. He could have imagined Jeremiah's response. No, he had not! Gathering courage from that, he continued. "Has Lung given you the impression that he understands—well, what you are thinking?"

"What I am thinking?" she echoed. Now she turned her attention from the Peke to Nick. "No," she said as if to herself. "You really mean that, don't you? I told you—Pekes have a very high intelligence. He could always make me understand things—"

"That's not what I meant—" began Nick when she interrupted.

"I know. You mean—like telepathy, don't you? Why do you ask? Has Lung been reading your mind?" She might have asked that derisively, but he thought her tone was rather one of deep interest.

"No. But I think that Jeremiah has."

"Jeremiah!" Linda gazed beyond the fire at the cat curled up now at Mrs. Clapp's feet, and her expression was not altogether approving. "They keep telling me, Jean and Mrs. Clapp, about how wonderful that cat is, how he can let them know when there's any of the People around, or a bad influence, or something like that. You'd think he was a marvel. Now you come and tell me that he can read minds! I think you're all crazy!"

"But," Nick persisted, "have you tried finding out if there is any change in Lung?"

"You mean there might be something in this place that does produce mind reading and all that? But why not us, then, instead of the animals?"

"I don't know." He had to answer with the truth.

"Lung." Linda shoved the filled bowl into Nick's hands. Her attention was on the Peke. "Lung—"

The dog gave another soft bark, put his front paws on her knee as she sat down cross-legged and held out her hands to him. Gathering him up, she held him as Nick had seen her do before, with those bulbous dark eyes on a level with her own. "Lung, can you read my mind?"

Nick watched them. Was she serious with that question, or was it a jeer aimed at him?

Linda was silent, staring intently into the Peke's eyes. The dog made a dart with his head, his tongue went out to lick her chin. The girl gave a muffled exclamation, pulled him tightly against her until he woofed in protest.

"You—you are right. Lung knows."

"How can you tell?" Nick demanded. Now all his own objections to such a belief came to life again. He did not want confirmation, he realized, he wanted denial.

"I know." She did not enlarge on that. "Nick—we have to get away—back home!"

She sounded so afraid Nick was once more startled. It was as if during that long moment of confrontation with Lung she had learned something that made her whole world unsafe.

"We can't very well leave now," he pointed out. "You know as well as I do what we'd run into out there."

"They—" Linda's voice became a whisper. "Their plan for hiding out here—Nick—that can't go on much longer. The food is very low. And as for going downriver on a raft—" The note in her voice underlined her honest opinion of that. "Nick, whatever, whoever is chasing all the drifters we've seen, it's got to be something everyone has good reason to fear. If we just stay on here—Nick, we can't!"

Those were his own thoughts put into words. But would she accept his only other suggestion—the city?

"Nick, if we went back—right back to where we were when it all began, do you think we could get back to our own world?"

He shook his head. "There was a history of disappearances in our world for a long time—and no returns. It could not be for want of trying, I'm sure of that."

She leaned forward so her cheek was against the Peke's soft fur. Her hair was tied back with the red yarn still, but a piece of it was loose enough to fall over her eyes like a half veil.

"Nick, I'm scared! I'm scared the worst I've ever been in my life."

"I think we all are. I know I am." He matched her frankness. "But we've got to hold on. I think *here*, if you lose your grip, you're really lost."

"Yes, that's what I'm the most afraid of now, Nick. They—Jean—Mrs. Clapp, Lady Diana—they all seem to be able to take it and it doesn't matter. Mrs. Clapp—she's old and thinks that this is like a test of her belief that being good will help a person. She's talked to me about it. And Lady Diana, all her life she's been fighting for things—Mrs. Clapp told me about her, too. She's done a lot for the village where she lived. She sort of bullies people into doing what they should. I can't imagine her being afraid. And Jean—you know, Nick, she's in love with Barry. As long as she's near him and all's right as far as he is concerned, then she doesn't care about anything else. All that hurts her is that he still wants Rita—

"But not one of them is afraid the way I am. And, Nick, I'm so afraid I am going to break wide open, and then all of them will despise me." Her head sank lower and the lock of hair now hid most of her features.

"Not one of them will!" Nick tried to find the right words. "You're wrong, Linda. If you *could* read minds, I'd swear to it you'd find every one of them has a limit of control. Maybe they haven't reached it yet—but it's there. You're hinting we ought to go by ourselves? But we have a better chance of sticking it out here, at least for now."

"I suppose so," she agreed dully. "But I wish—No, I can't let myself wish, can I? I have to accept what's here and now and go on from there. But, Nick, we can't possibly stay here and starve. What can we do?"

Before he could control his tongue he answered: "There's the city—"

"The city? What do you mean?"

"That's really safe—at least from the saucers. We saw that proven." Now he was driven to get her reaction to his half-plan. "Suppose we could get into the city—"

"We can, easily enough. Accept the Herald's bargain, as Rita did. But, Nick, the way they talk about that—there must be something terrible happens when you do."

"Not the bargain, Linda. But suppose we were able to follow the Herald in somehow. Or, get out of him how to do it." Nick's plan was still only a suggestion to which his thoughts continued to turn.

"I don't believe you could." Linda replied so flatly he was momentarily deflated. Then he reacted to the deflation as swiftly, with the determination that he would at least try. But he would not give her the satisfaction of a protest. Instead he started eating.

"Are you going to try something like that?" His silence appeared to irritate her.

Nick shrugged. "How can I? At the present time I don't see any chance."

"Of course not! And there never was!" With that parting shot she arose and walked over to join Mrs. Clapp who was plucking the feathers from Jeremiah's addition to their larder.

Nick finished the stew, washed his bowl in the dribble of water that came out of the wall in one of the small alcoves cut in the cave, a dribble that found its way out again along a trough chiseled in the floor. But he set the bowl down there and did not return to the center portion of the cave. Instead he edged along through a narrow slit Crocker had earlier pointed out, one indeed too narrow for Stroud to negotiate, which led to another cave and a passage, and finally a very narrow opening on the world.

Just now Nick wanted no company, rather a chance to think without interruption. He had a puzzle. Perhaps it could not be solved, perhaps it could. But it must be faced and struggled with.

Nick worked his way up to that slit opening on the world. But, as he placed his hand on the side of the opening to steady himself, earth and a stone gave way under his weight. He snapped on the flash from his belt and under its bright light he could see where other stones had been rammed in to close an opening once much larger. Those stones were no longer so well bedded, they could be worked out with a little effort.

He began to pick and pull, laying the flashlight on a projection of the wall to give him light. The barrier needed only a little loosening. He would crawl out to prove that and then wall it up more securely.

Nick thrust with his shoulders, kicked and wriggled. Then he was out. It was only in that moment when he had achieved his purpose that he became aware of more than the action that had absorbed him. Crouched, his hands on the ground, his back hunched, he looked down the slope.

A cloud shielded the brilliance of the sun. But it could not dim the splash of color there. As he slowly rose to his feet, Nick saw he had his perhaps dangerous wish. It was the Herald.

❋ 10 ❋

Nick's first impulse was to dodge back into the cave. But it was already too late for that. He knew the Herald had sighted him. And he did not want to reveal even more this back door to the cave. Nick moved farther into the open to face the alien.

To his eyes this was the same Herald he had seen riding over the ridge to the city. The man (if man he really was) matched him in height, though his body was more slender than Nick's. His green breeches and undercoat were dulled by the brilliance of the stiff tabard with its wealth of color and glittering embroidery.

The tabard was divided into four quarters, each of which bore a different intricate device. Over each shoulder was a small half-cape with the same designs repeated in miniature. His four-pointed cap, beneath which his hair was so sleeked against his head as to appear painted on his skull, was stiffened by a band of gold like a small crown circlet.

His face was expressionless, impassive, and his skin very white so that the bracketing of moustaches about his mouth might have been drawn in ink. He did not move at once, but before Nick was more than three or four strides from the hole he was on his way to meet him, his walk an effortless glide.

Thus they came face to face with only an arm's length between them. And in all that time the Herald kept silent, nor did his set, smooth expression change. When he did speak it was startling, as if a painted puppet had been given a voice.

"I am Avalon."

There was a pause that he did not break. Nick gathered it was his turn for self-introduction.

"I am Nicholas Shaw." He stated his name formally, sensing the occasion demanded that.

The Herald made a slight inclination with his head.

"To that which is of Avalon, and of Tara, of Brocéliande, of Carnac, may you be welcome, Nicholas Shaw, if it be of your own will and choice that this be so."

So, this was it, the stating of the bargain. Nick thought furiously—he must stall, try to learn all he could without giving a quick denial. But to play such a game with this stranger would, he was sure, be very difficult.

"This is not a land to make one welcome." He sought for words that might in return bring some of the answers he wanted. "I have seen things here that are dangers past my own world's knowing." Even as he spoke he felt a faint surprise at his choice of words. It was as if he tried to speak a foreign language, yet they were of his own tongue, merely ones he would not naturally have selected.

"This is a land of strangers. Those who accept the land will find that it accepts them, and there are, then, not the perils you have seen."

"And the manner of this acceptance?"

Avalon slipped his hand beneath the stiff front of his tabard. He withdrew it, holding a small box, which he snapped open. The box was round, and nested in it was a single fruit, a golden apple, gold that is for the most part, but with a beginning blush of red on one side. From it, or the box that cradled it, came an aroma to entice the sense of smell, as it also enticed the eyes.

"Of this you eat, for it is of Avalon. Thus Avalon enters into you and you are a part of it, even as it is a part of you. Having so taken Avalon, you are a freeman of all it has to offer."

"I have been told"—Nick was cautious but hopeful of perhaps gaining a shred of answer—"that if one does this thing, becomes of

Avalon, one is then apart from one's past, no longer the person one was before—"

Still the Herald's expression did not alter. "One makes choices, and each choice changes one a little. This is the way of life, one cannot avoid it. If you fear what Avalon has to offer, then you make one choice, and by that you must abide. There are those who will not become a part of the land, thereby the land rejects them, and they shall have no good of it, nor any peace."

"There is peace then in Avalon?" Nick tried to get disbelief into his tone. "What I have seen here suggests that is not so. I have watched men entrapped by others, I have seen wanderers who cannot claim any portion of this world for home."

"It was their choice to reject Avalon, therefore Avalon rejects them. They remain rootless, shelterless. And the day approaches when they shall find that, without roots, shelter, they are utterly lost."

"Those truly of Avalon will turn against them?" Nick demanded. Was what he had just heard a threat or a warning?

"There is no need. Avalon is no man's enemy. It is a place of peace and safety. But if one remains without, then comes darkness and ill. This has happened before, the evil lapping at the land. Where it meets Avalon and Tara, Brocéliande and Carnac, then it laps against walls it cannot overflow. But for those without those walls there is peril beyond reckoning. Alternately that evil flows and ebbs. This is a time of the beginning of the flow."

"Is it this evil that brings such as me into Avalon in the first place?"

"Such questions are not for my answering, stranger. Accept of Avalon and you will understand."

"I cannot decide right now—" Nick fenced.

Again the Herald inclined his head. "That is understood, for your race are not of controlled thought. Clear decisions come hard for you. I shall see you again."

He closed the box, put it once more under his tabard, and turned from Nick, gliding away at such a pace Nick could not have matched unless he broke into a jog. But he was determined to follow, at least a little way. The Herald was not mounted, surely Nick could trail him—

With only that idea in mind Nick pushed through bushes, trying to keep in sight the blaze of that tabard. Meanwhile he thought about what Avalon had said. Apparently he called himself by the name of the land as if he were its official spokesman, identifying himself wholly with it. And had he threatened, or merely stated, that some great danger lay ahead for all those who were not protected by the People?

The mass migration of the drifters gave part proof. And what Nick had witnessed of the attacks from the saucers underlined the safety of the Herald and his city. On the other hand there was the manifest horror of his offer that the English displayed, though their reasons still seemed vague to Nick.

It was all—

Nick halted. The blaze of color had also stopped. Nick ducked into a bush. There was someone rising out of similar cover to confront the Herald, holding on high a pole topped with a cross of dull metal.

"Demon!" The figure used the cross-pole as a club, seeking to bring it down on the Herald's head. But Avalon was not there to take the force of that blow. Instead his body was well to one side. Again that wild figure, wearing a tattered and mud-bespattered brown robe, with gray hair matted about his head and a beard of the same on his jaw, tried to do battle. This time the Herald vanished from sight.

"Stay!"

From behind Nick came a gust of foul odor, with a sharp prick in his mid-back to reinforce the order. A moment later the same voice called, in a thick gabble he could not understand, some summons.

The Herald's would-be assailant was still moving about where Avalon had last disappeared, ramming the cross-pole into bushes, crying out in a high voice words Nick could not translate. His attitude was one of rage fed by bafflement.

At a second hail from behind Nick, he finally stopped beating the bushes and came toward the American in a lopsided gait that still let him cover the ground with speed.

His dress, Nick saw, as he came to a stop, leaning on the pole of his cross, was that of a monk. And the eyes in his grimy face were the burning ones of a fanatic.

"Up!" Pain in Nick's back. The American got to his feet, raging both at the man behind him and at himself for being so blind as to be so easily captured.

The monk thrust his face close to Nick's. His breath was foul and the rank odor of his body and ancient clothing was enough to sicken the captive. The fierce eyes swept up and down Nick.

"Demon!" He raised the cross and Nick thought it was about to thud home on his skull. He ducked and was rewarded by a cuff on the side of his head that sent him sprawling to his knees, his head ringing, half-dazed.

They gabbled over him, his captor and the monk. Hands caught and held him, one twisted in his hair so that he could not move his head. Again the cross loomed over him. And this time it was lowered so that its tip bit painfully into the skin on his forehead. The monk held it so for a long moment and then snatched it away, bending close to Nick to survey the result of that contact.

He grunted as if displeased, then gave some order to the other. Nick was pulled to his feet, his hands twisted behind him and secured there by a cord, which cut into his flesh. Then his hitherto-unseen captor came around to face the monk.

Though in build he was much like Stroud, he was far removed otherwise from the Warden in appearance. His face was largely covered with a greasy mat of beard, which climbed so high on his cheekbones that it was nearly entangled with brows as full and shaggy. On his head was a metal helmet, dented, rust streaked, which sprouted a piece to hide his nose. The rest of his clothing was in keeping, rusty mail over leather so old and filthy that it was near black. His slightly bowed legs were covered with tight-fitting but hole-filled hose, and boots that were close to complete disintegration.

But he was armed. A sword was belted on, and a dagger nearly as long as Nick's forearm balanced that. Over his shoulder arose the curve of a crossbow. He had drawn the dagger and leered at Nick as he set it with the point aimed at the American's throat.

The monk shook his head with the jerky violence that characterized all his movements and spat some order. The other grinned, his mouth a broken-toothed gap in that noisome brush of beard. Seizing Nick by his shoulder, he gave him a shove after the monk who hobbled on, his cross-pole upheld as if it were both a banner and a threat.

That he had fallen into the hands of a drifter band was plain. Nick, shaken by his own folly in allowing himself to be caught, could not yet think straight. He doubted more strongly every minute that these people could in any way be appealed to as fellow refugees. The soldier, if soldier were his occupation, who kept him going with bruising slaps and punches, exuded such brutality as Nick had never before encountered. And the monk's attitude was, to his mind, no better.

They came into an open space by a small stream to meet the rest of this company. There were three more of the soldiers, as like his original captor as if they were all brothers. But the authority was not theirs. Rather it seemed divided between the monk and another who sat with her back against a rock. She was tearing at a piece of half-cooked meat from a supply speared on sticks and set to roast at the edge of a fire.

Grease glistened on her chin, dripped to the front of the laced bodice of her gown where it joined and reinforced the stiffened evidence of many other such meals. Her skin was gray with ancient grime, her hair braids lusterless with neglect. But her features were those which, had she been clean and well cared for, might have made her a beauty even in Nick's world. And her foully used dress was patterned with what once had been fine embroidery, just as her girdle and the rings she wore on each finger and thumb were bejeweled. There was a gold circlet on her head with a setting of a dull blue gem above her forehead. She was like some princess out of a fairy-book illustration completely degraded.

At the sight of Nick she threw away the bone she gnawed. Sitting up straighter, she pointed to him imperiously and uttered some command he could not understand. Yet there were word sounds in it that were familiar. When he did not answer, his captor cuffed him again.

But the monk waved the soldier away, voiced a furious objection. The vicious amusement that had come into the woman's face at her underling's correction of their prisoner dulled with disappointment. She shrugged and gestured. One of the other men hastened to uproot another spit of meat and take it to her.

However, the monk planted himself directly before Nick and spoke slowly, spacing a breath between each word. It was all incomprehensible and Nick shook his head. Now his captor advanced again. He addressed the monk with grudging respect, then he turned to Nick.

"Who—you?" The accent was very guttural but the question made sense.

"Nicholas Shaw—and you are?"

The soldier grinned evilly. "Not matter. You demon spawn." He spat. "We keep—demons see—They give us sword—we give you sword!"

Now the monk broke into speech again, plainly demanding some response from the soldier. The woman, licking her fingers, interrupted. At her words the four soldiers laughed heartily. But the monk whirled to face her, waving his pole. She continued to smile but remained silent under his spate of speech. However, the soldiers stopped laughing.

Nick was jerked over to a convenient tree, his back planted against its trunk and a length of twisted hide rope used to anchor him securely. The monk surveyed the operation with approval and satisfaction. Then Nick was left to his own devices and his thoughts, while the rest tramped back to squat by the fire and eat.

The smell of the meat made him hungry. The stew Linda had given him now seemed very far in the past. But he was even more thirsty than hungry, and to see the ripple of water beyond was an aggravation that increased as the afternoon passed.

It would seem that this party was in no haste to travel on. One of the soldiers (or, Nick decided, they might better be termed "men-at-arms" since their shabby trappings were certainly more akin to that time labeled "Middle Ages" than his own) went behind a screen of bushes to return leading a heavy-footed, uncurried horse, its ribs too plain beneath its hide, and a mule with one lop ear. These he guided down to the water and let drink, before herding them back into the bushes again.

The monk stretched out on the ground well away from the fire as the heat of the afternoon increased. His hands were crossed on his breast, under them the pole of his strange weapon. The men-at-arms, drawing away from their betters, did the same, though they took turns on guard, prowling in and out of the bushes.

Having finished her meal, the woman wiped her hands on a tuft of grass, the first gesture toward cleanliness Nick had seen her make. She went to the brook, drank from her cupped hands, wiped them this time on her skirt. She stood, eyeing the sleeping monk and the soldiers. Then she gave a quick glance at Nick before returning to her rock-backed seat.

But she did not settle to rest. Instead she lounged at ease, playing with one of her long braids, humming. Now and again she glanced at Nick meaningfully, as he was fully aware.

As he had felt the brutality of the men-at-arms, the raw fanaticism of the monk, so the evil that was in her was like a scent, rank and horrible. Nick's reaction to this party he could not understand. Never before had he had such an aversion to any person or persons, the sensation that he knew their feelings. It was like his comprehension that Jeremiah could understand him, a heightened power of which he had never before been aware. And this added to his fear.

That he was in a very bad situation there was no denying. They would slit his throat with ease and needed no urging to it. In fact he would swear the woman would relish it. He could gather only one idea—that he was to be kept as a bargaining point with those they called "demons." And since the monk had screamed that at the Herald, it was the People with whom they intended to bargain, to so threaten by their usage of Nick. The thought was freezing. For what would the People care if he were murdered here? He had refused the Herald's offer—or at least delayed answer to it—so he was no concern of Avalon's. The terms had been made plain to him: Avalon defended its own, the rest could meet the fate they had chosen.

Now Nick wished he had answered differently. It seemed to him that the Vicar's talk of changing, of the wrongness of that choice, was as nothing compared to being in these hands. Yet—there was in him a stubbornness of which he was aware—he would not be forced to a choice he did not freely give.

This whole venture had begun because he had wanted to get away, to be himself without outside pressures, without interference. Yet he had met with nothing but that. He had been swung by duty into guiding Linda. After their meeting with the English party they had to conform to their type of existence, simply because he was not informed enough to take risks—

The monk was snoring, but his small snorts were nearly drowned out by the deeper chorus from the men-at-arms. Their comrade on guard duty came into view and the woman beckoned to him, gave an order. He touched his rusty helmet with a forefinger and went off in the direction of the animals. She watched him go, then arose and went to the stream.

Cupping her hands she dipped up as much of the water as she could, and came, swift-footed, with dripping fingers, to Nick.

"Aqua—" She held it out just a little beyond his reach.

Latin! She had spoken Latin!

Her hands moved closer. His thirst was torment now that the water was here. But he did not trust her in the least. He did not believe that she had a sense of compassion. This was a game she wanted to play.

The moisture dripped on his shirt, he could dip his head and drink. But something in him said "no," and he heeded it.

Her smile pinched into nothingness. She flung what remained into his face. Then she went back to her rock, to return as swiftly with a small whip, its stock tarnished but set with rough-cut stones. Raising it she struck him across the face, the lash as sharp as a knife stab, leaving a hot line of pain behind.

Now she laughed, for in spite of his control Nick had gasped, and stood flicking the lash back and forth, watching him to see if he understood the threat of that. But if she planned other mischief she was again defeated by the monk.

He had sat up, now he gave voice to what could only be a roar of rage. One so vehemently expressed that it brought the men-at-arms awake and their hands to their weapons, pulled their fellow back through the bushes at a run to join them.

The woman stood her ground, waiting for a lull in the monk's shouts. Then she replied with a matching sharpness. But she left Nick. Apparently the monk's wishes still ruled. Nick only wished fervently he knew what those were.

As the shadows of evening drew in he thought of the cave. They must have missed him by now, but even if they found his exit they would have no idea of where he had gone. And for their own sakes they would not venture into the open without a guide. He knew he could not hope for any chance of rescue.

He had been trying at intervals to loosen the ties about his wrists. But they were past dealing with. His hands were numb, and the lack of feeling was spreading up his arms. The support of the tree trunk against which he had been lashed kept him upright, but his feet were also numb. And he was not sure he could move with any speed even if he were now, by some miracle, set free.

With the coming of twilight the men-at-arms were busied. They had had one fire during the day. Now they were bringing wood, making a second some distance away. The monk labored with some lengths of dried branches he had chosen with care. He chipped away with his belt knife, used twists of grass in a way to suggest that he had done this many times before, and fashioned some more crosses of wood.

These in hand, he approached the tree and Nick and proceeded to set them in the ground, as if by doing so he erected a barrier about the captive. As he worked he muttered, and Nick thought that he recognized now and then a Latin word. Having set up the crosses the monk methodically paced along that line, touching each with the metal of the one on the pole, chanting aloud as he went. Behind him the others drew together and their voices were raised now and then in response to the ceremony he was performing.

They then lit the second fire, which gave a light that grew as the darkness increased. The horse and the mule were brought out, once more watered, and then tethered between the fires, while their guardian hung about their bony necks cords with bits of broken metal fastened to them. Into the light between the fires moved the whole company. The men-at-arms drew their daggers, kept them in their hands as if they settled in to await a siege. But the monk thrust the pole of his cross into the ground and stood not too far from Nick.

Their whole attitude was one of expectancy, and Nick found himself listening, though for what he could not imagine. From time to time the monk muttered, those between the fires shifted, or showed other signs of fatigue, but they lost none of their vigilance.

Nick became aware slowly of a foulness like the odor that wafted to him from the members of this camp. Only this was not a foulness born of the body, but rather of the spirit. That was another sensation he had never known, yet was able to recognize it for what it was. Just as the farmhouse wherein they had sheltered had been a haven of good, so did that which was closing in now advertise its threatening evil.

And the others must have expected its coming. It was not of Avalon, Nick was as sure of that as if the fact had been shouted aloud.

Dank, heavy, a cloud of corruption— Then Nick heard the rasp of something ponderously heavy moving through the brush—a panting breath.

Those in the firelight raised their hands—the iron they held there visible. While the monk freed his cross-pole from the ground and made ready to use it, as he had tried to club the Herald.

Closer—Nick saw a bush quiver to his left. He turned his head to face what might issue from there. In the midst of the branches was a head. He made himself eye it, though fear battled his control and he shivered.

Gray-white, bestial, twisted—it was obscene, the epitome of every night terror. It leered, showed fangs, was gone. A serpent, or something with a serpent's body, writhed out from another direction. It had a serpent's body, but the head was that of a woman. And, as the thing came, it called in a hissing voice words that those in the firelight must have understood, for with a cry of horror and hate one of the men-at-arms plunged forward, aiming at the creature with his knife. It sliced into the body behind the smiling head.

But there was no wound and the man cowered back, with a crowing sound, his knife forgotten, his hands before his eyes, huddling in upon himself, while the serpent woman coiled and reared—until the monk lashed out with his pole and she vanished utterly. That was only the beginning of the siege.

✴ 11 ✴

There were monsters pacing on all fours, others humanoid in shape. They leered, hissed, spat, called, menaced, only to slip back into the shadows and let others come. So far none of this hideous crew attacked the firelit party. But their very appearance rasped the nerves, kept one tense. And it was plain that the nerves of the party were already badly worn, perhaps by earlier meetings with the same threat.

When something with a goat's head but very human body, save for a tail and hoofed feet, gamboled into the light, prancing and beckoning to the men-at-arms, one of them threw up his head and howled like a dog. The one who had captured Nick rounded on his fellow and knocked him flat. The man lay whimpering on the ground. Goathead snickered, leaping in the air and clapping his hoofs together.

The monk thrust out with the cross-pole and Goathead uttered a thin scream, staggered back as if in that lay dire threat. But there shot up in his place another with a human body that glowed with golden radiance, having white wings stirring from the shoulder blades. Mounted on the broad shoulders was the head of an owl. Its left hand lay loosely on the back of a wolf as large as a horse.

"Andras!" The monk appeared to recognize this apparition. "Demon!" Again he struck out with his weapon.

But this time his attack was not so efficient, for the owl beak in the feathered visage uttered a sound. The noise swelled higher and deeper, filling the night, one's head—Nick flinched from the pain as that cry went on and on.

The agony grew worse, until he was aware of nothing save that. And he must have been close to losing consciousness when he saw, dimly, that those between the fires had dropped their weapons, even the monk his cross-pole. They were holding their hands to their ears, their faces betraying their torment, and they tottered to their feet and staggered forward.

Not to meet the owl-headed one, for he was gone. No, they wavered and stumbled into the bushes, drawn by some force they could not withstand. Men-at-arms; the woman, stumbling in her long, dragging skirt; last of all, the monk, his face a tormented mask wavering out into the haunted dark. Nick felt the force, too, and struggled against his bonds, the cords cutting deep into his flesh as he sought to obey the command of that screech.

He fought desperately. There was no respite from the pain unless he obeyed that summons—he must go! Yet he could not. And at last he slumped, exhausted, only the punishing cords keeping him on his feet.

His captors had disappeared. The bony horse and the dejected mule remained. And both animals were attempting to graze as if nothing had happened. His own head was free of the pain, though he could hear, fading away, that torturing sound.

What would be the fate of those answering it? Nick did not know. But that any would return to free him, or kill him, he did not believe. He was dazed from the assault upon his ears, but he began to realize he was still trapped.

Bright in the firelight lay the daggers they had drawn for their protection. But they were as far from his use as if they had been in his own world.

It was then that he became aware of a sound overhead, and pushed his head back against the rough bark, striving to find an angle from which he could see what passed there. Was it a flying monster?

He caught only a fleeting glimpse. But he was sure he had not been mistaken. One of the saucers was swinging in the direction of the fugitives.

Was that sound intended to drive or pull those sheltered here into the open where they could be taken? Those monsters—the people seemed able to identify them, he remembered the monk had named the owl head—what had they to do with this? But such could be used to disarm and break down the nerves of selected victims.

But if the saucer people made their capture they would learn about him! Perhaps they already knew and believed him safely immobilized. He had to get loose!

At that moment Nick feared the saucer people more than any monster he had seen lurking here tonight. For the monsters could be illusions, but the saucers were real.

Get free, but how? The daggers—He had no possible chance of reaching those any more than he had of summoning Stroud, Crocker or the Vicar. Or of seeing the Herald—

The Herald!

Nick's memory fastened on the picture of the Herald as he had seen him from the cave entrance. The brilliant tabard seemed to flicker before his eyes. Slowly his fear ebbed. The stench of evil that had come with the dark was gone. What Nick now felt against his sweating face was the clean breeze of the woods, with it a pleasant scent.

But the saucer! Freedom before its crew could come here! He was too spent now to struggle against the cords that only drew tighter as he fought. His hands and feet were alarmingly numb.

The Herald—in spite of his need to think of a way of escape Nick kept remembering—seeing Avalon.

"Avalon!"

What had moved him to call that name?

The horse nickered. It flung up its head, called, was answered by a bray from the mule. Both animals ceased to graze. They stood looking toward the tree where Nick was bound.

Then—*HE* was there!

Another illusion? If so it was very solid-seeming.

"Avalon?" Nick made of that a question. Would the Herald

release him? Or, since Nick had not accepted the bargain, would he be left to whatever fate the saucer people had in mind?

"I am Avalon." Nick could hear that.

"Can you—will you free me?" Nick came directly to the point. Let the Herald say "yes" or "no" and get it over with.

"Each man must free himself. Freedom is offered, the choice is yours alone."

"But—I can't move—even to take that precious apple of yours, if I want to!"

As before the Herald's features were untouched by expression. There was a glow about him that did not come from the fires.

"There are three freedoms." Avalon did not produce the apple. "There is the freedom of body, there is the freedom of mind, there is the freedom of spirit. A man must have all three if he would be truly released from bondage."

Nick's anger rose. With time his enemy, he had no desire to waste it on philosophical discussion. "That does not get me free."

"Freedom lies in yourself," Avalon returned. "Even as it is within all living things—"

He turned a fraction then, his level gaze moving from Nick to the horse and mule. For a space as long as several deep breaths he regarded the two animals. Then both of them moved their heads vigorously, certainly with more alertness than the half-starved beasts had displayed before.

They walked to the bushes and thrust their heads and necks into the foliage, turning, twisting with obviously intelligent purpose. Their motions snagged on branches the thongs about their necks that were hung with metal bits. Now each lowered its head and jerked back, so those cords were drawn off, left to swing there.

Freed, they came directly to the Herald, lowering their heads before him. He reached out a hand but did not quite touch their halters. Those in turn fell away, giving them freedom from all man had laid upon them.

Yet they still stood and gazed at the Herald and he back at them, as if they communicated. At last the horse whinnied, the mule brayed. Together they turned and trotted off into the night.

"If you can free them," Nick said hotly, "you can do that for me."

"Freedom is yours, only you can provide it."

That there was some purpose in what he said more than just the desire to frustrate the captive, Nick now believed. The horse and the mule had had to rid themselves of "cold iron" that men had laid upon them. But all his struggles had only exhausted him. He could not free himself—that was impossible.

"How?" he asked.

There was no answer.

"You told the animals!" Nick accused.

Still the Herald was silent.

Freedom that only he himself could provide? Perhaps because he had not accepted Avalon's offer the Herald could or would not aid him more than in such oblique statements. Nick leaned his weight against the tree and tried to think. Undoubtedly there was a way. He did not believe that Avalon was tormenting him for some obscure reason. And if there was a way he must have the will, patience and intelligence to find it.

Futile struggles did not aid. He could not reach the daggers so tantalizingly within sight but not within reach. So—what remained?

Freedom of body he did not have. Freedom of mind, freedom of spirit—could he use either? Telepathy—precognition—there were powers of the mind—paranormal powers. But those were talents few possessed and he was not one of them.

The daggers—within his sight—freedom of mind—

Avalon waited. There was nothing to be gained from him, Nick was sure. What he had to do was wholly by his own will and strength.

The daggers—a use for them—

Nick stared with all the concentration he could summon at the nearest blade, the slender one the woman had dropped. Knife—cord—one meeting the other with freedom to follow.

Knife—cord—He must shut out of his mind all else but that slender, shining blade, red with the light of the now dying fire, the thought of the cord about him. Knife—cord—

Sweat trickled down Nick's face. He felt strange, as if part of him struggled to be free from his body. A part of him—like a hand—reaching for freedom. If he could not move the knife with his desire—what of his hand?

Nick changed tactics. A hand—an arm—free—reaching into the firelight. His body obeyed his mind in some things, would it now? Something was forming, thin, misty—touching the knife. So iron did not prevent this! Nick concentrated. A hand, five fingers—fingers and thumb to close about the haft. That grayish thing was there—clasped about the hilt.

There was the hand, but a hand must be joined to an arm or it was useless. An arm—he set himself to visualize a wrist, an arm. Once more there was the gathering of foggy material. It joined the hand, yet it also reached back to him.

Now!

He had never in his life centered on any act the intense will he now summoned. The long, long "arm" of mist began to draw back toward him. He must hold it—he must!

Nick's breath came in gasps. Back, draw back—he must bring the knife!

The blade was out of the firelight now, trailing across the ground in little jumps as if his energy ebbed and flowed. But it was coming! Nick knew no triumph, only the need to hold and draw.

Now the knife lay at his feet, misty hand, elongated arm collapsed, faintly luminous, coiled like a slackened rope. Nick was so tired—fatigue of a kind he had never before experienced hung upon him like a black cloak. If he let it get to him he was lost.

The knife must come up! The coiled substance thickened, loops melted into a stouter, more visible column with the hand at the top, the knife in it. Up! Nick's whole force of being centered in his desire.

By jerks the blade arose. Its point pricked his knee. He brought it higher to the first twist of cord. Cut! He gave the order—cut!

It moved slowly, too slowly. He almost panicked, and then firmed his control. Slow it was, but it moved—

Cut!

Feebly the blade sawed back and forth across the tough hide. If only the edge was sharp enough! Do not think of that—think of nothing but the action—cut—cut—cut!

A loop of hide fell at his feet. The column of mist collapsed, the dagger falling with it to the ground. Nick writhed furiously with all the strength he had left. His hands fell away and he toppled over, to fall headlong, spent and breathless.

He turned his head to look for Avalon. But the Herald was gone. Nick lay alone between the dying fires, one of the wooden crosses standing in crooked silhouette between him and the limited light. He was free of the tree, but his hands were still tied and his feet numb, his body exhausted.

His hands—he must free his hands. There was the knife. Nick lay watching it. Once more he tried to create the hand. But the power, whatever power had worked in him to produce that, was gone. If he would help himself now he must do it by physical means.

Weakly he rolled over, hunched along until he could feel the blade. Wedge it somehow—but his hands were numb. Wedge it! Scrabbling in the leaf mold he dug the haft with the weight of his body into the ground. There was a stone, move that—Patiently he worked until he thought the blade secure. Up and down, Nick moved his wrists, not even sure the blade bit the cords.

He was not certain until his arms fell to his sides and the torture of returning circulation began. Then he pulled himself up onto his feet. He leaned against the tree that had been his place of bondage. The knife on the ground—iron. Stiffly, steadying himself with one swollen hand against the tree, Nick stooped to pick it up. Though the effort of putting his fingers around the hilt was almost too much, he managed to thrust the dagger into his belt.

Once more the danger of attack gripped him. He used the tree as a support, slipping around it, away from the fire. But his feet stumbled, he felt as if he could not walk. The bushes—if he could roll into, or under those—

Nick tottered forward. Ahead, only half to be seen in the gloom, was a thicker growth. He went to his knees, then lower, pushing, edging under that hope of shelter until he could fight no longer, his last atom of energy expended.

It was not real sleep that overcame him then, rather an exhaustion of body so great he could not lift his hand an inch from where it lay beside him. He was held in a vise of extreme fatigue but his mind was clear.

He could not yet understand what he had done. The mechanics of it, yes. He had brought the knife and freed himself. But how had he been able to accomplish that?

There were natural laws. He had been taught in his own world to believe what he had just done was impossible. But here those laws did not seem to hold. The Herald had spoken of three freedoms. This night Nick had used one to achieve a second in a way he would have sworn could not be done.

Nick closed his eyes. Do not think now—stop wondering, speculating. Close off memory. He needed release, not to think, concentrate, act—

A lulling, a slow healing—The evil that had been so thick was gone. The earth under him hollowed a little to receive his aching body, cradled him. Twigs and leaves brushed his upturned face, their clean scent in his nostrils. He was one with the ground, the bush—He was safe—secure—held—The sleep that came to him was dreamless.

He did not waken all at once as when one is shaken out of slumber by alarm. Recognition of reality was slow, gentle, sleep leaving him bit by bit. He could hear faint twitterings, rustlings—

Nick opened his eyes. There were leaves about him, very close above him, the tips of some brushed his face gently. He began to remember the how and why of his coming here. There was daylight around.

His body ached, he was stiff and sore, and there were rings of fire about his wrists, yet he felt wonderful, renewed, as if his body's hurts did not matter. And he was content not to stir as yet.

This was not the feeling of peace and security that had existed in the deserted farmhouse. It was alien, but it was friendly, as if he had been allowed a step inside a door that gave upon a new and different life.

Hunger and thirst awoke, flogging him into movement. Nick crawled laboriously out from his refuge. His hands were still puffed and the weals about his wrists raw. The stream must lie in that direction.

On his feet he lurched forward. There were the burned-out fires, two of the daggers, the cross-pole, now sunbathed in the open. Nick passed the rock where the woman had sat, fell on his knees beside the water. Then he lay prone, to duck his face, lap at the moisture, dangle his hands and wrists in the chill water that stung his hurts. This roused him from his drowsy contentment.

By the strength of the sun he thought it must be close to midday. Could he find his way back to the cave? And had they come hunting him? Were the saucers out?

Gazing around Nick could see no evidence that the campsite had been visited after its people had been drawn away. He gathered up the other daggers, but left the cross-pole where it lay. Then he turned slowly, trying to guess the direction from which he had come, only to be baffled.

Trees would provide shelter from any hunting saucer, but woods also had strange inhabitants. He could follow the stream as a guide—but a guide to where? As far as he knew there was no such body of water running near the cave. And he was hungry—

The thought of possible fish in the stream was the factor in making his decision to travel along it. Though how he was going to catch any water dweller he had no idea. However, a short distance farther up he found berry bushes well loaded with fruit.

Birds whirred away at his coming, but settled again to their own harvesting. Nick pulled greedy handfuls of the well-ripened globes and stuffed his mouth, the dark juice staining his hands. Blackberries, he decided, and a growth of them that was very heavy. He rounded a bush, picking and eating avidly, and heard a snuffle. Farther along in this wealth of good eating a large brown furred shape was busy. Nick ducked back and away. The bear, if bear it had been, was fully occupied. Nick would keep to this side and let the woods dweller have that.

But in his sudden evasion he was startled by a sharp cry and jumped back. Fronting him, anger and alarm made plain, was—

Nick blinked as the creature flashed away, was gone behind a tall clump of grass. He made no move to follow, he was not even sure he wanted to see more of what had been there.

Only, to prove that he had seen it, there still lay before him a basket. Nick reached down to pick it up. He could just get two fingers through its handle and it was very beautifully woven of two kinds of dried grass.

The berries that had fallen out of it Nick carefully returned. In addition he added enough more to fill it. And he looked toward the grass tuft as he set the basket back on the ground—in full sight, he hoped, of its indignant owner.

"I am very sorry." He kept his voice hardly above a whisper, remembering the bear.

Then, resolutely not looking back to see whether the harvester ventured out of hiding, Nick went on. His amazement had faded. The Vicar had spoken of legends come true here. And there had always been stories of the true "little people"—elves, gnomes, dwarfs—but the latter were supposed to live underground and mine for treasures, were they not?

Nick no longer doubted that he had seen a very small man, or a creature of humanoid appearance, dressed in a mottled green-brown that would be camouflage in the forest. And surely that manikin was no stranger that anything else he had sighted here.

Dwarfs, elves—Nick wished he knew more. One should have a good founding in the old fairy lore before venturing into this world. Was Hadlett right in his connection that the People had somehow been able to go through the other way in the past, perhaps even been exiled in Nick's world, thus providing the seed from which the fairy tales had grown? Some of the legendary ones had been friendly, Nick remembered that. But there had been others—the black witches, giants, ogres, dragons—

The berries no longer tasted so sweet. He left the patch behind and forged ahead along the stream. But now he kept a sharp watch on the ground before him, as well as on the bushes. What was spying on him? Nick meant no harm, but would they understand that? And there might be drifters wandering here, such a vicious company as he had just escaped. Those would be enemies to the People, he was certain, and could the People in turn tell the difference between a drifter of good will and one to be feared?

He hoped that they all had protection like the Herald's. His sympathy for the manikin and his kind was strong. The Herald— Where had Avalon gone last night? And why had he left Nick? Though he had given the American the advice that meant freedom, he had left. Did Nick now have knowledge his own companions could use in their defense?

Nick turned slowly, trying to sight something that he could use as a guide. He wanted to get back to the cave, to tell his story. And they must believe him! Surely, having faced all the improbabilities current here, what he had to say would not seem a complete impossibility.

He thought his way led left. And the woods seemed less dense in that direction. If he struck through there—resolutely he moved forward.

There were some more straggling berry bushes and he ate as he went, snatching at the fruit. But under the trees the bushes vanished and he hurried, trying to rid himself of the belief that he was watched, almost expecting to have some forester with an escort of outlandish animals confront him. But if Nick were paced by unseen company, they were content to let him go. And he chanced upon a path, marked here and there with deer prints, which ran in the direction he wished. So, turning into that, he made better time.

Nick came out on the edge of open country in midafternoon. He hesitated there, searching the sky for any sign of a saucer. Birds flew, a whole brilliant-colored flock of them, crying out as they went. They were large and their wheeling, dipping flight formed a loose circle out over the plain.

It was as if they were flying around and around some object. Prudently Nick took cover and continued to watch. The sun was bright but he could see nothing—

Or could he? Was something there, rising skyward like the towers of the wondrous city? But it was of such transparency that it was virtually invisible—The longer Nick watched the birds the more convinced he was that this was so.

Then the flock, which had been circling, formed a line and descended earthward, disappearing one by one as if winked out of existence when it reached the point where Nick was sure something did stand.

He rubbed his hands across his eyes. It was—it was becoming more and more visible. Towers—like the city—but smaller, fewer of them. Before his eyes they took on an opaque quality, gained substance. What he now saw was a towered, walled structure resembling a medieval castle.

❈ 12 ❈

To all appearances the castle was now completely solid, but lacking in the coloring of the city. No rainbow lights played along its walls, climbed the towers, glowed into the sky. It was gray white as if erected from native stone.

Though the birds did not reappear there was movement. A portion of the wall facing his hiding place descended slowly to form a drawbridge, as if the castle were surrounded by a moat. Over that rode a brightly clad party.

There was plainly a Herald as leader. Nick could recognize the tabard at a glance. Behind him were four others, riding the sky-mounting steeds, two by two. These wore tabards of the same cut as their leader but of forest green. And only a single emblem, which Nick could not distinguish at this distance, was on the breast of each.

They rode easily at what seemed a slow amble but which covered the ground with a deceptive speed so that they swiftly drew close to Nick. He did not now try to conceal his presence, sure he was in no danger. And he wanted to learn all he could of this company and their visible-invisible castle.

But the Herald and his party had no interest in Nick. They rode with their eyes forward, nor did they speak among themselves. There was no expression on their faces. But as they approached, Nick saw two had hair that brushed their shoulders and one of them was Rita.

Their riding partners were not quite like the Herald but might have once been as human as the English girl.

Now that they were closer Nick could make out the designs embroidered in gold and silver glitter on their tabards. Each was the branch of a tree. The first male had what was unmistakably oak leaves and golden acorns carefully depicted. With him was Rita with her apple branch. The next couple sported patterns Nick did not know, both depicted in flowers of silver white.

Their passage was noiseless since the paws of their steeds made no sound. And they might have been caught in a dream with their sight fixed ahead.

Nick first thought to force a meeting. But their aloofness was such as to awe him to remaining still and silent to watch them go.

Just before they reached the woods their long-legged beasts began to mount into the air. As if that provided a signal there came wheeling from aloft a pair of birds, white winged, huge. Twice these circled the riders, then forged ahead of them.

Nick watched them out of sight. Then he turned to look at the castle. He had half expected it to fade from sight. But it was more solid-seeming in the twilight than before. Only the gap of the drawbridge had disappeared.

Curiosity worked in him. Enough to draw him to that structure? Nick hunkered down, his full attention on it. Was it real, or wasn't it? After his own experience he could not accept anything here without proof. Should he put it to the proof?

"Nicholas!"

The sharp whisper broke the spell. His hand was on the hilt of the dagger in his belt as his head jerked to the bush from which the sound had come.

"Who is it?" Nick had the blade out, ready, though never in his life had he used a weapon against another.

Cautiously a branch swung up and he saw the Vicar's face screened in the greenery. Nick pushed the weapon back with relief. He slid around his own cover and in a minute was confronting both Hadlett and Crocker.

"How did you find me?"

"Where have you been?"

The questions mingled together, Crocker's the sharper, with anger in it.

But the Vicar's hand closed about Nick's upper arm in a reassuring squeeze.

"How fortunate, my boy. You are safe!"

"Now," Nick returned. "If anyone can be safe here." It was growing darker with a speed he had not expected. A glance upward showed a massing of clouds. And in the distance was the lash of lightning fire, a distant rumble of thunder.

"What happened?" Crocker repeated his demand aggressively.

"I was caught—by some drifters—" Nick edited his adventures. With the Vicar he would be more explicit, but his past contacts with the pilot had not been such as to provoke confidences. He had not accepted the Herald's bargain, but he was just as sure that he was not the same person he had been in his own world. And if the English looked upon change as a threat and a reason to outlaw one of their own, there was no need to hand Crocker a good excuse to get rid of him.

There was a second deep growl of thunder, this time closer.

"It would be better to seek shelter," Hadlett said. "The storm is near."

"Over there?" Crocker pointed to the castle. Though it did not reflect light from its walls, there were sparks here and there along the towers as if lamps hung behind windows.

Nick wondered if the others had seen the castle materializing from thin air. Much as his curiosity was aroused, he was not drawn to this as he had been to the city.

"We can, I believe, reach a hollow I know before the rain comes." Hadlett ignored Crocker's question. "Providing we start now."

It was he, not the pilot, who led the way through the brush, edging west along the line of the forest. But the first of the rain hit with great drumming drops before they came to his hollow.

One of the giant trees had fallen long since and its upturned root mass had in turn been overgrown with vegetation. The curtain of this could be pulled aside to give on a sheltered place into which the three could crowd, though they must rub shoulders to do so.

A certain amount of seepage from the storm still reached them, but they were under cover. And they had no more than settled in before Crocker was back with his question.

"So you were caught—by whom?"

Nick obliged with a description of the band. Once or twice the Vicar interrupted him with a desire that he expand some portion of his story, namely when he spoke of the monk. But when Nick described the monsters that had held the camp in siege, he felt Crocker stir.

"Snake with a woman's head? Thing with an owl head? Do you expect us to—"

"Lamia—and Andras," the Vicar said.

"A what and who?" Crocker sounded belligerent.

"A lamia—a snake demon—well known in ancient church mythology. And Andras—"

It was Nick's turn to interrupt. "That was what the monk called him—or at least it sounded like that!"

"Andras, Grand Marquis of Hell. He teaches those he favors to kill their enemies, masters and servant. In the army of the damned he commands thirty legions." It was as if the Vicar read an official report.

"But you don't believe in—" Again Crocker began a protest.

"*I* do not, nor you, Barry. But if one did believe in a lamia come to crush one's soul with its snake body, or in Andras, Marquis of Hell, then what better place for such to appear in threat?"

Nick caught the suggestion. "You mean—the nightmares one believes in, those have existence here?"

"I have come to think so. And if that is true, the opposite ought to exist—that the powers of good one holds to will also make themselves manifest. But it is easier for a man to accept evil as real than it is for him to believe in pure good. That is the curse we carry with us to our undoing. To those poor wretches this is Hell but they have made it for themselves."

"They were evil." Nick used an expression that would not have come easily to him in his own world. "You didn't see them. That woman—she was—well, you might call her a she-devil. And the monk was a fanatic, he could burn heretics in holy satisfaction. The others—in our time they would be muggers—have their fun beating up people."

"Padre." Crocker might have been only half listening, more interested in his own thoughts. "If they thought they could see monsters and devils and did, do you mean we could think up such things, too?"

"It is very possible. But we come from a different age. Our devils are not born of the same superstition—they are not, as you might say, personal. Our evil is impersonal, though it is not the less for that. We no longer decry Satan and his works and emissaries. Rather we have the sins of nations, of wars, of industry, of fanatical causes. Impersonal devils, if you wish. We speak of 'they' who are responsible for this wrong and that. But 'they' seldom have a name, a body. Your monk was certain his devils had personalities, names, status, so they appeared to him in that fashion.

"We cannot summon our devils to plague us here because they lack such identity. There is and always has been great evil in our world, but its face and form changes with the centuries and it is no longer personified for us."

"What about Hitler?" Crocker challenged.

"Yes, in him our generation does have a devil. What of yours, Nicholas?"

"No one man, no one cause. It follows the pattern you spoke of, sir."

"This is all very interesting," Crocker cut in. "But how did you get away from that crowd? Did one of the devils cut you loose and then disappear in a puff of smoke?"

Nick was uneasy. This was getting close to what he hesitated to tell. One had to accept many improbabilities in this world, but would these two accept what had happened?

"Well?" Crocker's voice sharpened. "What did happen next?"

He was boxed into telling the truth, which meant bringing Avalon into it. And he had neglected to speak of his earlier confrontation with the Herald. That omission might make him a suspect.

"You are troubled, Nicholas." The Vicar's tone was as soothing as

Crocker's was a source of irritation. "Something has happened that you find difficult to explain."

Hadlett said that as if he knew it. And Nick believed that the Vicar would be aware of any evasion or slighting of the truth. He braced himself.

"It began earlier—" In a rush he told of his meeting with Avalon, afraid if he hesitated longer his courage would ebb.

"Repeat those names!" Hadlett's command brought him up short at a point which seemed to him to have little significance. But he obeyed.

"He said, 'Avalon, Tara, Brocéliande, Carnac.'"

"The great holy places of the Celtic world," Hadlett commented. "Places that are rumored even today to be psychic centers of power. Though Avalon, of the four, has never been completely identified. In legend it lay to the west. Heralds bearing those names—yes, the proper pattern—"

"What pattern?" Crocker wanted to know.

"That of ancient heraldry. The heralds of Britain take their titles from the royal dukedoms—such as York, Lancaster, Richmond. The pursuivants derive theirs from the old royal badges. And the Kings-of-Arms, who command all, are from the provinces—Clarenceaux, Norroy, Ulster and the like. If Nicholas has the correct information, there must be four heralds here, each bearing the name of an ancient place of great power in our own world—perhaps once an entrance-way to this. Tara lies in Ireland, Carnac and Brocéliande in Brittany—but all were of Celtic heritage. And it is from the Celtic beliefs that much of our legendary material about the People of the Hills and their ways have come. I wonder who is King-of-Arms here?"

"I don't see what that's got to do with us!" Crocker protested. "We all know what the Herald is and what he can do to anyone foolish enough to listen to him. You seem to have listened for quite a while, Shaw. What did he offer you—enough to make it interesting?"

Nick curbed his temper. He had expected the suspicion Crocker voiced.

"He offered me," he said deliberately, "a golden apple and the safety of this world. He foretold the coming of great danger; this has overrun the land periodically before, and is beginning such an attack again. According to him only those who accept Avalon will have any protection then."

"A golden apple," Hadlett mused. "Yes, once more symbolic."

"And deadly! Remember that, Padre—deadly!"

"Yes." But there was an odd note in the Vicar's voice.

"So you met this Avalon—then what happened? Did your men-at-arms grab him also?" Crocker brought Nick back to his story.

"They tried to, or to kill him—the monk did." He told of the fruitless assault with the cross-pole and the Herald's disappearance.

"So that was when they grabbed you. Now suppose you explain how you got away."

Nick went on to the sound that had been a torment and the disappearance of the drifters, the fact that he was left behind. He did not enlarge on his own fears, but continued with the return of the Herald, the scene with the horse and mule. Then, trying to pick those words that would carry the most emphasis, he told the rest of it.

They did not interrupt again but heard him out through his account of the rest of his wanderings until he had seen the castle materialize from the air and the emergence of the Herald and his four attendants.

It was then that the Vicar did question him, not as he had expected, concerning the actions he had been engaged in, or had witnessed, but about the designs embroidered on the green tabards of those who had accompanied Avalon.

"Oak and apple, and two with white or silver flowers," Hadlett repeated. "Oak and apple—those are very ancient symbols, ones of power. The other two—I wonder—But I would have to see them. Thorn? Elder? It is amazing—the old, old beliefs—"

"I find it amazing," Crocker said deliberately, "that you are still here, Shaw. You took the apple, didn't you?"

Nick had expected this accusation. But how could he prove it false?

"Do I show signs of the changes you mentioned, sir?" he asked the Vicar, not answering Crocker.

"Changes—what changes?" Hadlett asked absently.

"The changes supposed to occur in those who take the Herald's offer. I didn't. Do you want me to swear to that? Or have you some way of getting your proof? You have had more experience with this than I have. What happened to me back there—when I escaped—I cannot explain. The Herald told me about freedom, I just tried to use what I thought he meant. It worked, but I can't tell you how or why. But—I—did—not—take—the—apple—" He spaced the words of that last sentence well apart, repeated them with all the emphasis he could summon. Perhaps Crocker might not accept that, but he hoped Hadlett would.

"The changes," the Vicar repeated again. "Ah, yes, you refer to our former conversation."

To Nick he sounded irritatingly detached, as if this was not a problem that troubled him. But Nick believed he must have Hadlett on his side before he returned to the rest. Crocker's suspicions would, he was sure, be echoed by others there. Jean would support the pilot in any allegation he made. And Nick had no faith that Stroud would greet him warmly once Crocker had a chance to speak. But that the Vicar carried weight with all he was well aware. Get Hadlett to stand by him and he would have support to depend upon.

What he could do then, Nick had no idea. He did believe that the Herald spoke the truth when warning of danger ahead. His own experience with the drifters and their monsters, real or illusionary, as well as the threat of the saucer people, argued in favor of investigating more closely Avalon and its advantages. Safety, it seemed to Nick, was what they must seek. He had no faith at all in their plan to head downriver. They did not even have weapons to match those of the medieval group that had captured him. Slingshots against swords!

"I believe you, Nicholas."

He almost started. That pause before Hadlett's answer had been so prolonged Nick had come to expect the worst.

"Also I believe that what you have learned during your various encounters may be of future service to us all," the Vicar continued. "I think we shall have to make the best of this shelter until morning, but the sooner we return to the cave and discuss your findings, the better."

Crocker muttered something in too low a whisper for Nick to catch, even close wedged as they were. But he was sure that the pilot was not in the least convinced. Nick was, however, cheered. If he could depend upon the Vicar's support he was assured of a hearing.

Outside, the storm was impressive, with an armament of lightning, deafening rolls of thunder, and a curtain of rain. They were damp, but the main pelting of the downpour did not reach them.

Nick wondered about the Herald and his followers, were they now riding the sky through this natural fury? And the saucer people, how did storms affect their flyers? The cave would be dry, and certainly the city a good shelter. The city—

His old half-plan of using the Herald to win a way into the city and learn its secrets without surrendering to the terms of Avalon— Could it be done? He was far from sure, but he longed to try.

And the terms of Avalon— The Herald had saved him in the forest, not by any direct aid, but by stimulating him to save himself. Nick thought about that feat of concentration, and his hand went once more to his belt to finger the hilt of the dagger he had drawn to his aid in such incredible fashion. If one could accomplish that by concentrating—what else might one do?

Hadlett said that his late captors had produced their own hellish monsters to harass them because they expected to see such. Therefore your thoughts had reality beyond your own mind. Those had expected Hell and its inhabitants, so that was what they had to endure and fear. In mankind was the belief in evil stronger that the belief in good, as the Vicar had also said?

If one concentrated just as strongly on believing in paradise here, would that be true? And would it hold? Nick remembered the intense weariness that had closed in on him after he had fought for his freedom. The mind could demand too much from the body. To sustain any illusion for a length of time might exhaust one utterly.

The monsters, Nick decided now, must have been unconscious projection on the part of the drifters. Perhaps, if you continued to expect to see the same thing, you added reality to it, more substance every time it materialized. Would it then sometime become wholly real? That was both a startling and an unpleasant thought. What he had seen in that night of horror must not obtain real life!

Real, unreal, good, evil—The little man he had encountered in the berry patch, the visible-invisible castle, Avalon himself—real, unreal? How did one ever *know?*

Nick longed to throw some of these questions at the Vicar. But not with Crocker listening. He would only provide the pilot with more evidence that he was a dangerously unstable person—someone who, whether he had had treasonous dealings with Avalon or not, was better exiled from their company.

Though the great fury of the storm ebbed, the rain continued to fall. Nick and his companions, in spite of their cramped position, dozed away the night until a watery, gray daylight drew them forth. Crocker took the lead, saying little, guiding them on a roundabout way, keeping out of the full embrace of the woods.

Nick wondered if the castle was still visible, but he had no excuse to linger to see. He must remain prudently quiet on such matters pertaining to the People until he was sure he was no longer suspect. If Hadlett had time to think things over he might be brought to consider invasion of the city—

Nick was not prepared to bring the women into any council, though he knew that all three of the English party would have a voice in any decision. To Nick, Margo's influence on his father had been a brutal shock. She had set up barriers one by one so skillfully that it had been months before Nick was able to realize what had happened. When he knew, it was too late to do anything. Dad was gone, there was a stranger, friendly enough, but still a stranger who spoke with his voice, wore his body— Just as if Margo had manufactured an illusion to serve her purpose. That stranger made an effort now and then. Nick could look back at this moment and understand those advances, tentative and awkward as they had been. But they had meant nothing, because Margo's illusion made them.

And losing Dad, Nick had sealed off those emotions that had once been a part of him. Sure, he had gone out with girls, but none of them had meant anything. There was always the memory of Margo, of her maneuvering, her skill with Dad, to hold as a shield.

Linda was a part of the world in which Margo existed. She, too, was able perhaps to twist someone into what she wanted instead of freely accepting him for what he was.

So Nick wanted now to argue out any decision, not with the women, but with the men whom he believed he could understand. And perhaps in the end he would find more acceptance, he thought wryly, from Jeremiah and Lung. Were animals more straightforward, less devious than men?

They reached the cave as clouds were once more massing, threatening a second downpour. Lady Diana manned the lookout.

"I see you found him. You don't look too damaged to me, young man." Her voice was far from welcoming.

"Did you expect I might be?" Nick could not resist countering. He had respect for her sturdy abilities, but he could not honestly like her.

"The thought occurred to us, yes. Adrian, you are soaked. You must have a hot drink, shed those shoes of yours at once. Luckily Maude has just finished stitching up a new pair. Linda," she called down into the cave. "Come here, girl. They're back safe, and they have your boy!"

Nick stiffened. He was not Linda's boy! What claim had she made on him to these others? But when she did appear in Lady Diana's place, Lady Diana herself laying hands on the Vicar to urge him on into shelter, Linda did not look directly at Nick, nor did she speak to him.

He let Crocker pass him, wanting to say something in denial of any claim she had advanced. That this was perhaps not the time or the place for that, Nick was uneasily aware, yet he was pressed to do it.

"You're not hurt?" Her voice was cool, he might have been an acquaintance about whom she was inquiring for politeness' sake.

"No." His wrists were still ridged and sore but one could not claim those as real hurts.

"You were lucky," she observed, still remote.

"I suppose so." He might not be hurt, but he had certainly brought back problems that might cause more trouble than physical wounds.

"You know what they think." A light nod of her head clarified who "they" might be. "They believe that you may have made a deal with this Herald. You sneaked out—without telling anyone—after you were warned. And you seem to know things—"

"Know things?"

"What you said about Jeremiah and Lung."

"You told them that?" He had been right in not trusting her.

"Naturally. When they started to wonder what had become of you. Believe it or not, they were concerned. They are good people."

"You are trying to warn me, aren't you?" he asked.

"To let them alone! If you've made some deal, live with it. Don't involve them."

"Thanks for the advice and the vote of confidence!" Nick exploded and swung down into the entrance of the cave. But why had he expected any other response? This was a typical Margo trick, one he had met many times in the past. He had been put in the wrong before his case had even been heard.

❖ 13 ❖

But they did not cross-question him at once. Hadlett was the center of attention, concern for him blotting out all else, though Jean brought Nick a bowl of hot soup, which he ate greedily. She, of course, made more of a fuss over Crocker, though Nick believed she tried to make those attentions not too obvious.

Nick was back safely, something he would have given much to achieve last night, or earlier yesterday. Now—he did not know. Though the others were within touching distance if he wished, he felt curiously detached.

But he had made no bargain. Unless—unless in following the Herald's hint he had somehow crossed a line between the old life and a new. Nick put down the empty bowl, studied his hands as they rested on his knees.

They were scratched, dirty, stained with berry juice. The rest of him was probably in keeping. But he was human still and not a creature of the People.

He was still hungry. But knowing the state of their supplies, Nick did not ask for more. As he leaned over to pick up the bowl again, he saw Jeremiah. The cat had appeared out of nowhere after the fashion of felines, and sat watching Nick with probing intentness that could disconcert a human at times.

Nick stared back. There was some reason for the cat's singling him out, he guessed. What did Jeremiah want of him? If the cat could communicate, he was not trying now. Nick disliked that cool stare, but he refused to let it ruffle him.

"How much, Jeremiah," he asked in a whisper, "do you really know?"

On Nick's knee, beside his hand, there was a shimmer as if the air took on substance in a small whirlpool of energy. It thickened, held so for a moment, then vanished. But it had been there, and Nick knew he had in that moment seen a mouse.

Jeremiah! The cat could somehow use the same energy that Nick had tapped to free himself in the woods to materialize a representation of his most common prey. He was astounded. That an animal could—

Answering his astonishment came a cold thrust of near anger. Jeremiah's ears were flattened to his head, his eyes slitted.

"Animal? Who is an animal?"

The words did not form as such in Nick's mind, but some impulse brought them to the surface there. Indeed—who was an animal? In this place where all the old certainties had been swept away, could anyone make claims that could not be overturned?

Another idea came to him. Could—could Jeremiah's species (Nick tried to avoid "animal" and after all humans were animals, too) accept the Herald's terms? Was Jeremiah now a part of Avalon even though he stayed with Mrs. Clapp and the others?

Once more that swirl of air that was not air, the swift formation and disappearance of an object Nick had only an instant to sight—an apple! Then Jeremiah was—What? A spy?

Nick dismissed that at once. A guard? Against them? For them?

Jeremiah yawned, arose, and, with a flirt of his tail tip, which was firm dismissal of the whole subject, he stalked off.

"Now then." Mrs. Clapp came away from where she had settled Hadlett by the fire, his feet rubbed dry and newly fashioned moccasins on them. She stood over Nick, one of the handleless clay cups in her hand. An aromatic steam arose from it. "You drink this up! It'll roast the chill out. We want no lung fever hittin'."

She stood over him, in fact between him and the rest who were gathered about the Vicar, while he drank. And he found her gaze as searching as Jeremiah's had been. Did she know what her cat now was?

"You're a lucky lad, that indeed you are. With himself an' Barry out to hunt you."

Her voice was sharper than Nick had heard it before. He understood that, in her eyes, his late adventure was a disgrace, mainly because it had involved trouble for the Vicar.

"I know." Nick tried to be meek.

"Knowin' afterward is not doin't beforehand. I'm takin' it on me to say this—we've stayed together now for long an' we've managed. Because we think about how what we do is for all of us, not just for one. In this place you can set a foot wrong an' stir up trouble fast." The longer she spoke the softer her voice became. "There now, I've had my say. You'll hear it from the others without doubt, but they have a right to such sayin'—they knowin' all that's around us here. You—What in the wide world were you doin' to get that now?"

Her hand caught his, dragging it forward to bring his ridged, raw wrist into the full light.

"Oh, that happened when they tied me up." Nick tried to free himself from her hold, but she kept the grip with surprising strength.

"Raw that is—an' you could get a nasty infection. The other one is as bad too. You stay right here 'til I get some o' my heal powder."

Nick knew it was futile to protest. He waited and she was quickly back with two large leaves on which was spread a greasy salve.

"Should have us some bandages, but we ain't got 'em. These leaves work good though. Now hold up your hand, lad—that's the way."

She was quick and deft, and Nick soon had two green cuffs about his maltreated wrists. It was not until she had finished he remembered his own first-aid kit in the saddlebags. But already the stuff she had smeared over his abraded skin was drawing out the sting, and he was content with her treatment.

"Now." Mrs. Clapp tied strings of tough grass tightly enough to keep the wristlets in place. "You keep those on today an' tonight.

Then I'll have another look at 'em. Should be as good as healed. Those there herbs worked into fat, they've got a lot of good in 'em."

She did not go away, but stood there, her supplies in her hands. There was no sternness in her expression now, rather a concern that made Nick more uncomfortable than her scolding had done.

"You've had a bad time—"

He summoned a smile. "You might say I deserved it."

"Nobody deserves bad, 'less they give it. To my mind you're not one of those who do. But you're young, you don't want to believe what you hear 'til you try it out for yourself—"

"And," he interrupted, "in that trying I might hurt more than myself next time?"

"That I said an' meant it." Mrs. Clapp nodded. "But I'm thinkin' you're not a stupid lad. You don't need no second lesson once the first has been swallowed down."

"I hope, Mrs. Clapp, that I shall deserve that confidence."

"Maude!" Lady Diana called, and his nurse hurried back to the group about the Vicar.

Nick sat down once more, his leaf-enfolded wrists before him. They thought that they were safe here, perhaps they were. But with their supplies dwindling they might be forced out. And he had no faith at all in the river plan. He had not seen Stroud since their return and wondered if the Warden still skulked about the site of their raft.

Stroud did not return until evening. And it was with news to dash their faint hope of making use of the river. The land was alive with bands of drifters and the sky with saucers whose crews preyed upon those in the open. The Warden had witnessed the sweeping up of two such parties, one being a squad of men wearing British uniforms of World War I vintage.

"Couldn't see their badges," he reported between mouthfuls of the nut-flour cakes Mrs. Clapp had ready for him. "But I remember m' Dad had him an outfit like that. Just a nipper I was when he had embark-leave the last time. Off to Turkey for the fightin', he was, an' reported missin' in action. We never had no more news of him, though Mum, she up an' tried to get some word hard enough. They kept tellin' her after the war was over the Turks'd have to let their prisoners loose. Only after the war was over an' they did—m' Dad weren't one as they had any record of. Lot o' poor chaps never did get found.

"But I remember how m' Dad looked—an' these chaps those saucer tykes netted, they were wearin' the same sort o' gear, that I'll swear to! Could I have gotten close to 'em maybe we might've had a chance to get together." He shook his head.

"This migration and hunting has taken on unusual proportions," the Vicar observed. "Are the saucer people trying to make a clean sweep of the whole country?"

"Well," Stroud had finished eating, "there's that, of course. But I don't altogether think that's the right of it, Vicar. We've had hunts before, but not like this. It seems to me it's more like somethin' else started all these drifters on the move, something up north. They're comin' down from that direction an' they're not movin' slow at all, but pretty steady—like something was pressin' on their tails.

"Anyway, we'd best stay in cover, do we want to stay free. The saucers are takin' good advantage of all this movin'. To get out on the river in plain sight is as good as askin' to be caught."

"Nicholas." The Vicar summoned the American. "What did Avalon say when he warned you? Remember his exact words if you can."

Nick closed his eyes for a moment, summoning memory to provide him with the words Hadlett wanted to hear. He could see Avalon vividly. Now it was as if he could hear the Herald's emotionless voice so that he need only repeat word for word what the other had said.

"Avalon is no man's enemy. It is a place of peace and safety. But if one remains without, then comes darkness and ill. This has happened before, the evil lapping at the land. Where it meets Avalon and Tara, Brocéliande and Carnac, then it laps against walls it cannot overflow. But for those without the walls there is peril beyond reckoning. Alternately the evil flows and ebbs. This is a time of the beginning of the flow."

"Avalon?" Stroud repeated.

"The Herald." Crocker spoke up and there was silence. Nick knew they looked at him now, but he met no eyes save Hadlett's.

If the others accused him, and he thought that they did, that was not to be read in the Vicar's expression.

Stroud got to his feet and moved in until his weather-tanned face was not far from Nick's.

"You had words with the Herald now, did you?" To the Warden that fact must be of major importance.

"Yes," Nick replied shortly, adding no explanation.

"You was pally enough to have him give you a warnin'?" Stroud continued. All Crocker's disbelief was intensified in that red-brown face. The vast moustache bristled with antagonism.

"If you mean, did I accept his offer of safety," Nick returned, "I did not. However, he saved my life."

"That's not the way you told it before," Crocker cut in. "You got away by yourself—in a way that took some doing, too."

"He pointed the way." Nick kept the lid on his temper, but the irritation Crocker could ignite in him threatened his control. "If he had not—"

"It is all a very likely tale," Crocker snapped. "Let them listen to it—all of it—now. And see what they think of it!"

Hadlett nodded. "Tell them, Nicholas, from the beginning."

With the Vicar and Crocker listening, Nick could not alter his story, even if he wanted to. Which now he did not, that stubborn streak in him making sure that they must hear it as it happened and then believe or reject him.

Once more he told his adventure in detail from his first sight of Avalon to the meeting with Crocker and the Vicar. He had no more interruptions, but their full attention. As he finished, he waited for the voicing of disbelief, suspicion, complete rejection.

"You—you just thought—and you got that knife?" Stroud opened the examination.

Nick pulled the blade in question from his belt. He had already passed over to Hadlett and Crocker the other weapons dropped when the medieval band went to their unknown fate.

"I have this."

Stroud snatched it from him, studied it carefully, and then threw it to clatter on the rock floor some distance away.

"There's your miracle knife," he said. "Now let's see you get it back by thinkin'!"

A fair enough test, Nick gave him that. He turned to face the blade. Now he tried to set out of his mind everything but his need for the knife. He must have it—How had he done it before? A hand—a hand to take it up—and then an arm—

Nick concentrated on the need for the hand. But, though his mind ached under the lash of his will, nothing formed in the air. No mist thickened to put forth fingers closing about the hilt. He fought to produce that hand, but it did not come. There was something here that had not been in the clearing, a barrier against which his will fruitlessly beat.

"I can't do it." How long he had struggled he did not know. But something here short-circuited all his efforts. "It won't work this time."

"Because"—there was triumph in Crocker's voice—"it never did! That story was a lie from the start, I knew it!"

A hand grabbed Nick's shoulder with force enough to hurt and swing him around before he could fight back. Then Stroud's face thrust very close to his.

"You sold out to the Herald! Then you came back to get us. Not openly the way Rita did—you crawlin' worm!"

Nick tried to dodge the blow. His effort was enough so that Stroud did not knock him out, but sent him reeling, half-dazed—to bring up against the wall. He was dizzy from the force of the punch, only half-aware that Hadlett had stepped between them.

"Sam!" The Vicar's tone was a command, which the Warden answered with a growl. But he did not try to push past to be at his victim again.

"He sold out, came back to get us," Stroud said thickly. "You know that, Vicar."

"You are prejudging, Sam. All of you." Hadlett spoke not only to the Warden, but to the others who had moved in as if they were ready to join Stroud in whatever vengeance he proposed to take, their faces—ugly. Fear came to life in Nick. He had heard of the hysteria that gripped mobs. Was this the same horror?

"Listen to me carefully, all of you," Hadlett continued. "This is of the upmost importance—not just to Nicholas and to you because you propose to mete out what you conceive to be justice, but because it may also determine our future."

He was answered by a sound, not quite words of protest, but certainly expressing that. But they no longer moved forward, and Stroud dropped his ready fist to his side. Now the Vicar half-turned to address Nick.

"When you brought the knife to your aid you were alone?"

"As—as far as I know." Nick tried to control his voice to steadiness.

"There was no counter power of disbelief there," Hadlett commented. "But when you tried just now—what did you experience?"

"It was as if there were a barrier."

"Just so. A barrier raised by disbelief. Or so I think. Do you understand that?" He asked his question not of Nick but of the others.

Nick saw Lady Diana nod her head, reluctantly, he was sure. And Mrs. Clapp's lips formed a "yes." The others stood stolidly. But someone spoke from Nick's right.

"If we believe in him, then he can do it?"

Linda moved out. On one side of her paced Jeremiah, on the other Lung bounced along, his silky ears flapping.

"Nick." She did not wait for Hadlett to answer. "Nick, take my hand!"

That was no request but an order, and, without meaning to, he obeyed. She drew him away from the wall, and the others fell back to let them past. Once more they approached the knife. But Linda did not relax her hold. Instead she said:

"Try it again—now!"

Nick wanted to resist, but that seemed petty. Somehow, a new confidence was flowing into him. The knife—to move the knife—

Concentrate—see only that sliver of steel—a hand—fingers to grasp the hilt—pick it up—

There was still the barrier, but also—a new strength flowing into him. That came from the clasp of hands, from others—Linda—the two furred bodies at his feet. Nick had a moment of wonder and then shut that out. All he must think of was the knife.

Once more he saw that thickening in the air. From it developed the ghostly hand, building up finger by finger, not misty now— seemingly solid. From the hand his thoughts went to an arm. That, too, appeared inch by inch, a chain reaching from him to the hand.

"Come!" He thought that order.

The arm shortened, drew in toward him, and with it came the hand, fingers laced about the knife hilt. It drew back to his feet and then was gone. The knife clattered on the rock.

Linda's hand dropped from his. But it was she who rounded on the others.

"You saw that!" she challenged. "And I have been under your eyes all the time, *I* have had no dealings with Heralds! But I loaned Nick my energy to combat the wall of your disbelief, and so did these two." She stooped to scoop up Lung, laid her hand for a moment between Jeremiah's ears.

"Do you now judge all of us liars?" she added.

"Jeremiah!" Mrs. Clapp moved forward. The cat had turned his head at her call. She lifted him as if she feared him injured in some fashion and he moved his head to touch her cheek with his nose. Then he stiffened his forelegs, pushing himself out of her hold. But he stayed beside her, rubbing against her skirts.

"The two of you—" Hadlett began, but Linda corrected him instantly.

"The four of us! And I believe you can all do this—but you haven't tried. Nick had to, to save his life, and now you want to punish him for it!"

"He did it all right." The Warden picked up the knife, weighed it in his hand as if to assure himself that it was just what it appeared to be. "I saw it."

"Yes, he did it," the Vicar agreed. "My dear," he spoke to Linda, "you may be very right. We have never been put to such a test ourselves, so how could we know. Are you really sure about the animals?"

Nick had regained some of the strength the concentration had drawn out of him. He was not as worn by it as he had been the previous time, perhaps because the others had backed him up.

"The animals—they know—" He was puzzled—what could he say for sure that Lung and Jeremiah knew? His only contact had been with the cat. Would they believe Jeremiah had materialized a mouse? As for Lung's abilities, he had only Linda's assurances as to those.

"They know," he began again, "a lot—how much I can't say. Jeremiah can materialize things." Nick again braved disbelief and told of the mouse. But he said nothing about the apple, having no intention of turning against the cat the fury he had earlier faced himself.

"Jeremiah did that!" Mrs. Clapp gazed down. "But how—how could he, sir?" she asked the Vicar. "He—he's a cat. I've had him ever since he was born. He's old Floss's last kitten. She had a bad time an' she died. I couldn't let him, too—the poor mite! I got me a little doll bottle an' fed him milk an' egg an'—an'—Jeremiah's a cat!" She ended explosively, as if to think any differently would mean an end to all security.

"Indeed he is, Maude." Lady Diana put her arm around the bent shoulders of the older woman. "But it could be that this world changes animals somehow. See, he's worried about you now."

The big cat was sitting up on his hind legs, his forepaws reaching above Mrs. Clapp's knee, as he hooked claws in her skirt to balance himself. He opened his mouth in a soft sound that was not quite a mew.

"Jeremiah!" She hunkered stiffly down on the floor to gather him into her arms. This time he did not push against her to gain his liberty, but butted his head against her chin and sounded a rumble of purr.

"I don't care if he can do strange things," she declared a moment later. "He wouldn't do no harm, not Jeremiah. He did good—lettin' us know that the lad was tellin' the truth. Jeremiah's a good cat."

Hadlett and Lady Diana between them drew her to her feet, still holding Jeremiah.

"Of course he is, Maude. And like all cats," the Vicar continued, "he doubtless sees things in a more sensible way than do a great many humans. Don't you worry about Jeremiah."

Stroud brought attention back to Nick. "Look here, mate." He held out the hand which, fist hard, had left the darkening bruise on Nick's face. "If you want to dot me one for what I gave you, you're welcome to do it. I shot off then before I aimed. I'm willin' to say it."

Nick met the hand with his own. "No hard feelings," he gave ready answer. "I thought no one might believe me, I hardly believed it myself. And I don't want a crack at your jaw in return." He laughed a little too loudly in relief. "What I would like is for you, all of you, to listen to something I have been thinking about—"

Whether this was the time to be frank he did not know. But they were predisposed in his favor now just because they had been so quick to misjudge him. Suspicion might rise again and he had better make his plea while they still felt a little guilty and ill at ease.

"And what's that?" Crocker's voice was neutral. He, Nick guessed, was not feeling guilt.

"Just this—you heard me repeat what the Herald told me. Stroud has reported what he saw. You all know the drifters are on the move and that trouble seems to be coming from the north. There is only one place of real safety that we know of—the city."

Nick waited for their anger to rise again. What he was suggesting was opposed to all their ways.

"You mean—take the Herald's bargain?" Crocker asked fiercely. "I think not! You see what he's doing?" the pilot demanded of the others. "Just because he pulled that knife across the floor doesn't mean he didn't sell out! I say he did—let him prove otherwise!"

They had drawn away again. Nick had made the wrong choice after all. Would Stroud be as ready with his fists? And the Warden had a knife in hand—"How can I prove it?" Nick countered. Stroud was not looking at him but to the Vicar. "Best have him do that, if he wants to, sir. It'll stop all the trouble—"

"Yes." Hadlett sounded tired. "If you will come with us then, Nicholas—"

He did not know what they wanted of him, but as Stroud had suggested, he wanted the matter settled. Either they accepted him now or he would have to clear out. And he found himself disliking the thought of exile very much.

Stroud and Crocker fell in behind as the Vicar led the way into the small cave they used for storage, though the supplies there now were pitifully few. Inside Crocker spoke.

"All right. You said you'd give us proof. Strip!"

"What?" Nick was confounded.

"There are certain physical changes. I believe I spoke of them to you, Nicholas," the Vicar explained. "They appear very shortly after the bargain is concluded. It has been well over two days since you admittedly saw the Herald. If you have accepted his offer, you will reveal these."

"I see." Nick began to pull off his shirt. If they wanted proof they would get it now.

❈ 14 ❈

There was a fresh wind blowing and the morning was clear. Nick longed for binoculars. He had won his way this much—with Stroud he was back on one of the ridges above the city. They had traveled by night to reach this point, in spite of the Warden's reluctance.

But conditions around the cave had worsened. They were virtual prisoners there as saucers clustered to prey upon the drifters. And the still hazy plan Nick advanced, of trying to discover the secret of safety in the rainbow towers, had won some support. Now he was trying to line up enough cover on the plain ahead to give him a chance to scout closer.

Grass grew there but he judged, and Stroud agreed, that tall as that was, it provided no safe cover. And whether his own plan had any chance at all Nick could not know. Only he could not stall here much longer. Let a saucer home in on the city as Stroud said they did at intervals and they might be pinned down here for hours.

"All right, shall I try it?" Nick got to his feet. So much depended upon him now, upon his ability to use that wild talent. He had practiced with it, but hardly enough—

"You do, or we go back," Stroud returned. "We came to do it."

Did he believe that faced by a final choice Nick would back down? Did he hope for that? If he did, his disbelief had just the opposite effect: Nick was forced into action.

The Herald.

In his mind the American built up a picture of the Herald. Then that was not in his mind at all. He had done it! He had actually done it! Not captured the Herald physically as he had first thought to do, but projected him—

"I got him!" Nick was exultant.

"So it looks," Stroud agreed. "But can you keep him?"

"I'll have to. Here goes—"

Nick swung down the slope. The Herald was gone, winked out when Nick no longer willed him. But when it counted he could produce Avalon again—he had to. Stroud would remain behind, watch him into the city. They had not been sure whether this illusion of the accepted guide would hold for two, and since Nick's was the talent he went alone.

Now as he slipped and slid to more level ground he was excited, tense as one is before any testing. In a way his self-confidence had grown from that moment in the cave when he had been able to prove that he was not a traitor to his kind and his power had not been fostered by surrender to the People. Two days more he had tested it, and the others with him.

The Vicar had some ability to project, oddly enough Mrs. Clapp even more—though she tired easily. Crocker firmly refused to try. His antagonism to Nick had increased, Nick was sure, instead of diminished. The talent flared higher in the women—Linda, Jean (though she showed the same reluctance as Crocker), Lady Diana, could all produce some phenomena. Linda had formed a linkage with the animals again and produced stronger and longer-abiding illusions.

But all of them found it impossible to hold such for long. And the more one struggled to do so, the more one's energy was exhausted. Nick was not sure now how long he could hold the Herald, even if he could use that illusion for a key.

He did not believe that the People were active enemies of any of the drifters. From Avalon's words it would seem that when refugees from Nick's world refused alliance they were simply ignored.

However, if he were able to break through the invisible defense, enter the city, and be discovered there as an alien, would that indifference hold? During the past two days Nick had prevailed on the English to pool all their observations concerning the People and the city, even though they had shied away from that before.

It was from the city, or cities (they had seen others), that the Herald, or Heralds, issued. There were others of the People, such as the Green Man of the forest—some of these lived in water, more on the land—and these did not appear bound to the cities at all. Yet all were native, Hadlett thought, to this world.

The Vicar drew, as he readily admitted, on the half-forgotten lore of his own native country for his identification and evaluation of those he had seen here. Perhaps his guesses were of little value, but they were all he had to judge by.

In addition to those of the People who seemed neutral, there were others who were definitely a dangerous threat. But these in turn were bound to certain baneful portions of the land. And if one avoided those sections, refused to be drawn by such lures as the singing Nick had heard in the rain, they were no great menace.

Nick reached the level ground. He wished he could work his way closer to the city before he produced the illusion. But he had no way of telling whether or not he was already under observation. He concentrated with all the power he could summon.

Once more the Herald appeared. Nick did not try to make every detail of the illusion sharply clear. It was enough that the general appearance of his "guide" tallied with the real one. With the thing born of his will ahead, he started at a swift pace to the towers.

Stroud had pointed out where he might expect to meet the unseen barrier, and he was doubly eager to reach that, to make his entrance. Yet most of his attention must be on the phantom.

They were past the barrier point—though he could not be entirely sure, because Stroud might have been mistaken. Nick refused any triumph yet. The strain of keeping the Herald was beginning to tell. What if he could not hold? Would he be a prisoner on the inside of the barrier?

Doggedly he fought his own weakness, holding the necessary concentration. Then—

The city—he was in the city!

The transition was quick, as if the buildings had risen about him. Buildings—Nick forgot the Herald, his need for the illusion.

There were buildings, yes, towering up and up, doors, windows, streets. But where were the people? The streets were deserted, no one walked the white-and-green blocked pavement, no vehicle moved there. The doors were closed; the windows, if they were open, still had the appearance of being shuttered. The walls about him had glassy surfaces as if they were indeed crystal, backed by some opaque material. And up and down them ran those opaline changes of color, green, blue, yellow, red and all possible shadings between.

Nick hesitated. There was no sound in the city. He could be in a ruin deserted centuries ago. Yet this was no ruin, there was no sign of erosion, nor breakage, cracking—

Slowly he approached the nearest wall. He held out a hand hesitatingly so that just the tips of his fingers touched its surface. Then he snatched it back again. For what he had fingered was not cold stone or crystal, rather a substance delicately warm, alive with vibration.

Energy, some form of energy was encased in the walls. That would account for the radiance. The whole city might be a generator or storehouse of energy.

The avenue on which he stood ran straight. If Nick did not turn into any sideway how could he be lost? Summoning his resolution anew, Nick began to walk forward. But it was all he could do to hold control.

For he knew, was as certain as he was of every breath he drew, that the city, or those who dwelt here, knew him for what he was— an interloper. Twice he came to a stop, turned to glance behind. But no new wall had suddenly arisen, no guards were in view to cut off his retreat. The street was as silent and deserted as ever.

Where were the people? Had the population shrunk so that only a handful lived here at its heart? Or was the city really a city? Perhaps those terms from his own world did not apply here. This vast site might have some entirely different purpose. But the Herald came from here, he had returned with those who accepted Avalon. Nick had seen that happen.

He sighted ahead an open space with something standing within, flashing a brighter light, so bright that it hurt Nick's eyes and he wished he had Linda's dark glasses. To escape that he moved closer to a wall, tried to look up. But the tower rose so high it made him dizzy to attempt to see its tip against the morning sky.

Now, a little daring, Nick set hand to the door in the wall. This had a different texture than the wall. It seemed a single slab of silvery metal. And at close inspection Nick could see it was engraved with a pattern of many lines in intricate design. When again he tried to touch it, there was no vibration, but as his fingers moved along those lines he perceived a meaning sight alone could not give them, and they were more visible than they had been before.

There were queer beasts, some like the ones he had seen in the woods, a unicorn among them, and creatures that were humanoid. Around them, encircling them, were ribbon bands that bore marks unlike any lettering Nick knew.

As his fingers passed he could see them plainly for a moment or two. Then they faded so they were discernible only as faint scratches.

Having tried one door he passed to the next and once more put it to the test of touch. Again he saw pictures, though these were different in both form and arrangement.

What lay behind these doors? Nick gently applied pressure. There were no visible latches, locks, knobs, or any aid for their opening. And they remained fixed, immobile, against all his strength.

Locked doors, deserted city. Nick returned to the middle of the street and forged ahead. Though the belief that someone—something—was watching him held, Nick had regained a little confidence. He sensed no threat in this place. If he had violated some sanctuary then as yet those who guarded it had not made up their minds whether he was a threat to their purposes or not. And the longer they held off the more confident he felt. That in itself might be a danger, he began to realize.

Nick advanced resolutely toward the flashing point ahead, shading his eyes to its glare. So he came out into what might be the heart of the city, though he had no way of knowing if that were so. This was an open space into which fed five avenues, like the one he followed. The shape he could see was that of a five-point star, one street entering at each point.

Now that he was close to that which flashed, it did not glare as much as earlier and he recognized its shape. For this he had seen in his own world, and that it had a very ancient significance he knew.

Set up straight in the middle of the star was a giant representation of the Egyptian ankh—the looped cross. It appeared to be fashioned, not of the crystal of the towers, but of a ruddy metal. And in the mid-center of the two arms, on the arms themselves, and around the loop were shining gems. But could those be gems? Whoever heard of precious stones of such size they could not be spanned by two hands together?

It was from these that the light flashed, green, blue, white—but no red nor yellow. As those rays shot well over the level of his head, Nick judged that the height of the ankh was equal to that of a four-or five-story building.

From it came such a force of radiant energy that he felt dizzy, weak. He staggered back. Was this the source of the safety devices of the People? But what powered it? He saw no evidence of machines. Or was it some receiver or booster broadcaster?

Nick wavered. For the first time, stark fear broke through his wonder. This—this was overpowering. His skin tingled, his dizziness grew. He must get away.

But could he? The avenue—Somehow he managed to turn, though the gem lights nearly blinded him. There—get—out—Nick broke into a stumbling run, heading for the opening to the avenue. But it was as if he were trying to wade through deep mud. Something sucked avidly at his strength, his very life-force. He must get away!

He stumbled, fell, but somehow pulled himself to his hands and knees and kept on at a crawl. The buildings rose on either hand, he was within the avenue. But not far enough. And he was not going to make it—

Nick gasped, fought for breath. Now it felt as if the air about him was being sucked away, that he could not get enough into his lungs—he was choking.

He lay flat, his arms outstretched above his head, his fingers still moving feebly, trying to find some crevice between the blocks of the pavement into which they might fit and draw him forward, even if only for an inch or two.

"Come!"

Had he heard that? Nick still fought to move. There were hands on his shoulders, he was being dragged away from the star, down the avenue, out of the baleful influence of the ankh. He could not summon strength enough to look up and see who—or what—had come to his aid. Not the Herald—the Herald had been his own illusion. Stroud? His thoughts were weak, slipping from him. He no longer really cared who saved him.

The tingling in his flesh faded. But he was not regaining his strength. However, the hold on him relaxed and he made a great effort to roll over so he could see his rescuer.

She did not have that misty outline of light about her this time but looked thoroughly solid and substantial. Nor were there tears on her cheeks.

"Rita."

He must have said her name aloud. Or else, like Jeremiah, she could read his thoughts.

"I am Rita, yes." There was in her speech that same toneless quality that marked the Herald's.

But her face was not as expressionless as Avalon's. There was concern there, and something else. She studied him, Nick thought, as one might study a tool before one put it to service.

"You might have died—back there. You are not of the Kin." She made statements, she asked no questions.

"Are you alone here?" he asked.

"Alone?" Plainly that had startled her. She glanced from left to right and back again, as if she saw what he could not and was astounded by his speech. "Alone—why—" Then she paused. "You are not of the Kin," she repeated. "The sight is not yours. No, though you do not see, I am not alone. Why did you come if you would not be one with Avalon?"

"To find out what keeps the city free from attack. Your people—they are in danger. They need protection."

"There is no danger for the Kin, Safety those others can have for the asking. It is so. I have gone to them and they drove me out. They are blind and will not accept sight, they are deaf and they will not hear. They—" For the first time her voice trembled. "They will be lost because they choose it so."

"They say that you changed."

"Yes. I have become one with the Kin. See." She went to her knees beside him and laid her arm next to his, not quite touching.

Her skin was white, a dazzling white, and very smooth, without any fluff of hair along its surface. Against it his arm was coarse, rough, browned. She took his hand in hers and the sensation of flesh meeting flesh was not as he had known it before, but rather as if fingers and palm of sleek marble had grasped him.

"Thus it is with the bodies of the Kin," Rita told him. "That is how we go protected against the weapons of the flyers, and against other dangers here. There are evils that can destroy us, but those are evils native to this world, and they reach us in other ways than by wounds of the body. If your people accept Avalon, then they shall become of Avalon, as I now am."

"You are—hard—" Nick could not find another word for the feel of her flesh. "Yet—when you were in the woods—I saw Linda's hand pass through your arm."

Rita did not answer him. Instead she said with the authority of one who did not imagine she would be disobeyed:

"You have come where you cannot stay. If you accept not Avalon, then that which is of Avalon can kill. You have felt the beginning of that death. Get you out—this place is not for you."

She touched his forehead in much the same place as the fanatical monk had pressed the cross so painfully into his skin. There was chill to her fingers. But from them flowed into him a renewal of strength so he could stand again.

"You saved my life. Is there anything I can do for you?" Always, Nick thought, he would remember those tears and what lay in the eyes where that moisture gathered.

"What words can you use with them that I have not already spoken?" Rita asked. "Their fear lies so deep in them that they would kill before they will accept what I offer."

He expected her to stay, but when unable to find words to deny the truth of what she said, Nick started away, Rita matched step with him.

"I will go out of the city. You need not trouble—"

There was a trace of a smile on her face. "To see you to the door?" she ended for him. "But there is a need. I do not know how you entered, but you, being what you are, cannot win free again save that the door be opened for you."

Not all the strength drained from him had returned. Nick moved slowly along the silent, empty street. But to his companion was it either silent or empty? He believed not. That he could see her might be because she was originally of his kind. Or maybe she willed it so because she still felt a faint linkage with those outside. She did not explain, in fact Rita did not speak again until they reached the abrupt ending of the avenue, the beginning of the grassy plain.

Then again came her question delivered with authority.

"How did you enter through the barrier?"

Nick wanted to dissemble and found he could not. With her eyes upon him he must speak the truth.

"I followed a Herald."

"That is—impossible. Yet, I see that it is also the truth. But how can it be the truth?"

"The Herald was of my imagining. I pictured him into life."

He heard a hiss of breath that was a gasp. "But you are not of the Kin! How could you do such a thing?"

"I learned how to save my life. And it was Avalon himself who gave me the clue as to how it could be done. The others are trying it too—"

"No!" That was a cry which carried a note of fear. "They cannot! It means their destruction if they have not the power of the Kin. They are children playing with a raw fury they do not understand! They must be stopped!"

"Come and tell them so," Nick returned.

"They will not listen—"

"Can you be sure? Having used this power I think that they understand more than they did before. The Vicar, I am sure he will listen."

"Yes, he has a deepness of heart and a width of mind. Perhaps this can be done. I cannot but try again. But they must not attempt to weave the great spell. It can kill—or summon up that which it is better not to see. Avalon has some life in it that can answer one's dreams in a way to freeze the very spirit."

Nick remembered the devilish things that had besieged the party in the woods.

"So I have seen."

Rita gave him a long measuring look and then held out her hand. "Let us go."

As her cold, smooth fingers closed about his, Rita drew him along. So linked they went out into the open, heading for the ridge where he had left Stroud on watch. Would the Warden accept Rita? Had the prejudice of the party been so shaken by Nick's discovery that they would listen to the one they had cast out? Nick hoped so.

But he was not so sure when they did climb the ridge and Stroud was not waiting. Nick found the flattened grass where the Warden must have lain in hiding to watch him enter the city. But no one was there.

"Stroud!" Nick called, but he dared not shout as he wished.

An answer came in a croaking caw, as a bird burst up from the grass, beating black wings to carry it skyward. Once aloft, it circled them, still calling hoarsely.

"He has—he is in danger!" Rita watched the bird. "The balance has been upset, the force thoughts have released evil. You see—" She turned fiercely on Nick, her composure broken. "You see what such meddling can do? The Dark Ones hunt, run he ever so far or fast. And he, not understanding, will lead them to the rest!"

"Lead who?"

"All those of the Dark who are not bound to any place of evil. And all those they can command among the sons of men! You played with the power, erecting no safeguards. And they who do so open all doors, many of which give upon the Outer Dark. We must hurry—!"

Rita gripped his wrist again, her grasp biting into the still tender flesh so that Nick winced. But she did not note that as he strode forward, dragging him on.

Instead of skulking under cover Rita made her way confidently along the shortest route, heading for the cave. It would seem she had no fears of this land. But Nick did not share her confidence. However, when he tried to free himself from her hold, he found that as impossible as if her fingers were a metal handcuff.

He came to a stop, jerking her to a halt.

"Tell me exactly what we may be facing, what Stroud may have done, or what might have happened to him."

"Do not delay us!" Deep in the eyes Rita turned upon him was an alien glow. "He has fled—but you saw the Corraven where he had been. That is the creature of the Dark. It was left to warn us. It so declared this was not a matter for the Kin."

"Yet you are making it your matter," Nick pointed out.

"Yes, but that I cannot help. I am tied, heart-tied, and I have not been long enough among the Kin that those ties are loosed. Still do I care for those of my old heritage. I am free in Avalon, free of choice. If I choose to go up against the Dark, then none will step before me to say 'no.' For I choose, knowing what may be the price. But we waste time. Come!"

That she planned to be an ally in whatever lay ahead, Nick had no doubt now. And her urgency aroused his fear. He hoped that he had recovered enough from his ordeal in the city to keep going, as she began to run and he pounded with her, heading for the cave and what might await them there.

✳ 15 ✳

The sky that had been so bright was now overcast. Though it was summer a chill breeze blew, bringing with it a faint, sickening scent as if it passed over some source of stale corruption. Rita ran easily wherever the ground was clear enough to allow it. But Nick felt the effects of what he had faced in the city and would have lagged behind, in spite of his efforts, had not her hold on him lent that energy of hers.

He could see ahead the rolling hills among which was the cave. And there darkness gathered, clouds massed. While the air was alive, not with saucers, but rather things that flew with flapping wings, some feathered, some of stretched skin. There was movement on the ground, also, though Nick could not be sure of what or who caused that for it did not show clearly.

Yet Rita took no care in her going, as if no hint of ambush concerned her. She was as impervious in her attitude as the Herald had been when under attack from the saucer.

Before they reached the approach to the cave entrance she slowed to a halt. About them now, though Nick could see very little, he was aware of that same miasma of evil he had felt on the night he had been captive. A black-winged bird, with eyes of glowing red, blazing points of fire set in a feathered skull, planed down straight for them, uttering a piercing cry. Nick's free hand went to his belt, drew the dagger.

The bird, with a second scream, sheered away. And there was a small sound from Rita.

"Iron!" She pulled a little away though she did not drop his hand. "Keep that from me—you must! It will serve you, but to the Kin it is deadly."

In this dusk, which was increasing abnormally fast, her body showed the radiance he had seen before, her eyes were bright. There was an excitement about her as if just ahead lay an ordeal.

But he could also see that the ground, the bushes, around them were astir. Things peered at them in menace, yet did not make the attack Nick braced himself to meet. Rita still moved forward, now at a walking pace. There was a breathless quiet about them that those skulking around did not break. Were they real, or illusions? And if illusions, fostered by what enemy?

Ringing them around, moving with them as they advanced, were dwarfs. They were squat of body, furred with gray hair. They turned faces grotesquely human, yet so malignant of aspect as to be weapons in themselves, toward those they escorted, showing teeth that were those of carnivorous beasts in frog-wide mouths, which they opened and shut as if they spoke, or shouted, yet there was no sound.

Behind these stalked others man-tall, specter thin, their limbs mere bones covered with dry and dusty skin, their hairless heads skulls. Moldy tatters clung to them; they moved stiffly yet at surprising speed.

There were other things—some that might have been wolves yet had an obscene humanity about them, reptile forms, giant spiders— all things that might have haunted the nightmares of generations were here given form. But these were only the fringes of the company. And suddenly the air was split with shouts, arrows sang.

"Hurry now!" Rita cried, "I cannot hold double protection long."

Then Nick saw that the radiance from her body had spread to enclose him. Against that the arrows dashed, to fall. He heard more confused shouting. Other forms rushed at them, shrank from the bright mist.

There followed what could only be the crack of a rifle. Nick involuntarily ducked, but did not reach the ground as Rita's hold on him dragged him up and on. The mist was thickening but he was sure he could see through it men in black uniforms. They must be passing through a small army.

Evil it was, the loathsome scent the breeze had earlier hinted at was sickeningly strong. It formed a choking reek. But Nick could see dimly the rocks that were the outer guard of the cave.

There came the sudden chatter of a machine gun. On either side, as the besiegers reluctantly parted to let them pass, men fell. A machine gun! Where had the English obtained that?

"On!" Rita sounded breathless.

They scrambled among the rocks, up to the higher entrance. The rattle of gunfire was now constant, deafening—Perhaps it was turned on them. Nick did not know. But at least nothing penetrated the barrier Rita held. Though he could see that it was thinning.

With a last effort they tumbled into the hollow of the sentry post. The radiance dimmed. A man arose before Nick, aimed at him pointblank with a handgun.

"Illusion!" Rita cried. "It is an illusion!"

Real! The death before him was real!

"No!"

Nick thought to feel the impact of the bullet, but that did not follow. The man swung away from him as if he no longer existed. He was a stranger in battle dress. There were three defenders with a machine gun, aiming and firing at the Dark Ones. Nick stumbled after Rita, down into the cave.

"You!"

They were all there, even Stroud, though the Warden lay upon the floor, his coverall marked with dark stains. The rest stood as might those determined to fight to the end, meeting death but not capture.

It was Crocker who had cried out, his voice echoing through the cave. For the clatter of gunfire was now gone. Jean caught at the pilot's arm as he faced Rita, his eyes wide, his hand holding one of the daggers. He might have been warding off attack, though Rita had not moved. The glow about her was only a lingering glimmer.

"No!" That was Jean. "The gun—we have to keep the gun—"

Out of the shadows pranced Lung, heading straight to Rita. He leaped and barked before her, trying with all his might to gain her attention. If the others had no welcome, it was plain the Peke did not agree. His joy at her coming was manifest.

"Get out of here!" Crocker shook off Jean, moved toward Rita, the knife out.

"Stop, Barry." The Vicar stepped between. He looked to Rita, not the pilot. "Why do you come?"

"Do you not remember that I was once one of you? Should I not try to aid you now? You have done that which has brought the Dark Ones; you have dabbled in things you do not understand, to your own undoing."

"She's one of them! She wants to get at us!" Crocker pushed against Hadlett, but as if he did not quite dare to set the Vicar aside.

"I am of Avalon," she replied. Once more her features were composed, she looked as emotionless as the Herald. "But you have opened gates, which are of the Dark Side, and you have not that in you which can close them again. You have used powers and you have no defense—"

"And while we talk here," that was Lady Diana, "those out there will attack. We have to hold—"

"Your illusion?" Rita interrupted. "But that, which you strive against, is no illusion. Do you not understand? We of the Kin have our enemies. You have raised those. But you have not our weapons to defeat them. Look upon you—do you not already weary? It drains the energy to build an illusion. Granted that you now unite to do this and with some success—but how long can you continue? For those without are not bound by time, nor the frailties of bodies such as yours. They can wait and wait until you are brought down by your own lack of strength. And I say to you—better that you be dead than alive at the moment they overrun you.

"This is the beginning of the time of the Running Dark. From all the places of evil will come forth that which has been lurking there. Those it enspells become wholly its creatures. Others seek to run before it—those you have seen. And in the end it will be little better for them, for the sky hunters will take them.

"But to you have come the Dark Ones ahead of time. Avalon will not protect you, for you have refused its freedom. Put your iron to your throats, but even so there are those who can pour into your bodies, inhabit them, use them as clothing—"

"As you use Rita's?" Crocker's eyes were fires of fury.

"I *am* Rita. I am more Rita than I ever was before I accepted the freedom. Then I was as one asleep and dreaming, now I am awake— alive! Yes, I am Rita, though you will not believe it. I think that you cannot, for there is that in you which wants me to be the lesser. Is that not so?

"This day I have said to him who came with me that I was still heart-tied to you. Perhaps that was true—once. When I came to you before, my once dear friends, after my change, it was as a beggar, asking for your alms. But in that I erred. For what have you to give me now?"

"Perhaps nothing." Hadlett, not the pilot, answered her.

She laughed. "How well you sum it up. Still—there are those here—" Rita glanced from one to the next. "You have such courage, even if it is wrongly rooted. I know you all well, even these two new ones come into your company. And, though you may not believe it, I wish you well. What I can do for you, that I will. But I warn you— it can be but little. You have not the freedom. And what you have provoked is very strong."

"It was Avalon who gave me the first hint of using the mind power." Nick spoke for the first time. "If this was such a wrong thing, then why did he do it?"

He thought Rita looked a little shaken. "I do not know. The Heralds have their purposes under the King. This is a change time—"

"So," the Vicar said, "a time of alteration may bring things out of custom to pass? Logos once more faces Chaos. And you say that our strength will not hold to protect us?"

Rita shook her head. "It cannot. We with the freedom draw from Avalon itself. Look—it can be thus with us." She stooped to set her hand to the floor. Under her touch the rock crumbled, leaving the imprint of her fingers. "That is no illusion, set your hand within if you do not believe me. But its like you cannot do, for your gift is small. Unite if you will, as you have, and there is still a limit, for the land will not nourish you."

Lung, who had been crouched at her feet, leaped up again, and she smiled at his exuberance, laid her hand on his head, while from the shadows sped Jeremiah, wreathing about her ankles, purring so loudly they could hear. And for the cat, also, Rita had a touch. When she raised her head there was a faint trouble on her face.

"Some can accept freedom, others choose their chains. Why is it so?"

"Because," Crocker burst out, "we are ourselves! We don't want to be changed into—into—"

"Into what I am? But what then am I, Barry ?"

"I don't know. Except that you are not Rita. And that I hate you for what you have done to her!"

"But I am Rita, the whole Rita. Fear walks with hate. You hate because you fear."

Nick saw Crocker's face go tight. A man might look so when he killed.

"You see?" Rita spoke to Hadlett. "His mind is closed because he wills it so. We build our own walls about us. What is your wall, Vicar?"

"My faith, Rita. I have lived with it as part of me all my life. I am a priest of my faith. As such I cannot betray it."

She bowed her head. "You are blind, but your choice by your own standard is just. And you, Lady Diana?"

"Perhaps I can also say it is faith—faith in the past, in what made up my life—" She spoke slowly as if seeking the right words.

"So be it. And you, Jean? Yes, I can understand what ties you to danger and darkness."

The other girl flushed, her mouth twisted angrily. But she did not speak, only moved a fraction closer to Crocker.

"Mrs. Clapp, then?" Rita continued. It was as if she must force a final denial from each and every one of them in turn.

"Well—perhaps it's because I've been a churchgoing' body all m' life. If the Vicar thinks this wrong—then I'll abide by what he says."

"And you, Warden?"

"It's like Lady Diana said—you make your choice 'bout who you stand with. That's good enough for me."

"And you?" Rita turned now to Linda.

"If one chooses Avalon, is there any chance of returning to one's own time and world?" the American girl asked.

"That I do not know. But I believe that the will to remain will be stronger than the will to return. For one becomes a part of Avalon."

"Then I guess it will be 'no'! But has Lung chosen?" Linda's eyes were now on the dog crouched at Rita's feet.

"Ask."

"Lung—Lung—" Linda called softly. The Peke looked at her and came, moving slowly, but he came.

"They have their loyalty also," Rita said. "He will stay with you because he is heart-tied. Even as Jeremiah will share what comes to you, Maude Clapp."

She was going to ask him now. Nick braced himself, because he knew what he would answer and what would come of it. Why must he take on this burden? He had no heart-ties, as Rita called them, yet he must go against all his inclinations, and for no reason he could put into words.

"I stay," he said before she could ask.

Rita was frowning. "For you it is not the same. You say the words but something more may come of this. We shall see. However, in this much shall I aid you all now. That which waits without is but the first wave of what comes. Use your will with mine and I shall set a barrier—to hold for a little."

"We want nothing from you!" Crocker flared.

"Barry, this is for all to decide," the Vicar said. "I think, Rita, you mean this for our good. What say the rest?"

Crocker and Jean shook their heads, but the others nodded in agreement. So having decided, they linked their power, standing within the cave, not knowing what it wrought outside, but feeling, too, the fierce surge of energy from Rita.

"This will not hold. It will only afford you a brief respite."

"For as much as you have given us, we thank you," Hadlett answered. "And, my child, we wish you well."

Rita raised her hand and traced a design in the air that remained there for an instant, written in pale blue fire—the ankh.

"I wish you—peace. And that none may trouble you thereafter."

Once more she wept, tears on her white cheeks. Then she turned and went from them, the shining envelope of radiance closing about her so they could not see how she disappeared.

"She wished us death!" Jean exploded. "You know that, don't you—she meant that by her 'peace'—death!"

"She wished us the best she could foresee for us." Hadlett's voice was very tired. "I believe she spoke the truth."

"Yes," Lady Diana agreed heavily. She did not add to that but went to stand by the fire, staring into it.

But Linda came to Nick. "There can be a way back—" she told him, an eager note in her voice.

"Back where?" He was hardly aware of her.

"Back to our own world."

"How do you mean?" She had his attention now.

"If we can only get out of here—back to where we came in. Once there, why can't we make a door and go through? If we could make soldiers and a machine gun, as we did"—she waved to the cave entrance—"then we ought to be able to get back by willing hard enough—all of us together. Don't you see? It could work—it has to!" She ended as vehemently as if at that moment she could see such a door, the safe past behind it.

"Even if it would work," Nick countered, "how are we going to get back to the forest to try? If we leave here—do you realize what is waiting out there? We couldn't fight our way across country—not with those things waiting for us!"

"We can"—she was stubborn—"use illusions. Don't you see—it is all we can do."

"What is the only thing we can do?" Jean's voice, hostile in tone, cut in.

"We have to try to get back to our own world. I was telling Nick—we can do it! If we go back to where we first came through— to where the jeep is—then make a door—we can go through! It's a way we'll have to try. Don't you see, we have to!"

Her excitement grew as she talked. That she was wrong, Nick was convinced. But to his surprise he saw an answering spark arise in Jean.

"If it would work—" The English girl drew a long breath. "Yes, if that worked and he—we—could be free of everything here! It would be wonderful! That forest is a long way from here and with all that out there—"

"We've just got to try," Linda urged. "She—Rita—you heard what she said about worse coming. If we stay here we're caught. But if we can make it back—"

"Can't do it." Crocker had been drawn to their group. "If the country was free, yes, it would be worth a try. But we can't fight our way through now."

"So we just stay here"—Linda rounded on him—"and wait to be caught by those horrors? Is that what you want? There ought to be some way we can get through."

She looked eagerly from one to another. Perhaps in Jean she still had an ally, but Nick knew how impossible such a trek would be. He had come cross-country under Rita's protection and he had a very good idea that had it not been for that he would not have lasted long no matter how stiff a fight he had put up. With Mrs. Clapp, the Vicar, the wounded Stroud, to slow them, they would not have a chance.

"We have to get back," Linda repeated. "I—I don't want to die. And you were right, Jean. Rita wished us to die there at the last. She—the People won't do any more to help us. We'll have to help ourselves and the only way is to get back to our own world. Maybe—maybe you don't have to go to the place you came through after all. Maybe we could make a gate right here!" Her words came faster and faster.

Nick walked away. He was tired with a weariness that weighed on him like a heavy burden. He did not believe that Linda's suggestion had any hope of realization. And he was too worn out to argue about it. He sat down on the floor and was only aware of Mrs. Clapp when she handed him one of the wooden bowls that held some liquid with a sharp scent.

"Get that down you, lad. It'll perk you up. An' I want you to tell me somethin' true—no fancying it up because I'm an old woman as should be told only good things. I'm old enough to know that there are some things that have no good in 'em at all. Those are made for our bearin' when the time comes. Do you think there is anything we can do—you have been out an' seen it all—to help ourselves?"

Nick sipped the drink. It was slightly bitter, which was in keeping with the situation at hand. But as it slid down his throat it brought warmth—though it did nothing to banish the inner cold rooted in his mind and body.

"I don't think there is any more we can do than has been done. She said that the Dark Powers can draw men to help them. And I saw some out there that might be such. I don't know how long the barrier will last."

She nodded. "It is not what you've said, but all you've not. Well, there were the good years. But you young ones—it would be fairer to you if you had had longer. I wish Jeremiah had gone with her, an' the little dog, too. It's not right that good beasts have to be with us." She sighed and took the empty bowl he handed to her.

Nick longed to go and stretch himself out on his scanty bed. But who knew when the protection Rita had raised would fail? It might be well to check on what was happening out there.

He dragged himself to his feet and went to the entrance, pulling up to the sentry station. No phantom machine gun was there now. But before him, about five feet away, a shimmering cloud, very visible in the gloom, made a curtain. If anything moved beyond he could not see.

Not that he doubted they were still there. And there they would wait until the curtain failed. When that happened—illusions that could not be held and—

Nick put his arm across a rock, laid his head on it, and closed his eyes. But he could not close out his thoughts. Rita and the Herald were right; these stubborn English, he, Linda, were throwing away life for nothing. He did not believe that Avalon was evil.

The power radiating from the ankh in the city had nearly killed him. But there was nothing of evil in it. It was only that he, as he now was, was too frail, too flawed a thing to hold such energy.

Now the Dark Tide swept the land. Only in the city, in those places with the freedom of Avalon, would there be light. And those who did not accept the light opened a door to the Dark. They had tried to use the gift of the light to their own purpose, and in that, Rita said they brought worse upon themselves.

But why had Avalon, the Herald, given Nick the hint that had led him to the discovery of the power? Certainly there was a purpose in that, a test, perhaps—wherein he had failed by the way he had made use of his discovery. It could well be.

In any event he would now have to face what lay before him and make the best of it. Perhaps Rita was also right in wishing them a swift death as the best she could offer.

Nick thought about death. Was it an end or a beginning? No one knew, only hoped for the best with the part of him that feared absolute extinction above all else. Death could be peace, in such a land as this.

"Nicholas—"

He raised his head. By the glow of the wall he could see Hadlett, though he could not read the Vicar's expression.

"Yes, sir?"

"You were in the city, Sam told us. What is it like there?"

Wearily Nick spoke of the walls and streets, of those doors with their pictures that came alive at the touch, and, finally, of the great ankh and the energy that could slay when one was unprepared to face its force.

"The looped cross," said the Vicar. "Yes, the key to eternity, as the Egyptians called it when they put it into the hands of their gods. A source of energy that only those who have surrendered to it can absorb."

"They are not evil," Nick returned. "I have seen evil and it does not lie in the city."

"No. It is not evil, yet it demands the surrender of one's will, of what one is."

"As is also demanded by our own way of worship." Nick did not know from where he had those words.

"But that is an older way, from which we turned long ago. To surrender again to its power, Nicholas, is to betray all our own beliefs."

"Or to discover that there is only one source after all, but from it many rivers—" Again Nick was not aware of his words until he uttered them.

"What did you say?" Hadlett's tone was sharp, fiercely demanding.

16

Nick was not given time to answer. For, from beyond the shimmering barrier, now came a sound he had heard before—the compelling, head-hurting summons that had drawn his former captors. He clapped his hands to his ears, but the sound was in his head.

Only this time it was not so severe. Nick gritted his teeth, braced himself against obeying the summons. In the faint light he could see Hadlett doubled up against the rocks, his hands also to his ears, his white head bowed.

Fight it! Nick marshaled his will to do that. He did not know in whose hand was that weapon, but it was evil. Then he was aware of someone pushing past him. He threw out his arm, tried to deter that other, reeled back from a blow.

He watched Crocker head to the barrier. Behind him scrambled the others: Jean very close to the pilot; Lady Diana, her face twisted, her hands to her tortured ears; finally Stroud lurching along, his gait that of a drunken man, or one so weak only intense purpose kept him going.

The four came to the barrier before Nick could move from where Crocker had shoved him, passed through, to be hidden from sight. Hadlett wavered forward, but this time Nick was prepared. He sprang to tackle the Vicar, bearing the old man with him down toward the cave entrance.

Linda, Mrs. Clapp—he must stop them if he could. He pushed and pulled Hadlett into the cave. The torment in his head continued but he could master that—he had to. This time he was not tied to keep him safe.

By the light within Nick saw a scene of confusion. Mrs. Clapp lay on the floor, struggling to rise. Linda knelt beside her, not striving to aid her but with both hands on the woman's shoulders, holding her down, while Mrs. Clapp writhed and flung her arms about.

Before them crouched the two animals. Lung snarled in anger, the cat growled and lashed his tail. Both of them faced the women as if at any moment they would join the struggle.

Linda's face was twisted with pain, her mouth ugly as she moaned and cried out. Mrs. Clapp uttered meaningless sounds.

"Help!" Linda gasped as Nick came, pushing the staggering Vicar.

He gave Hadlett a last vigorous shove, this time taking no care, only heading the older man toward the interior of the cave. Then he ran to Linda.

"She—mustn't—go—"

"No!" he agreed. But his help was not needed, for Mrs. Clapp, with a last cry, went limp and still.

"No!" Now the protest came from Linda. She lifted the woman's head, held it against her, cradled in her arm, touched her face gently. "Nick, she can't be dead!"

"I don't think so. Watch her." He returned to Hadlett.

The Vicar had slumped to the floor, sat there with his legs outstretched, his head sunk on his chest, his arms hanging limp so his hands lay palm up on either side of his body. He was breathing in heavy gasps, but that was the only sign of life.

The clamor without was retreating. Nick could think more clearly, relax a little. The cat and the Peke were still alert, but had ceased their active objection. It was as if they were to be given a breathing space.

"She's—she's alive, Nick!" Linda glanced up from her charge. "But the others—they went out—where?"

"I don't know."

"That was—was more of the Dark Ones' attack?"

Nick had no answer to that either. "I don't know. It was what took the drifters who captured me. But I never saw what caused it—only them going."

"As they did here." Linda settled Mrs. Clapp's head more easily against her arm. "I wanted to go, Nick. But Lung tripped me, jumped at me. And Jeremiah pulled at Mrs. Clapp's skirt, tangled her up so she fell. They—both of them—helped me think straight, know that I mustn't go—she must not. But how did you and Mr. Hadlett get away, Nick?"

For the third time Nick had to admit ignorance. He only knew that, painful and compelling as that sound had been, he had been able to withstand it, not only that but somehow prevent Hadlett from being drawn also. He flinched away from imagining what might have happened to the others. For this moment it was enough to know that in so much they had beaten the enemy.

"Maybe because I heard it before and could not answer," he speculated. "It may lose impact the second time around. And Hadlett was with me. He did not move out at once, which gave me a chance to—"

"To save me, Nicholas." The Vicar slowly raised his head. His gaunt face was so haggard that he might have been mortally ill. As he spoke a twitch started beneath his left eye, a flutter of skin and muscle that drew his face into an unsightly grimace for a second. "To save me from the Devil's own work, Nicholas." He straightened and winced as if his body protested. "We must not allow the others to be taken by that—that thing! They are possessed—"

"Jeremiah!" Mrs. Clapp opened her eyes, looked up into Linda's face, her expression dazed. "Jeremiah—he jumped at me! My own old boy—he's gone mad!"

"No." Linda soothed her. "He wanted to save you, and he did."

The cat padded closer. Now he set both forepaws on Mrs. Clapp's breast, leaned down to touch her nose with the tip of his own. His tongue came out and he gave her face a small, fastidious lick.

"Jeremiah." Mrs. Clapp lifted one hand, laid it on the cat's head. "Why—"

"To save you," Linda repeated. "Just as Lung saved me, and Nick did Mr. Hadlett."

"But—" Mrs. Clapp struggled to sit up and Linda aided her. The old woman looked about. "Where're the others? Lady Diana—she was right here—and Jean—and Barry—"

"They have gone." It was Hadlett who answered. "And we have to do what we can to aid them, as soon as possible."

He struggled to his feet as if he would go running with the same unheeding recklessness as had taken the others. Nick moved between him and the entrance to the cave.

"We can't, not until we know what we're facing. It might be throwing away any chance we do have just to go blindly out in the dark."

For a moment, he thought the Vicar would give him a hot argument, even try to push past him. Then Hadlett's shoulders slumped and he answered dully:

"You are right, of course, Nicholas. But we must do something."

"I intend to." That was wrenched out of Nick. Again he was being forced to a decision he did not want to make, take a course he knew was dangerous. The sound had died away, his head was free of the pain. Did that mean that the menace had withdrawn with the prey it had so easily snared, or only that it had subsided to prepare for another and perhaps stronger assault? There was no use looking for trouble in the future, he had enough facing him now.

"Not alone." The force and vigor that had always been in Hadlett's tone was returning. "We must go together—"

"All of us," Linda broke in, "all together."

Nick was about to protest, and then he understood that perhaps she was wiser than he. To leave two women here alone, for he knew he could not argue the Vicar into staying, would be utter folly. When the barrier failed the Dark forces would overrun the cave. Linda and Mrs. Clapp would have no chance at all. And what he had seen of the besiegers made Nick certain that they must not face what had walked, loped, slithered out there.

Of course it was the height of stupidity to go out at all. But if he did not, he was sure Hadlett would set off by himself, or with the women. Nick must be as practical as this impractical situation allowed.

So he suggested that they make up packs, the heaviest to be for him and Linda, though both Mrs. Clapp and the Vicar insisted they shoulder their share. And the Vicar did offer experienced advice.

"Is there any other way out—besides the one I found earlier?" Nick asked.

"Along the stream, sir—" Mrs. Clapp looked to the Vicar.

Hadlett seemed doubtful. "That is a rough passage, Maude."

"Rough it may be," she answered stoutly, "but if it takes us out where those things ain't watchin', won't that be for the best?"

"I suppose—" But he did not sound convinced.

"Along what stream, sir?" Nick pursued the matter.

"An underground one. We never explored it far. But there is a place, Sam assured me, where one can scramble out. I believe some distance from this—" He gestured at the entrance.

"All the better." Nick was a little heartened. He would have suggested the back entrance he had found but he was sure that neither the vicar nor Mrs. Clapp could make it.

If they only had in truth the machine gun of the illusion, or weapons from their own world. He had the knife, and now he found in his saddlebags the camp knife he had almost forgotten. Since Hadlett had one of the daggers, he gave this to Linda. Iron—little enough for defense. They might as well, thought Nick savagely, go barehanded.

Mrs. Clapp looked about her. She had quietly stacked the wooden bowls, folded up some crudely woven mats. It was plain she believed it would be long before anyone returned here.

"A rough wild place it is, but it's been good to us."

"Yes, Maude," Hadlett answered gently.

"Sometimes—sometimes I dream about walkin' up the walk— seein' the roses an' those lilies Mrs. Lansdowne at the lodge gave me the settin' of. There's m' own old door an' Jeremiah's sittin' on the step watchin' for me. I dream like that, sir. It's as real as real for a while—"

"I know, Maude. I wonder if that bomb did hit St. Michael's. Five hundred and fifty years—a long time for a church to stand. It still stands for me."

"We got it all to remember, sir. That nobody can take away. An' you can close your eyes sometimes, when you're restin' like, an' see it as plain as plain. Maybe if we went back—Sometimes I think to m'self, sir, that I see it better'n it really was. You can do that, you know. Like lookin' back down the years to when one was a little maid—everything was brighter an' better then. The years were longer like, not all squeezed together like they seem to be now. An' there was a lot packed into every one o' 'em. Well, a clackin' tongue ain't goin' to get me, nor anyone else, goin'. But for all its roughness, this has been a good place. Come on, Jeremiah!"

Her speech ended on a brisk note. Linda moved closer to Nick.

"She makes me want to cry. Oh, Nick, I don't want to remember, not now. It does something to me, I get to feeling wild, as if I could just run about screaming, 'Let me out!' Don't you ever feel like that?"

"It depends," he answered as he shouldered his pack, "on what you have to go back to. Anyway there's no use looking too far ahead now. We had better concentrate on getting out of here."

"Nick," she interrupted him, "what can we do—to help them? Can we even find them?"

"I doubt it. But those two"—he nodded to the Vicar helping Mrs. Clapp over the rough footing in a side alcove of the cave—"won't give up trying. And we can't leave them to do it alone."

Linda caught her lip between her teeth, frowned. "No, I can see that. Will they ever admit it's hopeless? What do you think happened to the others, Nick?"

"Your guess is as good as mine," was the best answer he could give her. He was trying to control imagination which was only too ready to present him with horrors.

The way Hadlett guided them into was rough, and soon they had to go single file. Lung and Jeremiah had the best of it as they padded along with far greater ease than the two-footed humans and soon outpaced them. Linda called anxiously now and then, and was always answered by a single bark from the Peke.

After a very short time they hit a downward incline, dropping them well below the surface of the larger cave. Twice they had to stoop, proceeding at a back-aching angle. Nick's flashlight in Hadlett's hand lit up the worst of the obstructions.

Now they could hear the gurgle of water. And a last scramble brought them into a wider tunnel, one that water over the centuries must have carved for itself, though the present stream running along it was much smaller than the space through which it passed.

"This way." Hadlett turned left. Nick was pleased at that. Unless he was completely misled, any opening in this direction to the surface would be well away from the upper entrance. He wondered if the barrier there still held.

With that gone, would the enemy make a frontal attack? With no resistance they could enter the cave. At that thought, Nick turned uneasily to glance over his shoulder, tried to listen. But the sounds of the stream and their own journey effectively cloaked what might be behind. He wished that the Peke and Jeremiah had remained in closer contact. The animals had a far better range of hearing and could sound the alarm if it was needed.

Nick wanted to hurry, but he knew with Mrs. Clapp's stiff and painful legs and the Vicar's age, they could push on at no better speed than this. He drew his knife, always straining to hear any sound except that of the water and their going.

"Here—" Hadlett flashed the light to the left. There was a break in the wall of the tunnel. Then the light showed the surface of the water. They must splash through that to reach the cleft. Nick wondered how deep it was. He saw Jeremiah sitting on the other side. But Lung whimpered and ran to Linda, begging to be taken up. So the Peke thought the flood too deep or had some objection to splashing on. The cat must have jumped it. Nick took warning from Lung.

"Don't try to wade!" He crowded up beside the Vicar. "Give me the flashlight."

"You noticed Lung, yes." Hadlett passed over the light.

Nick squatted on his heels. The rest had flattened against the wall of the tunnel. He turned the light directly on the water. There were no signs of a swift current, and it looked shallow, but he was not a trained woodsman to know. The stream might be a trap the animals knew by instinct. Yet it was too wide for their jumping—they did not have Jeremiah's talents. It would be wade—

"Nick!" Linda dropped beside him. Now she swung her arm across his chest to point upstream.

The troubling of the current was plainly visible. And that was not caused by some rock nearly breaking the surface, for it moved toward them. Nick handed her the light.

"Hold that!" He was ready with his knife. For the sight made him believe he faced the alien.

The disturbance in the water ceased, but Nick breathed faster. That thing, whatever it might be, was not gone. Rather it had taken to what cover the water afforded.

"Nick!" Linda's cry scaled up to near a scream, but her quick reflexes saved them. The hand and arm flashing from beneath the water did not achieve its purpose. Webbed fingers grasped in vain. Linda now had the flashlight well out of reach.

The American stabbed down into the water with the knife. There was a flurry there. Then the head and shoulders of the being that had tried to rob them of light arose. This was no human. In the first place the creature could not be much larger than Jeremiah. Secondly it was covered with fur as might be an otter or seal.

It had great round eyes, a whiskered muzzle, a wild tangle of coarser hair like a mane reaching to its shoulders. The mouth opened, showing yellow fang-teeth. Then it snapped shut while it hissed much as might Jeremiah in a rage.

Nick advanced the blade he held. The water thing sputtered, made mewling sounds, but it retreated. This was one of the natives of Avalon he was sure. But it did not seem as one with the Dark forces. That it was hostile to his kind was plain, but it was not strongly evil.

"Wait, lad." Mrs. Clapp came forward. "Iron will keep that off, but there is another way also."

Nick glanced up in surprise as she fumbled in her bag and drew out a small length of branch. Solemnly, as if performing some ritual in the Vicar's vanished St. Michael's, she recited:

"Nixie, pixie—
The water is draining,
Your fine home awastin'.
Comes now th' cattle a-stampin', a-trampin',
Naught will remain.
By th' elder, by th' ash,
Begone—thrice!"

She struck the surface of the water three times with her branch.

The thing stopped in mid-hiss, watching her warily. But as she said "thrice," it gave an eerie cry and submerged. They could see it moving at lightning speed upstream. Lung ran along the edge of the water barking furiously, while Linda called him.

Mrs. Clapp laughed. "There now, I never thought to say that in a lifetime. M' old Aunt Meg, she was a proper one—more'n my auntie she was really, 'cause she was sister to m' great-granny. But she lived a long time. A hundred 'n' more she was before she took to her bed the last time. She had the healin' an' the Second Sight. Folks use to go to her for wart charmin' an' the like, 'fore it got so the young folks laughed at such.

"Aunt Meg, she could see the Gentry—that was what we called 'em in our bit o' country in those days—though she never talked much of that. Offered me a bite of yellow cake stuff once when I was little. Said it was Gentry-baked. My Mum struck it out o'm' hand an' beat it right into the dust when I fetched it home. She said it was silly, but she knew right enough about dealin' with the Gentry.

"That there was a nixie. Auntie, she said they were mischiefmakers. Live in bogs, some of them do, an' lead people astray. She learned me that spell an' told me about usin' elder. There's nothin' like elder an' ash to stand up to them of the Gentry as is for mischief. Yes, she learned me that when I was goin' for the milk up to Barstow's farm an' had to pass over a bit of bog there if I took the quick way home. I was old enough to keep m' tongue inside m' teeth, an' Mum never knew. Never saw a nixie, though, not there. But I always kept careful watch like Auntie said to."

"Will it be back?" Linda had caught Lung and was holding him.

"Not if we do it right." Mrs. Clapp appeared to have complete confidence in her method of routing the water thing. "First we see just how deep this is here." She used the elder branch for a measure. "'Bout knee-high, I would say."

"Now," she continued with authority, "we'd best take off our shoes, an' pull up m' skirt an' your pants. We can take a wettin' better than our clothes can, dry off sooner, too."

"A very wise precaution." Hadlett was already pulling off his moccasins, rolling up his trousers.

"An' this"—Mrs. Clapp held out the branch—"I'm goin' to stick in so." She pushed it down into the water and it stood there upright. "That there elder is goin' to be a cover for us."

Splash across they did, though Nick kept watch for any telltale line in the water that would mark the return of the nixie. He was the last across and Mrs. Clapp yelled to him:

"Bring the wand with you, lad. Don't know when I'll get m' hand on another good bit of elder. Don't seem to grow too plentiful hereabouts."

He pulled the branch free, dragging it behind him through the water as an added precaution against an attack, to hand it back to its owner. Mrs. Clapp flipped it to shake off the droplets along it and stowed it briskly away as if her past performance was as ordinary as eating or sleeping.

Now they climbed at a sharper angle than they had descended. It was difficult for Mrs. Clapp. At times all three of them boosted or pulled. She breathed heavily but she never complained. Sometimes she even made some cheery remark on their aid or her own clumsiness.

"Just ahead now. I had better turn this off." Hadlett pushed off the flash button. There was instant and smothering darkness, and Nick began a protest, but the Vicar was continuing:

"Wait until our eyes adjust. It is night out there but there should be some light—moon—"

"Let me lead now." Nick did not want to do that, but he certainly was not going to stand behind two women and an older man.

Something brushed past him and he nearly cried out. Then he knew it was Jeremiah.

Nick bumped into a solid surface with considerable force and realized there was a turn in the passage. Feeling his way with one hand, the knife in the other, he made the turn and indeed did see a pale spot ahead.

"Wait," he whispered, "until I make sure."

"Well enough," Hadlett agreed.

Nick took it very slowly. There was too much chance of tripping, or making some noise. If those who had besieged the other entrance to the cave had an outpost here they could be waiting.

That short advance was one of the hardest things Nick had ever forced himself to do. But at last he felt the cool night air, saw moonlight. He crouched and listened, wishing with all his might he knew what were the natural sounds one should expect to hear—and those that would mean trouble.

Then Nick sighted Jeremiah. The cat was in the open, his gray fur hardly distinguishable. And from him Nick gained one of those thought messages. There was no one threatening nearby—they had gotten free of the Dark Ones—for now.

Nick crept back to the turn and whispered the good news. The waiting three followed him. A moment or so and they were out of the slit into the night, standing under the stars, seeing the silver of the moon.

"Which way do we go now?" Linda wanted to know. She carried Lung, and Nick thought she did not trust the Peke not to run into some waiting danger.

"Ahead I would say." Hadlett held Nick's compass. "We should go east for a space before we turn south. Thus perhaps we can outflank those by the cave."

"If they are still there," Nick commented.

Having three prisoners, would they be waiting for the rest? He thought it more in keeping that they would only leave a token force and be on their way with their captives. If they were captives still and not—

He refused to accept what his imagination supplied. Not yet, not until they had proof, would he believe the others dead. They might lose time by following the Vicar's suggestion, but it was a sensible one. And the more they could avoid the ghastly crew he had seen the better.

Rita—had she returned to the city? She made it clear she would not come to their aid again. But that was only just. They had refused what she had to offer. And what had they gained in return—the loss of half their company.

"Nicholas." He turned toward that half-seen form that was Hadlett, now hand-linked to Mrs. Clapp, who had admitted her night sight was poor.

"What is it?"

"We are no longer alone." That was the chilling information Nick had feared ever since they had emerged from the cave's back door.

✳ **17** ✳

Nick sensed it also—the presence, or presences—but not the evil that had been such a foul emanation from the Dark Ones. He heard a mewling cry from Jeremiah.

Then once more he saw the cat. With him was Lung who must have escaped from Linda. The animals stood together and before them was one of the weird forest beasts, larger than either, but bending its head to touch noses with first the cat and then the Peke.

It was the one—or like it—that Nick had seen with the Green Man—the creature Hadlett had named "enfield." In color this had a golden sheen, misted as the Herald and the People appeared. And that radiance made clear its fox head, greyhound body, the taloned, eaglelike forefeet, the canine hindquarters and wolf tail.

What manner of exchange passed between the animals they had no way of knowing. However, the enfield raised its sharp-eared head and gave a cry that was neither bay nor bark, closer to song. It was answered from the darkness about in various notes and tones, as if the human party was now ringed by strange and alien creatures.

The enfield turned its head to eye them. In its skull its eyes were small yellow flames. For a second out of time it studied them. Then once more it voiced the call. When it was answered, it was gone, winked out as might be the flame of a candle caught by a puff of breeze.

"What—?" Linda began shakily.

But Nick knew, without words he knew.

"We have nothing to fear—from them," he said.

"The freedom of the woodlands," Hadlett added. "Perhaps we have not been given full seizing, that ancient right to estate under formal rule. But this much—"

"I don't know what you are talking about!" Linda burst out. "What was that—that thing? And, Nick, from the sound, they're all around us. What if—"

"We have nothing to fear," he repeated. "Not from them."

Could they dare to hope they had acquired an escort? Or would the unseen company of beasts merely remain neutral? He knew they were still there, though he did not sight them. And with the vanishing of the light radiating from the enfield he could no longer see either Jeremiah or Lung.

"We'd better get on," Nick added. What he did not say was that he wanted to see if other company would move with them.

"Yes!" Linda was eager to push ahead. Undoubtedly she wanted to leave the unseen behind. "Lung," she called softly. "Here, Lung!"

The Peke came to her readily and she scooped him up, holding him as if she feared he might be snatched from her at any moment. Then Nick felt the push of a furred body against his legs, stooped and gathered up Jeremiah. The cat wriggled up, draped his body about Nick's shoulders stole-fashion. The American was a little uncomfortable under the weight, but knew that he must be content with Jeremiah's choice.

Guided by the compass, they went east, skirting the open where there was need. But their pace slowed. Nick knew without seeing or being told that Mrs. Clapp was lagging, and he suspected it was little better with the Vicar. They would have to rest.

When he suggested a halt there was no objection, and, using a bush growth for cover, they dropped to the ground. Jeremiah leaped from Nick's shoulders to disappear. There was no measuring how far they had come, but Nick wondered if they should not now turn south, strive to cut across the trail of the missing.

Morning light would be better for a tracking attempt and he

pointed this out. To his surprise, the Vicar agreed. They planned to keep watch, the three of them, allowing Mrs. Clapp full rest, turn about.

Nick volunteered for the first sentry go. The moonlight somehow appeared dimmer and he had to depend more on his ears than his sight. He stuck the knife point down between his knees, resting one hand on its hilt, and tried to think.

There was, he believed, very little chance of them being able to rescue the others. But that fact they would have to prove to themselves. Afterward—what could they do? Would it be possible to slowly work their way back through a now totally hostile world to the place they had left the jeep and there try Linda's suggestion of opening a return door? Nick thought they might try, but the chances for success were close to nonexistent. What would remain then? A harried, ever-endangered existence as the prey of either the Dark Ones or the saucers. Perhaps they could get as far as that farmhouse again. But there was the matter of food—And life in a continual state of apprehension was no life at all.

The English had known that at home with the air raids, the constant threat of invasion. Nick had read about it, but that was all very far away and long ago. You could not understand such fear until you, yourself, were forced to live with it. And he and Linda, though the world they knew also had its violence, had not had to deal directly with it before.

The best answer was still the city. But if the Vicar and Mrs. Clapp continued to refuse—what then?

Nick tensed, jerking the knife free. He had heard nothing, he saw nothing—but there was something out there now. One of the alien animals? They had had no escort from that meeting, of that Nick was fully convinced.

Now he heard a small whine. Lung came from where Linda lay. His small body, when Nick laid hand on it, quivered as if he wished to run forth in greeting. Nick could sense no fear, only excitement.

There was a faint penciling of light in the air, outlining a figure. Nick arose to face who—or what—stood there. The light grew stronger, that figure more solid. Nick expected Avalon. But this was Rita!

"You! But—"

Then anger rose in him. "You gave us a very dramatic good-bye. Why return now?"

Her porcelain face was without expression. "For your purpose it will be enough that I have come at all. Those you seek have been taken by the flyers, not the Dark Ones. If you would have them forth, seek the sky hunters."

"Why are you telling me this?" Nick demanded. "By your own words you are apart from us, and Avalon cares nothing for us."

"True." Now there was a faint troubling of her expression. "But if you seek among the Dark Ones—then you shall be totally lost. I would have you save yourselves."

"And the others?"

Rita shook her head. "How can you save them? For those who have taken them are mightier than you can hope to be. They have weapons that are as far beyond those you have known as yours are beyond bow, sword, and spear. Those they take are gone, accept that."

Nick's anger, aroused by what he could not analyze, remained steady. At this point had Rita said the sun was bright, he would have denied it. At first he thought her information might be a trick. Then he was sure it was true.

"Was that sound one of their weapons?"

""Yes. It compels—draws—"

"Then why did it not take us all?"

"I told you—you are different. The Great Power touched you. Also he—and Maude—and the girl—they, too, believe, though they deny it. Maude and Adrian Hadlett have the old belief in their blood, their past. The girl—her dog has given her the open door. You each had a small defense against that weapon, and Lung and Jeremiah were fully armed. They are of Avalon in their own way."

He saw now by the glow of light about her that the cat and the Peke were seated at her feet, gazing up at her as if entranced. She stooped to touch fingertip to each furred head.

"Wise in their time are these," she said.

"Wiser than we?"

"Ask that of yourself, not me."

Her glow was fading, drawing about her. Nick moved.

"Wait!"

But she made no answer. Rita was gone.

"That's a good act." Linda was beside him. "Do you believe a word she says?"

"Yes."

"The trouble is, though I don't like her—in fact, if you want the absolute, down-to-earth truth, I think I hate her—I believe her, too. Which means what, Nick? Can we possibly help the others if the saucer people have them? I don't see any chance of doing that."

"Right now I don't either," he confessed. "They could have taken them anywhere."

"It is not as hopeless as it would seem." They were both startled by the Vicar's voice out of the dark. "Yes, I have been awake, saw and heard our visitor. And I also believe her. But, remember, we were brought to this continent as prisoners of the saucer people. They had then a headquarters here, not too far from where we were wrecked and freed. Surely any prisoners they take will be found there."

"But we haven't a chance of getting in," Nick protested. "Rita was right, you know. They do have weapons beyond anything we know. They stunned those men we saw netted. And that sound—the rays they turned on the Herald. We have no protection against such. It's crazy to think we can get them away." But even as he protested, Nick knew that Hadlett would remain unconvinced, determined to rescue the others, be that possible or impossible.

"We seem to have a partial defense against the sound." It was as if the Vicar had heard nothing Nick said. "What was it that Rita told you—Maude and I, through our blood and the past—now what did she mean?" Nick thought he asked that question of himself rather than his listeners. "Maude is of Sussex, very old Sussex. She was a Boorde before her marriage. And you heard her speak of her great-great-aunt who had the Sight and the powers of healing. As for me—we have been ten generations in Minton Parva, squires or churchmen, and I know the old ways—

"The old ways," he repeated. "Yes, Avalon, and the People, I have long heard of them. Iron and the Church drove them out, but they lingered for a space. Perhaps in England they were in exile, perhaps they were colonists. 'The Gentry' some called them—because they were indeed 'gentle folk' in the old meaning of the word, fair to look on, courteous, sometimes helpful to man."

"They had their faults, too, sir." Mrs. Clapp had been roused. "They disliked those who spied on 'em, an' there were them as made trouble. But they was known, leastways to the old folks. These here flyin' people, they're different, not like us at all. If they've got 'em—Lady Diana, Barry, Sam, Miss Jean—then how are we goin' to get them back, sir?"

It was as if her brisk question roused the Vicar from his thoughts.

"That will take some consideration, Maude."

"It will take more than consideration." Hadlett was not a man with whom to be brusque, Nick had known that from his first meeting with the Vicar. But he would not accept some unworkable scheme now. He worried too much about the powers of the saucers. Perhaps, in a way, he could understand those better so he really dreaded them more than the monsters he thought might be illusions, horrible as those were.

"You are right, Nicholas," the Vicar agreed.

"But," he continued, "we now know where we must search—to the north, not the south."

That he was going to be able to argue the English out of abandoning the search Nick already guessed was impossible. And to leave them—that he could not. It would be up to him to try to think up some telling argument, but at present his mind was a blank.

What he did do was question Hadlett methodically to learn all he could of what the Vicar had observed during their captivity in the saucer. That the flyers could stun their prey was the truth. Rendered completely helpless such prisoners were loaded into the saucers and it was some time before that effect wore off. When it did, they were locked into compartments meant to be prisons.

The escape of the English party had been a fluke which might happen perhaps once in a thousand times. Some motive power of the saucer had failed and it crash-landed.

The door to their cell had been sprung and the English had found at least two of their captors dead.

"Their helmets were shattered," Hadlett explained. "It is evident that they cannot breathe this air without the protection of the snout-masks that are part of their headgear. That is one advantage for us—"

A very small one, was Nick's conclusion. How were they going to break helmets in any battle when the enemy could stand off and ray them down? The more he thought about it, the more he was convinced this was a suicide mission.

"Were they all killed?" Nick asked.

"Yes. Barry and Sam went back to the ship—Barry had some hope of learning their method of flight. But all he could discover was that the ship was locked onto some homing device. What had caused it to crash he could not discover. But the crew were all dead. They were very small—dwarfish—and their skins blue. Barry and Sam did not have time to learn much, for they found another machine broadcasting what Barry thought was a distress signal. We hurried away, which was prudent, for we saw in the distance later another saucer—perhaps hunting the wreck."

"Locked into a homing device," Nick repeated. Then if one had access to a saucer it would take one to their headquarters—perhaps.

"That has some meaning for you?" the Vicar began and then added excitedly, "But, of course, it would be the perfect way, would it not, to enter the enemy stronghold undetected."

"The perfect way," Nick reminded him, "to walk straight into a prison and whatever the saucer people have ready for those they capture."

"Perhaps, perhaps not. It is a point to consider, Nicholas. Yes, an excellent point to consider. Think of it this way, my boy—if we were not altogether affected by their sound weapon, then it could just be we could allow ourselves to be apparently captured, to turn the tables—as the old saying goes—on our captors."

Fantastic! Did he really think that? It was the wildest suggestion yet. Nick's penetration into the city was as nothing beside this.

"Could we do it?"

Nick nearly rounded on Linda hotly. Somehow he had

unconsciously expected her to support him in any trial of wills in their small party, but listen to her now. "Could we use illusions for bait?" she continued.

Nick's annoyance faded. Though her face was only a blur in the dark he stared at her! An illusion for bait? Then perhaps an ambush of the saucer? No, it would not work—they had no weapons except their knives—

"Now that, m' dear, is right smart thinkin'. I do believe, sir, that Miss Linda has an idea that might just work—"

"And how do we jump them when they come down with the net?" Nick raised his voice in protest. Pressure—a sharp pricking against his leg. He exclaimed. Jeremiah had hooked his claws well into Nick, demanding attention.

"Jeremiah." Nick went to one knee, stroking the cat. "What is it?"

Foggy—like trying to see a picture through a dense mist— outlines that wavered back and forth, on which Nick tried to focus. Even when he concentrated, the pictures were odd, as if he saw through eyes that were not normal, having other qualities than his own. Lung—certainly that bouncing creature was Lung at his most exuberant. And there was the enfield, and behind it other weird, mixed things. The beasts of Avalon. Was Jeremiah promising now their help?

Yes! Thought answered his unasked question.

It would be a plan of many pieces, and much would depend on luck, on attracting a saucer, on timing thereafter. But maybe, just maybe, they could do it. And it was better than just blindly walking into trouble—which is what the Vicar might well do if Nick did not produce an alternate plan.

"Sir," Nick tried to bring all his power of persuasion to bear. "Do you think a plan such as this might work?" As he continued, he thought of new details, added improvements (he hoped they were improvements).

Thus it came about that hours later found them in the hot sun on the edge of the open. Having set their plan they had rested and then, with the beasts of Avalon guiding, they had reached this point.

Now they were linked, men, women, dog and cat together, with an ingathering of power. Perhaps they were again misusing that as Rita had warned. But it was their only key. They lay in hiding, but out in the open two figures walked very slowly. There was limit to their power of projection and Mrs. Clapp had suggested that instead of trying to reproduce their whole party they create only two illusions, that of the Vicar and herself. She and Hadlett had formed those figures, Nick, Linda, and the animals feeding them the sustaining energy.

Jeremiah and Lung were out there, pacing beside the slow-moving illusions. There were others concealed in the tall grass. Nick had suggested such were visible from above and there had been amusement beamed from Jeremiah. Perhaps the beasts of Avalon had some native protection against such sighting.

Now—all they needed was a saucer to take the bait. How long would that take? They might have to set this scene many times, for they could not hold any illusion long. How—

Not long at all! A saucer burst into view in one of those instantaneous arrivals. It swooped, to center over the staggering figures. Now! Nick gestured. The illusions slumped forward, lay full length. From the belly of the saucer the net broke, descending.

Nick could see twitching grass, the beasts were on the move. Surely the aliens would spot that suspicious movement! But if they did, they did not counter it. It was time for him to make his own move. He was sweating, and not from the heat of the sun. It all depended now on whether they did have any protection against the alien weapons.

He began to run, zigzagging as he went, though that might be no protection against attack. One of the suited crewmen was already sliding down the rope toward the inert bodies, a second swinging out of the hatch to follow him.

Then Nick was hit by a force from the saucer, as if a fist struck him. As planned, he gave way, falling—which was only too easy. They would think him a prisoner—perhaps he was. But he summoned up the strength of will that he had commanded in the woods. He could do this, his body was his own to order. He could move. And he did.

The grass was tall about him, hiding most of the scene around the net. Hadlett, Mrs. Clapp and Linda would hold the illusions on the inert figures as long as they could. If their plan was to succeed, they must hold until he reached the net. He saw now one of the aliens prepare to slip the net around the illusion of Hadlett. Behind the suited figure the grass moved. A small gray shape leaped, hit the shoulders of the alien, clawing at the helmet. It was joined by a flashing creature that could only be the enfield. The other alien, partway down the rope, turned to reclimb.

Out of ambush arose a thing to swing up the rope with the agility of its monkey body. Yet on its shoulders was an owl's head. With no difficulty at all it caught up with the alien, scrambling over his body, so the suited figure lost hold and fell back and down.

Nick was under the shadow of the saucer. The longer he had fought the force that tied his limbs, the easier it became to move. He reached the net. How many crewmen were still in the saucer? The owl-monkey scuttled over the ground leaving a crumpled body behind. The net was now burdened by a number of the beasts, weighting it down. With any luck at all they should anchor the saucer.

Up! Nick caught at the rope ladder. But the owl-monkey was before him, springing up as if this was a stairway. As it went, its outline blurred, it became one of the suited aliens. Nick began to climb. Was the party in hiding successful also? Was he now in the likeness of a helmeted dwarf? Up and up—he hardly dared believe he had made it this far. Now he was through the hatch, the owl-monkey-alien disappearing through a door beyond. Behind Nick came Jeremiah, able to use his claws on the ropeway.

Nick hurried after the beast. His impetus carried him into the control cabin of the saucer. Flame flashed, outlined the owl-monkey whose illusion had vanished. But the creature was as untouched as the Herald under the raying. Nick leaped—there were only two aliens, and the owl-monkey had beaten down the weapon of one, bearing him down into the seat from which he had half-risen.

With a crash Nick met the other alien, carrying the smaller figure back against the wall of the cabin. At the shock of being slammed against it, the alien went limp. Nick held him for a moment, making sure he was harmless. Then Jeremiah landed on the suited form, his snarling face pressed against the surface of the helmet. The eyes of the being inside were closed.

His fellow crewman was still struggling feebly but uselessly with the owl-monkey who proceeded to draw him hack to the door opening into the hatch space. Nick, apprehensive, searched the ship. But the four beings they had already taken were the entire crew. Nick was shaking a little from reaction, unable to believe they had done this thing.

Now he feared that the saucer might as suddenly vanish with him. The two aliens, both still alive, Nick thought, were lowered to the ground. Of the two who had been with the net, one was dead with a cracked helmet, the other a prisoner. Nick could not kill in cold blood, but to maroon them in the open country, prisoners of the beasts, unable to summon help, was the answer. And the sooner he got his own party on board, the better.

Hadlett and Linda could climb. But they activated the net to raise Mrs. Clapp and Lung. Once that was inboard the hatch snapped shut of its own accord, and the saucer quivered to life.

Nick ran for the control cabin, forced his larger body into one of the seats. He could not hope to use any of the levers and buttons before him. Like it or not they were on their way, locked into an enemy craft, their destination unknown. And now that he had time, he began to worry again. Their amazing good fortune with the ambush could not continue to hold forever.

18

"This is our chance!" Linda tried to fit herself into the narrow neighboring seat.

"Our chance to do what?" Nick had prowled the saucer ship twice. He made several finds of what might be weapons, but he dared not experiment with them inside the cabin. The only chance he could see was one so hedged by threats it was nearer to an invitation to disaster.

"To get back to our own world." She was impatient. "These saucers must go through. People have seen them back there. We have only to learn how, then we're home!"

"That learning how," Nick pointed out, "might take some time. Time we don't have. When this lands—"

"We can use illusions again." Linda dismissed such details as unimportant, her own goal the real one.

"You mean, we hope we can." Nick found the flight pattern of the saucer made him queasy, he wanted nothing more than to be free of the alien ship.

"We can. And we can get back, too!" Her optimism remained high.

"You're forgetting the time factor, aren't you?"

"What time factor?"

"These others—they thought they had only been here a few years. But it's been over forty. How long have we been here—days—a week—I've not counted. But how long have we been away?"

What had happened back in the world of the Cut-Off? How long before they had been missed and the search begun? What about Dad and Margo? Who had been hunting Linda? She had said no more about her past than he had. Who was missing her?

"Nick—" Her eagerness was gone, he might have struck her in the face. "Do you think—But it couldn't be! We can't have been gone months, we can't!"

He could give her no reassurance. Before, he had not really considered that point as it applied to himself or Linda. But now Nick faced it squarely and found that he really did not greatly care. All that had happened before their arrival in the forest seemed to be the past of another person and have very little meaning for the Nick Shaw that now was.

"Dave—" Linda stared ahead of her. "What will Dave do? What will he think?"

"Who's Dave?"

"My father, David. He's with NASA—on the Cape. I was staying with Aunt Peg for a vacation. But there's just Dave and me—we're a family!"

Linda hunched down in the seat her body did not adjust to. "Nick, we've got to get back. And the saucer people must know how."

"First things first—" Nick had only gotten that far, not knowing how he could make her see the impossibility of what she wanted, when the saucer began a vertical descent.

They had reached whatever goal had been set. Nick had had no control over the flight. Now it must be tested whether he had any defense over what they might encounter outside.

With a hardly perceptible jar the ship touched down and the vibration of its life ceased. Nick headed back to the area about the hatch. They had made the best plan they could and at least they would have surprise on their side.

Again he was to have the active part. The rest, using their combined concentration, would back him. As the side of the saucer now opened slowly to form a ramp, Nick drew a deep breath and walked forward.

He could not tell if his protecting illusion was in force, if he would indeed appear to anyone outside as a normal alien crewman. What he could see ahead was not too reassuring. There another of the saucer ships rested on stilt-legs, its ramp down. To the right was a section of ground in which huddled a group of drifters. Nick could see no walls, yet none made an effort to escape even though there were no visible guards.

To cross the space between the ship and the captives was an ordeal. Nick expected any moment to be challenged, or else simply rayed down. He studied the prisoners, tried to understand what kept them there.

Some distance beyond the captives a tall pole arose into the sky from a broad earth base. At its tip sprouted two fan shapes fashioned of glittering wires stretched over frames. Even as Nick sighted them they moved, the fans waving slowly upward until they joined above the tip of the supporting pole. Along the wires glowed light, deepening to a fiery red.

The air about Nick tingled with energy. It was like and yet unlike the broadcast of the ankh. Nick knew, without understanding why or how, some vast power was at work.

Now he saw those who controlled it. There were six of the suited aliens clustered about the base of the pole. What they might be doing there did not matter, the fact that they were so engrossed by it did, giving Nick a slender chance.

"Those we seek—there—" An impression from Jeremiah on his right side. Lung was to his left.

"Can't go through—a wall ahead—" For the first time he also caught the Peke's thought.

Nick walked forward with caution. Jeremiah moved before him, stopped, as if his nose touched an unseen barrier. A force field? One of the aliens need only look up—see him investigating it—

Though Nick put out his hand to touch what the animals said was there, he felt nothing—save that a bolt of energy nearly rocked him from his feet. With that how could the captives hope to escape? And how could he and his party hope in turn to reach them? If he knew how to control the ship perhaps they could lift it and drop it on the other side of the barrier. But that was beyond his skill.

The prisoners noticed him. He saw faces turn in his direction. Two of the disheveled figures got to their feet—Crocker and Jean. Did they see him as himself, or did the alien illusion hold?

Illusion—some wisp of thought he could not pin down exactly. What had Hadlett earlier said—that the illusions a man could produce were born out of his own particular thoughts and fears, that those from the medieval period who had taken him prisoner had seen the demons and devils of their own time. Demons and devils—what would be the demons and devils of the aliens? If he only knew more! Nick felt bound and helpless, with weapons just out of his reach, as he had been in the camp when he had first used the freedom of mind. He had no guide, no way of knowing what would serve as the proper demons and devils to evoke here.

Into his mind flashed a memory—that of the Herald riding unconcernedly along under the attack of the saucer. But he was no Herald, nor could he, Nick was sure, take on the seeming of one himself, even though he could create the image of one for a short space. He sensed that the Herald was too much of Avalon to be used here in human counterfeit. Also if this place was of Avalon, what had it to hold for these who were not subject to the People or their powers? What other fear or threat could he summon? Wait—there had been that time when another flyer of a different shape had attacked the saucer—

The cigar ship! Demons and devils! But could they produce that as an illusion?

In the prison compound Jean and Crocker were aiding Stroud to his feet with the help of Lady Diana. If Nick was right in his surmise he would have to drop his own cover, give all power to the illusion.

"Join!" Nick sent the message to Jeremiah in the linkage he could not hold direct with his own kind. The big cat crouched, his tail tip quivering as if he stalked prey. He did not glance at Nick but the man felt his message was received.

Lung bolted, skimmering back to the ramp of the saucer. How long did they have? Nick fastened his attention on the sky above that pole, tried to draw there the demon of the aliens—one of the cigar-shaped ships.

He—his message had gone through! Jeremiah—Lung—those in the ship behind him understood. There was the enemy that the aliens knew, hovering over their source of energy. He heard no sounds from the crew working below, but saw them freeze for a moment and then scatter, heading toward positions in the grass. They were about to defend their post desperately, as if it were paramount to their existence.

In his hand Nick held one of the weapons from the ship. It was a rod about the length of his forearm, with two buttons at one end. Being hollow in part he equated it with some type of gun. What it might do he had no idea, nor even if he could fire it. But the action of the aliens was a clue. If the fan-pole was so important, for they were firing rays into the hovering illusion to protect it, then if he could destroy it. . . .

Nick began to run. There was shouting from the prisoner pen, but he paid no attention. The pole was the important thing now. He came to a halt, raised the rod and took a chance, pushing the nearest button with his forefinger, aiming at the fans overhead.

He thought he had failed. There was no trace that the weapon had fired. Then—

The red glow of the wires above flashed an eye-searing white!

Nick flung his arm over his eyes. Was he blinded? And that roaring—enough to deafen one. The ground shook under him, rolled as if solid earth had vanished. He staggered around blindly, trying to head away from that holocaust, back to the ship. But where was the ship?

He was finding it hard to breathe, as if the air was being drained away. Then he was crawling through a world afire. This might be the ancient Hell of humankind—

Nick lay on the still trembling ground, pressed against it by a force like a massive fist weighing upon his back. He was being crushed and he thought he cried out feebly. Then came darkness in which the fires of Hell were quenched.

The ankh stood tall, glowing. From it streamed light, reaching out and out, and under that light was peace. The fan-pole stood and glowed balefully, it drew upon the life-force of Avalon, and the peace was broken. Things crept out of ancient places of the Dark to walk the land again.

Peace fled before the power of the pole, before the Dark, withdrawing into the city, into those places wherein Avalon nursed full strength. To and fro were harried those who were neither of the light nor the Dark—but were prey—

Little things, fleeing without purpose, pursued and attacked by their own fears made manifest and given foul life. They were blind to all but what they unknowingly summoned to their own torment.

The balance was disturbed. In the cities gathered the People. Rita, those others who had accepted Avalon. There stood the Herald who bore the name of this land, and behind him his four pursuivants, Oak and Apple, Thorn and Elder, each wearing the badge of his naming. To the fore of them all was Logos King-of-Arms. He was might, clad not in the brilliant tabard of a Herald, but in a robe of dark blue over which ran runes in silver that twisted, turned, formed words of deep wisdom, and then dissolved to form again. In his hands was a great sword, point down into the soil of Avalon from whose metals it had long ago been wrought. Up the blade of that sword were also runes. But these were fixed for all time, set in the metal by a forging of power in ways now long forgotten, even in a world where time meant little.

Two hands held the sword erect: wide shoulders held proud and straight, and above them a head—The face of one who could summon storms, bind wind and water to his will, yet who disdained to take power for his own desires. Silver hair, bright as the crawling runes. There was a name for this King, a very old name that Avalon knew, which was legend also in another world—

Merlin.

Now the Logos King-of-Arms faced outward from the city. His hands moved, uprooted the sword, raised its mighty weight with ease, pointing it out at heart level. His lips moved, but whatever words he spoke did not issue forth as sound—they were not for the hearing of lesser men or spirits.

The aliens' fan-pole lashed out with scarlet fire, which brought black smoke that settled to stain the land. Where those stains grew so did the Dark Ones spread, creeping toward the cities. And the drawing of the alien power weakened that of Avalon, so that life under it withered and lessened.

But—

There was a flare of force, so great that all that could be seen was swallowed up. All was red and then white. The world was gone, sight was gone. There was nothing.

"Nothing—nothing—" Nick heard that. Understanding returned sluggishly. "Nothing—nothing—" His own voice was repeating that.

He—he was Nick Shaw—and he was alive. But he did not want to open his eyes and see again the awful nothingness that had been the end of Avalon. How could he still live when all else, even a world, was dead?

"All dead—" He put this thought into words.

"No!"

He had not said that. Who was here? Who had escaped the end of Avalon?

"Who—?" he asked.

"Nick! Nick, please, look at me!" Someone—who?

"Who?" he repeated. He was not sure he cared, he was so tired—so very tired. Avalon was gone. In him there welled a vast sorrow. He could feel tears in his eyes, squeezing out under the lids he would not raise. He had not cried for a long, long time—Men did not cry, men could not cry. They could hurt as he was hurting, but they must not cry.

"Nick! Please, can't you help him. Do something—?"

"There is only what he can do for himself."

He had heard that voice before, long ago. In Avalon. But Avalon was gone. He had seen it die. No—worse, it had been his act that had finished it. Nick began to fit together painfully this scrap of memory and that, to form an ugly picture. He had fired upon the fan-pole with the alien weapon. There had been a vast explosion of power. And there had been the Logos King—Merlin—with the sword. But the blasting of the fan-pole must have overbalanced the energies on which Avalon existed. Avalon was gone and where he might be now Nick neither knew nor cared.

"Nick!" Hands were lain on him, their shaking hurt, but the pain of his body was less than of his spirit, the knowledge of what he had unwittingly done.

"Open your eyes, see, Nick, see!"

He opened them. As he thought, there was nothing, nothing at all.

"There is nothing. Avalon is gone," he said into that emptiness.

"What is he talking about? Is he—is he blind?" There was dread in that voice from nothingness.

"He is blind in his own way." Again that other voice from the past.

The Herald! Avalon! But the land was gone, erased into nothingness: How did the Herald still exist?

"Avalon, Tara, Brocéliande, Carnac—" Nick said over those names that had once had great meaning and that he had rendered meaningless. "Oak and Apple, Elder, Thorn, and the Logos King—gone."

"He—he doesn't know what he is saying—" The first voice choked as if someone struggled against crying. "What has happened to him?"

"He believes, and to him what he believes is," Avalon replied.

"You are Avalon," Nick said slowly. "But that is not true—for Avalon is gone. Am I dead?" There was no fear in him now. Perhaps death was this—this nothingness.

"No, of course not! Nick—Please don't be like this! Oh, you can help him. I know you could if you would."

"He must believe."

"Nick, listen!" Someone was so close to him he could feel a stir of breath against his cheek. Breath was life—so that other must be alive. But how could one live in nothingness? "Nick, you are here with us. You somehow blew up that power standard, or whatever it was. And then—everything just happened. The prisoners were able to get out. And the aliens all died. Barry says the backlash of power did it. Their saucers were blown open. Then—then the Herald came, Nick, you must see!"

Something stirred in him. This was Linda. He could give a name to her voice. Linda and Avalon were here with him. He could feel her touch as she held his head against her, he could even hear the beating of her heart. A beating heart was life also.

And if Avalon existed for Linda, how could it be gone for him? Once more he opened his eyes on nothingness. But there should be no nothingness—there should be Avalon!

Nick drew upon his will of concentration. Avalon—let Avalon be!

Sight did not return as it had gone in a burst of fierce light—but slowly. He saw first shadows darkening the blank white of the place into which he had been exiled by his own desperate act. Then those shadows took on substance. There were figures. As he had concentrated on creating illusion, so he concentrated now on the return of a world. Was this an illusion also? No, he must not give room to such a doubt.

There was Linda, watching, concern on her face, in her touch as she supported him. There was Jeremiah, unblinking eyes regarding him, and beyond, standing, so he had to raise his head a fraction to see the better, the blaze of color that was the Herald.

Brighter, sharper, more real with every moment, the world came back. Had he indeed lost his sight so that it had made him believe he had lost all else into the bargain? Nick did not know. All he cared about was that he had been wrong.

He was lying, he discovered, at the edge of what must have been a battlefield for forces, not men. Facing him, one of the saucers had flipped from stilt feet to its side, part of it plowed in a deep gash into the earth. The sight of that tore his mind from his deep self-consciousness to think of the others. He freed himself from Linda's hold, struggled to sit up and look around.

Linda was safe, and Jeremiah, and Lung, for the Peke was pressed close to the girl as if he feared they might be parted. But Hadlett, Mrs. Clapp—the prisoners in the pen—?

"The others," he demanded of Linda. "How are the others?"

She did not answer at once, only looked distressed.

"The Vicar—Mrs. Clapp?" What of those two who had shared this last adventure?

"Over—over there." She put out a hand to restrain him. But Nick pushed it aside and somehow got to his feet.

"Over there" was by the second saucer. There was a rent in its upper surface, its landing ramp was twisted. At the foot of it he saw Crocker and Jean. Mrs. Clapp and Lady Diana were on their knees beside someone stretched on the ground. Nick began to walk, though he felt very lightheaded and dizzy.

"Nick!" Linda was beside him. Before he could resist she had caught his arm, drawn it about her shoulders, steadying him. He did not try to push her away this time. If her help could bring him to the others sooner he accepted it.

He covered the gap, stood with Linda's support, looking down at the Vicar. Hadlett's eyes were open and when he saw Nick he smiled. "St. George," he said, "and St. Michael are supposed to be the warriors. I have never heard it of St. Nicholas that he went into battle, but rather that he was a giver of gifts."

Nick went to his knees. "Sir—" Until that moment he had not realized, though perhaps he had dimly suspected, how close were his ties with this man. Heart-ties Rita had called them. Now he could feel why.

"You won for us, Nicholas. And"—Hadlett turned his head just a fraction in Mrs. Clapp's hold—"I think it was perhaps a notable victory indeed. Have I the right of it, sir?"

Nick realized then that the Vicar spoke to someone behind, and turned his own head to see that the Herald had followed them.

"He has won the freedom of Avalon, and not for himself alone."

"There was a danger then for you as well as us," Hadlett said. "Yet we were not allies—"

"Only in part. Avalon has its laws, which are not the laws of men."

Hadlett nodded, a fractional movement of his head. "That was—" He paused and there was struggle on his face. "That was the truth that I had to abide by. Good may govern Avalon—but it is not—my—good—" A red bubble formed in the corner of his mouth. It broke and a trickle of scarlet came from it.

Nick turned on the Herald. "Help him!"

"No, Nicholas." It was not Avalon, but Hadlett who answered. "To every man his own season. And the season passes. You and I"— again it was Avalon he addressed—"know that. It is given few men to find peace. I am—content. You told me once, Nicholas, that there might be many rivers from a single source. That is also the truth, but we each choose our own. Now, let me enter into my own peace in my own time."

What he repeated thereafter were the words of his own priesthood and belief, the belief he might not surrender to Avalon. Nick could not listen. It was too unfair. The Vicar had given freely, and what came in return?

He pulled loose from Linda, moved away from the others, steadying himself with one hand against the bent support of the wrecked saucer. Before him stretched the open land with a crater rimmed in glassy slag to mark the site of the pole. Had that operated the gateway to the aliens' own world? If so it was closed, perhaps forever.

What would happen to him and his companions now? Would the Dark Tide Rita and the Herald warned of continue to flow? Or had his vision, dream, whatever it might have been, held the truth— that it was the force of the aliens that stimulated and released the Dark Ones, built up their power to spread over the land?

"Nick?"

He did not look around.

"You won't get back through any way of theirs now!" He struck out at her voice.

"No." But she did not sound crushed.

Nick turned his head. Linda stood there in worn and bedraggled clothing, her hair loose about her shoulders, a raw scratch on her cheek, Lung in her arms, as if he were now the only treasure she could ever so hold. She looked forlorn, lost.

"I hope—I hope Dave—" Her voice broke. "No—" She backed away as Nick took a step toward her. "Don't—don't try to tell me— We won't go back, ever. After awhile we're going to forget, I think. The past will all seem a dream. Maybe, Nick, I shall accept Avalon. I must! If I don't—I'll keep on remembering and that I cannot live with!"

"And what about them?" Nick gestured toward the others.

"The Vicar—he's gone, Nick." Tears spilled down her cheeks and she made no move to wipe them away. "And the rest—the Warden was killed in the backlash, as you might have been, Nick—as I thought you were at first." There was fear and horror in her eyes now. "The others—they know now what they must do. And you, Nick?"

"I always knew—after the city. There can be only one way of true life in Avalon. If we would be any more than those miserable human animals I saw in the woods, we must choose that."

He held out his hand, and Linda, cradling Lung against her with her other arm, let her fingers be enclosed in his. Together they started back. After all, Nick thought, in this choice the giving was not so much his. What he received was far the greater.

Avalon the Herald waited for them, the radiance about him very glorious indeed.

Yurth Burden

✵ 1 ✵

The Raski girl made Demon Horns with two fingers of her left hand and spat between them. That droplet of moisture landed, dust covered, on the rutted clay of the road just missing the edge of Elossa's stained travel cloak,, She did not look at the girl but kept her eyes turned to those distant mountain rises, her goal.

In the town hate was a foul cloud to stifle her. She should have avoided the village. None of Yurth blood ever went into one of the native holdings if they could help it. Broadcast hate so deep gnawed at one's Upper Sense, clouded reception, muddied the thoughts. But she had had to have food. A tumble on a stream's stepping stones in the past evening dusk had turned the supplies she carried in her belt pouch into a sticky mess she had jettisoned that morning.

The merchant whose stall she had visited had been surly and sullen. However, he had not had the courage to refuse her when she made a quick choice. All those eyes, and the waves of hate. . . . Now, when she judged she was well beyond the girl who had given her that last salute, Elossa walked faster.

A Yurth man or woman moved with dignity among the Raski, just as they ignored the natives, looking over and around them as if they were not. Yurth and Raski were as different as light and dark, mountain and plain, heat and cold. There was no common ground for their meeting ever.

Yet they shared the same world, ate the same food, breathed the same air. Even some among her kin had dark hair resembling that the Raski wore in tight rolls about their heads, and their skins were not unlike in color. That of the Raski might be brown by birth, but the Yurth, living as they did ever under the sky and the fierce sun, also tanned darkly. Put a Yurth, even herself, into the bodice and ankle-sweeping skirt of the girl who had so graphically made her hate clear, let her hair grow and twist it up, and she might have looked no, or little, different. It was only in the mind, the thought, that Yurth stood apart.

It had always been so. The Upper Sense was a Yurth child's from birth. He or she was trained in its use before plain talk came from the lips. For the Upper Sense was all which stood between them and utter annihilation.

Zacar was not an easy world. Storms of terrible force came in the bleak season, sealing Yurth clans into their mountain burrows, blasting, and overwhelming the towns and the dwelling on the plains. Wind, hail, freezing winds, rain in drowning torrents. . . . All life sought shelter when those struck. That is why the Pilgrimage was only possible during the two months of early autumn, why she must hurry to find her goal.

Elossa dug her staff point into the crumbling clay and turned aside from the road which served farms she could see, the houses squatting drably some distance ahead. For the road, such as it was, angled away from the mountains she must reach. She longed to be out of the plains, higher up into the places of her own heritage, where one could breathe air untainted by dust, think thoughts unassailed by the hate which clogged about any Raski gathering place.

That she must make this journey alone was in keeping with the custom of her people. On the day the clan women had gathered to bring her staff, cloak, supply bag, she had known a sinking of heart which was not quite fear. To travel out into the unknown alone. . . . But that was the heritage of Yurth, and each girl and boy did so when their bodies were ready for the duties of Elders, their minds fallow enough to receive the Knowledge. Some never returned. Those who did were—changed.

They were able to set up barriers between themselves and their fellows, sealing out thought talk when they wished. Also they were graver, preoccupied, as if some part of the Knowledge, or perhaps the whole of it, had been a burden fastened on them. But they were Yurth, and as Yurth must return to the cradle of the clan, accept the Knowledge, however bitter or troublesome that might be.

It was the Knowledge which would itself guide them to their goal. They must leave their minds open until a thought thread would draw them. The coming of that was the command they must obey. She had tramped for four days now, the strange urgency working ever in her, bringing her by the shortest route across the plains to the mountains she now faced, the land no one visited now unless the Call came.

She had often speculated with those of her own birth age as to what must lie there. Two of their company had gone and returned. However, to ask them what they had done, or seen, was forbidden by custom. The barrier was already set in them. Thus the mystery always remained a mystery until one was led oneself to discover the truth.

Why did the Raski hate them so, Elossa wondered. It must be because of the Upper Sense. The plains dwellers lacked that. But there was something else. She was different from the hoose, the kannen, all the other life which Yurth respected and strove to aid. She did not wear upon her body, slender beneath her enveloping cloak, dust plastered from the road, fur or scales. Yet there was no hate for her in the minds of those others. Wariness, yes, if the creature was new come into the places of the clan. But that was natural. Why, then, did those who possessed bodies like her own beat at her with black hate in their thoughts if she was forced by some chance to move among them as she had done this morning?

Yurth did not seek to command—even those of lesser and weaker minds. All creatures had their limitations—even as did the Yurth. Some of her kin were keener witted, faster to mind-speak, producing thoughts which were new, unusual enough to make one chew upon them in solitude. But Yurth did not have rulers or ruled. There were customs, such as the Pilgrimage, which all followed when the time was ripe. Still no one ordered that this be so. Rather did those obeying such customs recognize within themselves that this must be done without question.

Twice, she had heard, in the years before her birth, long ago by the reckoning of the clan, the King-Head of the Raski had sent armies to seek out and destroy the Yurth. Once those reached the mountains they had fallen into the net of illusions which the Elders could weave at will.

Men broke out of disciplined companies, wandered lost, until they were subtly set back on their path again. Into the mind of the King-Head himself was inserted a warning. So that when his brave soldiers came straggling back, foot worn, exhausted, he returned to his city stronghold, and did not plan a third mountain expedition. Thereafter the Yurth were let strictly alone and the mountain land was theirs.

But among the Raski there were rulers and ruled, and they were, as far as Elossa had been able to tell, the sorrier for that. Some men and women toiled all their lives that others might live free and turn their hands to no task. That this was a part of their otherness was true, and perhaps those who toiled had little liking for it. Did they hate their masters with some of the same black hatred that they turned toward the Yurth? Was that hate rooted in a bitter and abiding envy of the freedom and fellowship of the clans? But how could that be, what Raski knew how the clans lived? They lacked the mind-speak and could not so rove away from their bodies to survey what lay at a distance.

Elossa quickened pace again. To be away from this! She was fanciful. Surely no tongue of that black ill-wishing she had "seen" with the Upper Sense reached after her like the claws of a sargon. Fancies such as that were for children, not one old enough to be summoned for the Pilgrimage. The sooner, however, that she was in the foothills, the more at ease she would be.

Thus she walked steadily as the fields about gave way from ordered rows of grain to pasturage, well grazed by hoose teeth. Those patient animals themselves raised their heads as she passed. She gave them silent greeting, which seemed so much to astound them that here and there one shook its head or snorted. A younger one came trotting to parallel her way, watching her, Elossa felt, wistfully. In its mind she detected a dim memory of running free with no rein or lead cord to check that racing.

She paused to give it the blessing of food forage and pleasant days. Back to her came wonder and pleasure in return. Here was one ruled, and yet those who ruled it did not know what manner of life it really was. Elossa wished that she might open the gate of all these pastures, let loose those the fences kept in restraint, that they might have the freedom only one remembered so dimly.

Yet it was also laid straightly upon the Yurth that they must not attempt to change in any way the life of the Raski or their servants. To do so meant using the Yurth gifts and talents in the wrong manner. Only in some crisis, to defend their own lives, might the Yurth cast illusions before their attackers.

Now the pastures disappeared; she entered the foothills of the mountains. The way was rough, but to Elossa it was familiar. She threw off the last of the shadow which had troubled her since she had come through the town. Lifting her head, she allowed the hood of her cloak to slip back so that the wind might run fingers through her pale, fine hair, bring fresh breath to her lungs.

She found faint traces of paths. Perhaps the townspeople came hunting here or they fed their stock among these hills. Yet there was no sign that such trails had been recently used. Then, upon climbing the top of one ascent, she sighted something else, a monolith taller than she when it stood upright, as it must once have been. It was not native to this place, for the rock was not the dull gray of that which surfaced here and through the scanty soil, rather a red, like the black-red of blood which had congealed in the sun.

Elossa shivered, wondering why such a dark thought had crossed her mind when she sighted that toppled stone. She shrank from it, so with the discipline of her kind she made herself approach closer. As she drew near she saw the rock had been carved, though time and erosion had blunted and worn those markings. What was left was only the suggestion of a head. Yet the longer Elossa stared at it, the more that same stifling uneasiness which had ridden her in the town arose to hasten her breathing, make her want to run.

The face was Raski in general outline, still it held some other element which was alien, dreadfully alien—threatening in spite of the veil the wearing of time had set upon it. A warning? Set here long ago to turn back the wayfarer, promising such danger ahead that its marker had been able to give it that distinctly evil cast?

The workmanship was not finished, smoothly done. Rather the rugged crudeness of its fashioning added to the force of the impression it made upon the viewer. Yes, it must be most decidedly a warning!

Elossa, with an effort, turned her back upon the thing, surveyed what lay beyond. With eyes taught by all her mountain training to study and evaluate terrain she caught another remnant of the far past: there had once been a road from this point on.

Stones had been buried by landslips, pushed aside by stubborn growth of bush and small tree. But the very grading which had been done for the placement of those stones had altered the natural contours of the land enough for her to be sure.

A road of stone? Such were only found near the cities of the King-Head. Labor in making such was very hard and would not have been wasted to fashion the entrance into the mountains, in the normal course of events. Also this was very, very old. Elossa went to the nearest of the stones, its edge upthrust as it lay nearly buried in the grass. She knelt and laid her hand upon it, reaching with thought to read. . . .

Faint, too faint to make any clear impression for her. This had returned to the wilds very long ago. So far in the past that the land had accepted it back, laid its own seal upon it. She could sense the trail of a sand lizard, the paw touch of a bander; what lay behind those in time was nothing she could seize upon.

The pavement itself headed for the mountain she must climb, and to use the faint traces of it would lighten her way a little, aid to save her strength for the more difficult task ahead. Deliberately she turned into the roadway. Once a way of importance, it must have been sealed, forgotten, and the fallen monolith set to forbid entrance. Who had done this and why? The curiosity of Yurth minds possessed her; as she went she kept looking for any hint of what had been the purpose of this road.

The farther she advanced along the vestige of highway the more Elossa marveled at the skill and labor which had gone into its making.

It did not take the easiest way, twisting and turning, as did the game trails and footpaths of the mountains she knew, or the clay-surfaced roads of the plains, rather it cut through all obstacles, as if its stubborn makers would tame the land to serve them.

She came to a place where slides had, in a measure, covered what had been a cut into the side of the mountain itself, picking her way over the debris left by those slides with a stout aid of her staff. Still the road headed in her direction, and, because her curiosity was now aroused, she determined to see where it might lead. Though it could be, that before its goal was reached, she must turn aside to fulfill her own quest.

There were no more of such worn-off stones as that left below, but at intervals she did sight small ones, several still upright. On those there were traces of carving, but so worn that the markings were only shadows. None of these gave her the feeling of discomfort as had the one below. Perhaps they had been set another time and certainly for other purposes.

It was in the shadow of such a one that Elossa sat to eat at nooning. She need not even use the liquid in her water flask, for only a short distance away a rill from some higher mountain spring had made a runnel for itself. The murmur of running water was loud enough to be heard. She felt at peace, at one with what lay about her.

Then—that peace was shattered!

Her mind-seek lazily reaching out to engulf the freedom and quiet, brushed upon thought! One of the clans on the same Pilgrimage? There were other clans cross mountain with whom her own people had little contact save during wintering. No, in that short touch she had not caught the familiar recognition which would have signaled Yurth—even Yurth traveling with a closed mind.

If it was not Yurth, then it was Raski. For no animal registered so. A hunter? She dared not probe, of course. Though the Raski hatred was dampened by fear, who knew what might chance were a Raski, away from his own kind, to encounter a single Yurth? She remembered now those on the Pilgrimage who had never returned. There were many explanations—a fall among rocks, a sickness away from all help, yes, even perhaps death by intent from some menace they could not restrain by the Upper Sense. Prudence must be her guide now.

Elossa pulled tight the string of her food bag, picked up her staff, got to her feet, No more easy way by the road. She must put her mountain knowledge to the test. No Raski had the skill of the Yurth in the heights. If she was indeed the quarry now, she was sure she could outdistance her trailer.

The girl began to climb, not with any spurt of speed—who knew—this chase might be a long one and she must conserve her strength. Also she could not stretch the power too far, keeping in touch with the pursuer and still sense out any trouble ahead. That lightest of mind-probes could only be made at intervals, to be sure she was being trailed and not that the other was going about some business of his own on the lower reaches.

❖ 2 ❖

At a point well above the forgotten road Elossa paused to take a breath or two, allow her mind-search to range below. Yes, he was still on a course which brought him in her wake. She frowned a little. Though she had taken precautions against such a thing yet she had not really believed it would happen. No Raski ever hunted Yurth. This trailing was unheard of among her people since the great defeat of the King-Head Philoar two generations ago. Why?

She could stop him, she believed. Illusion, mind-touch—oh, yes, if she wanted to bring her own talent into use, she had weapons enough. But there remained what lay ahead of her. When one set out upon the Pilgrimage there was no hint given by those who had made it of what might be expected. However, there were some warnings and orders, the foremost of those being that she would need all her talent to face what lay ahead.

It was the nature of the Upper Sense in itself that it was not a steady thing, always remaining at the same force no matter how one used it. No, it waxed and waned, must be stored against some sudden demand. She dared not exhaust what she might need later merely to turn back a stranger who might come this way by chance and did not really trail her. Night was not far off and nights in the mountains were chill. Best find a place to hole up for the dark, cold hours. With eyes used to such a task, Elossa surveyed what lay ahead. So far this upward slope had not been enough to tax her strength greatly, but she noted that there were sharper rises beyond. Those she would leave, if she could, for the morning.

She now stood on a ledge which, to her right, widened out. Some drifts of soil there gave rootage to small bushes and grass. Bearing in that direction she came out into a pocket-sized meadow. The same stream which had given her drink near the ancient road fed a spring pool here. Her sweep of mind-search touched birds, several of the small rock-living rodents, nothing more formidable.

Dropping her staff and bag on the edge of the pool, Elossa knelt to splash the water over her face, wash away the clogging dust of the plains. She drank from cupped hands, then took from the breast of her jerkin a disc of metal depending from a twisted chain. Holding this flat on her palm, she gave a last survey, with eye and mind, of her immediate surroundings, making sure she dared to slacken her guard for a short time.

Nothing near which need be watched with caution, though perhaps she was indulging in folly to try this. Still, it was best she knew who or what did follow. If the climber was a hunter, well enough. But Raski acting out of tradition—that was something else again.

She looked down at the plaque of metal. Its surface was clear, but strangely enough did not reflect her face. The disk remained completely blank. Elossa drew upon her power of concentration. Try first to envision something she knew existed in order to prove what she might later see was not just fancy born from her own imagination without her being aware.

The pillar of warning. There was a ripple on the mirror-not-mirror she held. Tiny, a little fuzzy, since distance also influenced reception, the fallen block of stone with a malignant face, now in more shadow with the passing of day, appeared.

Well enough, reception was working. Now for her follower, which would be a far more difficult task since she had never seen him and must project from mind-touch alone. Warily, very slowly, she sent out the questing thought.

It touched, held. She waited for a long moment. If the trailer were conscious of the probe there would be instant response. She would then break that tenuous linkage at once. But he did not react to her delicate probing. So, she applied a stronger send, staring down into the mirror.

Far more fuzzy than the pillar, yes, because she dared not reinforce the linkage past the power she now exerted. But there was a small figure on the mirror. He was dressed in the leather of a Raski—a hunter surely, for he had a bow and a bow case, though he also wore a short sword. His face she could not see, but the emanations of the mind-touch suggested he was young. And. . . .

Elossa blinked, instantly broke the contact. No, the response had not been that of Yurth. Yet that other had come to know that he was under her inspection—not clearly. He had been alerted only into uneasiness.

She considered that with a small measure of unbelief. By all the standards of her own people such awareness among the Raski was impossible. If they had had any of the Upper Sense they could never have been deceived by illusions. Still she was also certain that what she had read in those few moments before she had severed linkage had been right. He knew! Knew enough to sense she was probing.

Which made him dangerous. She could, of course, induce an illusion. It would not last long, no one Yurth had the power to hold such; it required a uniting of energy of many to produce that. But, she sat back and stared into the beginnings of a sunset. There were several illusions useful, the materialization of a sargon for example. No man could hope to stand up to one of those furred killers who killed to drink blood, and which were known to den among the heights. So insane were they that even Yurth could not control them more than to turn them for a space from the path they followed. They could not be mind-spoke, for they had not real minds, only a chaos of blind ferocity and a devouring need for blood.

An excellent choice and. . . .

Elossa tensed. Sargon? But there was a sargon! Not downslope where she had thought to place her illusion, but up mountain. And it was headed toward her! Water—of course—water was needful to all life. This pool beside which she now sat might be the only water for some distance. She had noted the prints in its clay verge of wild birds as well as the lesser paw marks of the monu and mak. Water would draw the sargon.

Nor had this one eaten lately. The consciousness, such as this beast had, was all raging hunger near overwhelming thirst. Hunger, she must play upon that!

No sargon could be turned aside by illusion, and she could not alter its path either. The beast's hunger was too great. Swiftly she loosed mind-search. There was a rog, one of the dangerous beasts who also laired among the mountains. Was it too far away? Elossa could not be sure. It depended upon how hungry the sargon was.

Now working with precision, she fed into that swirling pit of ferocious desire the impression of the rog . . . near. . . . Not only would that mean food and blood to the rabid hunter, but rage at the invasion of what it considered its own hunting ground. For two great carnivores could not occupy the same territory without a battle—not two of these breeds.

She was succeeding! Elossa knew a flash of elation which she quickly dampened. Overconfidence was the worst error any Yurth might pay for. But the beast on the slope well above her had caught her suggestion, was angling away from the pool meadow. Now the wind blowing down mountain brought a trace of rank scent.

Rog, that way, she continued to beam. Yes, the sargon was definitely changing course. She must monitor, though, continue to. . . .

All this was a drain on her power which she had not foreseen.

Elossa held fast. The rank stench grew stronger. That the sargon could pick up her own body scent she did not fear. Long ago the Yurth had discovered various herbal infusions for both the skin and the inner parts of their bodies which destroyed the normal odors such beasts could pick up.

The sargon was running now, the momentum of downslope adding to its normal high speed when on a trail. Already it had passed the meadow and was well below her own position. It was time to withdraw that prick of mind-goad. There was a rog, sooner or later that. . . .

Her head jerked. The now gathering dusk in the lower reaches of the mountain might confuse sight but nothing could conceal that scream of rage and hunger. The rog so close . . . she had not thought it to be. . . .

Swiftly she strengthened her mind-probe and then froze.

Not the rog! Something to hunt, yes, but human! He who had come after her by chance or purpose had been in the right position to be scented. The sargon was after him.

She had sent this horrible death in that direction! Elossa felt cold flooding through her, following that realization. She had done the unthinkable, loosed death at a creature whose species she shared. Raski might be subjected to illusion, they could not be death doomed by Yurth. She had. . . . The horror of her act made her sick. For space of a breath she could not even think, just felt the terror of one loosing forces not to be controlled.

Then, snatching up her staff, leaving her bag of provisions where she had tossed it, Elossa turned back to the slope up which she had climbed. Hers the fault, if she went to death now it was no more than the payment she had so earned. That other had bow, wore steel—but neither could turn a sargon.

She slipped and slid, the skin of her hands scraped raw, intent on keeping her footing. No need to court a fall, which could serve nothing, save perhaps wipe out by death the memory of these past few moments.

Once more the sargon screeched. It had not yet closed in. But how much time had she? Her Yurth-trained mind began to shake free from the shock of knowing what she had done. To go down this way would avail her nothing.

Her staff was no weapon with which to face what would be there. There was only . . . the rog!

Elossa struggled to marshal her thoughts, gather strength. She stood on a small ledge, her back to the rock of the mountain, looking down. The stubby brush of the lower slope hid what lay there.

Rog! Like a summons a battle commander might shout when hard pressed her thought leaped out. It caught that other animal mind, fighter the rog might be and was. Ferocious, it was not insane as was the sargon. Now she thrust with power where normally she would have inserted an idea slowly, gently. Sargon . . . here . . . hunting . . . kill . . . kill!

The other huge carnivore responded. Elossa played upon its hatred, bringing that emotion to a pitch which would have burned out a human mind entirely. The rog was on the move!

Out of the dusk came a second cry—and that was human!

She was too late—too late! Elossa gave a dry sob. Once more she began the descent. There was no more need for the rog to be goaded into battle. It was ready. Now she must seek the man who might be already dead.

Pain, yes, but he still lived. Not only lived but fought! He had climbed to a height where the sargon could not yet reach him. But that would not serve him as a refuge for long. Also he was wounded, easy meat for a furred monster now making a determined effort to pull him down.

Rog. . . .

As if in answer to that thought a third cry sounded. Now she saw. Across the slope, angling straight for the brush-hidden parts below, came a huge dark shape. Standing taller than she at the shoulder, its thick body so covered with dense fur that its short legs were nearly hidden, it scrambled, its claws loosing showers of small rocks, earth and gravel.

Even among rogs this was a giant, old enough to be a wary fighter, for only the strongest survived cubhood. It was indeed a fit match, perhaps the only one for the sargon. As it came it bellowed for a second time, sounding a challenge which, Elossa hoped, might draw the enemy from its final attack upon its victim.

The challenge was answered by a screech. Elossa swallowed. Would the sargon attempt to make sure of its prey before it turned to do battle? She sought to enter the raging mind. Rog! She was not sure that her mental prod did any good now. The mind of the thing was an insane whirl of death and the need for destruction.

Rog! Her urging might be futile, but it was all she could do. She was sure that the man yet lived. For a snuffed life was never to be mistaken. That she would have felt as a kind of diminishing of herself.

Not such a blow as would issue from a Yurth death, still to be picked up.

The rog had halted, in a spray of gravel flying outward from its feet. Now it reared, to stand with its heavy fore-paws, the huge claws visible against its dark fur, dangling. Its head, which appeared to be mounted on no neck but resting directly on its wide shoulders, raised so that the muzzle pointed in the direction of the brush, jaws slightly agape to show the double row of fangs.

Then, out of concealment came the sleek, narrow head of the sargon. The creature screeched once more, threads of foam dripping from its mouth. Long and narrow as a serpent, its body drew together as might a spring. Then it launched itself through the air directly at the waiting rog.

⚜ 3 ⚜

The beasts crashed together in a shock of battle which reached Elossa not only by sight and sound, but as an impact of raw emotion against her mind to nearly sweep her from her own feet before she was able to drop a barrier against it. Rog and sargon were a tangle of death-seeking blows. Elossa crept on hands and feet along the slope above to reach a point where she dared descend. Her duty still lay in that danger spot below. She was certain that he whom the sargon had attacked was wounded. The stab of pain her mind-seek had picked up had been enough of a jolt to suggest he might be in grave danger still.

She slipped downward until the brush closed about her; any sound she might make in that passage was well covered by the clamor of the battle. Once hidden by the growth she got to her feet, using her staff to hold back branches and open a way.

Very cautiously she sent out the thinnest of probes. To the left, yes, and down! Elossa was sure she had the position of the other centered. Shutting her mind against the emanations of rage beamed from the struggling animals, she went on.

The brush thinned out. She was in the open where rocks clustered under the rapidly growing dusk. Though she had closed her mind and the noise from above was ear-splitting, Elossa caught the moan of pain. On the top of the highest of those rocks something half arose, to fall back again and lie, one arm dangling down the side of the

241

stone. Elossa set her staff against a shorter outcrop of rock and scrambled up. There was still enough light to see the limp body with a spreading stain down left side and shoulder.

She moved cautiously, for his body near covered the top of the perch he had found as his only hope of life. Then she knelt beside him to examine a wound which had slashed downward from shoulder to rib, tearing away flesh as easily as one might peel the skin from a ripe fruit.

At her girdle was a small bag holding Yurth remedies. But first, though he had not moved at her coming, she knew she could not work while consciousness remained. Not only was intense pain a barrier to what she must do—and the Raski knew no form of inner control to that—but also she could not heal where a conscious mind could well impede her out of ignorance. Drawing a deep breath the girl sat back on her heels. What she *must* do (for this hurt was her work) went against custom and law of the Yurth. Yet the obligation laid upon her was also ruled by even higher law. What she had harmed, she must try to help.

Slowly, with deliberation and great caution, as she was engaged in a forbidden thing, one she was not trained for, Elossa began to insert her mind-send.

Sleep, she ordered, be at rest.

There was a response. His head jerked against her knee, his eyes half opened. She had touched something, yes. He was still on the borderland of consciousness and was partly aware of her invasion.

Sleep . . . sleep. . . .

That fraction of consciousness faded under deliberate mental command. Now she inserted another order, willing away pain. It was still there, yes, but like a far-off thing. This she had done with animals found injured, with a Yurth child who had fallen and broken an arm. But the animals had trusted her, the child knew what she would do and was prepared to surrender to her. Would it also work for the Raski who looked upon her kind with hatred and suspicion?

Sleep. . . .

Elossa was sure he was past the threshold of consciousness. She could find in her delicate search no further alert against her invasion.

Now she drew her belt knife to cut away the rags of his leather jerkin, the shirt stiff with blood underneath that, laying bare a frightful wound which tore shoulder to hip. Out of her belt bag she took a folded cloth to spread flat upon her knee. Across it was a thick layer of ground, dried herbs mixed with pure fat.

With infinite care she worked to bring together the strips of torn flesh, holding them with one hand while with the other she laid the cloth, bit by bit, over the wounds. Though the blood had been flowing, yet, when that sealing cloth went on, there was no more seepage. In the end the wound was covered from end to end.

Elossa must release her mind-hold upon him now. All her power and skill with the talent had to be centered elsewhere. Slowly, as slowly as she had entered his thoughts, she withdrew. Luckily he did not rouse, at least not yet.

She laid her fingertips along the cloth. Focusing her will, she built a mental picture of healing flesh, clean healing. She must assume that Raski bodies were not too different from those of the Yurth. Blood, she commanded, cease to flow. Cells she stimulated to begin growth of new connecting tissue.

The drain of energy was such that she could actually feel it flowing out of her fingertips into the hurt. Heal! Back and forth her fingers passed, touching lightly the surface of the cloth, sending through that the force of the Upper Sense aimed at this one task alone.

She had reached the end of her endeavor, weariness was about her as an outer skin. Her hands dropped to her sides, her shoulders were bent. The dark had now so enclosed them that she could not see the face of the sleeping man save as a white blue. But he slept, and for him she could do no more.

Elossa raised her head with a great effort. Now she was aware that the clamor of battle was stilled. Her concentration relaxed. She wanted to seek out through the night, but the power was far spent, her whole body was so drained that she could not even move, only sat hunched beside the sleeper, waiting and listening in a dull way.

No sound. Nor did the feeling of aroused fury sweep toward her. She could not seek to penetrate the dark with mind-send. It might be a full day and night, or more, before she might draw back into her even a fraction of the talent she had used.

There was a sigh out of the night. Once more that head moved against her knee. Elossa tensed. She had paid her debt to the Raski but she did not believe that her care of him would in any way mitigate the inborn hatred of his kind for hers. Though she had nothing to fear from him in his present weakened state, still his emotions, if he roused fully, would shatter the peace and quiet she must have to recover her own necessary strength.

Very slowly she pushed away from the man. In spite of her great fatigue she knew that she must make an effort to get away, out of his sight. She slipped down from the rock perch, steadied herself against that while she picked up her staff.

With that to lean on, Elossa turned once more to the slope. Out of the veiling brush she caught the scent of blood, the reek of rog and sargon intermingled. There in the open rested a mass of torn fur, splintered bone, from which all life had fled. Here two monsters, equally matched, had fought to the death of both.

The girl pulled herself past that horrible battlefield, digging the staff in to support herself. There was the sound of sliding gravel, a hoarse clack of bird, a patter of feet Scavengers were coming out of the night. None of that noisome crew need she fear. They would find a feast awaiting.

Up and up. She had to pause often to gather her forces and settle her will the firmer. But, at length, she came into the cup of grass and growth where the spring pool lay. Wavering over, she plunged her face and hands into the sharp chill of the water. Then she fumbled with her provision bag, hunger gnawing within her.

She drank from the stream, chewed food she hardly tasted, struggling to keep awake while she ate. At last she could battle no longer. Around her neck she settled the chain of the seeing disc and that she put by her ear. Though she did not know the reason or the method by which that worked, it was tuned to her personally alone, and, when she set it so, it would rouse her against the coming of any danger.

Thus protected as well as she could be in this wilderness, Elossa stretched out on the tough grass, her traveling cape about her. There was no time tonight for the daily meditation upon all happenings which was a part of Yurth training. Instead she dropped into almost instant slumber as she relaxed her conscious hold on her mind.

Dreams could warn, could instruct, were of importance. For long Yurth minds had investigated, recorded, shifted and judged dreams. They had learned to control them, to pick from perhaps a muddling and puzzling sequence of dream pictures a scrap here, a fragment there, which could be carried over into waking and there answer some question, or propose one to be investigated in the future.

Elossa was very used to dreams, some vivid and alive, some so tenuous they were floating wisps she could not capture even with her training.

But. . . .

She stood on a road, a road of stone blocks fitted together with expert precision and art. Smooth and solid under her feet was that road. It wound on, arose by expert engineering into heights, until her questing eyes could no longer follow it. She began to move along the road, headed toward those heights. Behind her came another presence, but she could not look over her shoulder, she only sensed that it followed behind.

Her feet did not quite touch the surface of that stone way. Rather, she swiftly skimmed above the stones. Up and up the road led, and she went, that other always following.

Distances were lessened by the speed with which she moved. Elossa thought that she must have come a long way since she had first seen the road. Now she was among the mountains. Mists clung to her body, but with the road as a guide she could not lose her way. She passed so swiftly that all around was a blur. There was some need, some desperate need, that she reach a point ahead, though what was that need and where lay that point, she could not understand.

There were no other travelers along the road. Save for that one who came behind, whose speed was less than hers so he did not catch up. But the urgency which filled her was shared by him also. This much she knew.

Up and up, and then came a pass with mountain walls rearing

high and dark on either hand. When she stood in the pass the force which had carried her hither abruptly vanished. Below the mists clung and veiled the lower slopes, the road which lay farther on.

Then, as if a curtain had been drawn aside, those mists were pulled from immediately before her. She did indeed look down, and down, over such a drop as made her dizzy. Still she could move neither forward nor back.

Below were lights sparkling, as if a handful of cut gems had been spilled out. They shone from reaching towers, along walls, outlined great houses and buildings. This was a city far larger, far more majestic and imposing than any she had seen. The sweep of the towers was so marked that she thought at ground level they must seem to reach the sky.

There was life there but it was far away, dim in some fashion, as if another dimension besides distance lay between her and it.

Then. . . .

She heard no sound. But in the air there came a burst of flame as brilliant as an unshielded sun. This flame descended toward the city. Not to its heart, but at the far edge. The flaring outburst reached the wall there, spread over, to lick out at the nearest buildings.

Something hung above those flames. The fire sprouted from the bottom and a little up the sides of a dark globular mass. Down that came. The flames swept out, caught between the ground and the mass, fanning farther and farther.

She was too far away to see what must be happening to the city dwellers as this fate descended to crush and burn. Lights went out. She saw three towers break and fall as the mass riding the flames drew nearer. Then that rested part on the city, part without. Wall, towers and buildings must have been crushed under it.

More flames arose, spreading farther over the city. Elossa wavered where she stood, fighting against the compulsion which held her there. In her there arose a keening sorrow, yet she could not give voice to the great sadness which tore at her. This catastrophe—it was not intended—but it happened and from it came a sense of guilt which made her cringe.

Then. . . .

Elossa opened her eyes. She did not stand in any pass watching the death of a city. No, she blinked and blinked again. For the space of several heartbeats she had difficulty in correlating the here and now with the then and there. There had carried over from the dream the sense of guilt, akin to that which had possessed her when she had realized that she had unwittingly sent death to stalk another.

The first of Zasar's twin moons was well up in the sky, its sister showing on the horizon. The beams silvered the water of the pool, made all within the cup of that small mountain meadow either shadow black or moon white. One of the scavenger birds croaked as it arose sluggishly from its feast.

Elossa settled into a deliberate pattern of even breathing to steady her nerves. That her dream had been one of the important ones she did not doubt. Nor did it begin to blur and fade from her mind after the fashion of most dreams. She had witnessed the destruction of part of a city. But the reason why she had been given this vision she did not know.

She took into hands the seeing disc, being half minded to try a search. Did that city—or had it—ever existed here? Had that road she followed to the pass been the one time had nearly erased? She longed to know. Yet prudence counseled no, she must not again use her talent until she was sure within herself that she had an ample supply of energy.

Slowly she settled back, her hands crossed upon her breast under the folds of her cloak, and clasped in her right one the disc. But she did not fall again into slumber. The memory of her dream was like the dull aching of a tooth, prodding at her mind, plucking at her imagination.

Why and where, when and how? There was nothing in all the teaching she had absorbed from early childhood which suggested the existence of any such city, either past or present. The Yurth did not gather in large cities. Their life, to the outer eye, was primitive and rough. What they did inwardly was something very different. While the Raski, for all their liking to gather in towns and the city of the King-Head, had certainly produced nothing to equal what she had seen in her dream.

No, this was a mystery, and mysteries both drew and repelled her. Something lay within the mountains which was of importance—the very fact of the Pilgrimage testified to that. What would she find? Elossa looked upon the rising moon and strove to put her mind into the serene order demanded by her kind.

❊ 4 ❊

With the coming of day Elossa filled her water bottle, ate sparingly of her supplies, and began to climb again. The freshness of the mountain air drove away some of the shadow which had overhung the day before. There was only fleeting thought of the man below. She had done for him all that she could, the rest depended upon his own strength. To attempt to contact him now might betray herself and her mission.

On and on, the climb was a sharp one. She did not set a fast pace, conserving her energy by seeking out those places which were most easy to pass. Here the wind was chill. Already there were scarves of white snow along the upper peaks. Late summer, early autumn on the plains turned to winter here.

Once when she paused to rest, surveying curiously what lay about her, there was a quick flash of memory. Not too far ahead the rise of rock walls was such as she had seen before. She crouched on a narrow ledge she had been following because it gave good footholds and arose along the slope as if it had been chiseled there to offer a path.

However, this ledge was of natural formation. What lay beyond her perch came from the hands of men, or at least it had been built to answer the demands of intelligence equal to human. There stretched the remains of a roadway.

Surely this could be the same road she had seen leaving the foothills, while before it now lay the pass of her dream. Elossa hesitated. A dream of guidance, showing her where she must go? Or a dream of warning, to say this is not your path? She had no hint of which it might be. To try to learn she summoned the memory of the dream.

In that the road had not been a tumble of broken stone, but firm and whole. Though she had not actually trod upon it, yet it furnished her with a guide. Also a dream, for all the horror of the burning, dying city, had not seemed a threat to her. It was a sending, she decided. Though it had not been beamed by any one of her people, she would have recognized instantly the technique. Therefore. . . . A past shadow?

The theory and explanation of those was as familiar to her as her own name. Acts which aroused great emotion on the part of the actors could impress upon the scene of those acts pictorial representation of the events. These emanations might be picked up a long time later by any whose nature left them open to such reception. She had seen in the past the shadows of three of the King-Head's forces who had gone to their death from a rog attack. Yet those deaths had occurred generations before her own birth. And how much greater the death of a city would be—to imprint the agony of that loss upon the site!

Elossa dropped her head into her hands, forcing away the dream memory, reaching out for the compulsion tie which had brought her on the Pilgrimage. That was there, and it pointed her to the mountain gap! Gathering up her bag and staff, she descended to the ancient road and doggedly continued along that to the pass. She was farther than the length of her staff along that way before she swayed, set her teeth grimly upon her lip.

Though she retreated behind a thought barrier, that was no safe refuge as far as emotion was concerned. It was as if she were now buffeted by unseen blows, all sent to force her into retreat. What lay here had no substance, but to approach was like forcing a way through a knee-high swift current designed to sweep her from her feet.

More than wind flowed through the pass. Anger came, as deep and fierce as the mindless rage of the rog and the sargon, a cry for— for vengeance. Elossa was not aware that her progress became unsteady, that she reeled from one side of the way to the other.

Pulled forward, pushed back—it would seem that the forces here were near evenly balanced and she was the plaything of them both. But she did win forward, even though it was but a step, a half step, length at a time. Breath filled her lungs only in painful gasps. The entire world had narrowed to the broken road, and on that only a few lengths ahead.

Elossa fought. She was so enmeshed now in those two forces she could sense that she dared not even attempt to free herself. No, this she must see until the end.

On and up. Her own breathing filled her ears. Pain looped around her ribs ever more tightly. She would plant her staff in some crack a little before her, and then, by main effort, drag herself to that spot, look ahead for another anchor.

Time itself left her. This might have been morning, or hours near sunset, one day or the next. Beyond and around her now flowed life and time. She was near spent with every step.

At last she stumbled into a pocket of absolute stillness. So quick was the cessation of those two forces which had used her as an arena that she collapsed against a rock, hardly able to keep on her feet.

The girl was only aware of the heavy pounding of her heart, the rasping sound of her breathing. She felt as emptied of strength as she had after she had expended the talent to aid the Raski hunter.

At length Elossa raised her head. Then that harsh, heavy breathing caught in her throat. She was not alone!

Her efforts had brought her to the other end of the pass. As in her dream, mist curdled on the down slope, cutting out all view of the way below and beyond. But, stark against that mist, fronting her. . . .

In spite of control Elossa uttered a cry of terror, fear welled in her. She clutched the staff which could be her only weapon. A length of wood to use against—*that?*

In form it was roughly human. At least it stood erect on two limbs, held two more before it. One of those was half hidden behind the oval of a shield which covered it near throat to thighs. The other, a seared paw, still possessed enough charred bone of fingers to clasp a sword hilt. A skull, blackened by fire, to which strips of burnt flesh still clung here and there, was overshadowed by a helm.

It—it had no eyes left—yet it saw! Its helmed head was turned in her direction. Nothing, no one of her species who had been so burned could live! Yet this, this thing stood erect, the teeth of that horrible skull bared in what seemed to Elossa to be a grin of mockery, born from recognition of her own fear and loathing.

Nothing could live so! She drew several short breaths to steady her nerves. If this thing could not live (and reason came flooding back to her to make that assurance) then it was a thought form. . . .

The thing had moved. To her eyes it was three dimensional, as solid as the hand she herself raised in a gesture of repudiation. Thought form—from whose brain—and why? The shield had swung up to a position of defense, so now only the hollows of the skull's eye sockets appeared above its smoke-darkened rim. The sword was held steady. It was coming toward her. . . .

A thought form—if it followed the pattern of such things—then what it fed upon, to give it more and more solid substance, was her own fear and sickness. It was not alive—save in as much as it could build itself life out of her own emotions.

Elossa licked her lips. She had dealt with illusions all her life. But then she, or those of her kin, had built those. This was totally alien, born of a mind she could not understand. How then could she find the key to it?

It was an illusion! She caught and held that thought to the fore of her mind. Yet it moved toward her, its stained sword raising slowly, ready to cut her down. Every instinct urged her to defend herself with her staff as best she could. But to yield to that demand would be her loss.

Thought form . . . Beneath her first horror and revulsion another emotion stirred. Perhaps that had been born out of her dream. It was not the skeleton apparition before her which caused terror now. No, it was her memory of the destruction of the city which she had witnessed.

Some guard or warrior who had died there. But in whose

memory had such a thing lingered to be thrown against her now? And why?

Guard, of course! A guard who had died at his post. Maybe not a thought form born of any living mind, but rather a lingering of pain and rage so great that it could be projected long after the brain which had given it birth was dead.

"It is over." Elossa spoke aloud. "Long over." Words, what had words to do with this? They could not reach the dead.

But this was only a projection, knowing that she was safe—safe. . . .

Gathering assurance about her as she might the billows of her journey cloak she stood away from the rock against which she had sheltered. The guard was only the length of a sword thrust from her now. Elossa stiffened herself against any flinching, any belief that this might do her harm.

She went forward, straight in the way the dead blocked. It was the most dreadful test she had ever faced. On, one step, two. She was up against the figure now. One more step. . . .

It was. . . . She stumbled as that wave of raw emotion filled her, ate into her confidence, her sanity. Somehow she was through, one hand to her head which felt as if it were bursting with utter terror, terror which was all filling, which overwhelmed her thoughts, left only sensation.

Elossa had walked through!

Now she looked back. There was nothing. It was even as she had guessed. Both hands on her staff, leaning on that as her legs felt so weak that they might give way under her at any moment, the girl tottered on into the wet embrace of the mist which cloaked the descent from the pass.

There were—sounds. Visual had been the first attack, audible was the second. Screams, faint as if from some distance, but not from any animal; rather the last cries of torment and overriding fear too great for any mind to face without breaking. Elossa wanted to cover her ears, to do anything which would shut out that clamor of the dying. But to do that was again to acknowledge that these projections had power over her. She. . . .

Elossa saw a stir within the mist, movement near the ground. She halted as a figure crawled into clear sight. This one went on all fours, had no shield nor sword. Nor were the signs of fire anywhere on it.

Though its progress was that of a stricken animal, slow, painful, yet, it, too, was human. One leg ended in a blob of crushed flesh from which seeped blood to leave a broad trail upon the rocks. The head was raised, forced back upon the shoulders as if the crawler sought ahead of her some goal which was the only hope of survival.

For this thing coming out of the fog was a woman, the long hair, sweat plastered to temples, did not fall forward enough to hide what ripped clothing displayed, while that clothing bore no resemblance to the few scorched rags the guard had worn. Blood-stained and torn though it was, it had been a close-fitting body suit of a green shade, unlike any garment Elossa had ever seen.

The crawling woman reached forward to draw herself on. Then her mouth opened in a soundless cry and she fell, still striving to hold up her head, looking at Elossa. In her eyes there was such a plea for aid that the girl wavered, almost losing control of her own determination not to be misled.

The silent plea from the woman struck into Elossa's mind. This was no figure out of nightmare, but rather one to pluck at her pity in a way as deeply demanding of action as the fear generated by the guard had been. There was a feeling of kinship between them. Though this stranger was not of Yurth, or not of the Yurth blood, Elossa knew.

Help, help me! Unspoken, faint, those words in Elossa's head vocalized out of the emotion rising swiftly to fill her. Help. Unconsciously she knelt, stretched out her hand. . . .

No! She froze. Almost, this illusion had won!

To be caught in an illusion, the primary fear of the Yurth choked her. She hid her eyes with her hand, swayed to and fro. She must not yield! To do so was to surrender all she was!

But hiding her eyes was not the way. As she had done with the guard, she must face squarely this thing born from emotion, face it and treat it for what it was—nothing but a shadow of what once might have been. As the guard had been fed from her fear (and perhaps the terrors of others who had been drawn into this way before her) so would this other be fed by her pity and wish to aid. She must rein that in and not be moved.

Elossa got to her feet. The woman on the ground had raised herself a little, levering her body up with one arm, one hand planted palm down against the stone. The other hand she held out to the girl beseechingly, her need open in her staring eyes, her mouth working vainly, as if she could not force out words, but needs must try.

As she had done with the guard the girl gathered her force of will and determination. Staff in hand she walked deliberately forward. Nor did she look aside from the woman, for such an illusion must be faced in its entirety and without flinching.

On . . . on. . . .

Once more she was engulfed In a flood of feeling, pain, need, fear, above all the plea for aid, for comfort. . . .

She was through, shaking, spent. Once more the mist closed about her as she pulled herself on, striving to shake from her that upheaval of emotion which had attempted to net her a second time and in another and, to her, more deadly fashion.

It was well that Elossa had the road for a guide here as the mist was so blinding that otherwise she could have wandered from her path unknowingly. The badly broken way was sometimes hidden by slides of earth and rock, but ever, as she pushed ahead, she would find it again. Then the fog began to thin. She was coming out of that when again she halted, half turned to face up slope, toward the pass now hidden from her.

That was not illusion! She had been only half consciously casting about with the mind-search to make sure that other things beside the illusions did not hide here. So she had touched another mind, instantly withdrew.

Who?

She must know, even if probing would reveal her to whatever lurked above.

With the extreme caution she must use, Elossa stood on the moisture-slicked rock where the fog condensed some of its substance in drops, and reached out. . . .

It was. . . . He! The Raski she had thought left far behind. Why had he followed her? In spite of the healing she had brought to his wound, he surely had not recovered enough to make such a journey easy. But there was no deception possible in the contact she made. This was the same mind she had touched before. He was here—above. . . .

And. . . . She felt the wash of his fear. The guard—he must be confronting the guard. Without any defense against illusion (for he could not have that by his very nature) how was he going to fare?

Elossa bit hard upon her lower lip. Before, she had been to blame in part for his hurt and therefore she was bound by her honor to come to his aid. This time the situation was different. He had chosen this path of his own free will, not through any control set by her. Therefore she was not responsible for what might issue from his folly.

�֍ 5 ✧

Go forward, commanded logic reinforced by all her training from birth. Still Elossa lingered, unable to break that tenuous contact with the other's fear. Go forward! *This* is none of your concern. This you did not bring upon him. If he chose to come skulking behind, then he must face the result of his folly.

She forced herself to take one step, two, resolutely closing her mind to any more emanation, even though a buried part of her fought that decision. The last tatters of the mist drifted away; now she could see the country below.

And. . . .

Against all logic Elossa had expected to see what her dream had shown her—a city—the thing from the sky which had brought ruin to it. There was indeed the plateau which stretched near as wide as part of the plains she had crossed. At a far distance she could distinguish shadow shapes of other mountains. This range must encircle as a wall on three sides, like arms curved out in protection.

There was no city as such. But when she sighted certain hollows and rises in the plateau (all now cloaked in withering grass) the girl knew that there lay long lost and forgotten ruins. There even arose piles of stones which might be the last vestiges of walls. She turned her head a little to the north, to follow the winding of such a wall. What lay there was not in the city, rather farther away then her dream had shown it. Only a portion of it now arched above the surface, but a dome of top showed still. That was the thing which had descended from the heavens to wreck destruction here.

It was toward that that the Pilgrimage compulsion clearly drew her. The force of that was stronger, urging her to complete her journey as swiftly as she might.

Here the road angled along the wall of the mountain, taking a turn to the left. It was much broken, large portions of it shorn away by sideslips or avalanches. This path was not one for the unwary; one foot misplaced could send her sliding to destruction.

Elossa concentrated all her attention on that descent, taking care, her staff often an anchor over a treacherous bit of path. The journey was longer than she had thought when she had viewed her goal from the heights.

So the sun was well up and it was midday before she reached the level of the plateau. There she paused to eat and drink before she turned from those grass-matted stones toward the dome.

Just as the trail had been longer than she had expected, so now did the ruins loom larger. In many places the mounds topped her head. While from their mass below a chill wind which made her wrap her cloak more tightly about her.

As the ruins had grown taller so did the curve of the buried globe rise higher. In her dream the whole globe had been great enough to blot out a goodly portion of the city; now she could understand how. Judging by the dream, all which remained above the soil now was perhaps a quarter of its entire bulk. Still that stood as high as perhaps three of the Raski dwellings set one atop another to form a tower.

It was uniformly gray in color, not the gray of a natural rock, but lighter, resembling the hue of the sky before the approach of a summer rainfall. As Elossa moved toward it a sighing of wind, blowing through the ruins, produced an odd wailing note. Dared she loose her fancy she could believe that filled with the far-off keening of voices lamenting the dead.

No, she had had enough of illusion! Elossa paused long enough to tap one of the half-buried stones with the end of her staff. It was satisfyingly solid under that contact—no illusion. Wind often had its own voice when it blew around and through rock formations, whether those were natural or man-made.

As she went the ruins grew yet higher, threw their own broken-edged shadows here and there. She found that she must alter her path and go farther in among those mounds in order to reach her goal. Doing so made every nerve shrink, protest.

Death—this was the way of death.

For a long minute the very air curdled, became a curtain, drew apart She saw shapes with more substance than the mountain mist, still they might have been born of that. One such shape fled, the others were hounds behind it, wisps of arms raised. . . . While the shape which fled dodged and turned. . . . There was that in her which answered to it, knew the fear and torment which possessed it.

No! At once she clamped down her mind barrier. The shapes were gone, but Elossa never doubted that once such a hunt had crossed the path she must now follow.

Her energy had been drained, more than was normal, even though she had made that perilous descent of the mountain. She found she must lean more and more on her staff, even pause and rest, breathing fast to draw air into her lungs. She, too, might have been running at the desperate speed of that fog thing.

Her head jerked. The sensation that had come out of the air might have an unexpected blow, pulling her to the left. Now she saw a path winding westward among the mounds. In spite of her efforts at control the ordering of her own body was mercilessly rift from her. She turned, not by her will, but by a compulsion strong enough to override that other she had followed so far and long.

Elossa fought with every weapon of the Upper Sense she could summon. But there was no winning of this battle. She moved along that faint path, pulled by a cord she could not break. Still she also was very much aware that this was nothing of Yurth spinning—rather a contact totally alien to all she knew.

On she went. Now she no longer struggled to break free. The caution in which she had been drilled suggested that both her will and strength might be put to a stronger test in the immediate future and it was well to conserve them now.

The mounds of ruins grew ever larger, loomed over her, shutting out the view of the half-buried dome, sometimes closing off all but a ribbon of sky well over her head. It was in such circumstances that the path ended in a dark opening at the side of one of the mounds. Seeing that ahead and guessing full well that whatever (or whoever) drew her intended that she enter that threatening doorway, Elossa braced herself for a final struggle. So intent was she on marshalling her forces, that she was unaware of what crept behind her.

There came a blow, landing to numb her shoulder so that she dropped her staff. Before she could turn or disengage thought power to defend herself, a light burst in her head and she fell forward into dark nothingness.

Sounds first aroused her from that nothingness. There was the deep tone which made the very air vibrate, and that came at spaced intervals. Her body answered to that beat, quivering as the tone slowly died away, shrinking before the coming of the next deep sound. It was so hard to think again.

Elossa opened her eyes. No sky, no daylight. Here was dark, battled only feebly by a flickering of flame she could see from eye corner. Always that beat of sound enwrapped her, keeping her off balance as she strove to use mind-touch, discover where she might be and who had brought her here.

Now the girl strove to move her body, but she could not stir. She was not held in mind-thrall—very real bonds entrapped her. Rings prisoned her wrists, her ankles, a large one about both her legs at slightly above knee level, and one binding her breast. She was fastened to a hard surface over which she moved fingertips, to learn she lay on stone.

The pound of the sound ceased. Elossa turned her head toward the light. That issued from a lamp, the metal of which was wrought in the form of a monstrous creature sitting up on hind quarters, while the light within it streamed from open mouth and eyes.

So limited was the range of that radiance she could not see beyond the lamp. There lay a darkness as thick as the mist had been in the mountains. However, with that overpowering beat at last stilled, she found that she could gather strength enough to send forth a mind-probe.

The Raski!

There would be no question now of what she must do. Those on the Pilgrimage were pledged and conditioned that nothing must interfere with their quest. Successful accomplishment of such was needful to the Yurth as a whole, for each one who made it and returned added new vigor and strength to the clan. She, herself, had felt that inflow of shared power on past occasions when the Pilgrimage feast was given after a return.

She must complete what she was sent to do. If her success meant the taking over of this inferior and "blind" mind, then that she would do also.

Having located her quarry, Elossa used a strong probe to follow the light contact she held. And. . . .

What she found made her gasp. A layered mind—a double life lying side by side! The one which she sought to reach was guarded by the other. Guarded, or in thrall to? That was only a guess, however, something impressed her that the full truth might well be so.

But the Raski had no mind control, none of the Upper Sense! What stronger mind could be here? She dismissed at once the belief that another Yurth was present. Not only was it against all custom, except in the most dire occasions (such as the one she faced), but what she had probed in the quick instant before her snap of withdrawal had not been Yurth. Nor was it Raski to the extent of the man who had followed her. The possessor was another—another species?

She marshaled her defense, expecting a fierce return probe which would have been natural under the circumstances. What the Raski feared the most was not the tangible weapons a Yurth held but had discarded, rather the mind-send which the plains people considered unnatural and a kind of evil magic. Only now there came no return stroke. Nor did the Raski either move or speak.

Slowly once more Elossa sent out a tendril of mind-seek, not a strong probe, more like a scout sent to estimate the forces of the enemy. The Raski was quiet in body, in mind she touched a seething of force. Hate and vengeance—such as the illusion guard had broadcast on the mountain. A hate which had passed beyond the point of any reason. To all purposes the Raski was now mad, or rather held in the grip of a madman's thoughts.

There were those among the Yurth who could enter into the chaos now whirling in that other mind, bring to it the peace of unconsciousness, until the cause for its trouble could be remedied. But those were old in learning and far more powerful than she.

Elossa dared not maintain contact for more than an instant or so at a time, lest she be caught in that mad whirl of hate and lack of logic, infected in turn. She could not be sure of what she dealt with now. This matter of two different personalities which she was sure were present was unlike ordinary mental imbalance.

She could only continue to pick delicately, striving to find a way into the personality she knew from the mountain trail, discovering a path past the other to reach that. To so strengthen the man she had touched earlier might be a way to defeat the mad thing which had settled into his mind.

Hate, that was like a fire fanned into her face, burning her mind as real flames could reduce her flesh to that which still clung to the charred skeleton of the pass.

No! Do not think of the guard, such memories strengthened the mad thing. As did the illusion form, it could feed on such a memory, grow stronger. Was that what happened to the Raski? Had he made contact with the thought form, and in some way absorbed thereby what rode him now?

Do not speculate! There was not time for anything but to marshal her will against an invasion of hate and fear. Elossa stared up into the darkness over her, unable to see the Raski to focus upon him. She reluctantly withdrew mind-touch lest that other use her own bridge as a path for counterattack.

Emotion charged this space in which she lay securely captive. It pressed in upon her like the beat of the sound which had drawn her from unconsciousness.

She had done nothing to give rise to such loathing. No, that reached from the past, the far past. And it had fed on fear for a long time. Now it was feeding upon the Raski, and it would feed on her also—unless she could hold her guard against it—for a space.

In the dark above her formed a head, the charred bone head of the guard. Skeleton jaws opened: Not with her ears but her mind she heard the cry:

"Death to the sky devils! Death!"

Elossa stared back at the illusion. It began to fade, its jaws still moving to mouth the soundless words. She did have a tie with the Raski who lent his strength, willingly or unwillingly, to this manifestation. Her healing had gone into his body, she had touched his flesh, sending into him the force which was hers to give.

Deliberately she closed her eyes. With one portion of the Upper Sense she kept watch for any sly attack on the mind-touch level. With the rest she began to build an illusion of her own, concentrating into it most of her strength. She had never tried this action before, but when one is faced with a new form of danger one must accordingly change one's defense.

Slowly her eyes opened. There was movement in the air above her where the death's head had hung. But this was her doing. As a worker with colored clay might project upon a stone wall some vision which had before lain only in his mind, Elossa built upon the air the form of her illusion.

There stood the rock on which she had found the Raski, firm and sturdy, gaining solidity with every breath she drew. On it now her imagination, well harnessed and schooled, laid the body of the Raski as she had seen him, the torn flesh, the freely running blood. Then she brought herself into the scene to straightway relive those moments when she had fought to save his life, using all the skills she knew. It was clear, that picture.

As the woman in the vision worked, so did Elossa gather up within her the emotion which such a healer uses—sympathy, pity, the wish for skill to aid what she would do. All the emotions naturally opposed to that burning hate. In the vision she labored to save a life, not blast it.

So, as was always true, emotion fed emotion. The woman strove as she had done to aid the man. Now Elossa turned her head to face the corner in which he lurked. The woman in the vision arose—her hand rested on her breast and then moved outward, as if bestowing some gift freely and gladly. From the outstretched hands of that illusion Elossa strove indeed to make sympathy and good will speed to the one who crouched in the dark.

❈ 6 ❈

The girl continued to beam a sense of healing and that good will with all her strength. In return came only the flame of the mad rage rising higher as if it were fed anew. She could no longer hold her pictured illusion. It winked out as might a lamp puffed by the wind. But the emotion which it had contained she still broadcast.

Friend . . . aid . . . peace . . . freedom from hurt and pain . . . Her whole being was absorbed in sending forth that message.

There was only the very dim lit space above her, empty of any illusion. Into that came a head—not building up slowly as had the skull of her own vision. So dim was the lamp by her side that she could see only half a face, and that was drawn into a grimace which resembled the rictus of the dying.

No vision. This was the Raski who had shuffled to her side, and now stood looking down at her. She saw the working of his mouth, the one eye staring dully in the lamp light.

Peace . . . peace. . . .

A hand came into view, its fingers crooked into the form of talons, held about her as if to rake the flesh from her bones.

Peace—there is peace between us. . . . That hand wavered, clawed down at her, the nails scraping feebly at her tunic. There was little of the human in the face. Elossa was tempted to use the probe, thought better of it. That which possessed this man was alert to what she did.

There could be no hope of a victory fighting on its level. She must rather hold fast to her own, perhaps ineffectual, way of counterattack.

Peace—peace between us, man of the Raski. No harm from me— I have tended your wound, perhaps given you life. Peace between you and me now—peace!

His hand relaxed, fell to lie limply on her breast. Another form of contact! Such could carry a greater charge than thought alone. Now his head bent forward farther into the light. The terrible mad grin which had stretched his mouth began to ease away. That dull stare of the eye which was completely visible changed. Deep in it, she was sure, shone a measure of intelligence.

Elossa gathered all her force for a final attack upon the thing buried in him.

Peace! Though the word was but thought, it held all the power of a shout.

His head jerked as it might from a blow in his face. Now that eye closed, his features went utterly slack as he fell across her, his weight pressing her painfully against the stone on which she lay.

Elossa tried the probe. The rage had drained out of him, or else it had been pushed so deep that she could not reach him without giving that insanity a new gateway to the surface. He lay unconscious—open. Now she could do what would give her an only chance.

Into that open mind she beamed a command. His body arose by degrees, not easily, rather as if he resisted her even though he had no control. She had implanted a single order, and that with all the strength left in her.

Wavering, he swung away from her sight. She thought from a faint sound he must have gone to his knees beside the slab she was prisoned on. There came a metallic sound like unto the click of a shot bolt, the turn of some reluctant locking device. The bands which held her slipped away and she sat up.

The Raski huddled beside that table (or perhaps it was an altar of sacrifice; she suspected that the latter was the truth). He did not stir to impede her as she slipped over the edge of the opposite side and stood up, feeling stiff and sore as if her ordeal in that place had lasted longer than she knew.

But she was unharmed and she was free! Though how long? If she went on her quest a second time, leaving him behind, what was the chance that he would not again be claimed by the spirit which had used his body to bring her down? Very great, Elossa thought. Therefore she dared not go and leave him behind, little as she wanted to take him with her.

She was again breaking custom and the Law of her clan to contemplate such action, yet she could see no choice other than killing a helpless man. That deed would bring on her such a burden of wrong doing that she would be changed irrevocably into someone who could never more be any but an outcast wanderer.

Rounding the table she caught the Raski's head between her two hands, turned his face up into the dim light. The eyes were open, but without any spark of intelligence in them. His features seemed oddly shrunken as if some portion of his life force had drained away.

Elossa drew upon all remnants of her will. There were only remnants now, for the ordeal of her battle with the mad thing had near exhausted her. Holding him so, and looking down into his unseeing eyes, she loosed that which remained of her trained will in a second sharp command.

His body stirred. She held him fast for several breaths more, giving to this all she had left. Then, as she stepped back, he put his hands on the edge of the table altar. Bracing himself against that he got to his feet, stood, his blind eyes on her, his arms now dangling loosely by his side.

Then he turned, stumbling. On into the dark beyond the reach of the lamp he lurched, Elossa after him.

It would seem that this thick dark did not hinder him. She caught at one of the dangling tatters of the jerkin she had cut away from his body to tend his wound. With that tugging in her hand she could not lost contact.

She thought that they were traversing a passage underground, for a dank smell filled her nostrils. Then that ribbon of leather which united them pulled upward at a new angle. A moment later her toes stubbed against a step.

Up he climbed and she followed. The dark so pressed in upon

them that it was an almost tangible thing. What if her hold on the Raski's mind failed while they went this way, and the madness would possess him again here in the blackness? No, do not even think of that, for such thoughts could perhaps unloose in turn just that which she must keep at bay.

On and up—until at last they came to another level hallway. Ahead Elossa saw a grayish glimmer which gave her an instant of excitement and triumph. That must be a door to the outer world!

The Raski went more and more slowly. She read his reluctance. Still she did not try mind contact again. A probe, no matter how delicately used, could well break her hold on him.

They emerged from the fetid and musky darkness into the gray light of early day. Around them hunched the mounds, dark and menacing, like rog and sargon waiting to pull down those who invaded their jealously held territory.

With these so tall about her Elossa was not sure in what direction stood the dome which had drawn her here.

For a moment she hesitated. The Raski wavered on, free of the hold she had kept upon him in the dark ways. He did not turn his head or show any awareness of her. Elossa, with no better guide, came behind.

The mounds ceased abruptly to exist. Here instead was a section where the only signs of the one-time city were lines on the ground. Then even those ceased to be, and they were out in the open traversing an empty space.

Looming above was the dome, its surface dull in this subdued light. The Raski stopped short. His hands came up with one swift movement to cover his eyes. It could be that he refused to look upon the structure ahead, that it implied a threat to which he had no answer.

Elossa caught him by the upper arm. He did not drop his hands nor look at her. Though when she strove to draw him on he resisted her feebly. She had to guide him for he did not change the position of that blindfold of flesh and blood he had raised.

So they came to the foot of the dome. Elossa dropped her hold on her companion. Now. . . . She licked her lips. Though she had not been told what she would find here, she had carried one aid in the quest. She had been given a single word and told that when the time came for its use she would know it.

The time was here—and now.

Raising her head high, the girl fastened her eyes upon the swell of the dome and cried aloud.

There was no meaning in the word-sound—at least none that she knew. The sound itself re-echoed in the air about her.

Then came the answer. First with a harsh grating as if long rusted or deep set metal moved against bonds laid by time. On the surface of the dome, well above her, appeared an opening. That continued to enlarge until wide enough to admit a body. From that doorway sounded another complaint of metal, continuing, as there issued out a curving strip like a tongue aimed to lick them up.

Elossa retreated warily, drawing the Raski with her. The tongue of metal, which had issued with such effort, now curved down, touched end to earth a little to her right. She saw that it was a stepped way. So was she bidden to enter.

Again she dared not release the man with her. What lay within the dome must be the great mystery of the Yurth. But to allow this one free, perhaps waiting as a receptacle for returning madness, would be like setting a weapon edge to her own throat.

She laid hands on him once more only to meet stronger resistance. He voiced a word in a voice so faint that it might have come from a far distance:

"No!"

As she pushed him to the foot of the ladder ramp, wondering how she could force him to climb if he set all his strength against her, he cried out, to be echoed hollowly:

"Sky devil! No!"

However, he was still subject enough to her mind-command that he could not escape and so began to climb, every tense line of his body arguing his struggle to be free. They went slowly. Elossa could see nothing beyond that opening. Nor did she try to use the mind-search to learn what might await them there.

For now she was aware of something else; around her gathered and grew that mad hate she had twice faced and which now began a third assault. The Raski suddenly threw back his head, lifting his face to the sky. He howled, mouthing a cry which held no human note in it.

She feared he would break the mental bond, turn and rend her with the brainless ferocity of a sargon. But, though he howled once more and his fear and rage enveloped her, still her will subdued that in him which struggled for freedom and he continued to climb.

They came to the door. The Raski flung out both arms, caught at the sides of that portal, bracing his body as if this were his last stand against unnamable terror and despair.

"No!" he screamed.

Elossa, now afraid that he would swing around, throw her down the incline of that ramp-ladder, did not wait to send a mind-probe. Instead she thrust vigorously, her hands striking him waist high. Perhaps the speed of that physical attack made it successful. He stumbled, his head falling forward on his chest. Then that stumble continued and he crumpled, to lie motionless.

Elossa squeezed past him, turned and stooped, hooked her fingers in the belt which held his torn clothing to his body. Exerting her strength, she pulled him well into the hall.

Then. . . .

Instinctively she braced her body as one preparing for defense. For out of the air—not in her mind, but rather in words she could understand, though they had a different accent from true Yurth speech—there came a message.

"Welcome, Yurth blood. Take up the burden of your sin and shame and learn to walk with it. Go you forward to the place of learning."

"Who are you?" Her voice was shaken, thin. There came no answer to her question. Nor would there be, some sense within her knew.

The Raski rolled over on the floor, lay staring up at her. There was no cloudiness in his eyes now, rather a fierce, demanding intelligence. He pulled away, to sit up, looking about him as a trapped animal might search for a way out of a cage.

From the doorway sounded once more the scraping of metal.

The Raski whirled but he did not even have time to get to his feet. Inexorably the door slid shut, they were sealed into this place.

"Where are we?" He used the common tongue forged between Raski and Yurth.

Elossa answered with the truth. "I do not know. There was a city . . . in ruins . . . but that you know . . ." She watched him carefully. It was true that sometimes some inner safeguard could wipe from memory all trace of the immediate past—if that memory threatened the well-being of the mind. To her ear his bewilderment suggested this might have happened to him.

He did not answer at once. Instead he surveyed what lay about them, the smooth walls which stretched away to form a narrow hall, no break in them. He frowned as his gaze returned to her.

"City—" he repeated. "Do not tell me we are in Coldath of the King."

"Another place, older, far older." She thought that the King-Head's capital which he named might have been lost in this place when it had been a home for men.

He put his hand to his head. "I am Stans of the House of Philbur." He spoke to himself, she knew, rather than to her, reassuring himself of his own identity. "I was hunting and. . . ."

His head came up again. "I saw you pass. I was warned that when any Yurth sought the mountains I must be prepared to follow. . . ."

"Why?" she asked, disturbed and surprised. This was a breaking of an old tradition and had an ominous sound.

"To discover whence comes your devil-power," he replied without hesitation. "There was . . . surely there was a sargon." His hand went to his side where her plaster still clung to his flesh. "That I did not dream."

"There was a sargon," Elossa assented.

"And you tended this." His hand continued to rest upon his side. "Why? Your people and mine are ever unfriends."

"We are not unfriends enough to watch a man die when we might aid him." There was no need to explain her own part in his wounding.

"No, you are content to be murderers!" He spat the words into her face.

✻ 7 ✻

"Murderers?" Elossa echoed. "Why do you name us that, Stans of the House of Philbur? When has any of the Yurth brought death to your people? When your King-Head came hunting us, swearing to kill us all, man, woman, child, we defended ourselves, not with drawn steel, but with illusion which clouds the mind for a space, yes, but does not kill."

"You are the Sky Devils." He arose, bracing his shoulders against the wall of that hall, facing her as a man might face great peril when his hands were empty of any weapon.

"I do not know your sky devils," she returned. "Nor do I mean any harm to you, Stans. I have come hither by the custom of the Yurth and for no reason which means ill to you and yours." She was eager to get on, to obey the voice which had welcomed her here. That compulsion which had led her to the mountains, and, in turn to the dome, had become an overwhelming urge to go on to some inner place which would show to her what she must learn.

"The custom of the Yurth!" His mouth moved as if he would spit upon her even as had the girl in the town. Anger blazed out of him, but it was not that madness which had controlled him in the ruins. This was natural and not the result of possession.

"Yes, the custom of the Yurth," Elossa returned quietly. "I must complete my Pilgrimage. Do I go in peace to do that? Or is it that I must set mind-bonds upon you?" She believed that she really could not do so. Her energy was far too sapped by what she had called upon to aid her in escape. But she must not let him realize that, and she knew that, above all else, the Raski feared mind-touch for any reason.

However, she could not read any fear in him now. Had he realized in some manner that her threat was an empty one?

"You go." He stood away from the wall. "I also come."

To refuse him would mean a confrontation either at mind level (which she was very dubious about winning) or on the physical plane. Though her thin body could endure much, the thought of such a contact by force was one any Yurth would find revolting. Touch, except for very special reasons and at times when one was completely relaxed, no Yurth could long endure.

She did not know what lay before her; that it was an ordeal, a testing of her kind she did not doubt. What might it be for a Raski intruder? She could envision traps, defenses against one of another race or species which could slay—either mind or body or both. All she could do was warn.

"This is a sacred place of my people." She used the term which he must understand. Though the Yurth had no temples, worshiped no gods that had any symbols, they recognized forces for good and evil, perhaps too removed from human kind to be called upon. The Raski did have shrines, though what gods or goddesses those harbored the Yurth neither knew nor cared. "Do your temples not have sites of Power which are closed to unbelievers?"

He shook his head. "The Halls of Randam are open to all—even to Yurth, should such come."

She sighed. "I do not know what barriers for a Raski may be raised here. I warn, I cannot foresee."

His head was held proudly—high. "Warn me not, Yurth woman! Nor believe that where you go I fear to follow. Once my House dwelt in Kal-Nath-Tan." He made a gesture toward the door through which they had come. "Kal-Nath-Tan which the sky-devils slew with their fire, their wind of death. It is told in the Hearth-room on my clan house that we once sat in the High Seat of that city and all within raised shield and sword when they cried upon our name. I am the last to bear the sword and wear the name that I do. It would seem that Randam has ordained that I be the one to venture into the heart of the sky-devil's own place.

"Other men of the clan have come seeking. Yes, we have followed Yurth hither. One in each generation has been bred and trained to do so." He stood away from the wall, straight and tall, his pride of blood enwrapping him as might the state cloak of the King-Head. "This was my *geas* set upon me by the very blood within my veins. Galdor rules in the plains. He sits in a village of mud and ill-laid stone. While his House of Stitar was even not numbered in the shrine of Kal-Nath-Tan. I am no shieldman of Galdor's. We of Philbur's blood raise no voice in his hall. But it is said in the Book of Ka-Nath which is our treasure: there shall rise a new people in the days to come and they will rebuild what once was. Thus we have sent the Son of Philbert each generation to test the worth of that prophecy."

Oddly he seemed to grow before her eyes, not in body but in that emanation of spirit to which the Yurth were sensitive. This was no hunter, no common plains dweller. There was that in her which recognized a quality which she had not been aware any Raski possessed. That what he said he believed to be the truth she did not question. Nor was it beyond possibility. The very fact that he had been so possessed by the hatred and need for vengeance which hung like a cloud of swamp fog here could be because of some ancient blood tie with the long dead.

"I do not deny your courage, nor that you are of the blood of those who once dwelt in this place you give name to, but this is Yurth." She gestured to what lay about them. "Yurth may have set defenses. . . ."

"The which may act against me," he interrupted her quickly. "That is true. Yet it is set upon me—a *geas* as I have said—that I must go where the Yurth who comes here goes. Never before has one of us been able to penetrate within this place. Yurth has died, and so have those of the House of Philbur, but none of my clan have won so far. You cannot keep me from this now."

She could, Elossa thought. It was plain that this Raski did not understand the breadth and depth of Yurth mind control. Only in her at this moment there was not enough strength to take him over or immobilize him against his will. She schooled herself against any concern. He swore he would do this thing; very well, let any ill results from his folly be upon his own head. This time she was in no manner to be held in blame.

Elossa turned and started down the hall. She was aware, without turning to look, that Stans followed. It was time to forget about him, to concentrate all which remained of her near-exhausted Upper Sense on what lay ahead.

She opened her mind fully, waiting to pick up a guide. Elossa fully expected to find such, but nothing came in reply to her questing. The dome might be as sterile and dead as the ruins her companion had named Kal-Nath-Tan. The hall ended in what appeared to be blank wall.

Still this was the only way and she must follow it to the end. However, as she was still a step or two away from that dead end, the wall broke open along a line she had not seen, a part of it moving to her left and leaving the way open.

There was a light within this place which came from no bowl lamp or torch, rather from the ways themselves. So now she did not face darkness, rather a well in which a stair wound around to a center pole. Part of it went down, the rest climbed to disappear through a hole above. Elossa hesitated and then made her choice to go up.

The climb was not too long, bringing her out in a room where she stood looking around her with a heart which suddenly beat faster. This chamber was totally unlike the bare caves of the Yurth or their summer-time huts of woven branches, just as it was different from the squat, dull dwelling of the Raski.

It was not bare. Around the circular walls stood set boards covered with opaque plates. Before these, at intervals, were seats. While one section of the wall itself was a huge plate, much larger than all the rest, confronted by two seats side by side. Directly behind these twin seats was a taller one of such importance that it drew her eyes in compelling way.

Hardly knowing why she did, Elossa crossed to stand with her hand resting on the back of the chair. Her touch alerted at last what she had been seeking—a guide. Once more there rang the deep "voice" which had greeted their entrance.

"You of Yurth, you have come for the knowledge. Be seated and watch. No longer shall one of you look upon the stars which were once your heritage, now you shall see rather what was wrought on *this* world and what part those of your blood played in it. For it was recorded and it comes from out of memory banks—that you may learn. . . ."

Elossa slipped into that throne-like seat. Before her stretched the wide screen. Now she collected her whirl of thought.

"I am ready." But she was not; there was a rising sense of something far more potent than uneasiness, this was the beginning of fear.

On the opaque screen before her there was a flicker of light which spread out from a center point to cover the plaque. The light vanished. She looked out upon a vast stretch of darkness in which there were only a few clusters of tiny, brilliant points.

"The star ship Farhome, in the colony service of the Empire, Year 7052 A.F." Impersonal that voice, with nothing of human in it. "Returning from placing a colonial group on the third planet of the Sun Hagnaptum, three months out in flight from base."

A star ship! Elossa licked her lips. Stars there were to be seen, yes. Also she had been taught that far away and small as they looked in the night sky, they were in truth suns, each perhaps with worlds, such as this on which she now stood, locked in patterns of orbit about them. But never had it been suggested to her that man might actually cross the vast void of space to visit another of those planets.

"On the fifth time cycle," continued the voice, "there was radar contact made with an unknown object. This was identified as an artifact of unknown origin."

On the surface of the picture before her came into view a small object which grew quickly larger and larger, leaping toward the screen she watched until she involuntarily flinched.

"Evasive tactics proved valueless. There was crippling contact made. A quarter of the crew of the Farhome were killed or injured by that encounter. It was necessary to set down on the nearest planet, since the matter transferer was completely wrecked.

"There was a planet just within range which offered a possible refuge."

Now a globe snapped into view, grew larger and larger, until first it filled the screen, and then continued to enlarge in one portion, Elossa could see, until mountains and plains were thoroughly visible.

"A site away from any inhabited section was chosen for a landing. Unfortunately there was a human error in the data given the computer control. The landing was ill-chosen."

Another change appeared in the picture. Rushing toward her now were mountains, cupping a piece of level territory. Situated there—the city! Surely that was, though strange when viewed from the air above and so, to her, out of focus, the same city she had seen in her dream.

Faster and faster the picture produced more details, spread out farther. They were coming down on the city! No!

Elossa cried that aloud and heard her voice ring around the chamber. Fire spread outward in a great fan, bit down into the city. Then all was fire, and, in that instant, the screen went dead.

"More of the ship's people were killed by a bad landing," the voice continued. "The ship itself could not be raised from where it had crashed. The city. . . ."

Once more the screen came alive and Elossa looked upon horror. She could not even control her eyes to close them against that view. Fire—the impact of the globe ship itself—death spread outward from where it had set down.

"The city," continued the voice, "was slain. Those who survived were in shock. All they had left was mad hatred for what had been done to them. They were warped, maddened by the blow. Their condition was an infection, a disease."

Elossa witnessed, unable to turn away, other terrors. The issuing forth of the ship's people to try to aid, their hunting down and slaying by the insane natives. Then came degeneration of those natives, eaten by a trauma which spread outward from the dead city, infecting all that came in touch with its fleeing people, the fall of a civilization.

The people of the ship, the handful that remained, gathered together, accepted the burden of the wrong they had done. Though it was the fault of only one, yet they took upon them all the responsibility. The girl saw them using certain machines within the ship, deliberately turning upon themselves a power she could not understand, resulting in the punishment they sought. Never again could those so treated by the machines hope to rise to the stars. They were earthbound on the world they had ravished, whose people they had broken.

However, from the use of the machines which forbade them flight there came something else. Within them awoke the Upper Sense, as if some mercy had been so extended to lighten the burden of their exile.

"There is a reason for everything," the voice continued. "As yet Yurth blood have not found the final path they must walk. It is laid upon them never to stop the seeking. It may be given to you, who have made the Pilgrimage now, to find that path, to bring into light all those who struggled in the darkness. Search—for some time there will be such a discovery."

The voice was still. Elossa knew without being told that it would not speak to her again. There flowed in upon her such a sense of loss and loneliness that she cried out, bowed her head to cover her face with her hands. Tears flowed to wet the palms of those hands. It was such a loss which even the death of someone she was kin to could not equal. For among the Yurth there were no close ties, each was alone within himself, locked, she saw now, in a prison she had never understood before. Until this moment she had accepted this loneliness without being aware of it. That, too, the machine which had awakened the Upper Sense had left with them as dour punishment.

She could feel now, deep in the innermost part of her a glimmering of need. What need? Why must the punishment be laid upon them over and over, generation after generation? What was it that they must seek in order to be entirely free? If not to reach the stars from which they had been exiled, then here, that they need not always walk apart—even separate always from their own kind?

"What must we do?" Elossa dropped her hands, and stared at the dark and lifeless screen. She had not used mind-speech, her demand had been aloud, delivered to the dead silence of the room.

❈ 8 ❈

Elossa did not expect any answer. She was certain she would never hear that voice again. Whatever result might come from this widening of her knowledge would be born from her thoughts and actions alone. Slowly she arose from the chair. Just as the Upper Sense had been drained by her exertions to reach this end of her quest, so now was hope and belief in the future ebbing from her.

What was left for the Yurth? They, whose blood had once dared the star ways, were planted forever on a world which hated them—outcasts and wanderers. Of what purpose were they? Better that they take steps now to erase their existence. . . .

Bleak and bitter thoughts, yet they clung to her mind, made the world look gray and cold.

"Sky-devil!"

Elossa turned to meet the eyes of the Raski. She had forgotten him. Had he seen what she had been forced to witness, the destruction of the world which had been that of his blood and kin?

She held up her hands, empty and palm out. "Did you see?"

Had the pictures on the screen been for her alone, cast there by a mental force denied his kind? Now he tramped forward. The madness did not haunt his eyes, he was all man, not possessed by any emanation from the dead. His face was sternly set—and she could no longer use a mind probe to read his thoughts! It was as if he, too, had one of the barriers the Yurth could set about them.

"I saw." He broke the small moment of silence which had fallen. "This—" He slapped the back of the chair in which she had sat with force enough to make it quiver a little as if it were not firmly fastened to any base. "This—ship—of yours gave death to the city. But not only to the city." He paused as if searching for words to make his meaning very clear to her.

"We were a great people—did you not see? We were not then dwellers in ill-made huts! What were we, what might we have been had this not come to us?"

The girl moistened her lips with the point of her tongue. For that she had no answer. It was true that the city she had seen both in her dream and on the screen was something greater than any existing now on this world. Just as, and now she would admit it, in her eyes this Stans was different from the Raski she knew. In him must linger something of the ability which built Kal-Nath-Tan.

"You were a great people," she acknowledged. "A city died, a people were left in shock and despair. But—" She moistened her lips again. "What happened after?" Her own mind began to throw aside the heavy load of sorrow and despair which had clouded her thoughts.

"What happened here was long and long ago. Not in a few years does nature so overlay ruins—or this ship be buried so deeply. Why have your people not found again their stairway upward? They live in their mud huts, they fear all which is different from them, they do not try to be other than they are."

His frown was black, his lips parted as if he would shout her down, she felt his rage building. Then. . . . The hand which had been deep clenched upon the back of the chair loosened its hold a trifle.

"Why?" he repeated. She thought he did not ask that of her in return, but rather of himself.

The moment of silence between them stretched even longer this time. His intent stare had shifted from her to the now dead screen behind her shoulders.

"I never thought—" His voice was lower, the anger in him was yielding. "Why?" Now he demanded that of the screen. "Why did we sink into the mud and remain there? Why do our people bow knee to a King-Head such as Galdor who cares nothing save to fill his belly and reach for a woman? Why?"

Now his eyes came once more to her. There was a fierceness rising in him as if he would have the answers out of her by the force of his will.

"Ask that of the Raski," Elossa answered him, "not the Yurth."

"Yes, the Yurth!"

She had made a mistake, focusing on her once again his attention. Still, though there was still anger in him, it was not so great.

"What have you of the Yurth?" He watched her warily as if he expected her at any moment to produce some weapon. "What have you that we hold not? You live in caves and branch huts, no better housed than the rog or the sargon. You wear rough cloth such as cover our laborers in the fields. You have nothing of outward show— nothing! Yet you can walk among us and each and every one, even full of hate, will not raise hand to you. You weave spells. Do you then live among those spells, Yurth?"

"We might. We do not choose to do so. If one deceives himself then he loses everything." Elossa had never really talked to a Raski except on small matters, such as chaffering for food in some market place. What he said, yes, it was a puzzle. She glanced around her at the chamber in which they stood.

This had been made by Yurth, the same Yurth who now lived, as Stans had pointed out, in caves and huts far more primitive than the dwellings of the Raski. Cloth of her own weaving was on her body, and it was coarse and near colorless. She had never really looked upon herself, her people. She had accepted all as part of life. Now, drawing even a little apart, she wondered for the first time. Their life was deliberately austere and grim. Part of the punishment laid upon them?

The same years had passed for Yurth as for Raski. Even as the Raski had not regained what they had lost, so did the Yurth make no move to better the punishment laid upon them. Were both races to live ever so?

"Deceive himself?" Stans broke into her thoughts. "What is deceit, Yurth? Do we inwardly say, we of the Raski, great things were taken from us, so we dare not try to rise to such heights again? Is this our deceit? If so it is time that we face the truth and do not flee from it. And you, Yurth—you who had the stars, because one of your blood made a mistake long ago—are you to walk in penance forever?"

Elossa drew a deep breath. He had challenged her. Perhaps Yurth had gained much with the awakening of the Upper Sense. But, also, perhaps they had accepted that as much of life as they could expect. Now she had a question of her own.

"Have you never asked such questions before, Stans of the House of Philbur?"

He still frowned, but not at her, she guessed. Rather he was seeking some thought he had not tried to capture before.

"I have not, Yurth."

"My name—" Oddly irritated at his form of address, the girl interrupted him, "—is Elossa—we count no Houses in our reckoning."

He looked startled. "I thought—it was always said among us— that the Yurth never spoke their names."

It was her turn to be surprised. What he said was true! She had never known a Yurth to talk so easily to a Raski that names were exchanged. Thought the Raski, by custom, were always ready to give their own and that of the First Ancestor of their House. Yet to her now it seemed needful that he stop calling her "Yurth," perhaps because she knew that among his own kind that was a term which was unpleasant.

"They do not," Elossa admitted now, "to those outside the clan."

"But I am not of any clan of yours," he persisted.

"I know." She raised her fingers to press upon her temples. "I am confused. This—this is different."

He nodded. "Yes, Yurth and Raski, by rights we should be in arms against each other. I—I was so earlier. Now I am not." His astonishment was apparent. "In Kal-Nath-Tan there was a horror which entered into me and I did what that made me do. It was not me, and yet a part of me welcomed it. Now I can only wonder at that and see it for a part of the darkness which was, which has always lain there. I ask no forgiveness of you, Elossa." He stumbled a little in pronouncing her name. "For a man who is bred to a task must see it through to the best of his ability. I failed in part, but I do stand where none of my kind have before. I have seen yonder—" He pointed to the screen. "—of the beginning of our hatred, and, also, for the first time seen what I cannot yet understand, the lack in us which keeps us what we are—dirt grubbers who do not dream.

"Are dreams illusions, Elossa? Your kind spin them to aid you. But it seems to me that dreams can in a way serve a man better. He must have something beyond dull thoughts centered on himself and the earth under him to become greater. You Yurth conquered the stars. You are not sky-devils as we think. Now I know that. Rather you are people such as ourselves who had a dream of far voyaging and lived to make it come true.

"Where lies that dream within you now, Elossa? Has it been killed because of your feeling of sin and guilt? What do you think beyond yourselves and the ground under you?"

"Little," she answered quietly. "True we seek purpose in all dreams, but we do not use them to change our lives. We are as bound by ancient fears and fates as you. We use our minds to store of knowledge but only within narrow limits. To us the Raski are alien. But why?" She hesitated.

"Why should that be so? In the beginning because you would have been hunted and slain by those maddened by the catastrophe we saw pictured. Later, when your power of mind changed, you— you no longer thought us of any more account than beasts of the woodland. We two speak the truth here and now—is not that the truth?"

"We were lesser beings, children, to move hither and thither at your bidding when we crossed your path or caught your notice in some fashion. Can you not see that by such an opinion of us you fostered and kept alive the shadow born in Kal-Nath-Tan?"

Elossa accepted the logic of what he said. The bitterness of the city's destruction, the coming of a space-traversing race such as the Yurth destroyed and then replaced with another pattern of thinking. How—how arrogant the Yurth had been—were! They had locked themselves in that arrogance, seeking, they believed, to atone by their own self-exile and austerity. But what they did was sterile, worthless.

Granted that at first they could not live at peace with the Raski, granted that their employment of their machines had altered them irrevocably, yet as time passed they might have sought contacts, turned their talents to the service of the Raski instead of jealously using the Upper Sense for unproductive learning. Their pride of martyrdom was their abiding error. She recognized for the first time Yurth life for what it was, and knew sorrow that it had not been otherwise.

"It is so," Elossa said sadly. "We judged you, and you have been right to judge us. Repentance is necessary, but there are other forms of righting a wrong. In choosing our selfish one we have only compounded the original act many times over. Why have we not seen this?" She ended with rising passion.

"Why have we not also seen that we lie in the dust because we have allowed the past to bury us so?" he countered. "We did not need Yurth to build anew. Yet no man reached for the first stone to set as a foundation. We have been locked in our pride also, we of the House of Philbur, looking always to the past and seeking only vengeance for what dashed us from our throne. We have been blind and groping."

"We have been blind and not even groping," she matched him. "Yes, we have talents but we use them only in a little. What might grow here if we harnessed them to a freed will and a living cause?" It was as if she were awaking in this instant from a drugged and drugging sleep in which she had lain all her life, awaking to understand the possibilities which could be ahead. But she was only one. Against her the weight of tradition and custom stood strong, perhaps too stout a wall for her to hope to break.

"Where do we go now, and what do we do?" She was at a loss, seeing this new-found enlightenment as perhaps an even more weighty burden to bear.

"That is a question for both of us," he agreed. The tenseness had gone out of his body as he fronted her. "The blind do not always welcome sight thrust upon them. They must wish it or they will be frightened. And fear feeds anger and distrust. Between us lies too great a chasm."

"One which can never be bridged?" There was a lost feeling in her. In part this emotion was like that which had come upon her when she witnessed the Yurth farewell to the stars. Were they to be ever imprisoned in the narrow cleft of their misreading or responsibility?

"Only, I think, when Yurth and Raski can speak one with the other face to face, setting aside the past with a whole heart and mind."

"As we have done here?"

Stans nodded. "As we have done here."

"If I," she said slowly, "return to my clan and tell them what has happened, I am not sure I will be heard with any open minds. There are illusions here. We have both dealt with those, suffered from them. Those who made this Pilgrimage before me must have faced the same or their like. Therefore it can be said that I am suffering from a more subtle and deadly illusion. And," she was being honest not only with him but herself now, "I think that that will be said. At least by those who have made the Pilgrimage and know the nature of this place."

"If I," he echoed her, "now return to my people and preach cooperation with the Yurth I shall die." His words were blunt but that they were in truth she did not doubt.

"But if I return and do not share what I have learned," Elossa continued, "then I am betraying that part of me which is the deepest and best, for I shall testify to a lie which I might have threatened with the truth. We cannot lie, not and remain Yurth. That is another part of the burden laid upon us by the Upper Sense."

"And if I return and am killed for speaking the truth—" He smiled a faint shadow of a smile. "—then what profit do my people gain? So it would seem we must be liars in spite of ourselves, Lady Elossa. And if it be true that you indeed cannot lie, then you face even worse."

"There are mountains here," Elossa said musingly, "and I can live alone. Yurth blood has this—we are not bred to soft lying or over much food. Who can tell what may lie in the future? Another may come here on the Pilgrimage and see as clearly. A handful of such, from small seed do high-reaching trees eventually grow."

"You need not be alone. Our own enlightenment is not yet old. Maybe some thinking together upon ways and means can show the two of us how we can do better than stay in perpetual exile. I know that the Yurth choose to dwell apart. Do you still hold to that, also, my lady?"

He was using the address of a high-born Raski to one of equal breeding. She looked at him in wonder as he raised his hand and held it out to her. What he suggested countered every teaching of her life to this minute. But was it not that teaching which had laid hampering bonds upon all her and her blood? Was it not that which must be broken?

"I do not hold to that which would imprison the mind in a false way of thought," she replied. She put out her hand slowly, fighting the distaste for flesh meeting alien flesh. There was so much she would have to fight, and to learn, in the future. The time to begin was now.

✳ 9 ✳

There was a bite in the wind which wailed and moaned around the last vestiges of Kal-Hath-Tan, raised grit of sterile earth to add to the mounding which already half hid the death ship from the sky. Elossa, in spite of her life among stark heights, knowing well the breath of winter there, shivered as she stood at the foot of the walkway which led up into the ancient Yurth ship.

It was not only the chill of that wind which troubled her, there was an inner chill also. She, who had come here to seek out the Secret of Yurth after the custom of her people, had made a hard choice indeed. Learning the manner of the burden which death had laid upon her kind, she had deliberately thereafter chosen not to follow the years-old pattern and return to her clan but rather to try to think in a new way, to hunt a middle road in which Yurth might some day be at peace with Raski and the past be as buried as Kal-Hath-Tan and the ship.

"There is harsh weather to come." Her companion's nostrils quivered as if, like any of the feral dwellers in the heights, he could scent some change in wind which was a warning. "We shall need shelter." It was difficult for Elossa to believe, even now, that she and a Raski could speak together as if they were of one blood and clan. Most carefully she kept tight rein upon her thought-send, knowing that unless she was ever aware of that, she might unconsciously communicate, or try to, without words. While to the Raski such communication was a dire, abhorred invasion.

She must learn carefully, if not slowly, since they had made this uncertain alliance. Stans claimed to be of a House which had ruled in Kal-Hath-Tan, bred and trained himself for the task of revenge upon the Yurth. But he was also the first of his blood to enter the half-buried ship, and therein learn the truth of what had happened in the very long ago. Learning so, he had deliberately set aside his long-fostered hatred, being intelligent enough to understand that, grievous as the destruction of the city had been through an error of the Yurth space ship, yet upon his people also lay some of the fault. For what had happened since? They had allowed themselves to sink back from the civilization they had once known, choosing to be less than they might be.

Yurth and Raski—Elossa's whole person shrank from any close contact with him, even as he must find in her much which to him was unnatural and perhaps even repulsive.

He did not look at her now, rather he stood gazing out across the mounded ruins of the city toward that distant rise of hills and heights on the other side of the cup-like valley in which Kal-Hath-Tan stood. As tall as she, his darker skin and close-cropped black hair was strange to her eyes. He wore the leather and thick wool of a hunter, and the weapons he carried were those of a roving plainsman.

Accustomed to the standards of the Yurth, Elossa could not truthfully judge, she decided fleetingly, whether he might even be termed fair appearing or not. But his determination, his strength of spirit and resolve, that she accepted as fact.

"There is still time," she said slowly.

As if he, too, had the Yurth power of mind-speech, Stans answered her before she had put her thought entirely into words.

"To forget what we heard and saw, Lady? To go back to those who are willfully blind and who squat in the mud like children who are self-willed and resist all which they should learn? No." He shook his head. "There is no longer any such time for me. Yonder—" With one hand he sketched a gesture to the distant hills. "We can find shelter. And it is best that we strive to do so. Winter comes early in these heights and bad storms strike sometimes with little warning."

Stans did not suggest that they take refuge in the ship, or in that chamber in the mound where he had imprisoned her on her first coming into the ruins. In that choice he was right, Elossa knew. They must both be free of the ancient taint which stained all which lay here. Only away from the evidences of the past could they really confront the future.

Thus together they struck out from ruins and ship, While the star ship's entrance closed behind them, sealing the secret once more to be ready at the coming of another Yurth seeker. Perhaps a seeker who might also be persuaded to realize the truth that what lay in the years behind must not be held about one as a cloak to deaden in turn the future.

Clouds gathered overhead and the wind grew stronger, pressing at their backs, as they crossed the valley, as if it moved to expel them from both ruins and ship. Stans went warily, continually eyeing the terrain ahead as if expecting some attack. Elossa allowed her mind-search to range a little. There was no life here. But she felt it was best not to bring to the attention of her companion the results of a gift so dreaded and hated by all his kind. This, save for them, was a barren land, left to the long dead.

The pace Stans set was one she could match with ease, since the Yurth had long since been a roaming people. He did not speak again, nor had she any reason to break the brittle silence lying between them. Their companionship was too new, too untested. And she had no desire to do that testing.

Twilight was upon them well before they had even reached the foothills—though those were clear-cut now, looking as stark and barren as the plain over which they journeyed. Stans halted at last, pointing to the left where some stones stood tall as if growing tree-like from the ground.

"Those can be a windbreak, unless that changes direction." He spoke for the first time since they had left the ruins. "It is the best shelter we can find hereabouts."

Elossa eyed those stones more doubtfully. She had good reason to believe that they were no natural feature of the earth and plain, rather more ruins. The illusions which might cling to such a place were ever in her mind. Even though such manifestations were only hallucinations to be controlled by Yurth training, still the very vividness with which they could paint themselves on the air could not but stir fear, and fear works upon the stability of the most disciplined mind.

Only Stans was very right, they could not keep on going through the night which was coming so fast. Even a faint promise of shelter away from the wind was to be sought. These are stones only, she told herself. If they hold aught of emotion, an imprint on them strong enough to summon illusions to torment the sensitive, she must armor herself with the truth and dismiss such visions for what they were.

As the Raski had pointed out, they did afford a windbreak. So when the two travelers hunkered down among the rocks they were, for the first time, out of the push of that cold. Elossa opened her journey bag.

Food, drink, both were problems they must face now. The supplies she had carried were scanty and not meant to serve more than one for a few days. She broke one of the coarse meal cakes carefully apart and offered half to Stans. There was water in her bottle, though they must limit themselves to sips until they discovered some river or spring in those heights ahead.

He did not refuse her bounty and he ate slowly as one mindful that every crumb must be found and munched. Of the water he took very little. When he had done he nodded to the hills ahead.

"The Naxes rises there. Water and game. . . . Also. . . ." Stans paused, frowning, as if his own thoughts had become a puzzle. He rubbed his hand across his forehead and continued, but it was as if he spoke more to himself than to the girl beside him. "There is the cave—the Mouth of Atturn."

"The Mouth of Atturn," she repeated when he again fell silent. "You have knowledge of this place?" The tradition of his House had made him in this generation the guardian of Kal-Hath-Tan. Did he also know more of what lay about the city?

His frown was more intense. "I know," he said with such sharpness as to warn her off any further questioning.

So wrapped in their cloaks they slept behind the stones until

Elossa was jerked suddenly out of slumber by some inner warning triggered by the Yurth talent. Over her crouched the Raski hardly visible in the night's darkness. Some trick of the small starlight from overhead touched upon what he held—a bared knife.

Elossa rolled to one side as the knife struck down into the earth where she had lain. But the blow intended to bury steel in her flesh, now slicing into the ground instead, threw Stans off balance. She rolled again, setting between them one of the stones. Getting to her feet now, her staff in hand, the girl waited, her heart beating with force enough to shake her body.

Ruthlessly she reached out with mind-touch. The wildness of thought she so found was near as upsetting as that attack had been. This was like tapping a mind gone insane. Horror and fear held the Raski in tight grip. And she had a glimpse of a distorted monster. He—he thought that was she!

"Stans!" She cried aloud his name, striving to so awaken him. For it seemed to Elossa that only a man in the hold of a compelling nightmare could be so disoriented.

She heard an answering cry, wild and beast-like. Then she saw him beyond the stones. He was running, on into the darkness of the night. And he went like a man pursued by an unbelievable source of terror.

Shaking, Elossa put out one hand to the stone behind which she had taken refuge. What had happened? All she could guess in answer was that uneasy fear which had been hers earlier—that these stones might generate illusion and one such had worked upon the Raski strongly because of his very heritage.

There was no use in running after him. If the stones were the source of his terror, then once he was out of range, his sanity should again be in control. She opened her mind wide, sent out a questing which lasted only an instant or two since she had no desire to attract any influences which might abide here.

Stans—he was still in flight. She had no desire to try to compel his return. Such an attempt might only heighten his distortion of mind at present.

Once more Elossa settled down in the lee of the stones. To all her cautious probing these remained only rock. It would seem that if they did exude some illusions such were a menace to Raski only.

Though she was uneasy and wanted to stay on guard, she drifted once more into sleep. Then, for a second time, she awoke into dire danger. For she opened her eyes, instantly awake, only to believe for a second or two that she was still caught in some particularly vivid dream.

This was not the plain where she had fallen asleep by the rocks. Instead she stood leaning on her staff in a narrow valley between two rises of hills. There was a season-killed and dry looking brush about. But in the middle of that, directly before her, crouched a sargon, its snarling echoed from the hill walls as a heavy menace.

The beast was a young one, perhaps of this season's litter. But even so immature a sargon was more than a match for any human. While the creature seemed somehow to guess that she must be helpless prey.

Frantically Elossa summoned the authority of mind control. But it was as if her trained thought was over-slow. She could not hold this raving beast nor turn it! She was going to be torn by those claws. She was. . . .

Out of the air came a shrill singing sound. The sargon's flanks quivered as it gathered strength to launch itself upon her. But now it yowled and in its throat showed the shaft end of a crossbow bolt.

Elossa came to life. She unleashed at the creature the full power of her talent. While, at the same time, she flung herself to one side even as she had moved to escape Stans' attack.

The sargon squalled, clawed with one paw at the wound in its throat from which poured a flood of dark blood. Elossa flattened her body tight against the wall of the hill. Between her and the wounded beast there was only a thin growth of brush which the creature could easily break through. But with her thought she prodded as best she could.

As if it had not seen her part-escape moments earlier, the sargon charged forward, breaking down brush. Blood spouted, as its exertions speeded the flow. Again that wailing in the air and a second bolt drove into the body of frantic beast, placed behind one of its forelegs.

Sprinkling blood widely, the sargon whirled around. Once more it did see her. It was readying for another spring. She could not control this raging alien mind. No one could make a sargon do other than its own will—or. . . .

Perhaps it was the feeling that death was very close to her which speeded Elossa's own thought processes. She dropped her vain attempt to somehow divert the attention of the beast. Instead, with a burst of energy which she rose to only under the lash of fear, she created an illusion. A second Elossa (not too carefully depicted, but at least in the animal's sight enough like its intended prey to draw its attention) now stood before the sargon. The illusion turned and ran. The sargon squalling aloud in its pain and blood lust swung its heavy body around once more to pursue.

It must have so presented the unseen bowman with a better target. For with a third shrilling of flight a bolt found its target. The sargon flung up its head, opened its jaw for a great roar. But it was not sound alone which burst from the beast. Rather a second outpouring of blood fountained down to earth. The creature took one step and a second, and then toppled. Though it still fought to regain its feet and its cries sounded strongly, the end had come.

Elossa needed the support of the bank against which she had taken refuge. That last outpouring of her talent had weakened her as she had seldom been since the earliest days of her training. It would take much rest until she could once more summon even the lightest of mind-power to her service.

She lifted her head as pebbles and earth cascaded down the hillside across the narrow valley. Stans half slid down in their wake. She could not test his mood by her only defense, not in her present condition. Though if he meant her harm now he need only have allowed the sargon to have its way. Or was it that some touch of the ancient revenge bred in him still worked to the point that he must take Yurth life by his own hand?

She stood quietly. In fact she could not have fled, even if she so wished, all the energy having seeped out of her. He paused, watching her across the body of the sargon. Then, without word he knelt to work his bolts out of the still quivering carcass, deliberately cleansing each in a fashion by driving it point down into the earth and plucking it forth again.

He no longer looked at Elossa. It was as if she were invisible. Nor did he speak. What would happen now? Her distrust of the Raski had awakened once again. Perhaps there was too great a gulf between their two races for any amount of good will to bridge.

Restoring his bolts to their quiver Stans got to his feet again. Now he did face her. There was a shade of expression on his dark face but she could not read it.

"Life for life." He spoke those three words as if they had been forced out of him against his will. What did he mean? That this was in payment of the succor she had given him when he had been clawed by a similar beast on the journey to Kal-Hath-Tan? Or had he saved her now because his attempt in the night had failed and he would be quit of the memory of that? She felt blind when she could not mind-probe for the truth.

"Why," she said at last, "why would you take knife to me? Is your hate from the old days still so strong, Stans of the House of Philbur?"

He opened his mouth as if about to answer and then closed it firmly once more. There was about him an aura of wariness as if he were fronting a possible enemy.

"Why must you take my life, Stans?" she asked again.

He shook his head slowly. "I do not kill," he began and then his head came up proudly and he met her in a fast locking of eyes.

"It was not I. This is a haunted land. It had secrets of things we Raski have long forgotten, which perhaps even you Yurth, with all your dark powers, never knew. There was another will taking over my body. When it did not win what it wished, it left me. I—" Again he frowned. "I think it is different—not Raski as I know, not Yurth. . . . It is very dangerous—perhaps to the both of us."

That this world might have secrets was, indeed, not impossible. Elossa turned her head to look up at the hills about them. They could go back, put into some corner of their minds to be walled there, all that had happened, all they had learned concerning themselves and their people. But she did not believe that was possible. To go on was to venture into the totally unknown. Yet she had a certainty growing within her that this was what could be the only road for her.

"We must go on," Stans said. "There is that—it is like Kal-Hath-Tan—it draws. Or does not that drawing touch you, Lady? I know that you may have no trust in me now, yet in some manner we are bound together."

Elossa tried to summon the talent—to judge—perhaps to feel what he said lay upon him. But she was too exhausted. If she went it would be going blind for a space until her energy was renewed. Resolutely she pushed away from her support.

"I have found water, also the path to the Mouth," he said then. "It is not far."

"Then let us go." So she chose a new road for the second time.

10

So this was the Mouth. Elossa hitched the carry cord of her supply bag up higher on her shoulder, studying the opening before her. Undoubtedly the place had been, or was, some cave opening, natural in these heights to begin with. But there had been the work of man overlaying that of nature. A portion of rock surrounding the opening had been smoothed to provide a surface into which were deep carven, strange mask-like faces.

Or were those separate faces? Rather, it seemed to the girl that they were the same face expressing different emotions, mainly, she decided, malignant ones. Now she asked of her companion, breaking the dividing silence which had lain between them since they had begun the climb to this place:

"You name this 'Mouth of Atturn,' who then—or what then—is Atturn?"

Stans did not glance toward her at all. Instead he faced the dark opening of the Mouth, into which daylight seemed reluctant to reach, with a faint shadow of fascination on his face. The Raski did not answer at once, as if her words reached him so faintly he scarce heard them at all.

"Atturn?" Now his head did turn slowly, reluctantly. "Atturn—Lady, I do not know. But this was a place of power for the ruling House of Kal-Hath-Tan." He rubbed one hand across his forehead.

"One of your legends? But there must be more," Elossa prodded. Before she entered such a place she wanted to learn all she could. Her experience with Stans in that other underground place beneath the ruins was not such as to encourage her to try a new venture into unknown darkness.

"I—no, I have not heard of this place. But how could that be?" He was plainly not asking those questions of her, rather of himself. "I knew, knew the way to this place, that it lay here, that it was shelter. How did I so know that?" That last question was aimed at her this time.

"Sometimes things heard sink into the memory so deeply that only a chance happening calls them forth again. Since the House of Philbur, as you have said, was made protector of the secrets of Kal Hath-Tan it may well be true that this is another scrap of knowledge you ingested without remembering clearly."

"Perhaps." By his expression he was not convinced. "I only know it was necessary for me to come here." He stepped forward as one obeying an order he could not refuse, to pass under the band with its faces on into the Mouth.

But Elossa had one last trial to make. Though her store of energy had been sadly depleted, still she must draw what she could for this testing. She summoned mind-search and loosed a probe into the cave. Stans she could pick up instantly, though she made no attempt to contact him—he was merely a registration of consciousness. There were other flickers of lifelight—far down the scale—perhaps insects or other things for whom the Mouth was hunting ground and home. But nothing approaching larger beast or human.

So reassured, she followed on into the dark. For dark it was beyond the small apron of light by the entrance. It was not a cave after all—rather the door to a tunnel.

"Stans!" She paused to call out, having no mind to go blindly on alone. In these heights there must be other caves, ones unused by ancient custom, clean of any man-taint. She knew so little about Raski beliefs. But there was a fact which all Yurth accepted: a place which had been the focus for any emotional experience (and that included temples and ancient dwelling places high on such a list) gathered over

the years an aura of force to which those sensitive enough to possess
the talent of her people were drawn, maybe even influenced by.

Elossa, remembering that, instantly closed her mind. Until she
could be sure no such influences lay here she could only depend upon
her body senses. And she felt as one crippled as she hesitated before
the dark boring.

"Stans!" she called again.

"Hooooo!" The sound was so echoed and distorted that she could
not even be sure the Raski had voiced that call. Then it came again.

"Commmmeee!"

Elossa moved on, cautiously and slowly. She so longed to loose
the talent. As her eyes adjusted to the dark she saw very pale bits of
radiance along the way. One of those moved and she stopped,
startled, stared closer.

A moth or some like winged creature near the size of her own
palm was struggling in a web, fighting frenziedly for freedom. It was
the lines of that web which gave off the faint light. Then there
dropped down toward the fighting prisoner a blackish ball to strike
full upon the moth.

Elossa shuddered. Now she could see other spots of the pale
light—more webs spun to catch the unwary. Perhaps their light was
the lure to bring their victims closer.

She kept well away from the webbed walls as she went, still
slowly. Her staff was now her protection, for she swung that ahead in
a slow sweep from side to side to make sure that the way was open.
Imagination kept painting for her a picture in which such a web, only
a thousand times larger and thicker, might be set across the tunnel
itself.

Stans had gone this way, she told herself. Sense did now,
however, banish such erratic trails of fear. How had he gotten so far
ahead? He must have quickened pace considerably since he had left
her company.

Elossa longed to hear his voice, but something kept her from
another call. She walked a little faster. Now the lighted webs were
missing. Perhaps they only hung where flying things who had
blundered in from the outer world could be enticed.

The darkness was very thick. She felt as if she might reach forth a hand and gather folds of it into her grasp, as one did a shrouding curtain. But the air she breathed was fresh enough and she was aware that there was a small steady current of it now and then touching her cheek.

There came a glow—a sudden leap of red-yellow flames. After the time in the utter dark these seemed nearly as bright as full sunlight and she blinked to protect her eyes against that glare.

Stans stood there, and in his hands was a torch burning bravely. He was thrusting the butt end of that into a stone ring jutting out of the wall as if he knew very well what he was doing. His past denials of such knowledge now made Elossa doubly uneasy.

The torchlight revealed a chamber which must have begun as a cave. But here man's hands had also smoothed and labored to pattern the walls. What the light shone the strongest on was a giant face which covered near the whole of the wall directly ahead. The mouth about a third of the way up from floor level was wide open, a dark cavity into which the light of the torch did not penetrate far.

Eyes as long as Elossa's forearm were pictured wide open. Those did not stare blindly ahead as might those of a statue. Rather they had been fashioned of material which gave them a glitter of life so that she felt that the thing not only saw her but derived some malicious amusement from her presence.

Stans lighted a second torch which he pulled from a tall jar to the left of the face. When he placed that in a twin ring on the opposite side the light was enough to give even more of a knowing look to the stone countenance. The other two walls were bare so that all attention was focused entirely on the leering, jeering face.

Such objects in themselves have little or no natural evil—that comes from without. To say that a carving on the wall was evil was to impute to stone a quality it did not and never had possessed. But to say that an image which had been wrought by those who wished to give evil a gateway into the world was malign was not opposed to that basic truth.

Whoever had carved the face on the wall had been twisted mind and spirit. Elossa had stopped short only a step within the cave room.

The illusions which haunted the road to Kal-Hath-Tan had been horrible—born of human suffering to leave the imprint upon the very earth itself. This, this had been cunningly and carefully constructed, not out of great pain of body and shock of spirit, but from a deep desire to embrace all the dark from which man naturally shrinks.

Stans had taken a stand before that face, his arms hanging by his sides, gazing up into those knowing eyes with visible concentration. Almost, Elossa thought, as if he were indeed in communication with whatever power that brutish carving represented.

She kept tight rein upon her talent here, having a feeling that if she loosed even a little—sent out any probe—what might answer would be. . . .

Elossa shook her head. No! She must not allow her imagination to suggest terrors which could not exist. That this may have been a "god," the focus for some horrible and evil religion, and so have drawn to it the energy sent forth by the worshipers, perhaps even the terror of sacrifices, that was the truth. But in itself it was nothing but cleverly fashioned stone.

"Is this Atturn?" She felt the need to break the silence, to shake Stans out of that concentration. He did not answer. She dared to go forward, and, putting aside the distaste of the Yurth for body contact, she laid her hand upon his arm.

"Is this then Atturn?" she repeated in a louder voice.

"What?" Though Stans turned his head to look at her Elossa felt he did not really see her at all, that his gaze did not meet hers but in some manner still set upon the face.

Then there was a flicker of change in his expression. That deep concentration broke. That he came alive again was the only way she could explain the change in him to herself.

"What?" He swung away from her to look once more at the face, so well lighted by the torches he had set "What? Where? Why?"

"I asked . . . is this. . . ." Elossa gestured to the face. "Atturn. He . . . it . . . seems certainly to have a mouth."

Stan's hands covered his eyes. "I—I do not know. I cannot remember."

Elossa drew a deep breath. Last night this Raski had tried to kill her as she slept. In the light of morning, after she in turn had been possessed (for what other than possession had sent her sleep-walking then into the path of the sargon) he had saved her life. He had brought them here, plunging through the darkness of the tunnel as if he knew what lay at its end, lighted the torches with the surety of one who knew exactly where to find the waiting brands and the strike stone.

"You know this place well indeed," Elossa continued, determined to pin the Raski to some admission. "How else could you have found those?" She pointed to the torches. "A hidden temple for your ancient vengeance to which you have brought me for slaying."

She did not know why she chose to make that accusation; it was out of her mouth almost before she realized what she said. But the possible truth of it alerted her to a danger which might also be real.

"No!" He threw out his hands as if he were repulsing that gap-mouthed face, repudiating all that it might mean. "I do not know, I tell you!" His voice was heating with anger. "It is not me . . . it . . . is something else which makes me its servant. And . . . I . . . will . . . not . . . serve . . . it!" He said that last sentence slowly and with emphasis upon every word as heavy as a blow he might seek to deliver against an enemy's body. That he believed in what he said now Elossa did not doubt. But that he could summon any defense against the compulsion which had twice ruled him, of that she had no surety at all.

The Raski swung around, his back to the face. There was a demand for belief in his expression. His mouth firmed into a thin line of determination, his jaw squarely set.

"Since I cannot control this—this thing which moves me to its will—then it is better that we part. I should walk alone until I can be sure that I am not just a tool."

That made good sense—except for one thing. The night before she had in turn been moved unknowing, walking in her sleep, straight toward death. Yet her race had bred into them, or she always so believed, mental barriers against any such tampering. No Yurth could master the mind of one of his fellows, nor could he control even a Raski, who had no such safeguards, for more than the building of short-lived hallucinations.

This was not a matter of hallucinations, it dealt with mental power of sorts on a level totally foreign to Elossa. And that aroused a sickly dread within her. Yurth talent had always seemed supreme, perhaps they had grown unconsciously arrogant in what they knew and could do. Perhaps even, her mind produced a very fleeting thought, it was the burden of the old sin which hovered ever over them as a true necessity to preserve their code of what the talent might and might not be used for.

Was it because she had shrugged aside Yurth Burden that she had somehow also fallen under the command of this unknown factor which Stans recognized and which she must believe had some existence? If that were her fault, then it was true she, as much as the Raski, had assumed a new burden—or curse—and must learn either to dispel or bear it.

"It moves me also," she said. "Did I not nearly walk into the jaws of a sargon without being aware of what I did?"

"This is not Yurth." He shook his head. "It is somehow of Raski— of this world. But I swear to you, on the Blood and Honor of my House, I know nothing of even any legend of this place, nor how I have been led to where it lies, nor why I am here. I do not worship devils, and this is a thing of evil. You can smell its stench in the air. I do not know Atturn, if this is Atturn."

Again she must accept that he spoke what was to him the utter and complete truth. Raski civilization had ended once in the great trauma of the destruction of Kal-Hath-Tan, the which she had witnessed herself in a vision. Though the people lived on, some inner spring of their courage, pride, and ambition had been broken. Much which must have been known in the days before the Yurth ship had blasted their city certainly was now lost.

Yet they stood now in a center of power. She could detect its force, like small fingers sliding over the shield she kept upon her mind, as if something curious and very confident strove to find an answer to the puzzle she presented. The farther they could get from this place, the better.

Elossa swayed. Through that mental shield, seemingly through her body, too, with a flash of pain as might follow a stroke of enemy steel had come that cry, Yurth! Somewhere—not too far away—one of Yurth blood was in danger, had loosed the call which was the ultimate in pleas, that was used only when death itself must be faced.

Without thinking she instantly dropped her barrier, sent forth her own questing search call. Once more came the other, lower, far less potent.

Which way? She had swung around to face the tunnel opening. Outside—which way? She sent an imperative demand for the unknown to guide her.

For the third time the call sounded. But not from the direction she was facing at all. No, behind her. Elossa pivoted to front the face. The seeing eyes glittered with malice. That call had come from behind—from out of the face! Yurth blood spilt here in some ancient sacrifice, leaving a strong residue of emotion which another Yurth could tap? No, it was too vivid in that first summons. Surely she would have sensed the difference between a reminder of the dead and a plea formed by the yet living. There was a Yurth in peril here somewhere—behind the wall and the evil, open mouth of Atturn.

✷ 11 ✷

Now it was Stans' hand which caught at her.

"What is it?"

"Yurth," Elossa answered distractedly, so concentrated on trying to trace that cry that she did not even try to free herself from his unwelcome touch. "Somewhere there is Yurth blood in trouble. Somewhere—there!"

The girl went to her knees before that open mouth in the wall. Recklessly she aimed a thought-probe.

Yurth! Yes, but—something else also . . . alien. . . . Raski? She could not be sure. She forced herself forward and lifted the staff, pointing one end of it into the mouth as if it were a weapon both to attack that which might lie waiting in the shadowed pit of the opening, or defend herself against that which might issue forth.

The shaft slipped in and in. That opening was no shallow one. It was as if it were a second entrance leading perhaps to another way through a maze of threaded caves. She must know. . . .

Elossa closed her eyes, drew steadily upon what energy had returned to her. Yurth—where waited Yurth?

Her thought touched nothing, no mind. Still she was very sure there had been no mistaking that first cry. Where then? A sound shattered her concentration. Startled, she glanced up from where she crouched with nearly all of her staff fed into the open mouth. Stans swayed, his hands clawed at the breast of his jerkin as if those fingers would forcibly strip the clothing from him, while his face was such a mask of mingled fury and fear that Elossa started back, jerking the staff free of the mouth to hold ready in her own defense.

As he weaved from side to side she gained a strange impression that he was fighting, fighting something she could not see, perhaps something which lay within himself. A small fleck of foam appeared at one corner of his twisting lips. He gasped, hoarse sounds at first, then words:

"Kill—it would have me kill! Death to the sky-devils! Death!"

Now it was he who went to his knees. As if he could not control them, his hands shot toward her, fingers crooked, reaching for her throat.

"No!" That cry was close to a scream. With a visible and terrible effort he swung his body half around, brought both fists down on the upper lip of the stone mouth. There was a crack opening in that stone, blood on his knuckles. The stuff of the face crumbled as if it were no more than sun-dried clay. It sloughed away, not only that protruding portion of the lip where the full force of his blow had fallen but more and more—cracks running up and down—away from that point of contact. Shards of what had seemed solid rock cascaded down into rubble on the floor.

Even those eyes shattered with a high tinkling sound as might come from the cracking of glass. Those, too, sloughed away, fell to become a powder-glitter. The face was gone. Only a hole framing darkness, into which no bit of the torchlight appeared to enter, marked now the mouth of that god—or devil, or whatever the face on the wall had been intended to portray.

But with the crumbling of the mask there was a change in the chamber. Elossa straightened, feeling as if she had just loosened, to drop from her shoulders some burden she had not been aware until that moment she carried. What was gone was the presence of evil, vanished with the destruction of the face.

Stans, still on his knees before the hole, shivered. But now his head came up and the conflict which had distorted his face was gone. There passed a shadow of bewilderment across his features and then came purpose.

"It would have made me kill," he said in a low voice. "It would drink blood."

Elossa stooped and picked up a bit of the rubble. It seemed strange that Stans' single blow had brought about such complete destruction. Between her fingers this bit had the solidity of stone. Though she applied pressure she could not crush it further.

She might not understand what had happened, but what must be done now was plain. If she were to answer that plea from Yurth to Yurth, she must enter what had been the Mouth of Atturn. Though every instinct in her arose in revulsion against the act.

"You did not kill." The girl once more picked up her staff. "Therefore it did not rule you, even though it tried." She had no idea what that "it" might be. In this place she was ready to accept belief in some force, immaterial perhaps, wedded to the face. Why Stans' blow had been enough to send it into oblivion (if he had, the chance might well be that this freedom was only a temporary thing) she might not understand. But she must accept a fact she had witnessed.

He stared straight at her. His frown was one of doubt.

"This I do not understand. But I am myself, Stans of the House of Philbur! I do not answer to the will of shadows—evil shadows!" There was both pride and defiance in that.

"Well enough," she was willing to agree, "but there lies the road for our taking now."

Elossa had not the slightest wish to crawl into the mouth. Only that age-old compulsion laid upon her race—that no cry for help sent mind to mind could be disregarded—was such that she could not deny it.

It was Stans who wrested one of the torches from its holder and who then, with that in hand, got down to crawl through the mouth. Elossa hesitated only long enough to seize upon another of the unlit brands stacked in the corner of the cave. With that, and her staff under one arm, she followed.

The light of the torch was dimmer somehow than it had been in the cave room, while the passage remained both low and narrow, to be negotiated only on hands and knees. Stans' body half blotted out the light ahead, but there was very little to see, save that the walls of this rounded way were smoothed and the flooring under them, though stone, was also free of even dust or grit.

Elossa had to struggle against a rising uneasiness. This was not to be recognized, as she had the atmosphere in the cave room, as from any real cause. It was rather that she was aware that over and around her was solid stone, the weight of which was a threat. The memory of how that which had appeared firm in the form of the face had so easily shattered under Stans' single blow was ever in her mind. What if an unlucky brush against ceiling or side wall brought about such a collapse here, to bury them without hope or warning?

Then she saw Stans' dark body disappear. But the light he had carried, after a swing out of sight, swiftly dropped again to guide her from that worm's path into again a larger space.

There had been no attempt here to trim walls or smooth flooring. This was a cave nature had wrought. A drift of sand and gravel lay at her feet as the girl stood up beside the Raski. Perhaps one time water had washed its way through here as some earth-hidden stream.

Stans swung the torch back and forth. Its light did not reach to any roof over their heads; they might well be standing at the bottom of a deep chasm, while the side walls showed faults and breaks in plenty. There was no indication which of those might mark an exit.

Once more Elossa shut her eyes and centered her talent upon a seeking-thought. No answer. Yet she was sure that that Yurth cry had not been followed by death. That ending would have reached her as a shock since she had held her mind open to pick up the smallest hint of response.

Stans moved slowly along the walls, deliberately shining his torch into each fissure he passed. But Elossa had sighted something else. The drifted sand on the floor did not lay smooth and unmarked in all places. Though it might be too soft to hold any recognizable print yet she was sure that what she sighted well to the left were traces left by the feet of some traveler.

"There." She indicated them to the Raski. "Where do those lead?"

He held the torch closer, then followed the scuffed marks. Those headed directly to another fissure, seemingly no different from the rest.

"This is deeper," he reported, "well able to be a way on—or out."

At least this time they did not have to go on hands and knees, though the way was a very narrow one and in places they had to turn sidewise to struggle through, the rough rock scraping their bodies. Nor did the path run straight as the two others they had followed.

Sometimes they had to scramble up a steep rise, climbing as if the way were a chimney. Again there came a sharply right-angled turn left or right. Then a last effort issued them into a second rough cave.

The torch was sputtering near its end. Elossa was well aware that they had been traveling a long time. She was hungry and, though they had taken sips of water from their journey bottles (filled to the brim at the stream Stans had found before they entered the mouth) there was a dryness which seemed to come from the very air of this maze to plague their mouths and throats.

This new cave was small and what they faced along one side was a wall, plainly built by purpose to be a barrier. The stones which formed it were not laced together by mortar. But they had been wedged and forced solidly into a forbidding mass.

Stans worked the butt of the torch into a niche at one end of that wall, then ran his hands along its rough surface.

"It is tight enough," he commented. "But. . . ." He drew his long-bladed hunting knife to pick carefully with the point at a crevice between two rocks near his shoulder level. "Ahhh. . . ." Holding the knife between his teeth, he wriggled the larger of the two stones back and forth and then gave a sudden jerk which brought it out of its setting.

With that gone two more rattled down and Stans kicked them back toward the way they had come. "It looks stronger than it is," he announced. "We can clear this without trouble, I think."

The space was cramped so that only one might pick at the wall at a time. They took turns at that labor, passing the freed chunks to the other to be cleared away. Elossa's arms and back began to ache. She was as hungry as one at the mid-winter fasting. But at present she had no wish to suggest that they pause either to rest or to share the fast dwindling supplies she carried. To be out of this underground hole was far more important.

When they had cleared a space large enough to squeeze through Stans collected the torch once again. He thrust that ahead of him into the aperture and a moment later Elossa heard him give a surprised exclamation.

"What is it?" she demanded trying to edge closer.

He did not answer; instead he forced his way beyond and she was as quick to follow. Again they passed from cave to man-made way. Not only were the walls of this new and wide passage smooth, but they also appeared to have been coated with a substance which gave off the sheen of polished metal. The torchlight brought color to blaze also—ribbons and threads of it wove long, curling strips on the smooth surface. Gem bright those appeared—scarlet, deep crimson, flaunting yellow, rust brown, a green as vividly alive as the new leaves of spring, a blue as delicate as the shading on the snows of the mountains.

There was no design in it Elossa could see, just a rippling of long lines and bands. Nor did the color of any one of those remain the same—yellow became green, blue deepened to red.

At first she had welcomed this change, finding in it a certain relief after the drab gray of the rock. Then she blinked. Was there something alien about those bands, threatening? How could color threaten?

She remembered the colored towers, palaces, walls of Kal-Hath-Tan as it had stood in her vision before death descended upon it. The city had appeared a giant chest of jewels spilled idly across the land. Just as bright as these bands. But there was a difference.

Stans swept the torch closely along the wall fronting them. The bank he chose so to illumine began green, became abruptly scarlet, continued orange, then yellow. He reached out and tapped a nail against that colorful ribbon and Elossa, in the silence of this passage, heard the faint answering click-click.

"This is of Kal-Hath-Tan?" she asked. She shielded her eyes a little with her hand. It appeared, she thought now, that the colors held the torch-light, brightened it. It certainly could not be only her imagination that her eyes smarted as if she had gazed too long into some source of light far stronger than the torch.

"I do not know. It is unlike anything I have ever seen. It—it seems as if it should have a meaning of importance, and yet it does not. Only there is the feeling. . . ."

She did not know how sensitive one of his race might be to influences designed by his own kind. But that this place made her more and more uncomfortable could not be denied. The sooner she—they—found a way out the better.

"Which way do we go?"

Stans shrugged. "It seems to be a matter for guessing."

"Right, then." Elossa said quickly, since he made no move to do any of that guessing.

"Right it will be." Almost like a fighting man on parade he gave a half turn and started right.

The passage was much wider, they could walk abreast without any difficulty. But they went on in silence. Elossa took more and more care to keep her eyes strictly ahead, trying not to glance at the bands of color. There was a pull there, like the beginning of some illusion.

Also, the farther they went, the wider the bands became. Those which had been the width of a finger at the point where they had broken into the passage were now palm size. Others could span her arm, shoulder to wrist.

The colors could not glow any brighter, but their change from one hue to another was far more abrupt, creating a dazzlement which reacted more and more on her sight. She walked now with hands cupping eyes to cut out the side view.

Perhaps it was affecting Stans also, though he said nothing, for he was quickening pace, until they moved at a steady trot. As yet they had discovered no break in the walls, and in the shadow beyond the reach of the torch the way seemed to continue endlessly.

Elossa uttered a small cry, staggered toward the wall on her right.

Yurth call—so loud and clear that he or she who had uttered that cry might be standing just before them. Only there was no one there.

"What is it?" Stans' hoarse voice held a note of impatience.

"Yurth—somewhere close. Yurth and danger!"

Now that she was so certain that they must be very close to that which had drawn her here, Elossa called, not with the mind-send this time but uttering one of the carrying summons which her people used in their mountain faring, each clan having its own particular signal.

There was movement in the shadows which lay ahead. Stans held the torch higher, took a step or so forward to see the better.

A figure, yes. Human in that it stood erect and came walking toward them. Elossa's hand arose in the greeting between Yurth and Yurth.

❈ 12 ❈

Yurth in feature the stranger certainly was. But his clothing was different. In place of the leggings, the coarse smock, the journey cloak, all of drab coloring which made up the uniform body covering of her kind, this newcomer's slender form was covered with a tight-fitting suit which left only the hands and the head from the throat up bare. It was of a dark shade which could have been either a near black-green or blue, and so fitted to the flesh and muscles it covered that it seemed another skin.

She had seen such before.

Elossa's hands tightened on her staff. Yes! This she had seen before, both in the pictures painted by the hallucinations guarding Kal-Hath-Tan and in those she had witnessed in the sky ship when she had learned the true meaning of the Yurth Burden. This Yurth wore the dress of the ship people—as if he had not been here generations but had this very hour stepped from his space voyaging ship, now half buried in the earth which was Raski world.

"Greeting . . . brother. . . ." She used the speech of her people, not the common tongue which they shared with Raski.

But there was no lightening of expression on that other's face, no sign that he knew her as one of common heritage with himself. Rather there was a glitter in his wide-open eyes, a set to his mouth, which awoke in her the beginnings of uneasiness. She tried the mind-speech. There was—nothing! Not a barrier, just nothing she could touch. Her amazement was so great that she was frozen for a second or two, while the hand of the Yurth moved, bringing into line with her breast a rod of black which he held.

"No!" Stans crashed against her, the weight of his body bringing them both down on the hard stone under their feet with a bruising force. Across where she had stood moments earlier there swept a beam of dazzling light. Heat crackled through the air so that, even though Elossa lay well below where the beam had sped, still she felt the touch of its fire through her thick clothing.

It was not the shock of the attack which had rendered her helpless for the moment, rather the understanding that nothing, no one, had fronted her. By the evidence of the mind-send there had never been any Yurth there at all! But the weapon? That had been no part of any hallucination—surely it could not!

She gathered her wits, struggled against the hold that Stans had on her. There was no Yurth—there could not be! She pulled around to find she was right. The passage was empty. But—on the floor— only a little beyond where she lay now with Stans' weight still half over her, was the tube weapon the stranger had carried.

"He . . . it . . . is gone!" Stans loosed her and arose to his feet. "What . . ."

"Hallucination." she said. "A guardian. . . ."

Stans bent over the tube but did not touch it. "He was armed— he shot fire with this. Can a hallucination do such things?"

"Such can kill, yes, if he or she who sees them believes that they are real."

"And they carry such weapons—real weapons?" Stans persisted.

Elossa shook her head. "I do not know. It is not known to my people that they can do so." She eyed the tube. It had not vanished with its owner, or user, but still lay there, concrete evidence that they *had* been fired upon.

To take that up would equip her with a weapon far better than any defense she had ever had. But at the same time she could not bring herself to touch it. She got to her feet, leaning on her staff for support Stans reached for the tube.

"No!" she cried sharply. "We do not understand the nature of that. Perhaps it is not of our world at all."

Stans sat back on his heels and looked up at her, frowning a little.

"I do not understand this talk of hallucinations. Nor can I believe in a man who stands there, fires death at us, and then vanishes, leaving his weapon behind. How does Yurth come into the Mouth of Atturn, and what does he here, besides striving to put an end to us?"

Again Elossa shook her head. "I have no answer for you. Save that it is best not to take to yourself anything such as that." With her staff she pointed to the tube. "And. . . ."

But she just caught sight of something amid that banding on the wall. There was a difference in the texture there—yes! And directly across from it, on the opposite side, another such spot. She reached out with her staff and, not quite touching the wood to the wall itself, outlined a square on either side about breast high and the size of her two palms flattened out together.

"Look!"

Stans slewed around at her command, gazing from one side of the corridor to the other.

"Did not the Yurth stand between these two?" the girl demanded.

His frown deepened. "I think so. But what of it?"

"Perhaps not a hallucination." She was trying hard to remember fragments of old stories from her people. Though they had never spoken of Kal-Hath-Tan and the Burden of Yurth to those who had not made the Pilgrimage which set upon them the seal of responsibility and maturity, yet they had tales of long ago. She had always known that there was little in common between her people and the world on which they were uneasy prisoners. They had had a far more glorious past than they dared hope to achieve ever again.

On the buried sky ship she had learned just how adept the Yurth had been in strange powers. It could be that what they had seen here had not indeed been a hallucination after all, but a real Yurth transported by some means now beyond her comprehension to defend a hiding place against Raski invasion—transported by mechanical means and now returned to his hiding place.

If the Yurth in such concealment had had no contact with the rest of their people then to such a one she would seem a Raski even as was Stans, thus an enemy. How could she communicate with these hidden Yurth?

But, why had the mind-touch registered as if there had been no one there? Could she begin to imagine what powers these ship people had had in their time—the knowledge they had put aside when they had taken up the heavy burden of what they believed to be their great sin against this world?

"If it were not a hallucination," Stans broke into her absorbed whirl of thought, "then what did we see? A spirit of the dead? Do spirits then carry weapons which they can use? We might have been cooked by that fire!"

"I don't know!" Elossa snapped, out of her own ignorance and awaking anger. "I do not understand. Save there are plates on the wall here and here." Once more she indicated those with her staff. "And he whom we saw stood between them." Now she dared to use her staff to probe at the rod on the floor, turning it over. Even in the limited light from the bands on the wall they could both see now that, though it had thrown a lethal beam at them, it could never do so again. The under side of the cylinder so exposed showed a hole melted, as if some great heat had eaten away the metal.

"It must have been very old," Stans drew the first conclusion from that evidence. "Too old to use—as old as the sky ship."

"Perhaps." But the useless weapon was not the important thing. That was the appearance of the Yurth, and that cry for help which had brought her here. She had not been mistaken in that. Somewhere Yurth still had being and was in danger.

"You must know more," she rounded on Stans, "of your own history, seeing those of your House were pledged to watch Kal-Hath-Tan, to seek out Yurth who came and demand satisfaction from them for your city's death. Where we stand you say is the Mouth of Atturn. Who is or was Atturn? What had Yurth to do with such a place? If this was a temple. . . ." She drew a deep breath, remembering now some of the things which had flitted ghost-like through the mounds of Kal-Hath-Tan—the hunting to horrible deaths of the ship's people who had tried to render aid to the city they had destroyed by chance. Had Yurth been dragged here, to be sacrificed in torment to some Raski god or force? Was that the plea, sent thundering down the years by dying men and women, which indeed lingered now to entrap her also?

"Was Yurth blood shed here?" She ended her demand harshly.

Stans had risen once more to his feet, though he kept a careful distance, she noted, from the two plates in the walls, apparently having no desire to pass between those.

"I do not know," he answered quietly. "It may well be so. Those of Kal-Hath-Tan were maddened, and they carried into madness their hatred. I cannot remember anything of Atturn nor why I was drawn to the Mouth. In that I speak the full truth. Enter into my mind if you wish, Yurth, and you will see that is so."

He called her "Yurth," she noted; perhaps their precarious partnership might not long survive. But she did not need to obey his suggestion and mind-probe. It was an offer he would not have made if he had anything to hide. The Raski hated too much the powers they believed Yurth used ever to speak as he had except in complete truth.

The corridor still stretched ahead. To retreat might be the way of safety. Only with the Yurth call still in her mind Elossa could not take the first step back. Too long had those of her blood been conditioned to support each other, to answer to such a plea with all the help they might give.

"I must go on." She said that to herself rather than to the Raski. But now she added to him, "This is no call that you are in honor pledged to answer. You saved me from flame death which some manifestation of my own people turned upon me. If you are wise, Stans of the House of Philbur, you will agree that this is no quest of yours."

"Not so!" he interrupted. "I can no more turn from this path than can you. What drew me to the Mouth still works in me."

He was silent for a breath or two, and when he spoke again there was the heat of anger in his voice. "I am caught in something which is not of my time. I know not what power holds me but I am surely as captive as if I wore the chains of an overlord on my wrists!"

He was eyeing her with the suspicion and rage which had been a part of him when they had fronted each other in the sky ship. The fragile meeting of minds which they had carried from that encounter might be entirely broken, Elossa decided unhappily. To face the unknown with a potential enemy by one's side was to compound all peril lying in future. Yet surely they were tied together in some strange fashion.

"It would be best," she suggested, "not to pass directly between those." Once more she indicated the plates on the wall. Crouching, she obeyed her own warning by going on hands and knees under the setting of the squares. Without hesitation the Raski followed her example.

They went more warily, Elossa herself now keeping a keen eye on the walls, glancing ever from one side to the other, in search of more such insets as that which had marked the coming of the Yurth in ship's clothing. She retained a close rein on her mind, blanketing down as best she could all emanations which another might pick up if some wide-flung mind-search were in progress.

According to the message left in the sky ship the development of Yurth talent had been a latter thing with her people, a deliberately fostered attribute which the ship's equipment had set upon them after the great catastrophe. Perhaps some of the Yurth who could might have fled before that plan had been enacted, might have escaped similar development. Yet the call had been on mental level only.

Even if there had been a body of survivors from the ship come into hiding here in the heart of these mountains, how many generations were they away from the first of the refugees? The man she had seen wearing the ship's clothing—clothing which looked untouched by time. . . . No, he *must* have been an illusion.

They went warily, at a pace which gave them a chance to survey carefully the passage ahead. That continued to run straight, the color lines on its walls, growing wider until their edges met and there was no neutral background to be seen. Elossa felt an ache develop behind her eyes; to survey those colors as she thought it needful to do hurt so that her eyes teared and smarted.

In a queer fashion the colors themselves made her feel ill and she slowed yet more, finding it necessary to pause now and then, closing her eyes to rest them. Stans had said nothing since they had started on, but suddenly he broke the silence between them:

"There is—"

He had said no more than those two words when, in the air, suspended without a visible support, there appeared a mist which whirled about, gathering substance as it moved. From a small core it grew larger until it filled the full passage from the rock under their feet to that which roofed them overhead, spreading in turn from one side wall to another.

As it solidified it became the same monstrous mask which had surrounded the mouth hole giving passage into this underground territory. The eyes of the mist face held the same malicious glitter—even, Elossa thought, more awareness than those set in the rock. Once more the mouth was agape as if providing a door to some threatening way beyond. Though through it she could see no spread of the corridor, only deep darkness.

"Atturn!" Stans gave the manifestation a name. "The Mouth—it waits to swallow us!"

"Illusion!" The girl countered with a firmness she could not altogether feel.

There was a stir within the open cavern of that month. Though the rest of the face was now appearing very solid, the mist which it formed no longer moved as far as she could see. Out of the opening there licked a tentacle of darkness, as if some great black tongue quested for them.

Elossa, without thinking, reacted on the physical level, stabbing at that with her staff. Then she realized her mistake. One did not fight such as this with force of arm—rather force of mind. But before she could ready such counter the staff had passed through the tongue without any visible effect. And that lash of darkness closed about Stans, closed tightly and clung. In spite of his efforts to free himself, the Raski was drawn forward to where the lips quivered, awaiting him. There was an avid excitement in the eyes of that face, a kind of terrible greediness to be read about the waiting mouth. Atturn would feed and this food was now within its power.

Elossa caught at Stans, taking firm hold of his shoulder. There was no disguising the pull which drew him with a strength which they could not match, even linked in common struggle. But the girl needed that contact in order to apply her own answer.

"You are not!" She cried aloud in her mind to that face. "You have no being here and now! You are not!" She launched her arrows of denial even as she would have sent ones of wood, metal-tipped, from a hunting bow. If only Stans could help her! This manifestation must be of Raski, even as the other had been of Yurth.

"It is not there!" she cried aloud. "This is a thing of illusion only. Think of it so, Stans! You must deny it!" She returned to her own fierce denial by force of mind.

The strength of the tongue appeared limitless. Stans was nearly at the verge of those lips opened even wider to engulf him, while Elossa had been drawn also through the hold she kept on the Raski.

"You are not!" Now she both cried that aloud and thought it with all the force she could summon.

Was it only her imagination, or did the awareness in those great eyes flicker?

"You are not!" She had not said that. It was Stans who had uttered that breathless, low cry. He had stopped fighting against the loop of darkness about his body, instead, with upheld head and defiant gaze he faced the eyes boring down at him.

"You are not!" he repeated.

There was no general loosing of his bonds. Instead the face, the tongue which held him, the whole of the illusion vanished in an instant between one breath and another, so quickly that they both stumbled forward, carried by the very impetus of their resistance when the source against which they fought disappeared.

❋ 13 ❋

Not only had the face which barred their passage vanished, but so had the passage itself. Those smooth walls with the bands of color winked out. In their place was a sweep of dark on either side. The torch which they had forgotten when they had worked their way through into the band-lighted passage was no longer alight to give them any idea of the extent of this pocket of deep dark.

Elossa stood very still, shivering. She had the impression that they were no longer in any confined corridor. Rather there must stretch about them, for some distance, an area which might hold deadly snares for any who blundered on. The fear of the dark unknown which was bred into her kind sought now to send her into panic, and she needed all the resources of spirit she could muster to remain self-disciplined, turn in upon what senses of hearing and smell she might draw upon, since sight was denied her.

"Elossa." For the first time her companion spoke her name. She was startled in that his voice seemed to come from some distance away. Yet, though that one word echoed hollowly, there was no trace of fear in it.

"I am here," she returned, schooling her own voice as best she could to the same level. "It remains—where are we?"

She nearly cried out as, from the smothering darkness, a hand fell on her shoulder, slipped down her arm. until fingers found and tightened about her wrist. "Wait. I have still the fire-strike." Those fingers which had gripped her, perhaps in mutual reassurance for an instant, loosed hold.

She heard the click-click of what could only be a striker in use. There followed a small flare of flame. That grew and she saw, with a thankfulness she did not try to put into words, that Stans had not abandoned his torch, though she had not remembered now seeing it in his hands as they passed along the corridor.

Such a small light hardly pressed back any of the dark. Still it illumined their two faces, and, in a way, built up a measure of defense against the pressing blackness. Stans held it between them for a long moment as if so to reassure them both that they did indeed have it. Then he swung it away, out before them, nearly at shoulder level.

The flames flickered, leaped and fell. Elossa could feel against her own cheek currents of air which puffed, flowed, then were gone again. But the light did not touch any wall, on either side, before, or behind. They might have been dropped on a wide open, lightless plain. Under foot was a solid surface of dark rock, the only stable thing they had yet sighted. Had the corridor been entirely illusion? Elossa, for all her awareness of how the conscious mind might be manipulated and tricked, could hardly accept that. If it had not been illusion in entirety then how had they been transported into this pocket of eternal night?

"There is a current of air. See, the torch," Stans said. "Our best guide may lie with that."

It was true that the flames were blown away from the head of the brand he held. His suggestion was undoubtedly the most sensible one. They turned to face that current, the flames pointing toward their own breasts.

But they kept their pace slow. Now and then Stans paused, holding the torch out to this side or that. There were still no walls to be seen. Finally the light shone out on the lip of a drop. There the Raski lay belly down, to crawl cautiously to the edge of that, holding the torch out and down. There was nothing to see below but a chasm apparently so deep that their light was quickly lost in it.

Yet it was from across this that the current of air blew.

Stans sat up. The small part of his face Elossa could glimpse by the weaving flame was set. However, she saw no suggestion of wavering or weakness in his frowning gaze as he turned his head slowly from left to right surveying the rim of the drop on which they crouched.

"With a rope," he said as if more than half to himself, "we might try descent. We cannot otherwise."

"Along the edge then?" Elossa was privately very dubious that they would find any way of bridging that gulf. On the other hand there just might be a faint chance that the break itself would eventually narrow so that a leap could take them over.

He shrugged. "Right or left?"

It was all a matter of chance. One way might be as good as the other. During the moments of rest here she had been sending out short mind-probes, striving to find even the most minute suggestion of other life here—life which might have its own paths and ways to reach again the surface of the world she knew. The puzzle of the Yurth cry for help still troubled her mind.

"It matters not to me." She returned from the emptiness in which her probe had been lost and useless.

"Left then." The Raski got to his feet. He waited until she, too, stood up, and then turned in the direction he had chosen, keeping near enough to the edge of the drop so the rim lay ever within the light of the torch.

There was little way to measure distance traveled, save in the fatigue of their own bodies. Elossa found herself counting steps under her breath for no good reason, save that such a sum of their journey quieted the ever-present fear that there was no way out.

Then—

Stans gave a sharp exclamation, strode forward. The light of the torch had caught a projection out from the rim of the chasm, extending over the dark emptiness of that drop. It was of the same rock as formed the flooring over which they had traveled, and narrowed as it went. Not worked stone of any man-made bridge, Elossa thought. Yet. . . .

Her companion swung the torch closer to the surface of that projecting tongue. Though there were no marks of tools smoothing this path there lay something else. Deep carven into the floor was another representation of that face, while extending from it was the bridge in the form of a tongue thrust forth. Elossa halted just beyond the edges of the carving, having no wish to tread over the wide lips of the mouth. But Stans apparently felt no such repugnance. He stepped onto the tongue where it issued from between the lips at its widest extent. Then he knelt and, torch in one hand, began to crawl out on the bridge itself, if bridge it was.

Elossa had no desire to follow. There was that about this continual appearance of Atturn's face which disturbed her. It was wholly of Raski, and yet Stans insisted that he knew little of it. There was also the fact that whoever had wrought the representations of it she had seen had continually accented the malice, the evil. Atturn had not been a god—or ruler—or energy—who had been engaged in any good for her own kind.

She watched Stans creep along over the drop, longing to summon him back. Yet she knew better than to disturb the concentration displayed in his whole tense figure. While the tongue bridge, though it narrowed, did seem solid enough as far as the torchlight reached.

Stans paused, for the first time glanced back at her over his shoulder.

"I think we can cross," he called and there was a distorted echo from below uttering his words so garbled they might have been from the throat of some beast. "It seems to continue. Let me see the other end."

"Well enough." Elossa dropped down just beyond the edge of the face, watching as he once more advanced slowly but steadily ahead. Around her the dark thickened as the torch was carried farther and farther away. She could hardly make out the details of the tongue passage, save that it seemed to her that it was narrowing to an extent where Stans might not even find width enough to support both knees at once.

The Raski's advance was very slow. Though he held the torch up to illuminate as much as he could of what still stretched before him, his other hand grasped the edge of the bridge in a grip Elossa did not have to see clearly to realize was tightened by the very real presence of fear. Then he moved so that now his legs dropped, one on either side of that path which had become so narrow his own body more than spanned it.

He began to hitch, his legs swinging over nothingness. Elossa, without being conscious of what she did, pressed one fist tight against her mouth, until the pain in her pinched lips made her aware. The torch had certainly not caught any sign yet of the other side of the chasm. What if the tongue became a tip and Stans slid off it into the depths?

The malice of the carven face certainly promised no more than harsh disaster for anyone daring to trust to it. She longed to shout to the Raski to return, but at the same time feared that any sudden summons might send him off balance, to fall.

She blinked, hardly sure that she did see that hint of a ledge of rock reaching out toward the tongue tip from the far side. Was there a space between the two which could not in the end be bridged? Or did the very tip of the stone span actually rest upon the ledge? It was too far—the light too confined by the distance—for her to make sure. Her heart was pounding, she had risen to her knees, staring out at that small flicker of flame which was so perilously distant.

Stans made a convulsive movement—a fall! Her breath caught in a choking gasp. No! He was getting to his feet, and now the torch was swinging back and forth like the flag of a victorious army waved to signal triumph.

He started back, down once more on the thread of stone, edging along, holding the torch before him. Her own body ached with tension as she watched him make the slow return trip. She only breathed deeply and fully once more when he arose to walk the last few steps to gain the lips of the face from which that incredible bridge issued.

"It is very narrow toward the end . . ." He breathed in short gasps and in the torchlight she could well see the sheen of sweat across his face. That journey had not been an easy one. "There is but a very small margin of meeting between bridge and the edge on the far side. But it is a crossing."

"As you have proved." She tried to make her face impassive. There was no escape save this very risky path. All her life she had known mountain trails which were narrow, where one must walk with the greatest of care, the highest dependence upon one's balance and skill. Yet the worst of those was as nothing compared to the ordeal before her now. She needs must shut away fear, and with it that other feeling of repugnance for the form of their only escape. To her the face carried such a sensation of sheer evil that to trust her body to the tongue was nearly more than she could force herself to do. The thing was stone, it had no life—except that illusion it might be able to foster in those who feared it—yet there was deep in her a sick hatred born from the need to touch its substance.

A picture haunted her, a vision of the tongue curling up and around, as that tongue of fog had wreathed the Raski. A stone tongue to hold her securely a prisoner, draw her back into the gaping mouth of. . . .

Elossa shook her head. To allow such a vision any place in her mind was to carry out the very purposes of those who had created Atturn—whatever he was. She held her head high and was pleased that her voice was so steady as she asked:

"How do we go?"

Stans had been looking back along the path he had taken once.

"I think I go first—if we only had a rope!"

Elossa managed a laugh which did not sound too ragged. "Uniting us? To what purpose in disaster save that it would mean the loss of us both then. I do not believe that either of us could sustain the weight of the other were that one to slip. If it must be done, let us get to the doing of it!" Perhaps with that last outburst she had revealed her dismay. If so he did not let her realize, by even a look, that he knew how fear ate at her.

Instead, holding the torch close enough to him that the light shone well over his shoulder, he set forth with an air of steady confidence to again cross the tongue. Staff in hand, her cloak held tightly about her, Elossa followed.

It seemed only too soon that they must descend from walking to crawling on hands and knees. She tried to keep her eyes only for the stone way that the flame showed. But those edges drawing ever more closely together were a torment to watch. Maybe she was lucky in that complete darkness did fill the chasm. Was it better not to see? Only then imagination could paint what the eyes did not distinguish.

"Astride here," his words floated back.

Elossa hitched high her robe, bunching it about her waist. The stone, rough and cold, chafed the skin of her inner thighs as she edged slowly along, and the perch on which she rested grew ever more narrow. Her dangling legs appeared to gather weight, making her ever afraid of over-balancing.

Then Stans seemed to give a leap, if one could so express his quick thrust forward from a sitting position. The torch flashed down. He had laid its butt on a ledge, the flames out over the gulf. On his knees, he turned to reach both hands to hers.

Somehow the girl loosed her grip on the stone. The staff she had held across her lap she snatched up, angling it to him. He seized the length of wood, then there came a steady pull, to drag her over what was indeed the most shaky of supports—the very tip of the tongue, a bit of stone no wider than her hand, where it just touched the ledge.

She sprawled forward, her body landing full on Stans, pushing him back across the stone. For a moment or two she could not move at all. It was as if the demands she had put on her body and her courage had weakened both at once, leaving her as weak and empty as one who has been ill for a long time.

Stans' arms closed about her. She was hardly aware of that fastidious dislike for touching another which was so much a part of her heritage. Elossa only knew at this moment the warmth of his body close against hers sent rushing back into the darkness of the gulf all the fear which had gnawed at her. They were across—there was stable rock under them.

Then the Raski loosed her as he made a lunge for the torch which was sputtering. He swung it up through the air so the flames took on new life. Elossa felt tears runneling the rock dust on her cheeks, but she bit back any sound. Using the staff for a support she was able to drag herself up and stand, though it felt to her for some space out of time that the solid rock which was her footing swayed from side to side.

Stans, torch in hand, held out that brand. There was no mistaking the way those flames were borne back toward them. Just as the current of air, which seemed to her as fresh as the wind from a mountain tip, blew from some space before them. There must be some way out waiting for them.

Elossa was hungry, her body ached from the journey. But she was in no mind to suggest that they halt, drink of what they carried in the water bottles strapped to their girdles, or eat the rest of her crumbs of journey bread. If there was a chance of winning out of here in the not too distant future, that was all that mattered.

The size of ledge on which they stood did have limits. It might not be as clearly defined as the tongue for a bridge, but there was space to be seen on either side. Only, before them loomed a new opening in a rock wall, unworked natural stone. It was down this passage that the air came.

Stans had thrown back his head, was drawing in deep breaths.

"We must be close to the outer world," he commented. "There is no underground taint in this wind."

He must feel as heartened by the thought of escape as she was for he moved on with a hasty stride and she hurried to catch up with him.

❈ 14 ❈

They emerged into a night near as dark as the passage from which they came. Clouds massed overhead heavily enough to shut out all signs of moon or stars. And there was a wind which carried in it more than a promise of the winter season now not so distant. Having found their door they were not so determined to use it yet, at least not until they knew more of the world into which they had come. In mutual consent they withdrew again into the passage and, finding a niche which protected them somewhat from the wind, they crowded into its shelter, deciding to wait out the hours of dark there.

Elossa brought out the last of her journey cakes—a mass of crumbs. And they had the water in the bottles. Having eaten, they drank, and then agreed, though they lacked any method of telling time, to share sentry duties.

Stans arbitrarily claimed the first watch period and Elossa did not dispute him. The ordeal of the bridge crossing still was with her. She was content for now to huddle within her cloak and just rest. But sleep came upon her then with the suddenness of a blow.

When she roused from that state it was to feel Stans' hand on her shoulder, shaking her into wakefulness. He grunted some disjointed words she did not clearly catch and settled down himself in the dark leaving her to look out upon the strangeness of this over-mountain country. At first she sharpened her sleep-drugged wits by trying to place their present position. Their crossing of the valley had been mainly an east to west trail. But when Stans had sought the Mouth he had certainly gone north. Had their journey also within the interior of the heights been northward? She was certain that was so. As her eyes adjusted to the dark she believed that they were surrounded by peaks higher than the foothills among which they had earlier traveled. There was no mistaking a certain feel to which she was sensitive from her life among the heights.

Now that the pressure of the journey, the need to escape, was gone, she tried to marshal what little she knew, what she had observed and felt, into a logical sequence from which she might reason possible future action.

Two heritages had been very much in evidence in the way of the Mouth: Raski—even though Stans denied that he knew much of Atturn—Yurth in the mysterious figure who had attempted to slay them with the ancient weapon of her own people and then had vanished.

Yet because of their very heritage there was no reasonable motive for such a melding of menace. Until she and Stans had stood in the sky ship and made their own uneasy alliance there had been, to Elossa's knowledge, no pacific meeting between Yurth and Raski.

She fumbled in folds of her clothing and brought forth the mirror pendant. There was no light of moon to give it life; she was able to see only a disc, and that very shadowy in her hand. Also to use that would open her mind, leave her defenseless to any other who had mind-send, mind-probe. Restlessly she fingered it, longing to put it to use, caution acting as a brake on her desire.

That Yurth call—concerning that she had not been mistaken. If that were only a mental illusion, to match what had been visual ones, then she was indeed lost. A chill of fear crawled along her body, far worse than any cold brought by the wind and the stone surrounding her. Mind must control illusion. But if the mind itself were to be invaded by such—against that not even the most strongly armed Yurth could stand! And she did not claim the completely trained powers of her elders.

She raised the half-seen mirror to her lips, breathed upon it. Then holding it at eye level she concentrated.

Yurth—if there was Yurth here then that call would bring, should bring. . . .

Elossa could see the disc only as an object between her fingers. She had never tried before to use it in such an absence of light. There was—no, she was not mistaken! The disc grew warm—it was activated!

Yurth! Urgently she beamed out that call.

No answer, though she put into her mind-send all the strength she could summon. If Yurth had ever been here then her people were now gone. Dare she try Raski? As Elossa hesitated, the memory of the Mouth was sharp in her mind. Better not play with forces she did not understand. That looping shadow tongue which had near taken Stans was something beyond her own knowledge. Regretfully she clasped the mirror between her palms, loosed all concentration, then stowed it carefully away.

There was a lighting of the sky beginning, and, judging by that, they were indeed facing north. How long did they have before the first storms of the cold season would close in? Though the Yurth had their log huts and stone caves, their storage houses, yet that season was never easy for them. She and Stans had no supplies, no shelter as yet. Both must now be their primary concern.

Dawn broke at last and Elossa could see the new land lying below, for the passage in which they had sheltered part of the night fronted on a slope well above the floor of a valley. Unlike the wide expanse which had held the destroyed city, this was relatively narrow. But it ran east and west and she was sure that she caught a glimpse of a stream of some size forming a ribbon down its center. There was growth of dark vegetation on the lower slopes, rising to stunted trees. But there was something unwholesome about the look of that.

Still a source of water was important. Only, where there was any stream, they could also expect to find a come and go of life. Sargon, such as had already near made an end to her over mountain, and kindred beasts of the heights might well roam here. Stans carried a hunter's weapons, she had nothing save her staff. Nor had she ever taken life herself.

"Darksome. . . ." Stans moved out to join her. "This is no country to welcome the traveler. Yet there is water. So it may well be good hunting territory."

They left the entrance to the tunnel to proceed down slope. Without any spoken agreement they both made good use of all cover as they went, while Elossa opened her mind a little, striving to pick up any hint of life.

"Two-horns—" She spoke in a whisper gauged just to reach the ears of the man moving hardly an arm's distance away.

He shot her a startled glance.

"To the west." She pointed with her chin. "There are four—they graze."

He nodded swiftly and turned in the direction she had indicated. His crossbow was in his hands. Elossa felt a little sick. At least she had not tolled a helpless animal within striking distance. But her betrayal was little the less. How true was it that one was allowed to slay in order to live? She could defend herself against attack—but a two horn was no attacker. She. . . . No, in this much she must face the necessity of breaking her own creed. To starve because one would not kill—a stronger person might face that rule, she fell far short of such strength.

Also, since this was of her doing, she must force herself to watch. So, like Stans, she slipped along.

The brush which cloaked the slope gave way to a stand of grass which waved tips near as tall as the shoulders of the animals who grazed there. Four two-horns. Elossa had read the emanations of life forces aright. There was one female, a half-grown yearling, and two males—one with the wide-curved horns of a herd leader of more than ten seasons.

Stans shot. The younger male gave a convulsive leap forward, a red stream shooting from its throat. The other male cried aloud in a great bellow and herded the female and her yearling before him into flight. The wounded animal had fallen to its knees as the bolt in its jugular drained it of blood. Stans raced on, knife in hand, to swiftly end its struggles.

Sick at what she had seen, Elossa made herself advance to where the Raski was busy butchering the kill. She stooped and thrust her fingers into the congealing blood. Then she drew on her forehead the scarlet sign of her sin. So must she wear that for all to note until in some manner she might atone. She looked around to see the Raski, pausing in his bloody work, watching her action with open amazement.

"It is through me the innocent had died," she said, not wanting to explain her shame, but knowing that she must "So must I wear a killer's blood token."

His surprise did not lighten. "This is meat, we must have it or die. There are no fields to be harvested here, no fruit ripe for the picking. Do not the Yurth eat meat? If not so, how do they live?"

"We live," she said bleakly. "And we kill. But never must we let ourselves forget that in killing we take on ever the burden which is part of the death of another, be it man or animal."

"You did not blood yourself with the sargon," he commented.

"No, for then the fight was equal—life risked against life—and that is left upon the balance of the First Principle, not upon any better skill or trick of ours."

Stans shook his head and his expression was still one of bafflement.

"Yurth ways—" He shrugged. "It remains, we can eat."

"Dare we light a fire?" The girl looked on to the end of the meadow which bordered on the stream. Across that swift flow of water (and it was swift, bearing with it sticks, masses of wrack as if there had been a storm somewhere higher up and the hurrying flood had picked up much debris along the way) there were standing rocks and sand, none of the vegetation which grew on this side.

"What do your Yurth talents tell you?" he countered. "If you can so find a beast to give us food without searching far, can you not also tell us whether we are alone here?" He sat back on his heels, his face impassive.

Elossa could not be really convinced whether he asked that without latent hostility. They were so different in their heritage—dare she ever be certain that there did not lie some other motive under any speech he made to her?

She hesitated. To reveal her weaknesses when she could not be sure of this Raski—that might be the height of stupidity. Yet she must not, on the other hand, claim powers which in a time of emergency she could not summon. That might well be worse in the future than admitting now there were limits to what she could do.

"If I use such a mind-search," Elossa said slowly, "and there is a mind equally trained within range, then instantly that other will know of me—or us."

"It would be a Yurth mind which could do so, would it not?" he asked. "Do you then fear your own people?"

"I travel with a Raski." She picked the first excuse she could light upon. "They do not hate nor fear your kind, but I would be so strange because of that."

"Yes, even as I company with Yurth!" He nodded. "Most of my own blood would send such a bolt as this—" He touched what he had taken from the wound—"through me without question."

She made her decision, mainly for the reason that hunger was strong in her; still she could not think of putting raw flesh into her mouth. A poor reason, in which the needs of her body overrode all else, yet the body must be fed or the mind also would perish.

Kneeling a little away from where Stans had gone back to his butchery, Elossa again brought out her mirror. The sun was up now, and the surface of the disc she held was bright as it had not been in the night time. She looked down into the pool of light, for that was what it seemed to become in her hold.

"Yurth!" She aimed the thought sharply into the disc. "Show me Yurth!"

There was—yes! It came—a rippling on the surface of the disc. Then she saw—but very faint and hard to define—a figure which might have been that which had fronted them in the corridor. Her mind-send reached out and out. Life . . . far. . . . But was it Yurth? She met no answering spark of mind. It was more like Raski—closed, unknowing.

"There is nothing close." She slipped the disc back into its carrying place.

"Good enough. There is drift along the stream—dry enough to give us a good fire, and also that which will not cause much smoke."

Leaving him to finish his bloody task, Elossa went down to the water and began to gather those bone-white, water-polished sticks which had caught in the rocks above the present rise of the water, though, she noted, that was creeping higher now even as she watched.

They roasted chunks of the meat speared on sharpened pieces of drift and held over the flames. Elossa forced herself to eat, applying mental discipline against her half nausea. Stans was licking his fingers one by one as he spoke disjointedly:

"We should smoke what we can—to carry with us."

He had said only that when Elossa was on her feet staring across the stream at the other rock-covered bank. Just as the strange Yurth and the face had both appeared without warning in the passage, so now had a figure winked into sight there.

She gasped. Not Yurth as she had half expected. Like Stans the man was dark skinned, dark haired. But—his face! He wore a living countenance of flesh and bone but it was still the one of Atturn. Nor was his clothing the hide garments of the hunter, even the clumsy ill-woven robes of the city men, or the primitive armor of the Raski soldiers who patrolled the plains.

His body was covered with a black, tight-fitting suit, not unlike those worn by the Yurth in their shipboard life, save that the black was scrolled over by patterns in red as if so drawn by some point dipped in fresh blood. Those patterns glowed, waned, and glowed again, their brightness speeding from one part of the body they helped to clothe to another. From his shoulders hung a short cloak of the blood red, and that was patterned in black, reversing the order of that on his other clothing. His head was surmounted by a towering crest of either thick black hair set in some invisible helm, or else his own locks stiffened and allowed to grow to a height of more than a foot above his skull, In all he was the most barbaric figure Elossa had ever seen.

Instinctively she had sent forth a mind-probe. And met—nothing.

The stranger raised his hand and pointed, while his lips—the thickish, sneering lips of the Mouth of Atturn—shaped words which sounded heavily through the air as if the words themselves were bolts from some weapon dispatched to bring down the two on the other side of the river.

"Raski, *si lar dit!*"

Stans cried out. The appearance of the man had caught him kneeling, now he was on his feet in a half crouch, his hand tightly grasping the hilt of his knife. Like the stranger who wore Atturn's face his features were alive, but his expression was that of defiance.

"Philbur!" He made of the name of his house a battle cry. It was as if he met red hate with a rage as great and overpowering.

Without clear thought Elossa's hand grabbed her mirror from its hiding place, the swift jerk of her pull breaking the cord which held it. Then, swinging it by what was left of that cord, she spun it through the air.

Was what happened then chance alone or some intervention of power she did not realize she could call upon? A beam of searing red fire had shot from the pointed finder of he who wore Atturn's face. It struck full on the disc of the mirror and was reflected back—its force of beam increased. The black and red figure vanished.

15

"Who was that?" Elossa found words first, Stans was still staring bemused at where that stranger had stood.

"It was—no!" He flung up one hand in an emphatic gesture of denial. "It could not be that!" Now he turned his head a little to look at the girl and his look of astonishment was still plain. "Time does not stop—a man dead these half thousand years cannot walk!"

"Walk." She gazed at the mirror which had so providently, almost impossibly, deflected whatever it was the stranger would have hurled at Stans. The disc was cracked, darkened. A vigorous rubbing against her cloak did not free it from that discoloration. Without even trying it she could be sure it was now useless for her purposes. "Walk," she repeated explosively, "that strove to kill!" For Elossa did not doubt in the least that had that beam of light struck Stans he would have been as dead as she would have been had the Yurth weapon in the corridor cooked her flesh from her charred bones.

"It was Karn of the House of Philbur—he who ruled in Kal-Hath-Tan. He is—was—of my blood, or I of his. But he died with the city! It is so—all men know it! Yet, you saw him, did you not? Tell me—" His voice was near a fierce shout—"you did see him!"

"I saw a man—a Raski if you say he is so—in black and red, but he wore the face of the Mouth of Atturn and you said you did not know it." Stans rubbed his hand across his forehead. He was visibly more shaken than she had yet seen him.

"I know—what do I know—or not know?" He cried that question, not to her, she knew, but to the world around them. "I am no longer sure of anything."

Then he took a leap in her direction, and, before the girl could move, he had seized her shoulders in a hurtful grip and was shaking her as if he would so reduce her to a kind of slavery.

"Was this of your doing, Yurth? All know you can tangle and play with minds, as a true man can toss pebbles to his liking. Have you so tossed my thoughts, bewitched my eyes—made me see what is not?"

The girl fought him, tearing herself free by the very fury of her resistance. Then she backed away, holding up to him at eye level the blackened and near destroyed mirror of seeing.

"He did that—with the beam that he threw! Think you, Raski, how would you have been served had this not deflected that power!"

Stans' scowl did not lighten but his eyes did flicker at the disc.

"I do not know what he would have done," he said sullenly. "This is an evil land and—"

He got no further. They came boiling out of the rocks across the water, splashing through, some of them covering the distance between with huge leaps. Not Yurth, not Raski. . . . Elossa gave a cry of horror, so alien were these creatures to any normal life that she knew.

Twisted bodies, limbs too long or too short, heads with horribly misshapen features—a nightmare of distorted things which vaguely aped the human yet were totally monstrous. It was this alien horror which kept both Elossa and Stans from instant defense. Also the creatures attacked without a sound, surging on in a wave over the water toward them.

Elossa stopped to catch up her staff; Stans still had his hunting knife to hand. But they had no chance. Evil smelling bodies ringed them in, hands which had four fingers, six, boneless tentacles for digits, seized upon them, dragged them down. The terrible revulsion which filled Elossa as she looked upon their distorted and deformed bodies and faces weakened her. She fought, but it was as if nausea weighted her limbs, deadened her powers of constructive thought.

They poured over the two by the fire like an irresistible wave, bearing them to earth. Elossa shuddered at the touch of their unwholesome flesh against her own. The fetid odor they wore like a second skin made it hard for her to breathe, she had to fight to regain consciousness. There were bonds pulled cruelly tight about her wrists and ankles. Still one of the creatures squatted on her, using the force of its weight to keep her quiet.

And the worst of that (Elossa had to close her eyes against the horror of that leering, drooling thing) was that it was obviously female. For their attackers wore but little clothing—scraps of filthy stuff about their loins the extent of their body coverings, the females among them as aggressive and bestial as the males.

The silence in which their attack had been carried out was broken now. Grunts, whistles, noises not even as intelligent as sounds made by far more cleanly living animals broke out in an unintelligible chorus.

Elossa, the center of one circle of captors, could see nothing of the Raski. She forced herself to look at these ringing her in. While they indulged meanwhile in small torments, pulling viciously at her hair, tweaking her flesh until the nails—of those which had nails— near met, leaving raw marks which bled a little.

There appeared to be, she began to understand, some argument in progress among them. Twice one party of the creatures strove to drag her away from the river, while others jabbered and screamed and fought over her to bring her back.

She waited for the man named Karn to appear, somehow sure that he must have been the one to unleash on them this frightful band. But there was no one but the things themselves. One had thrust a stick into the fire, whirled it around in the air until the end blazed and now limped, for one of its legs was shorter than the other, toward her, the fiery point manifestly aimed at her eyes.

Before that reached the goal the would-be torturer was tackled by a much taller and heavier male, whose tentacle fingers fastened about its fellow's thin, corded throat and dragged him back, flinging him away with callous force.

Before the jabbering creature could reclaim its stick there was a sharp outcry from those nearest the river. Now the large male waded into those about Elossa cuffing with fists, kicking out with feet on which there were no toes, growling hoarsely.

Having battered near half of her captors away, the male stooped and caught at a great handful of her hair. By this painful hold he dragged her to the water's edge. Then, seizing her by the middle of her body, he raised and flung her out.

She did not land in the water, but rather in some kind of a boat which rocked perilously under her weight, but did not turn over. A moment later Stans landed half on top of her, hurled in the same manner.

The Raski lay so limp Elossa feared he was dead. His weight across her body forced her into the bottom of the boat where there was a wash of slimy water. She had to struggle to lift her head so that would not lap into her face.

Under them the boat lurched and then floated free. But none of the horrors on the shore made move to join the prisoners in it. They were being sent alone, bound and helpless, into the full force of the current. Elossa's struggles made the boat rock dangerously. But she had achieved a few inches of room which did just keep her face above the water.

Caught in what was indeed a swift current, the boat rode dizzily, sometime spinning half around. Much of Elossa's range of sight was curtailed by Stans' body. She could really see only straight up where the sky held a thin, promising sunlight. But, as they were borne along, walls began to rise on either side, those same walls closing in toward the river. They cut off much of the sky. All she could soon see was a strip forming a ribbon between two towering stretches of dark rock.

The sound of rushing water was ever present. Now and then the boat grated against some obstruction beyond Elossa's curtailed range of sight and she waited tensely for their craft to rip apart on a sunken stone, or be over turned, allowing them to drown. Meanwhile she struggled against the cords about her wrists. Those were well under the water which washed in the boat and she wondered if the continued immersion might loosen the ties. But she was afraid to fight too hard lest her movements endanger the buoyancy of their clumsy craft.

A groan from Stans heartened her a little. Perhaps if he could regain consciousness they might have a slightly better chance. Then she saw the seeping of blood from his shoulder. That nearly healed wound which he had carried from his brush with the first sargon must have been wrenched open once again.

"Stans!" She called his name.

A second groan answered her. Then a muttering which was near lost in the sound of the water. Imagination was busy nibbling at the grip she held tight upon her emotions. Given the swiftness of the current here what might well lie ahead? Rapids which no such leaky craft as this could hope to ride, or even a waiting cataract or falls?

"Stans!" Perhaps she was wrong in trying to arouse the Raski—what if he should make some sudden move which would overbalance them?

But the water was washing higher now. It flicked in small waves against her chin. If he did not shift his weight In some manner she would be past the ability to keep her face above its surface much longer.

His body did move a fraction and the boat dipped. The water swirled up and she choked as it entered her nose without warning.

"Be—be quiet!" Her voice arose nearly to a shriek in her fear.

"Where. . . ." His voice was weak, she thought, but it sounded as if he were conscious.

"We are in a boat." She tried to outtalk the river sounds. "I am partly beneath you. There is water here. I must keep my face above it."

Had he understood? He made no immediate answer. She tried to wriggle away from him to the bow of the boat, hold her head up. Her neck ached and it was becoming more and more difficult to do that.

Then his words came clearly enough. "I shall try to move away," he said. "Be ready!"

She braced herself, took a deep breath to have her lungs full if she were to be ducked. His weight did move, slid a little down her body toward the stern of the boat. That rocked wildly under them, and the waves she feared did wash over her face. But through some favor of providence the craft did not overset.

Once more he moved. And then she felt free. Now it was her turn.

"Be ready," she warned. "I shall try to edge away, get my shoulders higher."

After a fashion she did. Her chin was jammed down into her chest, but the water was now well away from her face. Also she could see that he, in turn, was wedged across the boat in part, his head and shoulders against one side, his legs and knees trailing down the other.

The current was still fast but the boat seemed to ride it a little more steadily. Elossa knew very little of boats; they were never used by the Yurth. Perhaps their changes of position had something to do with the alteration.

From her present place she could see that the river must fill a very narrow gap between two very steep banks. It was as if they passed so through a mountain canyon. Even if they were free, and managed somehow to get out of the water, she greatly doubted that there was any way either of those natural walls could be climbed.

Once more she cautiously tried the ties about her wrists. And, to her overwhelming excitement, they gave a little. The water's soaking must have helped. She passed her discovery to Stans. He nodded, but it did not seem to interest him. Under the darkness of his skin there was a greenish color. His eyes closed as if it was beyond his strength to keep them open, and he lay inert. It might have taken all the energy he could summon to have made the move which freed her.

But her own determination and will were growing stronger. The extreme effect of those horrible attackers had faded. Alone, bound and helpless though they seemed to be, she could begin to search for some hope. To get her hands free—that was what she must first do.

In spite of the pain in her wrists, she flexed and relaxed, flexed and relaxed, tugging at intervals, though that repaid her with torment in her flayed skin.

Stans continued to lie with closed eyes and the girl believed that he had again lapsed into unconsciousness. She wondered how long their voyage down the river would continue. She was able to force her head up another few inches to see that once more the walls of the cut through which they were traveling were beginning to descend—the cliffs were not so tall and forbidding.

A last effort and she jerked one hand free. Her puffed fingers had no feeling in them. Then the agony of returning circulation made her want to scream aloud. She forced herself to flex those swollen and blood-stained hands in spite of the pain. But she could also use them to cautiously lever herself up farther in the boat, release her head and neck from the strain put upon them.

Though it was hard to make her fingers obey to any success she picked at the ties around her ankles. The thongs had cut deeply there and puffed rings showed bloody. Then she remembered that the creatures who had taken them captive had not searched her. And, using both hands together, she hunted within the bosom of her robe for that concealed pocket where she carried the small knife to serve her at meals.

It nearly fell through her nerveless fingers, but she managed to saw away at the thongs. As soon as those parted she edged warily around to see what she could do for Stans. Sitting up in the boat she had a better view of the river. Here it was much narrower than it had been in the valley, which might well add to the speed of the current.

The boat itself was blunt bowed, rising high on the sides. It appeared to be made of a wooden frame over which was tight stretched hide so thick it must come from some beast beyond Yurth knowledge. That was also scaled on the outside as she could see where it had been brought over at the edge and laced down. And she did not doubt that it was perhaps far tougher than any wood.

There was a feeling of age about it, as if not of her time at all. And she marveled at how buoyantly it rode.

Using both hands she shifted Stans a little, with a catch of breath as the boat dipped ominously. But at least she was able to saw at the cords near buried in the flesh of his wrists where they had been drawn so cruelly tight.

His ankles had fared better than hers for he wore the boots of a hunter. And there was more give to the bonds there. Once he was free she settled him as best she could to steady the boat. The blood stains from his shoulder had not spread, she could hope that the wound had stopped bleeding.

Now—without any oar, paddle, or means of controlling their craft—what could be done to better their present state? Elossa drew a deep breath as she turned her attention back to the river.

16

She did not have long to so wonder for the end of their wild voyage was very near. The higher walls about them sank swiftly, until they came out of the canyon into another valley—if valley it was and not a plains country beyond the mountains. At least this level land, clothed in the autumn hued grass, spread like a sea as far on out as Elossa could distinguish ahead.

The river which carried them did not flow so swiftly here, and its way across the plain was marked by stands of water-nourished brush and small trees which were the only vegetation to rise above the level of the thick grass. For the rest this seemed a deserted land. It was close to sunset as far as Elossa could judge and there was not a bird to be seen, no grazing animals in sight.

While the dull hue of the grass and the faded colors of the tree leaves gave a forbidding cast to the whole of this land, it appeared as if all vibrant life had been drawn out of it, and only withered remnants left. Looking around she shivered, more from inner than outer chill.

A groan from Stans drew her attention back to her companion. His eyes were open and he had shifted his position a little. When his gaze met hers his eyes were still open. It was plain he realized at least some of what had happened. With his hand he touched his shoulder carefully and winced. But at least he was fully conscious. Now he looked out at the plain into which the river was carrying them.

"We are beyond the heights." It was more a statement than a question.

"Yes," Elossa answered. "Though where we may be I have no idea."

He was frowning and now he rubbed his hand across his forehead. "Was it a dream—or did we see Karn back there?"

Elossa chose her words. "We saw a man. . . . he had a face like the Mouth of Atturn . . . you called him Karn."

"Then it was not just a dream." Stans spoke heavily. "But Karn is long dead. Though, yes, he was priest as well as king and in his own time men whispered behind their hands—a dark legend but one even I have heard remnants of. Karn dealt with forces most men did not even believe existed. Or so they say—and said. It is true I cannot remember clearly." Now he shook his head. "I feel that I should, but that some wall stands between me and the truth. Karn. . . ." his voice trailed away.

"If that was your long dead king," Elossa cut in sharply, "he has taken to himself some evil followers. The monsters who brought us down were no true blood of men."

"Yes. And them, of them I have no knowledge at all. But why they loosed us to the mercy of the river and this boat. . . ." He moved again and his face twisted with what must have been a grievous twinge of pain. But he had hitched up farther and was gazing around as if now intent upon assessing their situation clearly.

"No oars," he commented. "It is plain we are not meant to command any part of the future. But. . . ."

Elossa, who had looked back at the river and what lay ahead, gave an exclamation. There seemed to be a wall of brush now directly above the water, though that flowed unimpeded beneath it. It was evident that bearing down upon the barrier as they were, there was no other chance but that the boat would be brought up against it.

Carefully she got to her knees, balancing with difficulty as the boat bobbed and moved under her weight. Even if he stood, Elossa guessed, she could not have reached the top of that obstruction across the water.

The boat rocked again as Stans raised himself higher. He gestured to the river itself.

"Swim for it?" he suggested.

Though Elossa had splashed about in mountain pools and knew that she would be at a loss in this current-driven river. She hesitated. Perhaps, were they to bring up against the mass of the barrier, that could be better climbed. Yet the presence of the barrier itself was an implied threat. It had not simply appeared there as some freak of nature, of that she was sure. Made—it brought to mind the question of its makers and the purpose for which they might have erected it.

In the end they were given no choice at all. For even as the boat neared the barrier, there dropped, seemingly from the very air over their heads (though Elossa knew it must be the result of some well trained casting) a net which entangled both the boat and its occupants.

She and Stans were fighting that entrapment when those who had so arranged their capture appeared out of the brush and trees on either side of the stream. Unlike the misshapen monsters of their first encounter with the mountain dwellers, these were straight of body, well formed. And—they were Yurth!

Elossa cried out for help. These were kin, her own blood. But— were they. Some wore the coarse clothing of the mountain clans, enough like her own to have come from the same looms. Others had on the tight-fitting body suits she had seen in the pictures the ship had shown her, the same that Yurth who had aimed the ancient weapon at them scarce a day ago had appeared in.

Elossa sent out an imperative mind-call. To be so startled in return that she cried out. These were closed—tight guarded against her touch. Yurth they might appear in body—they were not Yurth in mind.

Also she saw now their faces more clearly—they were blank eyed, without expression. Nor did they speak to one another in any words as these on the left bank drew the net and so the boat and its two occupants toward them.

"Yurth," Stans said. "Your people—what would they do with us?"

Elossa shook her head. She felt so strange and at a loss—meeting closed minds, blank faces where she had the right to expect something far different—that she now had the sensation of being caught tight in some nightmare, or else laid under so strong a hallucination that it endured in spite of any attempt on her part to break it.

"They look Yurth—" She spoke her bewilderment aloud. "But they are not, not the Yurth I know."

If they were not her people, they were well used to handling prisoners taken in their odd net and water trap. And there were too many of them for either Elossa or Stans, weakened as he was by the reopening of his wound, to put up any defense. Even though her first attempt at communication had failed, the girl tried twice again to launch mind-send at their captors. But it would seem that none were receptive.

In the end, their hands once more bound behind them, she and Stans were marched away from the river and the boat, now tied at the bank, striking out across the dull emptiness of the plain. At sunset they camped where a circle of stones set to confine fire to a much blackened and ash-piled piece of ground suggested that this was a well used halting place.

The Yurth had marched in silence, speaking neither to their prisoners nor each other. Elossa had come to feel a shrinking from contact with any of them. They might well be only hollow shells of the people she had known, sent to obey the will of some other, without a spirit of their own remaining in their bodies.

At least those bodies remained human in their need for food and water. For supplies were produced and shared with their prisoners, unbound for the purpose, but watched closely while they gnawed on lengths of what seemed dried meat, as hard to chew as wood, and allowed to drink from journey bottles. Even the water had a strange, stale taste as if it had been in those storage containers for a long time.

"Where do you take us?" In the general silence of that camp Stans' voice rang out unusually loud. He had spoken to the Yurth who was rebinding his hands.

The man might have been deaf for he did not even glance up as he tested the last knot with grim efficiency before he turned away. Now the Raski looked to Elossa.

"They are of your stock, surely they will answer you." There was an odd note in his voice. Almost, Elossa thought, as if he had already identified her wholly with his enemies, in spite of the outward trappings of captivity which she wore.

She moistened her lips and launched the one appeal she had thought upon during that dusty journey to reach this place. To do this before a Raski went against all her conditioning from birth—Yurth affairs were theirs only. Still she must break through to these of her kin; that need had become the most important thing in her whole world.

Again she ran her tongue over her lips; her mouth, in spite of the water she had drunk, felt bone dry, as if she could not shape any words.

But this must be done—she had to know. So she began the chant in words so old that even their meaning was now forgotten. Out of some very dim past had those words come, and their birth must have been of abiding importance to all which was Yurth for the fact still remained that they must learn them, intelligible or no.

"In the beginning," she said in that tongue now forgotten, "was created Heaven and Yurth," (that last was the only understandable word in her chant), "and there man took being and. . . ."

On sped the words, faster now and uttered with more power and authority. And—yes! One of the Yurth, one wearing the clothing like her own, had turned his head to look at her. There was the faint trace of puzzlement dawning in his blank face. She saw his lips move. Then his voice joined hers in the chant, lower, less strong, halting at times.

But when she had done he saw her, really saw her! It was as if she had shaken out of sleep this one, if not the others. His eyes swept from her face down to the wrists again bound, the end of that cording looping out to twist about the arm of another of the guards. The attention in his expression became hopelessness.

"To Yurth the burden of the Sin." He spoke harshly as might a man who had not used his voice for a long time. "We pay, Yurth, we pay."

She leaned forward. None of the others had appeared to note that he had spoken.

"To whom does Yurth pay?" She tried to keep her voice as level as might one carrying on a usual conversation.

"To Atturn." His last faint trace of interest flickered out. Now he turned away and got to his feet.

She sent a mind-probe with all the force she could summon, determined to break through the barrier she had found, to reach the real man within the shell. Maybe she troubled him a fraction, for his head did turn once more in her direction. Then he strode off into the growing dusk.

"So Yurth pays," commented Stans.

"To Atturn," she snapped in return, desolated at her failure when she had begun to think that she might have actually learned more. "Perhaps to your Karn." She ended, not because she believed what she said. "But if Atturn rules, why does a Raski go in bonds?" she flung at him in conclusion.

"Perhaps we shall soon have a chance to learn." He showed heat to match her own.

With the dark the Yurth settled themselves for sleep, each captive placed carefully between two of their guards, cords looping them in contact so that Elossa guessed that the least move on her part would alert either one or the other, or both, of the men who boxed her in. He who had spoken to her was across the fire and settled early, his eyes closed, as if the last thing he wanted to see was Elossa herself.

She slept at last, rousing once to see one of the Yurth feeding the fire from a pile of sticks which had been stacked there waiting for their coming. Stans was only a dark form nearly engulfed in the shadows and she could not tell whether he waked or slept.

There was an uneasiness in her now which made her adverse to any casting of mind-seek. That these Yurth were perhaps bound to another's will was the only explanation which made sense to her. The "Burden" which the ship had loosed on her had ridden her people heavily for generations, that was true. But that it had reduced any to this state was not normal—Yurth normal. He and the others who had worn the clothing like her own—were they those who had earlier made the Pilgrimage and had never returned? Instead of death in the mountains they had found this life-in-death.

But there were the others who wore the ship's clothing. It had certainly been too many years since the crash of their spacer and the

death of Kal-Hath-Tan for any of them to have lived to this time—
again, unless someone had found the secret of prolonging life far past
any scale of years known to Elossa's reckoning. Had there been
another ship, a later one?

There was such a surge of excitement through her at that thought
that she had to will herself fiercely to lie still. It was the same
excitement and racing of the blood which had visited her when she
had watched in the wrecked ship the scenes taken in space before the
crash.

Another ship—a later one—perhaps sent to find Yurth, to take
them home. Home? Where was home then? Lying here she could see
the stars strewn across the sky. Was one of them the sun which
warmed the fields and hills of Yurth Home?

She drew a deep breath and then that excitement changed.

Those around her, she knew they were not free. If they had come
to save, then they in turn had been caught in some trap and made
captive. Yet they could not have been conditioned by the machines in
the ship as all those of her own blood and kin had been. She longed
to be able to crawl over to Stans, to shake him awake if he did indeed
sleep, force him somehow to tell her more of Atturn, of the Karn who
had stood wearing Atturn's face and who had launched the fire bolt
at them, who might have set upon them the monstrous creatures who
had pulled them down. There was too much she did not know, could
not know when the mind-seek refused to serve her.

Shortly after dawn, having eaten meagerly again of the dry stuff
and been allowed to drink, they were marched on steadily across the
plains. Stans walked well ahead of her. He seemed unsteady on his
feet and now and then the Yurth beside him put out a hand to aid
him with the impersonal manner of a machine doing some set duty.

They halted at intervals to rest, and were offered water at each
such halt. The dry grass grew long here, sweeping to their knees and
Elossa could trace no path in it. Still the party certainly moved as if
they trod some well known trail and did not have to fear getting lost.

There was something about the horizon ahead, a kind of haziness
she could not account for. But shortly before noon, or so she judged
it to be by the sun, they reached the explanation for that. The plain

ended almost abruptly in a cliff. It would seem that this level country was really a large plateau and to proceed they must descend to a country lying below, a far different country.

Whereas the plain forecast the swift coming of winter, the growth they now looked down on was lush, thick with leaves as it might be at the height of a good growing summer. Trees stood so close together that all one could really see for the most part was their tops, the leaves ruffled by gentle winds.

The leading guard went to the left a little and stepped onto the beginning of a stairway which had been cut back into the stone of the cliff. They followed single file, going down into that waiting lower land.

❊ 17 ❊

The luxuriant growth of vegetation in this lower land was beyond anything Elossa had ever known. Those valleys and plains in the east which the Raski cultivated to the best of their ability would seem desert borders compared to this. As the stair down the cliff side gave way to a road wide enough for six such guards as surrounded them now to walk abreast Elossa continued to wonder at the difference in this country.

Overhead trees arched, completely, she guessed, cloaking the road under their canopy. While the trees themselves were of new species. Between their trunks and lower branches climbed and looped thick vines which branched into stems so heavy with a bright purple fruit that they drooped downward near to breaking.

Around the fruit flew and climbed countless feasters—some feathered, some furred. Their squawks and cries led to a continual rise of sound. Yet none of the guard marching below glanced upward or seemed to notice any part of what lay on either hand.

There was a dank lushness to the very air of this woodland, scents both rank and fragrant hung as heavy as the fruit, clogged the nostrils and made the breath come faster as if one labored to catch lungfuls of the keener and more sterile air of the heights. The road underfoot was well laid and Elossa noted that, for some reason, none of the thick undergrowth so much as hung out above it. Those blocks might in themselves generate some warn-off quality which kept the forest from intruding on the work of the builders who so challenged nature.

But the way did not run straight. There were some trees of such a girth that it appeared their rooting could not be disturbed, so the road curled east or west about their bulk. When this was so and one glanced back it seemed that the road itself had disappeared from sight beyond each such curve.

Beads of sweat gathered along the edge of Elossa's hair, trickled down her face. This heat reached out to wrap her around until it seemed that every place her clothing touched her body the coarse fabric fretted and chafed her skin. Still the Yurth guard, having set on this path, did not pause or in any way abate their pace.

But all roads must in time have an end and this one came as they rounded an isle of earth which gave root space to three giant trees, so smothered in vines and towering ferns that the whole looked as solid as a rock wall.

The crook in the road ended in an open space, also paved with the firmly laid stone blocks. Set flat in the surface of the center was an opening, square and without doors. Now they came to more stairs but this time the descent ran into depths below the surface of the ground.

It was darker as they went; still there was enough light to see about them. The stair curled around, leading ever down but following the walls of this well-like space in a spiral pattern. The lower they went the more the lush rich air of the forest thinned, though there was a current which Elossa could feel and it was fresh.

She tried to count the steps, hoping so to gain some idea of how deep this burrow went. But it was easy to lose count. And she disliked the atmosphere of the place more and more. Yurth life was mainly led in the open, under the sky, and with fresh winds about one.

They reached the end of that descent to face a passage running straight from the foot of the stairs. Along it at intervals torches set in rings fastened to the walls smoked and flared, the acrid scent of their burning strong.

That hall ended in another arch and Elossa near missed a step. Once again they fronted the same—or twin—stone face of Atturn, its open mouth stretched wide awaiting them.

Two of the Yurth dropped to hands and knees and crawled through. Then pressure on Elossa's shoulders forced her down into the same humble position, indicating that she must follow suit. Angrily she obeyed, shrinking as far as she could from any contact with the walls of that mouth opening.

There was a wide chamber beyond, walled as well as floored with stone. As she scrambled to her feet she saw that there was a dais at the other end of the room and on it a seat high of back, wide of arm. Yet as large as that throne was it in no way dwarfed or belittled the man seated on it.

Red and black, crest of roached hair held high, this was he who had fronted them before the attack of the misshapen creatures. He was smiling as Elossa's guards dragged her forward, watching her as a sargon, had it more than rudimentary intelligence, might watch helpless prey advance within paw-crushing distance.

The girl held her head high, something in her responded with instant defiance to that smile, to the arrogant confidence the lord exuded, though to meet him stare for measuring stare was all she might do now.

The Yurth who had brought her there were as blank faced as ever. They were—maybe they were only now extensions of this Karn's will, his things, in truth swallowed up by Atturn.

"Lord." It was Stans who broke that silence. He elbowed past Elossa as if she were invisible, taking a stand Immediately below the single tall step of the dais. "Lord King. . . ."

The dark eyes of the man broke contact with Elossa, turned to the Raski, so like him in body. That smile did not fade.

"You make common cause with Yurth. . . ." In Karn's voice that last word took on the sound of some degraded and degrading obscenity.

"I am Stans of the House of Philbur." The Raski had not knelt, save for the address of courtesy, he stood as one addressing an equal. "The House of Philbur—" he repeated as if those four words were in some manner a talisman which would admit him to the dominate company of Karn. "Is it thus that the Lord of Kal-Hath-Tan speaks with his kin?" He jerked his shoulders as if to point home that he went bound as a prisoner.

"You company with Yurth filth."

"I bring you Yurth for you to do as you will. Your servants took no time to ask."

So! Her vague distrust of Raski, in spite of all their seeming need of one another had been right! Lies—lies ran behind him to the very moments on board the wrecked ship when he had apparently agreed that they had common cause in questioning all tradition had built in the past of their two peoples.

Karn's probing stare was sharp. Elossa felt another probe—not Yurth contact clean and clear, no. This was a furtive nibbling at the outer defense of her mind, a desire to violate her inner being without the power to force the rape.

"Interesting," Karn remarked. "And how knew you of the Kal-Hath-Tan which is, Raski?"

"It was—is—that laid upon the House of Philbur, that we take blood price for Kal-Hath-Tan. In each age we take it."

"There is a blood price for Kal-Hath-Tan of a different sort, Raski." Karn made a slight gesture to indicate the two vacant-eyed Yurth before him. "Yurth filth here is slave. More bitter is this than death—is that not so, Yurth?" Now he spoke directly to Elossa.

She made no answer. Still Karn—or some alien power in this place—was seeking a way past her mind shield. She found such fumbling feeble so far, but that did not necessarily mean that it could not build in force, perhaps without warning.

Karn's lips, so like those of Atturn's mouth, moved in what might be silent laughter. His gaze on her was worse than any blow which he might have dealt physically.

"Yurth breaks—yes, Yurth breaks. And I find it good that this, your gift to me, kinsman, is female. Breeding of our humble slaves is slow—we lack many females. Yes, I find your gift good." He raised his hand again and the Yurth to Stans' right took a step backward and freed the Raski's hands with a quick slash of his bonds. "You claim

House Blood of Philbur, kinsman. That also interests me. I thought that all our blood was gone.

"As for the Yurth—take it to the pens."

Elossa did not need the jerk on the cord about her wrists to bring her around. The hidden evil of this place was like a stinking mud rising about her feet, seeking to drag her down. She was willing enough to see the last of Karn and his "kinsman."

They left the audience chamber by a second door and traveled through such a maze of shorter and narrower passages that, though she tried to set each turn and twist in memory, she despaired of ever finding her way through them again.

At length she was shoved through a door into a room where there were more Yurth—women. None of them raised eyes to look at her as she half fell forward, being unable to help herself as her hands had not been freed. Instead those half dozen females of her own race stared blank-eyed before them. Two, she noted with horror, Karn's threat returning, had the big bellies of the pregnant. But they were all slack faced, as if empty of mind.

None of these wore the suits of the ship people; rather their robes could be the journey dress of the Pilgrims. But she recognized none of them as missing members of her clan. And she had no way of telling how long they might have been here.

Then the woman nearest her slowly turned her head. Her gaze fastened dully on Elossa's face and the horror of the mindlessness it suggested made the girl hurriedly edge away as the woman arose sluggishly to her feet and advanced toward her. To be touched by this—this *thing* wearing the guise of Yurth brought a scream very close to her lips.

But the woman passed behind her and a moment later Elossa felt a fumbling on the cords which bound her. Those fell away. Still blank of face the woman shuffled back to the pile of unsavory, stained couch pillows where she had first crouched and subsided again in the same position. Elossa, rubbing her wrists, moved back until her shoulders touched the wall and there dropped down to sit cross-legged.

Her gaze kept returning to the woman who had freed her. To look at this fellow prisoner suggested that the stranger was no different from her companions. Still, something had led her to come to Elossa's aid. Letting her head fall back against the support of the wall, Elossa closed her eyes.

That fretting at the edge of her mind-shield was gone. Very tentatively she released a small questing probe of her own. Nothing close to hand. If these here in this room and the other Yurth she had seen in the common dress were captured during the Pilgrimage then they had come here with powers equal to her own. Still those had seemingly been drained from them, leaving them empty and useless.

But the Raski had no such power. At least those of the outer world had not. They could be manipulated by Yurth hallucinations should just cause for such arise. What *was* Karn that he had been able to enslave those with gifts none of his race could claim?

"Karn is Atturn. . . ."

Only discipline of mind kept Elossa quiet. Who had sent that thought?

"You—where?" she shot out.

"Here. But be warned. Karn has his ways. . . ."

"How?"

"Atturn was a god. Karn is Atturn," came the not clear response. "He has ways of breaking minds—but not all. Some of us were warned in time . . . retreated. . . ."

Elossa opened her eyes slowly, looked to the woman who had freed her. This must be the one.

"Thank you. But what can we do?"

"I am not Danna." The correction came quickly. "She is broken. But still she can respond—a little. We work—we who still are true Yurth—to repair. But there are so few of us. No, do not look for me—we meet as mind speaking mind—we do not know each other otherwise lest in some ill chance the truth be riven from us. That death which came to Kal-Hath-Tan had strange, evil results. You have seen the twisted creatures who obey Karn in the first valley, those who trap all that wander into the inner lands.

"They are of the blood of Kath-Hath-Tan, but the ruin of the fire which blasted forth tainted them. They bear children from time to time as monstrous as themselves. Karn was worked upon otherwise;

he was already learned in a strange way in secrets known only to high priests and rulers. Of them a handful were in a secret inner place when the end came to the city. Karn became deathless, the incarnation so he believes—so his people believe—of Atturn who was never a deity of any grace or good. Karn I has outlived those who survived with him, always they sought what is Yurth power—that of the mind. But they sought it their own way—in order to deaden the spirit of others. And much did they learn through the passing years. Now. . . ."

As if a door had been slammed between her and the one who spoke there came instant silence. Elossa closed her eyes but did not attempt mind-probe again. The interruption had been warning enough.

Then speeding straight to her like a spear thrown in anger came another mind-touch.

"Kin." It was not that word which was heartening, it was the very force with which it came to her. Here was no evasion or warnings. Yet, dared she respond? The small scraps of information she had been fed suggested that Karn had resources to meet Yurth power. Perhaps he could also, in some perverted way, ape Yurth call.

"Come in."

Fair invitation, or trap? Still she hesitated. How deep had the rot reached in the Yurth who slaved for Karn; could one of them serve him thus, too, helping to betray some newcomer to actual takeover? Elossa felt that she could not depend upon her own judgment. With Stans she had been more than half convinced that he was willing to step free of the prejudices of his people, even as she had seen in that time of revelation in the ship the narrow folly—or what seemed so—of hers also. Yet Stans had indeed brought her here to Karn. Perhaps he had known from the very moment they left Kal-Hath-Tan where they were bound and why. He might have so betrayed others making the Pilgrimage before her.

"Come in," urged that other mind, laying open the door in a way which even Yurth seldom did and then only to those they trusted above all others. It was such an intimacy, such an invasion of the inner being that it only came at times of high peril—or honest shared emotion.

"Come in." For the third time and now it did not ask, it demanded in some impatience, even anger.

Elossa drew upon the full sum of her energy. She might be making the worst mistake of her life, or she might be finding a defense against the worst Karn had spoken of with his vile suggestion. She shaped a mind-probe, only hoping that she would have the power to jerk loose in time, if again she had trusted wrongly. With that probe she did as the other ordered—she went in.

❊ 18 ❊

But she was so startled as that other touch met hers that she nearly broke contact by an instantaneous retreat, a blocking. For it was not a single mind which had demanded liaison with her. No, this was a combination of different personalities! And Elossa had never known this kind of union herself. The one acting-in-concert which her own clan had done was for building of some hallucination when extra strength was needed to hold such for a length of time. Even then, she, not having made the Pilgrimage, had never been one so called upon to lend her power to the general good.

Her momentary resistance vanished, she became a part of this union, and in her grew an exultation, a feeling of such confidence as made all her other small triumphs of the past seem as nothing at all.

"We are together!" It sounded as if those others, too, felt the same surge of near invincibility. "At last, kin, we are strong enough to move!"

"What would you do?" she asked that which she could not even yet sort into separate individual personalities. "We act!" came the firm answer. "For long have we joined one to another, and yet another. We have hidden behind the slave covers Karn set upon us. For we needed more and more strength before we could go up against him. What he controls is alien to us; he has created such a barrier that we could not blast through. But now—now, kinswoman—with your strength added we await the final battle.

"Soon they will come for you that Karn may make you even as he thinks we are. Wait, go with them, but wait. When the moment comes—then we shall be ready!"

It was in Yurth blood to be cautious, ever wary, mistrusting of one's self for fear the power might seduce one to a downfall. All this distrust was aroused in Elossa as she listened. Yet she was impressed by the utter confidence of the multi-voice. And there was that in its argument which seemed logical. If Yurth, taken from the Pilgrimages—and perhaps elsewhere (she had no explanation yet for those wearing the ship's clothing)—had indeed pooled their strength, added force one to another, who knows what such an accumulation might accomplish. It would seem that this was indeed her best hope of escaping the fate she saw before her in this room of beaten women. She had a flash of speculation as to which of them were allied now in this composite voice.

"We must not act until Karn is about to use his own power," the voice continued. "We do not know if he can learn in any way from his own methods what we would do. Therefore, do not use mind-touch, kinswoman, until we come to you."

The voice was gone. Elossa shivered at its vanishing. While it had been with her she had felt warm, at peace. Now that it had gone she could worry once more, foresee only too many ways in which failure lay. She closed her eyes again and drew upon her will, upon those techniques for conserving and strengthening inner power which she had been so carefully schooled to use.

But she was not given long to so arm herself, for the door opened and the grate of its opening aroused her, though it was not the Yurth she expected to see, those guards who would come to make her submit to Kam's unholy slave making. Rather it was Stans.

He slipped inside and closed the door behind him, standing then with his shoulders against it as if he would use his body to reinforce a barrier. None of the other women looked up, their faces remained blank. But he was staring straight at her, and she saw his lips move with exaggerated shaping as if he would send her some message which he must not say aloud. She tried to read as twice he went through that, and the third time. . . .

"Come in."

The same message as that other. But was he Karn's instrument? If she obeyed the Raski's order would it mean enslavement? This was not what the multi-mind had warned her of, but that did not mean that this was not as great a peril as what her kin had here faced and lost to.

That a Raski should summon mind-touch was so against all the customs of his race that she could not believe in this. But for the fourth time he was shaping the words, and his expression was one of strain. He had turned his head a fraction so one ear rested against the door as if he must listen for some danger without.

It was trust he demanded. Elossa weighed her present feeling for Raski against the facts of their journey together. They had saved each other's lives, yes. How much did that count against his words to Karn? Her inbred caution warred with another emotion she was not prepared to understand, which she wished to press out of her mind altogether but could not.

At last she did as he wished. She sent a mental probe. Just as she had reeled and tried to withdraw from the multi-mind's meeting so did she know instantly that strange revulsion moved in him at her invasion. Yet as quickly he steadied himself, even as a man facing impossible odds for some point of honor which was even greater to him than life. She could read. . . .

And. . . .

Her strange instinct was right. What he had said to Karn—that had been a weapon of sorts, all he could seize upon at that moment. She read and learned.

Karn the impossible, the man who in the destruction of his city ages ago had, as she had earlier been told, continued to live, because he had already been deep in strange practices of the mind, disciplines of the body learned by chance by an obscure priesthood. They had wrought such changes, not by their own inner striving, but by the use of drugs and strange practices of control which could force hallucinations until the unreal became permanently real.

Fleeing the destruction of Kal-Hath-Tan a handful of priests, and

Karn, had reached this other sanctuary—one they knew of old—to which even then they had retired at intervals with victims for their researching into unhealthy paths. Karn had lived—or was it a hallucination of life? At any rate here he ruled.

The Yurth from the ship—some had been captured, brought here, subjected to Karn's processes of domination. They too, lived. But they were indeed the hollow shells of what they had been. For they had not been subjected to that change which Yurth brought upon themselves when they assumed the burden of what they considered their irreparable sin.

When the new generations made the Pilgrimage some had been drawn into Karn's net by the same method he had used with Elossa— the call for help uttered in Yurth mind-touch. Thus the hidden master of the over-mountain land had built up his forces.

He had had no failures—outwardly. So he became in his own eyes, undying, all powerful, Atturn himself—that entity which had been the core of the research. One by one the priests had died, or Karn had brought death to them. But Karn remained ever in power. Now, now he had thought to gather his forces, to extend his rulership. He had been questioning Stans—striving to learn what lay open to his taking in the plains lands to the east

"He read your mind?" Elossa demanded. For if Stans had lain as open to Kara as he was now to her then what hope had either of them for rebellion?

"He could not," Stans returned. "He was angry, and—I hope— troubled. But I am not one with him in Atturn. However, the fact that we are kin may not keep him from striving to break me. He has all which worked for him long ago—the drugs—the other things. But that takes time—he had not had me long enough in his hands."

Elossa made her decision. "Do even as you have done—play his liege man."

"But he will take you soon. You will become as these." Stans made a slight gesture to indicate the women about her, none of whom had seemed even yet to note his presence.

She might trust him from what she had read in his open mind, but it would be better not to provide him with any other information, unless she could hint that within herself lay some defense she had not yet tried.

"It may be that I can stand to him. If he holds in thrall all these Yurth then that must be exhausting to whatever power he summons. I am fresh come—and. . . ."

Stans stiffened. He turned to face her fully, his hands now balled into fists.

"They are coming!"

"They must not find you here." She was quick to recognize the additional peril in that. "Behind there." She pointed to one of the low couches on which the women sat. There was a small space between it and the wall—a very poor hiding place. But if they took her quickly—and she distracted their attention—it might serve.

He shook his head but she crossed swiftly and seized upon his sleeve.

"If Karn's men find you here then what good will you do either of us?" she demanded fiercely. "Hide, and later do what you can. Be Karn's man—perhaps he will bring you to see how he can enslave me. Then we can well have a chance there to act together."

Stans did not look convinced, but he did push toward the divan. The unmoving women still did not lift their eyes as he flattened himself into hiding there as best he could. Elossa, chin up, summoning her best appearance of confidence, stood not too far from the door as if she had been pacing up and down as might a new taken prisoner.

It was not the Yurth who came for her, rather two towering, shambling creatures, distorted, demonic-headed Raski, plainly of the same breed as those who had first captured them, the tainted city stock.

They had to stoop to enter for their heavily muscled bodies were those of giants among their kind. And they slobbered from half-open mouths. Their near naked bodies gave off the stench of unwashed, even diseased flesh as they closed in upon her, each gripping an arm and dragging her toward the door. Nor did they glance around. Stans, she thought, was safe.

Once again she passed, firmly held by her two monster guards, through a number of passages, until they came into a room near as large as the presence chamber in which Karn had first greeted them. Here his throne was to one side, less impressive. The middle of the room was occupied by a huge representation of Atturn. From the open mouth of that puffed, irregularly, trails of smoke, thin trails which did not rise to the ceiling, but rather wreathed around the mask-face as if it willed their clinging touch.

Elossa smelled the strange odors of the place. Was the smoke one of the mind-bending drugs Stans had mentioned? If so there was no way for her to escape at least some of Karn's infective devices.

The master of this maze had directly before him a brazier of gleaming metal, along the edge of which played those lines of light as had been on the walls of the corridor behind the first of the Mouths. In this, also, burned something which gave off smoke, and he leaned forward, was inhaling that, like a man gulping down some life-renewing fluid, his mouth open.

And. . . .

His face was changing. She watched, sure that she was viewing some hallucination achieved by the methods of the Raski priests. His countenance when she had entered had not been that of Atturn. Now, under her gaze the flesh stretched, altered, he was becoming Atturn once again, claiming the outward seeming of his god.

His eyes closed, he straightened up. The smoke from his brazier had died away. Whatever burned there might be utterly consumed. But his mouth hung open in Atturn's malicious grin. Even the tip of his tongue protruded over his lower lip until he was the exact copy of the huge face before which her guards had stationed her.

Now, without opening his eyes, Karn spoke—his words strange to her, rising and falling with the steady beat of an invocation. Words and rhythm were a part of building hallucination as she well knew. Her own defense against this instantly clicked into action. She refused to look—either at the man or the face before her. Her eyes closed, she held them so with all the firmness of her will. Still the desire to open them, to see the face, gripped her.

It was moving—she knew it! The lolling tongue within the mouth was reaching out to grip her as had the mist tongue near taken Stans in the mountain corridor. No! That was not true—it was only what

Karn tried to insert into her mind. Stans—she thought of the Raski—built his face up as a picture to fit over that of Atturn. Stans who had allowed her to read his thoughts in spite of all the horror his kind felt for such an act—Stans. . . .

To her vast astonishment that face she held in her mind became alive, not just a representation she used as a part shield against Karn's devilment. The lips moved, and in her thoughts a small and weak sound—wholly alien to Yurth touch—spoke:

"I . . . come. . . ."

Karn's trickery? No, she felt that had the master of this den managed to slip past her barrier his message would have been far more compelling. But Raski did not have the talent, that was Yurth's, and perhaps, combined with drugs and hallucinations, Karn's. Then how had Stans reached her?

She felt the beat of the words Karn mouthed, and now she crooked her fingers, altered the rhythm of her breathing, did all she could not to fall into the insidious trap that offered to make her own body betray her.

There was a sudden check in the rhythm—Elossa opened her eyes. Stans was indeed there, within touching distance of Karn. The man who wore Atturn's face had not looked at him, but the face itself changed again. From assured maliciousness it began to register growing rage. The eyes snapped open.

Stans swayed as if those eyes were weapons, had flashed out at him some shattering force. And at the same time:

"Now!" So loud was that voice in her brain that Elossa, in turn, wavered, took a step or two toward the face in order to catch her balance again. But she was no longer aware of her body at all—all that did matter was the huge face confronting her, still wreathed in those tenuous trails of sickly smelling smoke.

Her will, all the talent which lay within her, joined with those others at the summons. She was no longer a person, a living being; instead her body became only a holding place in which the power being fed to her grew and grew. She wanted to scream, to fight back—to force out of her this monstrous thing which was crushing her. But instead she was a part of it, she could not deny it entrance.

It seemed that in her torment she would burst apart, that nothing formed of human flesh and blood could contain what gathered, strengthened, made ready. Without her knowing it her mouth opened in a soundless scream of torture. She could hold no longer. But it had gathered, become full grown to the greatest force it might ever obtain—and now—it struck!

❈ 19 ❈

It seemed to Elossa that she actually saw that spear point of pure energy speed outward from her. Did indeed that light become real to her eyes, or did she see it only by the Yurth sense?

Straight for Karn that was hurled. His hands moved so swiftly that she hardly saw the gesture until they were in place, palm outwards, shielding from her his Atturn face. Now she swayed where she stood, for her body shook and quivered as the force of the Yurth gathered in her, solidified there, then sped out.

There was no Karn, no Atturn there now.

What curled in the place of the man were flames, both black and red. Outward flared those flames. The heat from them crisped her hair, was searing torment to her flesh. Flames swallowed up the spear of force, strove to destroy it utterly.

Still she did not cook away to nothingness. But her consciousness retreated further and further. Elossa was near gone, what trembled and wavered here was only a vessel to collect and then dispense energy.

The flames of Karn were fierce flags whipping about her. From behind those there beat steady sounds, each of which struck her like a blow.

And. . . .

That which gathered in her, melded to speed forth, it was

weakening, the flow was no longer steady, while the roasting heat of the Karn fire was something she had no strength to hold at bay.

On the very edge of her vision there was movement. Elossa could not turn her head to see what chanced there—she must hold steady— if she could hold.

Sound slashed as might a wood axe brought against a young tree. The sounds which had beat upon her. . . . Elossa steadied, somehow made a plea, and gave herself a last fraction more freely. The power arose in her—for the last time she knew.

She held it, held it as long as she could, until she knew that her battered mind could contain it no longer. Then, as might a warrior in battle release a shout of utter defiance—tinged with despair—she loosed that final up-flowing of Yurth talent—hurled it outward. . . .

The flames flared out and up. But this time she could see the spear of light out through them, break upon hands, hands which appeared in the heart of the flames.

"Ahhhhhh—"

Was that shriek of mingled pain and fear real, or part of a hallucination? Elossa wavered to her knees. She was empty! The power went out of her so suddenly that it was as if the very bones which supported her flesh had been withdrawn, leaving her no firmness of body at all. She braced herself with her hands upon the floor, her arms as tautly straight as she could hold them.

The flames died, were utterly gone. She had failed! Karn stood there still erect, invincible. Behind him in a half crouch was Stans. The Raski's face was set in a grimace, his lips were pulled a little away from his teeth, he looked at that moment as one rendered near as monstrous through torture as the misshapen creatures they had been captured by in the valley.

His breath came in great gasps, as if he could not draw enough air into his lungs. But now he launched himself at Karn, his hands out, his fingers crooked as if they were claws to tear the undying king into bloody shreds.

He moved jerkily as if he were in some manner crippled, yet was so will bound to what he would do that he could make even a maimed body obey in this last small attack.

His strength came against Karn. The king had taken no notice of his kinsman, but had stood statue still in the same position in which Elossa had last seen him, erect, his hands before his face.

Now those hands dropped, not as if he had lowered them, but as if there were no longer any strength left in the muscles which held them so. The flesh covering them appeared pallid, shriveled.

As his arms hung limp at his sides Karn took a step forward, then stumbled, fell to his knees on the floor beneath the one-step dais which had held his second throne. He was within touching distance of Elossa now.

But, seeing his face, she cringed away. Though his eyes were open, set, only white showed between the lids. There was a terrible, sickening change in his face, a writhing between Atturn and Karn, as if a last struggle between two personalities were in progress within him.

He began to crawl and Elossa pulled her body out of his path, edging around herself to watch him. Though he seemed blind, yet he was led toward the screen, the mouth of Atturn.

"No!" Stans sprawled down after the king. "He must not enter!"

As the king, he crawled, seemingly with little strength left. His strained face was also turned to the waiting Mouth.

"He must not . . . go . . . to . . . Atturn!" he gasped.

Elossa strove to draw upon any remnants of energy still in her. She opened her mind, sent out a plea for that which had been hers. But there came no answer. Had the multi-voice been riven forever?

Stans crawled on, and so did Karn blindly advance. Then the Raski launched himself once more in attack, sending his body before the path of the king as a barrier. When Karn reached him Stans grappled, holding the king by main force against struggles which, Elossa saw, Karn aimed not at his captor but rather to free himself.

His blind-eyed face was ever toward the stone image, his neck strained until his head was at a strange stiff angle. But Stans kept his grip on the struggling body of the king. As much as the Raski tried to hinder him, still Karn pulled forward, winning the length of a finger, the width of a palm, with dogged push.

Stans raised a fist, drove it full force into Karn's face. Elossa heard the dull sound of that blow, saw the involuntary rock of the head when it landed. Yet the blankness of expression did not change, the eyes remained rolled up and blind.

"No!" Stans' voice shrilled. "Not . . . to . . . the Mouth!"

His frenzy of struggle was enough to bring Elossa crawling toward them also. There must be a reason for Stans' need to keep Karn from the representation of the "god"—if god the Mouth was. She reached forth a hand and caught at Karn's arm, digging her fingers into the black and red fabric which covered it. But what she so held might well be made of metal, so unyielding was the substance of his tense flesh.

However, her effort, small though it was, when added to Stans', seemed enough to halt the crawl for an instant. Then, in their hold, Karn appeared to go mad. His struggles were the writhing of something totally divorced from reason. He flung his head around and down, snapping at Elossa's hand with his teeth. The pain of that wound loosened her hold and he jerked free.

With one great final effort he flung himself forward, beating Stans flat against the flooring with that lunge. One arm was thrown up and out. His hand curved around the edge of the lolling tongue. The girl saw the strength of the pull he exerted to use that to draw himself on and up into the Mouth.

Stans got up to his knees. He joined his hands together into a single fist. Raising that above his head he brought it down in a hammer blow on the nape of Karn's neck, even as the king had caught at the tongue with his other hand and was well on his way to drawing forward into the Mouth.

Karn fell, his forehead hitting the tongue. There was a sound then which cut through Stans' panting, a sound which seemed to Elossa to echo sickeningly through the whole room. The body, which a moment before had been taut, tense with effort, relaxed, slipped down, though the one hand still lay, fingers laced about the edge of the tongue.

Stans lurched away. There was a dull horror in his eyes.

"He . . . if he had gone through . . ." he said in a shaking voice.

"He could have lived and lived and . . . lived. . . ." His voice scaled upward and his body was shaking so that he could not control his hands but held them out in front of him now, quivering, staring at them as if he had never seen them part of him before.

There was another sound in that chamber, though it did not cancel out that of the blow which still echoed to Elossa. She looked up at the face and then cried out. Enough strength returned for her to clutch at Stans, dragging him back and away from the Mouth.

For the representation of Atturn was crumbling, falling in great jagged pieces of stone. These thudded down on the head and shoulders of Karn, hiding near half of his body.

Elossa pressed the back of her hand tightly across her mouth to stifle a scream. For behind that screen, as she thought the Face and Mouth had formed, there was. . . .

Nothing! Rather a curtain of darkness which negated all normal light. It did not reach to either wall of the chamber, rather was like a section of utter black forming an inner structure of its own.

The Face and Mouth had gone. Now the darkness itself was rifting apart from side to side. Objects within they could see dimly, without knowing what such might be. But as the darkness tore and vanished, so did that which it had held go with it. Now they could sight bare wall behind.

The shadow dwindled, seeped into the rock on which they crouched. Then all that remained was the half-buried body. Elossa could not turn her gaze from that. The defense of the Yurth had been torn from her.

Stans had crawled to her side. Now he pulled at her, thrusting his face close to hers.

"OUT!" He mouthed that order, jerking her toward the door through which she had been brought.

Somehow his order carried weight enough to get her started. But she retreated on her hands and knees, his hand impatiently urging her along whenever she grew faint.

Then they were out of the place of sickly scents, of death, and such illusions as she could no longer raise the strength to battle.

"Free. . . ."

No loud voice in her mind now, instead a whisper of near exhaustion.

Stans turned his head from where he had collapsed against the wall, only that support keeping him from sliding directly prone.

"Free. . . ." But he had said that aloud—and the other had been the multi-voice.

They were free indeed—but Yurth could not have done it without Raski. It had been Stans' actions back there in Karn's chamber to which much of the triumph belonged.

"Yurth," she said slowly, "and Raski. . . ."

He gave a sigh. "This. . . ." His glance went beyond her as if viewing all the length of the burrows underneath the earth. "Was evil of Raski—we did not stand guiltless after all. Raski and Yurth—perhaps something may now come of that thought we two shared in Kal-Hath-Tan after all."

She was so tired, so tired it was an effort to raise her hand from where it lay limp beside her knee. But this time she was the one to hold out palm and fingers in a gesture of union. Nor did she shrink, even in her mind, when his grasp closed about hers.

"Raski and Yurth—and freedom for both."

"True." The voice in her mind was stronger, a little eager, life was flowing back.